THROUGH SEETHING STRUGGLE AND SAVAGE
PASSIONS, THEY BLAZED A WAY IN THE
PERILOUS WILDERNESS . . .

Jessica Maclaine—A Highland beauty and lady's maid to
the governor's wife, she struggled to fulfill her dream in
the harsh land of New South Wales, but would surrender
everything for the love of handsome, powerful Justin
Broome.

Justin Broome—Illegitimate son of brave, strong-willed
Jenny Hawley, he lived for the untamed adventure of the
frontier—and the love of one passionate woman.

Jenny Hawley—Her courage had sustained her through
long, hard years in the virgin wilderness. Now her faith
and determination would fulfill her greatest dream.

DARING LOVERS,
BOLD CONQUERORS,
BUILDERS OF A NATION,
THEY WERE . . .

THE EXPLORERS

THE AUSTRALIANS

Vivian Stuart
writing as William Stuart Long

The Explorers
Volume IV of The Australians

Futura

A Futura Book

First published in Great Britain in 1982
by Futura Publications, a Division of
Macdonald & Co (Publishers) Ltd
London & Sydney
Reprinted 1985, 1987, 1990

ISBN 0 7088 2236 3

Printed and bound in Great Britain by
BPCC Hazell Books
Aylesbury, Bucks, England
Member of BPCC Ltd.

Futura Publications
A Division of
Macdonald & Co (Publishers) Ltd
Orbit House
1 New Fetter Lane
London EC4A 1AR

A member of Maxwell Macmillan Pergamon Publishing Corporation

This book is for Johnny Lane of
Phoenix, Arizona

Acknowledgments and Notes

I acknowledge, most gratefully, the guidance received from Lyle Kenyon Engel in the writing of this book, as well as the help and cooperation of the staff at Book Creations, Incorporated, of Canaan, New York: Marla Ray Engel, Philip Rich, Glenn Novak, Marjorie Weber, and Charlene DeJarnette.

Also deeply appreciated has been the background research so efficiently undertaken by Vera Koenigswarter and May Scullion in Sydney.

The main books consulted were:

Lachlan Macquarie: M. H. Ellis, Dymock, Sydney, 1947; *The Mountain Men,* Vol. 3: Bay Books, 1979; *Australian Explorers:* Kathleen Fitzpatrick, Oxford University Press, 1958; *The Life of Vice-Admiral William Bligh:* George Mackaness, Angus & Robertson, 1931; *Bligh:* Gavin Kennedy, Duckworth, 1978; *Rum Rebellion:* H. V. Evatt, Angus & Robertson, 1938; *The Macarthurs of Camden:* S. M. Onslow, reprinted by Rigby, 1973 (1914 edition); *Mutiny of the Bounty:* Sir John Barrow, Oxford University Press, 1831 (reprinted 1914); *A Book of the Bounty:* George Mackaness, J. M. Dent, 1938; *Description of the Colony of New South Wales:* W. C. Wentworth, Whittaker, 1819; *The Convict Ships:* Charles Bateson, Brown Son & Ferguson, 1959; *Captain William Bligh:* P. Weate and C. Graham, Hamlyn, 1972; *History of Tas-*

mania: J. West, Dowling, Launceston, 1852; *A Picturesque Atlas of Australia:* A. Garran, Melbourne, 1886 (kindly lent by Anthony Morris).

These titles were obtained mainly from Conrad Bailey, Antiquarian Bookseller, Sandringham, Victoria. Others relating to the history of Newcastle and Hunter River, New South Wales, were most generously lent by Ian Cottam, and extracts from the *Historical Records of Australia* were photocopied for me by Stanley S. Wilson.

My gratitude for her efficient help in speeding typescript across the Atlantic goes to my local postmistress, Jean Barnard; and I owe an immense debt of gratitude both to my spouse and to Ada Broadley, who, in the domestic field, made my work on this book easier than it might have been.

Readers of previous books in *The Australians* series will note that the final *e* has been omitted from the name of Colonel George Johnston. The reason for this omission is that papers pertaining to his trial by court-martial at Chelsea Royal Hospital, London, in May 1811, all refer to him as "Johnston," although in some earlier documents the name is spelled with a final *e*.

Truth, it is said, is sometimes stranger than fiction. Because this book is written as a novel, a number of fictional characters have been created and superimposed on the narrative. Their adventures and misadventures are based on fact and, at times, will seem to the reader more credible than those of the real-life characters, with whom their stories are interwoven. Nevertheless—however incredible the real-life characters may appear—I have not exaggerated or embroidered the actions of any of them.

Finally, I should mention that I spent eight years in Australia and traveled throughout the country, from Sydney to Perth, across the Nullabor Plain, and to Broome, Wyndham, Derby, Melbourne, Brisbane, and Adelaide, with a spell in the Islands and the Dutch East Indies, having served in the forces during World War II, mainly in Burma.

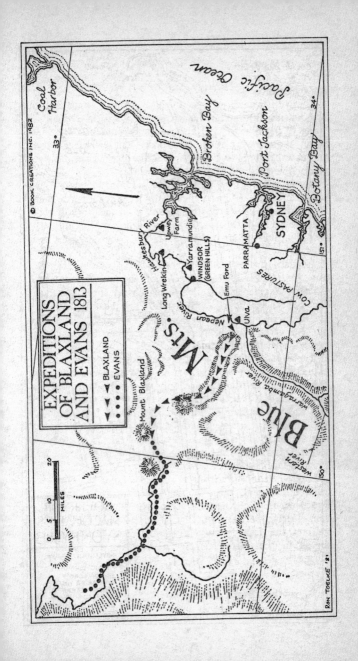

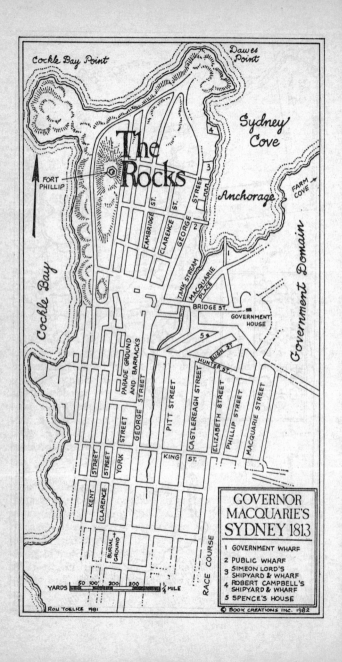

GOVERNOR
MACQUARIE'S
SYDNEY 1813

1 GOVERNMENT WHARF
2 PUBLIC WHARF
3 SIMEON LORD'S
  SHIPYARD & WHARF
4 ROBERT CAMPBELL'S
  SHIPYARD & WHARF
5 SPENCE'S HOUSE

Cockle Bay Point

Dawes Point

The Rocks

Fort Phillip

Sydney Cove

Anchorage

Farm Cove

Cockle Bay

Government Domain

Kambridge St.
Clarence St.
George Street
Tank Stream
Macquarie Place
Bridge St.
Government House
High St.
Hunter Street

Parade Ground and Barracks

Kent Street
Clarence Street
York Street
George Street
Pitt Street
Castlereagh Street
Elizabeth Street
Phillip Street
Macquarie Street

King St.

Burial Ground

Race Course

YARDS 50 100 200 300 ¼ MILE

Ron Toelke 1981

© Book Creations Inc. 1982

PROLOGUE

It was hot and airless in the confines of the empty storage cupboard, and dusty, too, now that the kit bags and packing cases had been removed, preparatory to being loaded aboard the waiting transports, which lay at anchor in Yarmouth Roads.

Crouched in the concealing darkness, Jessica India Maclaine heard the rapid thud of booted feet and shouted commands and breathed a small sigh of relief. The storage cupboard was situated beneath the stone staircase leading from the married families' quarters on the upper floor of Colville Barracks to those occupied by the regiment's non-commissioned officers on the floor below. Jessica had hidden herself late the previous evening when her stepfather announced that embarkation orders had been received, and she slept there, in desultory fashion, until reveille had sounded soon after dawn.

They would not look for her here, she was certain, and soon, when all the men had mustered on the parade ground outside and the roll call had been taken, His Majesty's Seventy-third Regiment would march down to the harbor and her ordeal would be over. Like her brother, Murdo, she would be free, with the regiment on its way to New South Wales and her stepfather gone from her life.

She had planned no further ahead than this. Just to escape from the misery of existence under her stepfather's roof was enough. She must get away from him and from the brutal beatings and never-ending humiliation he constantly heaped on her. If she starved, Jessica thought bitterly, if she had to beg bread in the streets, life could be no worse than he had made it for her.

For her *and* for Murdo, she reminded herself. Murdo had run away three months ago, before the regiment left Scotland, to be carried on board four Berwick smacks and driven by gale force winds to Gravesend and then to Yarmouth, Isle of Wight, to await the arrival of the transports that would take them across twelve thousand miles of ocean to exile, on the other side of the world.

That was how the whole regiment thought of the unwelcome posting. Even the officers spoke of it thus, as exile. The 73rd had served in India for twenty-five years; they had come home, expecting to fight their country's battles under Sir Arthur Wellesley in Egypt, Spain, or Portugal, or even, if need be, in the fever-infested West Indies, should the French seek to effect new conquests there.

But going to New South Wales was different. It was a penal colony, and even the knowledge that their commanding officer, Colonel Lachlan Macquarie, was to become Governor and Captain General was of little consolation to proud Highland fighting men dreaming of military glory.

Jessica sighed, remembering the talk she had heard, the angry complaints, the sense of injustice which even the new recruits had felt. She herself, after a childhood spent in India, had not been averse to the prospect of another long voyage, no matter what was at the end of it. She would have gone, willingly enough, with her mother . . . but not, O dear God, not with her mother's second husband! Not with Company Sergeant Major Duncan Campbell, even if her life were to depend upon it.

"Jessie . . . Jessie lass, are you there?" The voice was low, scarcely above a whisper, but Jessica recognized it as her mother's and stirred uneasily. The regimental families, the wives and children, would, she knew, be the last to embark, but even so . . . She drew in her breath sharply. The men had not yet marched off the parade ground; she could hear the throbbing of the drums in the distance, but the pipes were still silent, and the shouts told her that the calling of the roll was not yet completed.

"India," her mother persisted, using the name her own father had given her and which Duncan Campbell would never utter, save in mockery. "Open the door, child. I must speak to you."

"But they've not gone, Mam. I dare not. He will be coming back and—"

"He *is* coming back, lass. He was taking his belt to me . . . I had to tell him where you were."

There was shame in her mother's soft Highland voice, pity and regret mingled in the admission, and hearing this, Jessica's dreams of freedom faded. She stretched out her cramped legs and dragged herself to the door of the cupboard. She had placed a wedge against the back of it to prevent its being opened from the outside, and for a moment she hesitated. But the wedge would withstand only a casual push; it would be no defense against Duncan Campbell's brute strength, if he came in search of her.

"All right, Mam. Wait, if you please. I will open it."

She offered no reproach, aware that her mother had not willingly betrayed her hiding place, and when the cupboard door swung open, she was thankful that she had not. Elspeth Campbell stood facing her, swaying a little, her youngest child, Flora, on her hip. She was very pale, her lips swollen, and a livid bruise disfigured the right side of her lovely oval face. She raised her free hand in an attempt to hide the bruise, but it was evident to Jessica that she had suffered a more than usually severe beating.

And it had been on her account. "Did he hurt you badly, Mam?" she asked contritely.

Her mother shrugged, evading the question.

"I was thinking to spare you, lass. If you are coming with me now, we can walk down with the other women and nothing need be said. They are all assembled below, waiting for the word, and I have left Janet with Mrs. Macrae. We can be joining them. He will not touch you whilst we are all together. And once we are on board the ship you will be able to keep out of his way."

Perhaps she would, Jessica thought, but it would not be easy. The ship would be crowded, the quarters for the ninety wives and eighty-seven children the regiment was permitted to take with it would be spartan and lacking in places to hide. The empty barracks offered more scope.

"I could run from here," she began. "Upstairs, perhaps—"

"He will search until he finds you, child," her mother put in wearily. "You are knowing what he is like. And it is a matter of pride with him—he is determined to keep the family together, lest the officers think ill of him. And since Murdo ran away, he is more than ever determined that you shall not."

Four-year-old Flora, tiring of their low-voiced conversation and her own exclusion from it, set up a plaintive wail.

"Oh, quiet, Flora!" Jessica begged. The little girl was Duncan Campbell's favorite; he spoiled and indulged her even more than his elder child, the pretty, elfin Janet, and the sound of her weeping was calculated to bring him running, angry and reproving. "Stop crying, do!"

Flora ignored her pleas as, of late, she was tending to do. "Mam," she sobbed, "can't we go to the ship now? Let Jessie stay if she's wanting to."

"In a minute, baby," her mother soothed. She looked at her eldest daughter pityingly, taking in the signs of strain in Jessica's small, pinched, and tired face, knowing and understanding her longing to escape. But she was barely seventeen; to abandon her, perhaps forever, as she was being compelled to abandon her runaway son, went painfully against the grain. Murdo was a boy, and boys were better able to look after themselves. He would find work; he was strong for his age and well grown, while Jessie, who did not eat enough, was neither. She knew Duncan had no love for Jessie, and certainly no compassion. He was a hard man, there was no denying that, a very different man from the handsome, happy-go-lucky young soldier she had first married, who had enticed her away from her Highland croft and with whom she had voyaged to India and lived, in perfect happiness, for almost nine years.

But he had been killed in action at the battle of Seringapatam on May 4, 1799, when the Seventy-third Regiment had been in the forefront of the assault on the supposedly impregnable fortress of the ruler of Mysore, the infamous Tipoo Sultan, and she . . . Elspeth Campbell felt the familiar ache in her heart which the memory of him never failed to evoke.

She had been left a widow, with a son of barely five and the pretty, dark-haired little daughter of seven, whom her husband had insisted on calling India. Jessica India . . . an absurd name, but one he had delighted in and by which he had always addressed her.

The prize money for the capture of Seringapatam had amounted to over a million pounds, of which, Elspeth recalled, the commander in chief, General Harris, had received one hundred thousand . . . sums so vast that they were beyond her conception. As a humble corporal, Murdoch Maclaine had been entitled to a mere seven pounds. She had been paid this in gold, together with the few shillings the sale of his kit had raised from his comrades. However, she had soon found herself in financial difficulties. The British Army in India made no provision for widows; they were expected to marry again or eke out a precarious living in other, less respectable ways. If they were young and comely, there was never any lack of suitors, and she . . . Elspeth stifled a sigh.

She had still been in her mid-twenties and comely enough in those days, well thought of in the regiment, and there had been a number of offers. She accepted that of Duncan Campbell for many reasons. He was a corporal, as Murdoch had been, but with more ambition, marked out for future promotion, and was known as a man of strong religious principles and of sober habits. He had courted her with ardor, but perhaps what had weighed most with her at the time was the fact that he was in the quartermaster's store and there was less chance of his going into battle and being killed or wounded. They had wed when the regiment returned to its peacetime quarters in Madras, and—

"Mam, listen!" Jessica's voice broke into her thoughts, shrill with alarm. "The pipes . . . they'll be moving off!"

So they would, Elspeth's mind registered as she, too,

heard the skirling of the pipes. The regiment, parading for the last time in the glory of tartan and scarlet on British soil, would swing majestically into the rhythm of the march "Hie'land Laddie," as the drums beat it out and, crossing the parade ground, would start proudly down the hill to the harbor and the waiting ships. Duncan had told her with bitterness that the kilt was not to be worn in the colony of New South Wales, that the 73rd Highlanders would be indistinguishable from any other regiment of the line. They would be issued with white duck trousers, like its present garrison.

She should have been there, with the other women, watching them, but . . . impatiently, almost angrily, she grasped Jessica's hand, seeking to pull her forcibly from her hiding place.

"Come, lass, in God's name! I'll not leave you here, I cannot, whatever you say."

"But they're moving off, Mam," Jessica protested. "He'll be with them—he must be. He'll not look for me now, he'll not get leave."

"He will be seeking permission from the adjutant if he has need to," her mother answered. "If he is not seeing us there. All of us," she added forcefully. Flora's round, rosy face deepened in color, she drew a deep breath, screwing up her blue eyes preparatory to emitting another wail, but it was cut short by her mother's unexpected slap.

"Quiet!" she demanded. "Bide ye quiet!"

The child obeyed her, and in the sudden silence as the sound of the pipes and drums faded into the distance, there came another sound—that of booted feet on the stone stairway—and Elspeth Campbell whispered urgently, " 'Tis him, India! Out of that cupboard, as quick as you know how, and stand beside me. Your bundle, too . . . Oh, lass, reach for your bundle or he'll not believe you were coming with me!"

Jessica attempted to do as she was bidden, but her long sojourn in the cupboard had rendered her whole body stiff and leaden, and she was still tugging at the bundle which contained her few possessions when her stepfather came striding into the storeroom, roaring her name.

He was a formidable figure at any time, standing over six feet, with a broad-shouldered, muscular body in keeping with his height. Now, in full uniform, the tall regimental feather bonnet giving him the stature of a giant, and his gaunt, heavily jowled face suffused with angry color, he scowled, and Jessica shrank from him in terror. Her mother, bravely seeking to come between them, was thrust aside, her despairing "No, Duncan, no!" contemptuously ignored.

"Let the pulin' wee girl speak for hersel', woman!" he thundered. "Come on now, Jessie—what have ye tae say?"

Sergeant Major Duncan Campbell, unlike the majority of men in the 73rd, was a Lowland Scot, and the harshness of his accent grated unpleasantly, as it always had, on Jessica's ears. She backed away until, finding the door of the cupboard barred any further retreat, she cowered there speechless, unable to find words with which to defend herself. Her stepfather had a rattan cane in his right hand, she saw, and he was tapping it impatiently against the bare brown knees below his immaculately fitting kilt.

"Weel?" he persisted. "Were ye thinkin' tae hide from us, then? Were ye hopin' we'd sail without ye? And what, in the name of God, do ye suppose would have befallen ye, if we had? Come on now—speak up! I'm wantin' the truth, Jessie—and I'll have it, if I've tae beat it out o' ye!"

She knew he meant exactly what he said and, finding her voice at last, whispered miserably, "Aye, that . . . that was what I'd been hoping. I'm not wanting to come with you."

"Feyther," he prompted resentfully. "I'm your feyther an' dinna forget it."

Jessica bowed her smooth dark head but was silent, refusing to give him the name he had demanded, and her silence unleashed the anger that was burning within him.

"She's asked for it, wife," he flung at Elspeth. "And, by God, the damned wee huzzy will get what she deserves!"

The cane, in Duncan Campbell's big, powerful hand, was a cruel weapon, and he used it cruelly, caring little where his blows fell. Flora clung shrieking to her mother, but her cries and Elspeth's pleas failed to deter him, and it was not until Jessica fell to the floor, her hands covering her face, that the sight of the livid weals which now criss-crossed her arms gave him pause. Breathing hard, he tucked the cane under his own arm and growled, without contrition, " 'Twas only what she deserved. Tidy her up and follow me down tae the parade ground, the pair o' ye. I'll take the babby."

Flora went to him unwillingly, but his tone changed as he held her to him. "There, there, ma wee hen! Ye've nae-thing tae be feared of, for your dada loves ye. Ye ken fine that Jessie's been a bad lass and had tae be punished. Dry those tears now and ye shall ride doon on your dada's back." He hoisted her onto his broad, scarlet-clad shoulder, and the child's sobbing obediently ceased. "Make haste now," he bade Elspeth and bent to pick up Jessica's dis-carded bundle. "Is there no' a shawl in here ye can wrap round her?"

On her knees beside her elder daughter, Elspeth took the bundle from him, careful to avoid his gaze. She extracted the shawl and rose slowly to her feet.

"This will not hide what you have done to her," she said accusingly. Receiving no answer, she asked, tight-lipped, "Will the families not have gone already?"

Duncan Campbell, on his way to the stairs, turned briefly to shake his head. "I am in charge o' them. They'll not move off until I gie them leave. But bestir yersel', woman. I canna keep them waiting much longer."

So he had always had it in mind to come back for poor Jessie, Elspeth thought dully. He must have volunteered to take charge of the families, and probably—since it was not a duty many relished—the adjutant had been glad enough to leave the task to him. Biting hard on her lower lip, she did her best to obey his injunction to tidy up the outward signs of his savage assault on her elder daughter, but the cane had cut deep, and the girl's face and neck, as well as her arms, continued to bear mute witness to the brutal pun-ishment he had inflicted on her.

"You will be needing to hold this round you, lass," she said, offering the shawl apologetically. "But once we are on board the ship, I will cleanse these cuts and beg some balm for the bruises."

Jessica, who had borne her punishment with stoic resignation, staring emptily into space, turned pleading eyes on her mother's face. She had made virtually no sound as the cane bit into her yielding flesh, but now she burst out tearfully, "On board the ship! Oh, Mam, must I go on board the ship? Can I not bide here—surely he will not come back again, if he has the families in his charge?"

"No, he will not," Elspeth conceded. "But it will be I who will be blamed if I do not take you with me. And you are knowing what he will do."

She knew, from bitter experience; Jessica grasped the shawl and stumbled to her feet, recognizing that her cause was lost. Her mother put an arm around her, and together they descended the stone stairway, their shuffling footsteps echoing from its emptiness.

The women were waiting with the patience they had all learned over the years, their children as docile as they, held by the hand or carried, a few perched on top of the laden handcarts drawn up on the barrack square in front of them. The soldiers detailed to push the cumbersome carts came to attention in obedience to Sergeant Major Campbell's stentorian command, and the women moved off in a straggling line, Jessie and her mother having to run in order to catch up with them.

No pipes or drums lifted their hearts or gave them a step to which they could keep time—the regiment was long since out of sight and hearing—and they shuffled slowly along, only the shrill voices and excited cries of some of the older children giving vent to their feelings.

Morag Macrae relinquished Janet to her own mother's care and indicated, with a jerk of the head, that Flora had been placed on one of the baggage carts.

"The wean is sleeping," she said. "And 'tis as well, for you'll not be needing to carry her, Elspeth." She asked no questions as to the reason for their delay, but her shrewd dark eyes ranged swiftly over both of them, and from the pitying tone of her voice, Jessica sensed that she knew—or had worked out for herself—all that was to be known. Her husband was a sergeant, a kindly, elderly man, to whom she had been married for over twelve years, and six of their eight children had died in infancy—two on the voyage home from India. She was pregnant now, but this in no way impaired her energy or detracted from her willingness to help others, and her two surviving children, both boys, took after her.

"Thank you," Elspeth acknowledged. "We will walk with the cart, in case she is waking up."

They took their places behind the baggage cart, Janet with her hand in her mother's and Jessica, with bowed head and the shawl draped round her, following in constrained silence at their heels.

There were two ships tied up alongside the outer quay when they reached it, the men of the regiment still filing up the wooden gangways, with bulging kit bags balanced on their shoulders, and capes and haversacks strapped to their backs.

One of the ships was a naval two-decker, spruce and smart in her black and yellow checker paint. As the last company of soldiers trooped on board in regulation single file, the group of married families, similar in size to their own, moved toward the foot of the gangway.

"Our ship is the *Dromedary*," Elspeth said to Jessie. "She is an army transport, so that she will be larger than the *Hindostan*. But it looks as if we shall have a while to wait yet, before we can board her . . . that is Number Three Company preparing to embark. Are you all right, Jessie dear? If you are feeling faint, why do you not go and sit upon the baggage cart beside Flora?"

"I am all right, Mam," Jessica insisted. It had been a long walk and she was dropping with fatigue. The whole of her bruised and tortured body was aching, but to yield to weakness would be to concede defeat, to give her hated stepfather ascendency over her, and that, at whatever the cost, she would not do.

She glanced about, wondering where he was, and then saw him, striding self-importantly along the quayside, to come to a halt beside a small group of officers, his hand raised in an impeccable salute. One of the officers was Captain Henry Antill, who, she had been told, was to be aide-de-camp to the new Governor, Colonel Macquarie.

Antill was one of the regiment's heroes, having as a young ensign carried the colors into the breach at Seringapatam, and his gallantry was still talked of whenever the battle was a subject for discussion among the older men. He had been kind to her mother after she was widowed, Jessica recalled, and to Murdo and herself as children; but since the regiment's return to Scotland, he had been on furlough and they had seen little of him.

"Captain Antill is promoted to command of a company," her mother said, following the direction of her gaze, a pleased smile lighting the habitual gravity of her face. "And it may well be ours, I am thinking, since Major O'Connell is to take command of the regiment after we are landing at Port Jackson."

"Then Captain Antill will be with us on board the ship?" Jessica suggested. She had shown no interest in such matters hitherto, expecting that they would be no concern of hers, but she found the prospect of Captain Antill's presence oddly heartening. "On board the—what is it called? The *Dromedary*, Mam?"

"Yes, indeed," Elspeth Campbell confirmed. "And the new Governor also, with his lady and their servants. They will embark when we reach Spithead." She added thoughtfully, her smile fading, "They will be strangers to us, of course, Jessie—Colonel Macquarie has never served with the regiment. His own was the Seventy-seventh, but he was at Seringapatam, and they say that he is a good officer and in every respect a Highland gentleman. He is from Ulva and related to Maclaine of Lochbuie. His lady—" She broke off. "Ah, now, it would seem that our waiting is nearly over. They are moving, thanks be to heaven! I must waken poor wee Flora. Can you—" She eyed her elder daughter anxiously. "Can you manage both our bundles, if I am picking her up?"

"Of course I can, Mam. Do not worry your head on my account." Jessie held out her hand for the second bundle and did not wince when it was given to her. "I am fine now, truly I am."

But for all her brave protestations, she came near to fainting long before the slow-moving procession of women and children reached the foot of the *Dromedary*'s stern-most gangway. Her mother, with the two younger girls, mounted it ahead of her, and as Jessica leaned, regaining her breath, against the gangway's single rail, Captain Antill came up, with a young ensign and her stepfather in attendance.

He looked at her for a moment without recognition and then exclaimed, smiling, "Why, it is Jessica India Maclaine, is it not? And sorely burdened for one so small and young. Well, we must rectify that." His beckoning finger brought a soldier in fatigue dress to his side, who relieved Jessica of her bundles. She started shyly to thank him, keeping the shawl draped about her neck and shoulders, and then cold anger filled her, as she heard her stepfather say ingratiatingly, "The lassie is my stepdaughter, sir. Show your respect for Captain Antill, Jessie—where are your manners, girl?"

He wanted her to drop the young captain a curtsy, Jessica knew, and she hesitated, torn between her own natural good manners and her fury at his interference.

Finally Antill himself resolved her quandary for her. He said crisply, "Damme, Sar'nt Major, can you not see the poor child is exhausted? A puff of wind would blow her over. Come, India, have you forgotten the pick-a-back rides I used to give you in Madras? Arms round my neck now and we'll negotiate this gangplank together."

He bent and picked her up, and Jessie clung obediently to him as he carried her up to the *Dromedary*'s entryport and gently set her down. To the soldier carrying her bundles he said in the same crisp, authoritative tone, "Take her below to the families' quarters. Her mother is the company sar'nt major's wife, Mistress Campbell. Tell her that the girl is—" The shawl had slipped aside, Jessica realized in panic, and Captain Antill's eyes reflected his horror at what this had revealed. She jerked the garment back into place, the unhappy color rising to suffuse her cheeks.

"Tell Mistress Campbell that the girl is ill," he ordered, his thin, good-looking face suddenly stern and forbidding. "She will know what is to be done and whether the surgeon should be called." To Jessica, he added, forcing a tight-lipped smile, "I will see you again, India. A night's sleep will help to restore you."

The soldier was young, a recruit, judging by his appearance and the bewilderment in his eyes as he looked at her. But hefting both bundles onto his back, he offered Jessica his arm. "Lean on me," he invited in Gaelic. "We have a way to go to what they are calling the orlop deck."

The families' quarters were, despite the size of the ship, cramped and overcrowded, lit by lanterns which hung, at intervals, from the overhead deck beams. Wooden bunks, in tiers of three, occupied most of the available space, with scant room to pass between them, and mothers with babes in arms and very small children found themselves allocated only one—or, at most, two—of the bunks.

As the wife of a senior noncommissioned officer, Elspeth Campbell had been given a tier of three, each furnished with a straw palliasse and a single blanket, and situated in a recess to one side of the iron, wood-burning cooking stove. A stained curtain, hung on rings from a sagging wooden rail, gave the recess a measure of privacy, but that was all, and Jessica, when her escort left her, found her mother surveying her surroundings with something approaching dismay.

"These are quarters for sixty of us, not ninety," she asserted. "And hark to the children—it is like Bedlam out there! Or like a transport for convicts . . . and they are saying that the men are worse off than we are, with hammocks slung just a few inches apart. In bad weather, it will be unbearable."

Jessica said nothing. She felt lightheaded and racked with pain, scarcely able to concentrate on what her mother was saying. The concealing shawl fell from her shoulders as, unable to stay any longer on her feet, she slumped down on the lower bunk beside Flora, who, seemingly undisturbed by the shrieks and cries of the other children, slept as deeply as she had on the baggage cart.

Elspeth once again was made aware of the appalling severity of the beating her elder daughter had suffered, and was instantly contrite. She sent Janet to Morag Macrae, with instructions to remain with her until she was sent for, and when the child had gone, she lifted the sleeping Flora onto the upper bunk and went in search of water. Returning with a bowlful and some soothing ointment she had contrived to borrow, Elspeth set expertly to work cleansing and dressing Jessica's cuts and bruises, clicking her tongue with distress as the full extent of her injuries was revealed.

"He had no call to treat you so," she exclaimed indignantly. "And I've a mind to report him for it, truly I have. He is not knowing his own strength."

"He would never forgive you if you did report him," Jessica objected. "And they would do nothing. He would tell them that I had deserved it, and at most, he would receive a reprimand. You know what the officers are like, Mam." Captain Antill was not like the rest, she thought, but even he would not interfere in what would be regarded as a family matter.

Elspeth's capable fingers were trembling as she wiped the surplus ointment from their tips.

"I have done the best I can," she said. "But by rights I should be calling the surgeon to you."

"No!" Jessica's refusal was emphatic. "Please not, Mam. I feel easier now. Let us keep this between ourselves."

"Very well," her mother conceded. She rose from her knees, her thin face obstinately set, the jar of ointment still open. "I've a few bruises of my own to heal. But bide where you are, dear lass, and sleep for as long as you can. The weans will all be settled in their bunks soon, and maybe we shall get a little peace."

The *Hindostan* and the *Dromedary* sailed for Spithead next morning, and after a brief delay caused by the *Dromedary*'s running into a sandbar off Old Castle Point, they dropped anchor some four miles off the town of Portsmouth. There they both remained for a week, with much coming and going between the frigate *Hindostan* and the shore, but little activity on the part of the *Dromedary*'s civilian officers.

It was hot and airless in the families' quarters, the overcrowding a cause for constant complaint. Jessica slept

through most of the weary waiting, oblivious to both heat
and noise, but gradually her strength returned and her
bruises started to fade. A visit from the ship's master, Captain Pritchard, attended by several of his own and the regiment's officers, resulted in the rigging of a canvas contrap-
tion, supposedly intended to channel fresh air from the
upper deck to the depths of the orlop. It did little to disperse the fetid atmosphere or reduce the heat and smoke
emanating from the cooking stove, and as their children
grew more fractious, the women's complaints were redoubled.

On May 19, the *Dromedary* weighed anchor and brought-
to off St. Helen's, and word spread that the new Governor and his suite would come on board that day,
their arrival timed for five o'clock in the afternoon. That
morning, the 73rd's adjutant—flanked by the regimental
sergeant major, his orderly room sergeant, and two
clerks—made his appearance in the women's quarters.

"Gather round," he bade them officiously. "I have an
announcement to make that concerns you all. There have
been complaints of overcrowding on board this ship, and—"
He was interrupted by a chorus of indignant voices, as the
mothers reiterated their complaints, shrill with anger.

Coldly, he held up a hand for silence, and when the hubbub ceased, he made his announcement. "Your conditions
have been investigated and your objections to them are
held to be justified. I am therefore directed by Colonel
O'Connell to inform you that we shall transfer thirty of the
rank and file to His Majesty's ship *Hindostan*. In addition,
two officers, fifty other ranks, and forty women and children
will be set ashore and given accommodation in Portsmouth,
until such time as a convict transport bound for the colony
of New South Wales is able to embark them. The names of
those of you who will accompany your husbands ashore
will be read to you, and the ship's boats will commence
loading in two hours' time."

He motioned to one of the clerks, who cleared his throat
nervously and began to read. The first name on the list was
that of her mother, and Jessica caught her breath on a sob
as she heard it.

"Elspeth Campbell, wife of Company Sergeant Major Duncan Campbell of Number Four Company, and three children . . ." His voice droned on, but Jessica was not listening. She seized her mother's hand in a convulsive grasp and whispered, shaken, "Oh, Mam, Mam! Must we go, with *him*?"

"I must, with the weans . . . you know that. But you . . ." Elspeth hesitated, her dark brows knit in a worried pucker. The adjutant was addressing the assembled women again, giving them instructions as to the disposal of their baggage and where they must wait for the boats to take them ashore, and, her frown deepening, Elspeth led her daughter aside. Out of earshot of the rest, she said urgently, "The men will be going first and your stepfather with them. He'll not be able to come looking for you, Jessie, if you're wanting to stay on board."

"I'd need to hide again, Mam," Jessica whispered uncertainly. "And—" Tears came to ache in her throat, as she visualized the probable consequences if she disobeyed the order to leave the ship. "He will take it out on you, when he finds out I'm not with you. He—"

"That is of no matter, lass," Elspeth put in sharply. "You'll be gone, and the ship, too—if you've the courage to be going on your own. Mrs. Macrae will be here; she will be watching out for you if I ask her. And 'twill be to a new land that you'll be going, with friends, not strangers, for all the women know you well. That is surely to be preferred to what you'd have had to face if you had stayed in Yarmouth, once the regiment had left, is it not? You would have been truly alone then, Jessie."

That was indeed true, Jessica thought, but she continued to cling to her mother's hand, the pain and fear of parting coming to torment her anew.

"I'm not wanting to leave you, Mam," she managed, in a choked voice.

"You were ready to leave me when I found you hiding in the store cupboard," her mother reminded her. Her fingers tightened about the girl's small hand. "Besides, 'twill not be a long parting, dear lass. We shall be following after you as soon as there is a ship. You—" She broke off, as the adjutant and his clerks, their business finished, moved toward the companionway.

Pausing at its foot, the regimental sergeant major, a big man with heavy black whiskers adorning his dark-complexioned face, roared out a reminder that the shore boats would be ready to leave in two hours' time.

"Be sure that you are ready," he warned, "for they will not wait. And your husbands will have gone before you."

"You heard him?" Elspeth questioned.

"Aye, Mam, I heard him," Jessica acknowledged. Her heart quickened its beat. The voyage to Port Jackson would, she knew, take upward of six months. To be free of her stepfather's unpleasant company for six months was a tempting prospect. Her teeth closed fiercely over her lower lip, in a vain attempt to still its trembling. "I'll away and find a place to hide," she said, "if you are sure, Mam. If you—"

"Hush!" her mother whispered, cutting her short. "He is here. Go you and make a show of packing our things. You may leave me to speak with him."

Jessica obeyed, but as she watched the tall figure of her stepfather stride purposefully across to where her mother waited, she was seized by panic and had to fight against the instinctive urge to take to her heels and run . . . run anywhere, so long as it was away from him. Somehow she controlled herself, her eyes downcast as she thrust shawls and dresses, with the children's clothes, at random into her mother's wooden trunk. Small Flora, seated on the lower bunk, watched her in bemused sleepy silence; she had not noticed her father's arrival, but Janet had and she ran to him eagerly, both arms held out. Duncan Campbell's expression relaxed; beaming, he swept her off her feet and held her in a warm embrace, the picture of a loving father with his child.

Jessica again lowered her gaze and went on with her packing, filled with bitter resentment, and when he carried Janet back to the bunk, she did not look up, fearing to meet his gaze, lest she betray herself.

He said, an aggressive edge to his voice, "Your mam says you've learnt your lesson, Jessie. Be sure you have or there'll be trouble. I'm awa' now, wi' ma men, but see you're in guid time for the shore boat."

She inclined her head in wordless acquiescence, still careful to avoid his searching eyes and conscious of his mistrust. In the presence of the other women and children he dared not strike her, but he put out a hand, gripping her shoulder painfully.

"Did ye hear what I said?" he demanded.

"Yes, I heard," Jessica mumbled. There was a dress of her mother's to be folded; she held it up, like a barrier between them, her face hidden behind it.

"Yes, *Feyther*. Say it, you damned wee beezum!"

She said it into the folds of the dress, and he let her go. Thankfully she heard his heavy footsteps receding, and when she let the dress fall, her mother was beside her, white of face and breathless.

"You will be needing to hide yourself well, Jessie," she warned. "He says he will have a man posted at the entry-port, to make sure you leave the ship."

"I will hide," Jessica promised, her resolution hardened and her courage returning. "I will hide where no one will think to look for me."

She had no clear idea of where she would find the hoped-for concealment; the families had only twice been permitted access to the open deck since sailing from Yarmouth, and she had stumbled up in the wake of a mob of excited children, paying little attention to the decks they passed on their way. But, she recalled, one of the corporal's wives had pointed enviously to a row of white-painted wooden doors, two decks above the orlop, which occupied most of the stern part of the ship, and made some remark about officers' cabins and the differences between the accommodations they enjoyed and those of the married families.

If she was careful, she could probably find them again, and . . . Jessica drew a quick, uneven breath. If she took refuge in Captain Antill's cabin, he would surely not force her to go ashore. He had seen what her stepfather had done to her, and if she told him her reasons and threw herself on his mercy, he would listen to her at least. Although there was a risk—he was an officer and he had his duty. It would be safer, perhaps, to find an empty cabin, if she could. And . . .

Her mother, busy completing the repacking of their wooden trunk, gestured to her to assist with its closure.

"They will be coming to lift the heavy baggage soon. We must be ready." The trunk shut, and Elspeth sat back on her heels, brushing the perspiration from her heated face with a relieved sigh. "That is the worst of it—the rest will not be taking us long. I have been thinking that the best plan will be for you to come with the three of us to the entryport, Jessie, so that you can answer when the roll is called . . . and so that the soldier posted there will see you. Then you may go and hide when his back is turned. Once the last boat has gone, you will be safe." She added, with a mirthless little smile, "Remember to leave your own bundle here, for you will be needing it. And we will say our farewells here, before they call us."

When the order came for them to assemble at the entryport some two hours later, Jessica went with the rest, and her escape, after the roll had been called, proved a good deal easier than she had anticipated. A brief, surreptitious squeeze of her mother's hand and she slipped away, seemingly unnoticed in the confusion, as the forty women and children, with their baggage, were transferred to the waiting boats.

No one challenged her when she tiptoed up the deserted companionway to the deck above and found herself facing the two rows of white-painted cabin doors that had been her objective. All were closed, and the first four cabins, whose doors she opened warily, bore obvious signs of occupation.

The fifth was empty, devoid of personal belongings and evidently prepared for a single passenger, and after a swift glance up and down the passageway to ensure that she was unobserved, Jessica entered and closed the door behind her, her heart pounding. Gradually it resumed its normal steady beat and she looked about her, noticing for the first time that the cabin possessed a porthole, through which it was possible to look down on the entryport. Her small face pressed against the glass, she watched three boats, in turn, pull away from the ship's side, each with a cargo of despondent women and excited children, and the tears came, bitter and anguished, when she recognized her mother, with Flora on her knee.

Then they were gone, swallowed up in the blue haze of sea and sky, but she did not move, fearful of discovery should her footsteps be heard by the legitimate occupant of one of the neighboring cabins, for only a thin wooden screen separated one from the other. But no one came to dispute her occupancy of this one, and some time later— she had no idea how much later—she saw two of the boats return, piled high with baggage. The new Governor's, Jessica decided, and that of his suite, for there were leather, brass-bound trunks of superior quality, hatboxes, uniform cases. And . . . had not her mother said that Colonel Macquarie and his lady would board the ship at Spithead?

The third boat brought more baggage; then all three were hauled inboard and a barge was lowered, manned by seamen in uniform striped vests and white duck trousers, with two officers seated in the sternsheets. The boat for the Governor . . . with so much gilding on it, it could be nothing else, and despite her increasing weariness, Jessica watched eagerly for its return.

It came at last, heralded by the firing of a signal gun and the pounding of running feet on the deck planks above her head, followed by shouted orders and the grounding of arms—a guard of honor, she thought, accustomed to military ceremonial and able to visualize the scene taking place on the quarterdeck. Pressing closer to the glass of the porthole, she was able to make out the slightly stooping figure of an officer with graying hair, dressed in a gold-laced scarlet coat and with a field officer's cocked hat balanced on his knee, its plumes ruffled by the rising offshore breeze.

Colonel Macquarie, Governor-designate of the colony of New South Wales, Jessica told herself, peering down at the approaching barge, and less impressed by his appearance than she had supposed she would be. Seated on either side of him were two ladies, both muffled in dark cloaks. The one who looked to be the elder was, perhaps, in her early forties, with a round, smiling face and some wisps of coppery hair escaping from the confines of a severely practical bonnet, which was tied firmly beneath her chin.

The younger—only a few years older than herself, Jessica judged—was slim and pretty, wearing a bonnet that, by comparison with her companion's, was in the height of fashion. There was another gentleman, in civilian dress, but his face was turned away, and all she could see that was of interest to her was that he sported a very elaborate brocaded waistcoat and wore his hair powdered and tied in a long queue.

The barge came alongside, cut off partially from her line of vision by the bulging curve of the ship's side, and she stepped back, as the high-pitched shrilling of naval pipes told her that the new Governor must have stepped on board. It was then that she yielded to sudden panic, reminded of the precariousness of her own situation. The cabin in which she had taken refuge was a small one, prepared for a single occupant, who, clearly, had not yet come to claim possession of it. But it was on the officers' cabin deck and there would be little doubt that the owner—a staff officer, perhaps, or a valet or lady's maid in the Governor's service—would shortly put in an unwelcome appearance and order her removal.

Worse still, he or she might question her and, having done so, might report her to the adjutant or the orderly room sergeant and . . . Jessica's heart plummeted. There might still be time to send her ashore, for the ship had not yet weighed anchor. She moved to the door of the cabin, careful to make no sound as she opened it. From the quarterdeck came a chorus of resounding cheers, as the men of the regiment welcomed their new commander, and she heard the skirl of Highland pipes, playing a tune she recognized as "The Red-Tartaned Army." These compliments to the new arrivals would give her a little time, she thought, but would it be sufficient to enable her to return unobserved to the orlop deck? And if she did manage to return there, could she be sure that none of the women would report her? There were always one or two who, out of malice, were bent on making trouble, even for their own kind, but . . .

Biting her lip, Jessica pulled the door fully open. There was no one to be seen in the dimly lit passageway, and she had little choice but to risk swift and instant flight, back to the orlop. Discovery here would have worse consequences by far. She gathered up her skirts and ran, only to be brought abruptly to a halt by a tall, scarlet-clad figure which, turning into the passageway from its far end, now blocked her escape.

She stood, wide-eyed with fear, looking up into the stern, unsmiling face of Captain Antill. Recognizing her, this time without hesitation, his expression relaxed.

"Jessica India! Well, damme, I thought you had gone ashore with the sar'nt major!"

She stared up at him in mute despair. Then, finding her tongue at last, she said, in a faltering whisper, "I could not . . . go with him, sir. I *could* not."

"No," he conceded gently, "perhaps you could not." His fair brows met in a pensive frown. Finally, as if coming almost reluctantly to a decision, he opened the door of the cabin beside which he had been standing and gestured her to go inside.

"This is my cabin, child. You may stay here until we weigh anchor, which will be within the hour. Hush now"— he cut short her stammered thanks—"for both our sakes. I have not set eyes on you, and before heaven, I do not see you now! But I trust I can count on you to go back to your own quarters once we are under way?"

Having to fight back tears of gratitude, Jessica gave him her promise.

The young captain paused at the door, suddenly smiling. "I will do what I can do for you, India. Mrs. Macquarie is needing a second maid—if I were to recommend you to her, would you be willing to serve her?"

The tears came then and Jessica could not prevent them. "I would, sir," she sobbed. "Indeed I would!"

Next morning, with the *Dromedary* and the frigate *Hindostan* butting their way through a Channel gale, she entered the service of the lady with the copper-colored hair and the unfashionable bonnet and scarcely knew how to count her good fortune.

After an uneventful voyage of more than two months, the ships came to anchor on August 6, 1809, at Rio de Janeiro, where they were joined by the transport *Anne*. Mrs. Macquarie's personal maid, Mary Jones, gave notice and was put ashore—in order, it was widely believed, to join a soldier of the 73rd who had deserted soon after the *Dromedary* made port.

Jessica, invited to take her place, did so gladly and found herself, with strange irony, the legitimate occupant of the cabin in which, two months earlier, she had sought to hide from officialdom.

It was in Rio that she heard the first mention of the deposed Governor of New South Wales and of the military rebellion that had apparently taken place there. Brushing her mistress's lovely, glowing hair, in preparation for an official attendance at the Opera House at the invitation of the Prince Regent of Portugal, she listened to Mrs. Macquarie's account of two visitors to the ship who had called that morning, ostensibly to pay their respects to the new Governor.

"The frail, white-haired gentleman was Dr. Jamieson, late surgeon general of the colony. And his stout companion is also a surgeon—Dr. John Harris—who showed us sketches of the splendid house he owns in Sydney. They are an odd pair, seemingly wealthy and engaged in trade here . . . and both, on their own admission, took part in the rebellion against the late Governor, which was led by the military commandant, Major Johnston." Elizabeth Macquarie paused, her smooth brow pensively creased. Jessica went on brushing and her mistress continued, speaking more to herself than to her attentive but silent listener.

"They told Colonel Macquarie that Commodore Bligh was a cruel tyrant, who had to be arrested and deposed to ensure the colony's survival. And they said that he had broken his promise to return to England, as they are doing, so that the matter may be investigated fully by the home government. It seems that Mr. Bligh has taken the King's ship in which he was given passage—taken it, not to England, but to Van Diemen's Land, where he remains! And his daughter, Mrs. Putland, is with him."

She smiled into the mirror, meeting Jessica's dark and puzzled eyes in their joined reflection.

"But Mrs. Putland, from all accounts, is a young lady very much after my own heart. Dr. Harris said that when the troops marched to Government House under arms, for the purpose of effecting her father's arrest, she stood alone at the gate, defying them to enter, and with a parasol as her only weapon!"

Jessica echoed her mistress's smile, conscious of a feeling of admiration for the unknown Mrs. Putland.

"The young lady must be very brave, ma'am," she ventured.

Elizabeth Macquarie laughed, her laughter warm and expressing a genuine delight in the tale she had recounted. "You are not the only one to think so, Jessica India," she asserted. "Colonel O'Connell was much impressed by the description both gentlemen gave of her . . . and Mrs. Putland is a widow. I confess I am awaiting his meeting with her in the most sanguine anticipation, and, indeed, I am eager to make her acquaintance myself. That is, of course, if she and the commodore are still in the colony when we arrive there. I am, however, less eager to meet the late Governor, if all we have heard of him is true. He was in command of the *Bounty* when his crew mutinied against him, and according to Dr. Jamieson, during his term of office in New South Wales, he engaged in a merciless persecution of one of the colony's most successful and prosperous sheep farmers, a Mr. John Macarthur."

As if suddenly conscious of her surroundings and her audience, the new Governor's wife made a little grimace and rose to her feet, taking the hairbrush from Jessica's hand. "This is all over your head, is it not, child?" she said indulgently. "But never mind, you have done my ringlets beautifully and your brushing is very soothing. All the same, time is passing and I must attire myself for this evening's affair. It would never do to keep His Highness the Prince Regent and his consort waiting, would it? Although, if his appearance is anything to go by, the Prince is a far worse monster than Commodore Bligh . . . and he must weigh twenty stone at least! But, like my dear husband, Jessica, I have my duty to do. Fetch my ball gown, if you please, child, and see if you can lace it as skillfully as Mrs. Jones used to."

"Yes, ma'am," Jessica answered obediently. "I'll do the best I can, ma'am."

"I am sure you will, Jessica India," Elizabeth Macquarie affirmed, her tone warm and approving. "And who knows, perhaps in you I shall have found a treasure I shall never want to be without!"

"I hope so, ma'am." Jessica brought the elegant black gown, lifting it carefully from its hanger, her cheeks glowing.

In that moment, she was happier than she had been since her early childhood, and remembering how she had seen Mary Jones's expert fingers apply pressure to the gown's lacing, she set purposefully to work.

It was still a long way to Port Jackson and the rebellious colony of New South Wales . . . and she could learn, she told herself.

"That is too tight," her mistress reproached her gently. Jessica loosened the offending lace and began again. She *would* learn, she vowed silently, God helping her, she would learn. . . .

CHAPTER I

"Out oars! Give way together!" the gig's midshipman ordered. He glanced up at the small guard of scarlet-uniformed marines and the gang of fettered convicts, who had paused in their labors to witness the boat's departure, and added crisply, "Remember you're from a King's ship, my lads—let fall together!"

The oars splashed into the sun-dappled river water, but not in unison, and the faces of the four seamen from His Majesty's sloop-of-war *Porpoise* were sullen and resentful . . . the faces of men wholly lacking in enthusiasm for their task.

"I'm sorry, Mrs. Putland," the midshipman said, lowering his voice and aware that his crew's behavior would be a matter of some distress to his passenger. She was, after all, the widowed daughter of His Excellency Commodore William Bligh, the deposed Governor of the colony of New South Wales and his present commander. In an attempt to show his sympathy for her, Richard Tempest laid a diffident hand on hers. "We've all been here for too long, ma'am. It's hard to keep up the men's morale."

"I know that, Mr. Tempest," Mary Putland acknowledged. "You have no need to apologize to me."

She had been conscious of the seamen's feelings as soon as she had stepped into the gig, and after over eight months of frustrating inaction—spent for the most part at anchor in the mouth of the Derwent River and off Hobart Town—she had come perilously close to sharing their resentment.

Only the loyalty she bore her father sustained her now, as she glanced astern at the cluster of white-painted weatherboard huts and cottages, huddled haphazardly along the shoreline and clinging to the low hills beneath the snow-capped shadow of Mount Table. The residence of the Lieutenant Governor, Colonel David Collins, was as primitive and ramshackle as the rest, and Mary was glad to be leaving it, for all the dazzling natural beauty of its surroundings and the pleasantly temperate climate which the whole of Van Diemen's Land enjoyed.

To her, Hobart Town would always be a place of exile, a prison that only initially had offered the illusion of freedom. And Colonel Collins, with his lewd-mannered convict mistress, would always be an enemy, in spite of the courtesy he had displayed toward her personally and the hospitality he had insisted on offering her. She could regard him in no other way, since he had allied himself with the rebels in Sydney—those same traitors who, on January 26, 1808, had marched with three hundred bayonets behind them in order to arrest and overthrow their lawful governor.

Mary shivered and drew her cloak more closely about her shoulders. The events of that terrible day would continue to haunt her in memory, she thought bitterly, until the day she died. The sight of the glistening bayonets, borne by soldiers in the King's service, with their officers and their colors at their head, had filled her with terror, for she had feared for her father's life.

But they had spared his life, only to subject him to the infinitely less merciful humiliation of house arrest, when his dignity had been eroded and his pride humbled into the dust. They had held him thus for a year, while a succession of the regiment's commanding officers governed in his stead—first Major Johnston, who had led the rebellion, then Colonel Foveaux, and finally Colonel Paterson—and no help had been forthcoming, from England or even from India.

The gig pulled away from the wharf and out into mid-stream, to circle the sterns of two whaling ships at anchor, their crews hard at work flensing their malodorous catch, their decks slippery with blood and blubber. Mary held a handkerchief to her nose until the stench was blown away and then again returned to her earlier train of thought.

It was small wonder, she reflected, that when Colonel Foveaux had offered him a King's ship, on the condition that he should board at once and set course for England, her father had instead decided to sail his command to Hobart.

To Hobart, in search of help and support. As His Majesty's officially appointed Governor General and commander in chief, such help should surely have been readily accorded to him by a loyal Lieutenant Governor when it was requested, in the circumstances in which her father had made his request. Yet—Mary's small, firm mouth tightened. Colonel Collins had refused.

True, his initial reception had been correct, even cordial. He had received the deposed Governor with full honors, had opened his house and his town to her father and his officers, permitted the seamen shore leave, and supplied the ship with water and provisions. But then had come letters from the rebel administration in Sydney, with demands from Foveaux and accusations from Paterson, which claimed that "the late Governor," as they had the effrontery to describe her father, had broken the promise he had given them that he would return to England.

"A promise, extracted under duress by rebels and mutineers, could not," her father had declared, "be deemed valid or binding. Until His Majesty's government orders me to relinquish my office and leave the territory I was appointed to govern, I cannot do so."

He had issued a proclamation to this effect, but Hobart's Lieutenant Governor, instead of publishing it, had caused the rebel administration's counterclaims to be read out in church by his chaplain, the Reverend Robert Knopwood, and this . . . Mary's eyes filled with tears, as she recalled the unhappy occasion. This had been done when she herself, together with some of the officers of the *Porpoise,* had been present to attend divine service, as if deliberately to add insult to injury. And it had been followed by a blunt and discourteous refusal, in writing, to continue to supply His Majesty's ship *Porpoise* with provisions.

"I beg pardon, ma'am. . . ." Midshipman Tempest's voice broke into her thoughts, and Mary turned to look at him in mute question, her eyes still misted. For answer, he gestured astern of them in the direction of Mount Table, about the summit of which a sudden flurry of clouds had started to gather, their edges tinged with the red-gold of the sunlight they had obscured.

Mary Putland had been in the Derwent estuary long enough to recognize the danger signs and to know that these were frequently the prelude to the rising of a strong, gusting wind from the mountain, which swept down to lash the normally smooth surface of the river into a wilderness of storm-wracked water. Such storms were brief and localized, but to a small oared boat, like the one she was in, their effect could be disastrous.

"Have we time to reach the ship before that squall strikes, Rick?" she asked apprehensively, addressing the young officer by his Christian name. It was a measure of her anxiety that she did so in the hearing of the gig's crew, and she corrected herself hastily. "Mr. Tempest?"

Richard Tempest studied the distant, fiery-crested mountain with narrowed eyes and shook his head. He was some seven years her junior, but he had been at sea since the tender age of eleven, and her father—whose standards were extremely high—considered him, Mary knew, a competent and reliable officer.

"The ship is in Adventure Bay, Mrs. Putland," he told her, "not in the channel. If you were not with us, I might take the risk—but His Excellency would see me scuppered if I permitted any harm to come to you." He put his tiller over, his mind evidently made up. "Undermount Cove's just ahead of us—we'll pull in there and wait till it blows over, if you don't mind the delay, ma'am. It's better to be sure than sorry. Come on, my lads—pull!" he urged his crew. "Put your backs into it!"

This time the seamen plied their oars with a will, their former reluctance to exert themselves forgotten. To Mary's relief, they brought-to beneath the shelter of a curving, thirty-foot-high wall of basalt a good ten minutes before the first icy blast of wind struck the broad expanse of water astern of them, setting the two whalers they had passed in the outer harbor rocking violently at their moorings.

About a mile downriver, but clearly visible to those in the *Porpoise*'s gig, a small fishing or sealing vessel tacked from under the lee of the land with all sail incautiously set and, receiving the full force of the squall, was thrown on her beam-ends. She appeared in imminent danger of capsizing until her people managed to take in sail and bring her head to the wind. Then, looking like a toy ship at that distance, she lay wallowing in the wind-whipped swell under a single flapping headsail, and Mary, watching as tensely as the rest, expelled her breath in a gasp of relief.

"You made the right decision, Mr. Tempest," she offered, smiling. "For all the time I've spent at sea during these last few years, I confess I am no sailor and I dread these sudden squalls."

Midshipman Tempest echoed her smile. She was, he thought admiringly, one of the most courageous women he had ever met and, with her pale, oval face and brilliantly blue eyes, also one of the most beautiful. But she was very much her father's daughter, possessed at times of his quick and alarming temper, and he knew better than to presume on the kindly condescension that had made friendship between them possible.

"Then," he suggested diffidently, "you'll not be looking forward to rejoining us on board the *Porpoise*, ma'am?"

"I could not have remained under Colonel Collins's roof even an hour longer, in the circumstances," Mary Putland answered with asperity. "And, I assure you, I do not regret leaving Hobart." She added, a distinct edge to her voice, "You heard, I suppose, that Colonel Foveaux's last dispatch demanded that my father should be placed under arrest?"

"Lieutenant Lord told me, when I was waiting for you on the wharf," Richard confirmed. He moved closer, cup-

ping his hands about his mouth so that his passenger, and
not his boat's crew, could hear him above the now muted
assault of the wind. "I fear there will be fresh trouble in
store for us, on Colonel Collins's account, when he learns
about his son, ma'am."

"His son?" Mary stared at him in surprise, thinking initially of the noisy brood of unmannerly children—the offspring of Colonel Collins's convict paramour—whose riotous behavior had frequently shocked her during her stay
in Hobart's drafty, mud-floored Government House. Then
she recalled the fifteen-year-old boy whom, when relations
had been cordial, her father had accepted as a midshipman
on board the *Porpoise*.

This had meant a great deal to Hobart's Lieutenant Governor, she knew, for the boy was the apple of his eye, and
even when he had told her father, with cold formality, that
neither he nor his ship's company would, in future, be permitted to set foot on shore, he had not asked for an exception to be made for his son. Rather he had offered one, in
her own case. . . . Mary sighed, remembering his words.

"Mrs. Putland may remain as my guest in Hobart for as
long as she wishes to do so, Commodore Bligh," he had
said. "In return, you will, I trust, sir, treat my son as you
would treat any other officer serving under your command. I am anxious for him to make a career in the King's
service."

"Do you mean Colonel Collins's eldest son, Mr. Tempest?" she asked. "The one who is called after him . . .
Midshipman David Collins?"

"Yes, that's who I mean, ma'am. But he's no longer a
mid—he's been disrated, and the colonel will be getting
him back tomorrow morning," Richard Tempest answered
dryly. "The silly young idiot got roaring drunk when he
went with a boarding party to intercept a trader, from
which we—er—commandeered supplies. Our young Mr.
Collins commandeered his own, and it appears he drank a
lot while his boat was being loaded."

"Oh, dear!" Mary exclaimed, distressed. "How foolish of
him."

She had seen enough of naval discipline to guess what

the consequences of such foolishness were likely to be, particularly if her father had witnessed the boy's fall from grace, and Richard Tempest confirmed her unhappy foreboding when he added disparagingly, "He stove in two oars when he brought his boat alongside and talked back to the officer of the watch when he was reprimanded for his lubberliness. We might have covered that up, Mrs. Putland—indeed, we tried to, not for his sake but to avoid causing any more friction with Colonel Collins. Unfortunately"—he shrugged resignedly—"we couldn't. I think myself that the idle little scallywag was looking for trouble. He's not cut out for the service, and I fancy he'd had enough—he was trying to do what the pressed men sometimes attempt, to work his ticket."

Mary nodded her understanding. Men taken by the press gang often resorted to desperate measures to prove themselves unsuitable for the King's service, in the hope that they would, as a result, be discharged from it—with ignominy, if need be. But David Collins was only a boy, a boy of fifteen accepted for training as an officer, for whom conditions were infinitely better than those prevailing on the lower deck. Sensing that there was more to come, she prompted uneasily, "What else did he do? I hope he did not incur His Excellency's displeasure?"

"I'm afraid he did, ma'am," Richard Tempest admitted ruefully. "The young fool went to sleep on watch. His Excellency was on the quarterdeck, with Captain Porteous, and almost literally fell over him, and then, believe it or not, he had the temerity to argue the toss with both of them! I wasn't there, it was my watch below, but . . ." He repeated his shrug. "I heard from those who were present that it was a pretty hot exchange while it lasted. His Excellency, as you know, ma'am, is not one to take lip from a junior officer—least of all from a volunteer mid, who was appointed only as a favor to his father. That's what convinced me that young Collins was deliberately looking for trouble. But he went too far, and I don't imagine he bargained for just how much trouble he was going to land himself in."

Mary frowned. Clearly her own urgent summons to return to the *Porpoise*—for which there had been no explanation—must stem from the decision to dispense with young David Collins's services. But, if Rick Tempest's conjecture was right, this was the outcome the boy himself had wanted and no blame could accrue to anyone else.

She started to say so but broke off when, turning to face him, she saw the midshipman shake his head. "That's not quite all, Mrs. Putland," he warned.

"Not all? For goodness' sake, Mr. Tempest, what more is there?"

He eyed her uneasily. "Collins was sentenced to twenty-four lashes. The sentence was to be carried out this morning, but I—I was glad to miss it. Having the boat duty, I—"

"He's been *flogged*?" Mary interrupted, staring at him in disbelief. "Oh, dear God!" Officers of the Royal Navy were never flogged; that was a brutal punishment reserved for the lower deck. When a young gentleman was deemed to be in need of corporal punishment, this was carried out in the privacy of the midshipmen's berth by one of his seniors—and with a cane, not the dreaded cat, which marked a man for life.

Such treatment, meted out to the son for whom he had such high hopes, would anger Colonel Collins beyond endurance, Mary thought and, for the first time, found herself questioning her adored father's judgment. The relationship between the two men was sour enough, in all conscience, but this . . . She drew in her breath sharply and then asked, keeping her voice very low, "Mr. Tempest, did His Excellency impose the sentence? Did *he* order Mr. Collins to be flogged?"

"Oh, no, ma'am!" Richard Tempest's denial was emphatic. "It was the captain who ordered it."

Lieutenant John Porteous—captain by courtesy, because he commanded the *Porpoise*—Mary reminded herself, had always been guilty of disloyalty to her father's cause. The rebel administration in Sydney had given him a substantial grant of land in the Bringelly district, on which he had intended to settle, and he had returned reluctantly to his command, after her father had placed his successor, Lieutenant Kent, under arrest for dereliction of duty.

They had both been guilty of that, she thought with resentment. During the long weary months, when she and her father had been held under armed guard in Government House, the *Porpoise* had come back to her anchorage in Sydney Cove, after running the rebels' errands to Norfolk Island, Coal River, and Van Diemen's Land, and although there had been ample opportunity for them to do so, neither Porteous nor Kent made any attempt to support their lawful Governor or free him from arrest.

Rather they had supported Major Johnston and Colonel Foveaux from the very outset, dining in the Corps mess, receiving hospitality from its officers and from the Macarthurs and . . . Mary frowned, remembering. Captain Porteous had even accepted appointment as a magistrate, when the rebel administration had offered it. Had he now, she wondered, from the depths of her own disillusionment, an ulterior motive in imposing so harsh a sentence on a fifteen-year-old midshipman, merely because he was who he was—the son of Hobart's Lieutenant Governor?

Colonel Collins's reaction was predictable. He would be furiously angry, and he would lay blame for the whole unhappy affair at her father's door. And that being so, he could be expected to redouble his efforts to drive her father's leaking, unweatherly ship out of the shelter of the Derwent estuary and back to sea . . . back to England, perhaps, as her whole ship's company so evidently desired. Facilities for the repairs the *Porpoise* needed to make her seaworthy had been declared conditional on her commander's assurance that she would leave the port as soon as they were completed . . . an assurance that her father had forbidden Captain Porteous to give.

Feeling tears come welling into her eyes, Mary bit her lip in an attempt to regain her accustomed composure. There had been so many betrayals, so many acts of disloyalty both before and since the military garrison's rebellion . . . surely, she reproached herself wearily, she should be used to that by now. When the allegiance of King's officers could be bought by illegal gifts of Crown land, and when the desire for personal enrichment overrode the claims of duty, what else could one expect, save the betrayal her father had suffered?

"I suppose," she managed quietly, avoiding Midshipman Tempest's concerned and sympathetic gaze, "it will all be over, by the time we reach the ship?"

"Yes, ma'am," he agreed gravely. "Hands were being piped to witness punishment when my boat was called away."

There was a brief, tense silence, broken by the bowman's relieved shout. "Squall's blown over, I reckon, sir!"

Richard Tempest turned, shading his eyes with a slim brown hand. The sealer was setting sail again and getting under way, and the clouds had vanished from the flat, snowcapped summit of Mount Table as swiftly as they had appeared.

He inclined his head. "I reckon it has," he confirmed. "Right, lads—out oars! Let fall together! With a will now—pull!"

Mary huddled in her cloak and closed her eyes, her thoughts winging their way ahead of her to the distant ship.

On board His Majesty's ship *Porpoise,* the sixty officers and seamen mustered in a hollow square in the waist came stiffly to attention and removed their headgear, in obedience to the shouted command.

The shivering young prisoner, whose punishment they were about to witness, stood between the master-at-arms and the marine drummer, clad only in white ducks and a striped jersey, his lower lip trembling visibly. But few of the men spared him a pitying glance or a murmur of encouragement; as an officer, young David Collins had failed to win their esteem, still less their liking, and almost to a man, they deemed his punishment deserved.

None saw its incongruity or imagined any sinister purpose behind it; rather they were enjoying the unusual spectacle of an upstart young bully being served in the manner in which they were served when they offended against naval discipline or tradition. And he was one of them now, his officer's privileges taken from him—disrated to ordinary seaman, for all his father was Lieutenant Governor of Hobart and a colonel in the Royal Marines.

The *Porpoise*'s commander, Captain John Porteous, thin and lantern-jawed, stepped forward, his cocked hat tucked beneath his arm, to read the charge and quote the requisite Article of War under which it was brought.

"You have been found guilty of the offenses as charged and are sentenced to receive twenty-four lashes and to be dismissed from His Majesty's service and from this ship," the captain stated coldly. "Have you anything to say on your behalf?"

The boy drew himself up, suddenly finding defiance, if not courage, his dark eyes blazing with fury.

"I say you've no right to flog me—my father will make you pay dearly for it! There'll be no water and no supplies smuggled out from the shore, because I'll tell him how it's done and he'll put a stop to it! Then you'll have to leave here and good riddance. And . . . and I hope they hang you for a tyrant when you reach England, Mr. Bligh!"

He pursed his lips and, turning quickly, ejected a stream of spittle in the direction of Governor Bligh, who, a silent spectator, was standing a little apart from the group of officers on the larboard side of the deck. Whatever else the boy had intended to say was abruptly cut short when the shocked master-at-arms thrust a big hand, none too gently, over his mouth, jerking his head back so that he stumbled and fell to his knees.

"Seize him up!" Captain Porteous snapped. As the order was being obeyed, he ventured a covert glance at the Governor, but the older man's expression offered no indication of his feelings. It was as if he had not heard the angry youngster's outburst or, if he had, was indifferent to the threats it had contained.

He simply stood, a stocky, undeniably dignified figure, hands clasped behind his back, his gaze fixed on the tree-grown shoreline of Bruni Island. William Bligh had first entered this bay in 1777, when serving as Captain Cook's master in the *Resolution,* Porteous recalled, and again when in command of the ill-omened *Bounty,* eleven years later

. . . it must hold many memories for him. But even so, his attitude was odd, his silence difficult to comprehend.

Bligh held no brief for Colonel Collins's unpleasant young son and had not questioned the sentence imposed on the boy, although his own had been less harsh. Porteous frowned. What had he said, after the fracas on deck?

"That young man will never make an officer. He has no regard for discipline and no sense of duty. Have him disrated and sent back to his father, Captain Porteous. And, when he appears before you, make sure that the error of his ways is made clear to him—and to the ship's company."

Well, he had done that, John Porteous reflected grimly . . . although the suggestion of a flogging had come from his erstwhile second-in-command, William Carlile Kent, still held under open arrest and confined to his cabin by Commodore Bligh. Poor Kent! His motives were self-evident, even transparent . . . he wanted the ship to leave Hobart and sail for home, so that he might put his case to a court-martial, and if flogging the Lieutenant Governor's insolent brat of a son achieved that aim, there was not a man—save Commodore Bligh—who would not cheer his head off at the prospect. The ship's company had long since wearied of the sight of Adventure Bay and D'Entrecasteaux's Channel, and of the hand-to-mouth existence they led, dependent on incoming vessels for supplies, of which, in the King's name, the commodore ordered them to be robbed. Indeed, His Majesty's ship *Porpoise*—*his* ship—was now committing acts of piracy for which there could be no justification, and—

"Sir!" The chief boatswain's mate was standing at attention in front of him, the cat removed from its red baize bag, its nine knotted tails ominously dangling. "Two dozen, is it, sir?"

John Porteous glanced again at the commodore, but Bligh had pointedly turned his back on the proceedings. He was leaning, epauletted shoulders slightly hunched, on the rail, and he continued to stare with absorbed attention at the line of surf breaking on the distant shore.

"Two dozen," the *Porpoise*'s commander confirmed. "To be laid on well. Do your duty, bo'sun's mate!"

He nodded to the surgeon, who at once stood back, yielding his place at the pinioned prisoner's side. The marine drummer beat a roll on his drum; the boatswain's mate swung the whip behind his head and brought its thong hissing across young Collins's naked back with practiced skill. The first stroke raised a series of ugly red weals across the tautly stretched skin, the second drew blood, and before it fell again, Collins was screaming hysterically for mercy, all the defiance he had displayed earlier knocked out of him.

The men gave him no sympathy. The older hands, accustomed to more stoicism in those condemned to punishment, turned their heads away in disgust as he struggled to free his arms from the ropes binding him to the wooden grating, his high-pitched shrieks rising above the hissing of the cat.

"Six lashes, sir!" the master-at-arms called out. Captain Porteous looked in mute question at the surgeon, who shook his head without speaking. The whip was raised again and Porteous saw the commodore turn, his face still devoid of expression.

"That will do," he said, with crisp decisiveness. "Cut him down and let the surgeon have him."

"Cut him down, sir?" Porteous echoed, unable to conceal his surprise. "But he's only taken half a dozen, sir, and I—"

"I said that will do, Captain Porteous." The deposed Governor's tone was icy, his blue eyes as cold and uncompromising as his voice. "When you have dismissed the ship's company, have the goodness to call away the longboat with Mr. Fortescue in command."

"The . . . the longboat, sir?" His mind still on the abruptly terminated punishment, the *Porpoise*'s commander stared at him uncomprehendingly. "Is it your intention to send Mr. Collins back to Hobart right away, sir?"

"No, damn your eyes, sir, it is not!" Bligh retorted irritably. "Are you blind as well as deaf? Look over there, devil take it, man!" He gestured toward the flat, faraway summit of Mount Table, with its crown of menacing, red-tinged clouds. "There is a strong squall blowing up in the estuary, and my daughter's on her way in the gig. Forget about your blasted flogging and the scurvy reason for it. . . . You and Mr. Kent have done all the harm the pair of you intended, rest assured of that. Dismiss the muster and call away my boat, if you please."

"Aye, aye, sir," Porteous acknowledged, feeling suddenly defeated and ill at ease. Unable to meet the accusation in his superior's eyes, he lowered his own and gave the required orders with less than his accustomed authority.

Only when the longboat had pulled away, with Commodore Bligh in the sternsheets, did he seek out Lieutenant Kent in the after cabin in which he was confined.

"We pulled no wool over His infernal Excellency's eyes, Willie," he said sourly. "He knows—or he hazarded a damned accurate guess! Although, before heaven, I'd swear that little rogue Collins asked for everything he got."

"Wait till we get him back to England, John," William Kent returned, a gleam lighting his dark eyes. "We'll have an array of the most distinguished witnesses to testify against him . . . damme, Admiral Hunter; my revered uncle, Governor King, if he recovers; the officers of the *Buffalo;* and, of course, that poor unfortunate, devil, Joseph Short. And these, in addition to John Macarthur's people and, not least, George Johnston's highly influential father."

"Who is Johnston's father?" Porteous asked, and added, with an attempt at humor, "I didn't realize he had one."

"Oh, but he has, my dear fellow," Kent assured him, with conscious malice. "Our George is a by-blow of His Grace of Northumberland, no less—or so my uncle, *post-Captain* Kent, recently revealed to me in a letter. Indeed, I have the letter somewhere. It's confidential, of course, but I see no reason why you should not glance at it."

John Porteous read the letter. "D'you know, Willie," he said, his round, red face wreathed in smiles, "I do believe we'll have the *Bounty* bastard over the proverbial barrel, if we could only get him to go home."

"We may yet," Kent suggested, also smiling. "There are

moves afoot in the Colonial Office at long last, my friend, and a great deal of pressure to have him recalled. And his successor as Governor of the colony of New South Wales has been chosen and should reach Sydney by the end of the year."

"Who is he?" Porteous questioned. "The new Governor, I mean."

"A certain Colonel Lachlan Macquarie of the Seventy-third Foot, about whom nothing is known, save that he's bringing his regiment with him in a fifty-gun frigate. An old India hand," William Kent added. "Staff officer, but that's all I've heard. He wasn't the home government's first choice."

Captain Porteous rose thoughtfully to his feet. "At least," he said, "he could scarcely be worse than his predecessor, could he, Willie?"

He did not wait for William Kent's reply but left the cabin, closing the door carefully behind him.

more who is the Colonial Office of Long Jan, as it was, and a man that of you're as these impregnate. And the successor as Governor of the colony of New South Wales has been chosen and sworn Lecked Storey by the end of the war.

Yemen, he? Bottoms, concluded. "I'll now Governor Lennox.

"A certain Colonel Zachton Macpheson of the Seventy-third Regiment opposition nothing." I'shdiya, say to that I was minging the regiment with him is with you're orders. Ay his long hand." William Keat added. "And, officers, but that's all I've heard. He want," the horse scratching it, "that cholis.

Captain Hogonus cried thoughtfully, to the Keel. "Mr. Shaw." he said. "He and his subaltern he wore that his predecessor could have with it."

He had me well for William Keat's sake, but felt captain at owing me close enough to hand him.

CHAPTER II

The morning of Thursday, December 28, 1809, was dark and stormy, with a strong, gale-force wind veering from west to west-northwest, which brought the temperature plummeting.

During the previous night there had been a severe thunderstorm, with hail and lightning, and although the convoy of three ships bringing the new Governor to Sydney had signaled the South Head watch for a pilot, there was little chance, Justin Broome knew from experience, that the ships would be able to make port until the wind dropped.

He had left the cabin of his own small command, the *Flinders* cutter, at first light, hoping that now that he had the facilities of Mr. Robert Campbell's shipyard at his disposal, he would be able to complete the repairs he was making to the vessel within twenty-four hours. The slender new mast was there, the sheerlegs ready; but Campbell's workmen had failed to put in an appearance, and his shipwright, Sammy Mason, had shrugged resignedly when questioned, and gestured to the lowering clouds.

"You'll not find men willing to work in these conditions, Justin lad," he had stated, in a tone that brooked no argument. "Take a run ashore, why do you not, and drown your sorrows like most of us do?"

It was no use resenting Mason's attitude, Justin told himself, resenting it nonetheless. The shipwright was a good man, first-rate at his job, and the laborers Robert Campbell employed were not convicts who could be compelled by an overseer's lash to carry on with whatever task was assigned to them, without regard for the weather. But . . . He swore as he looked up at his stubby remnant of a masthead. It had sprung and finally snapped off at the cap when he was attempting to round Barrenjoey Head, his hold crammed with settlers' wheat and his deck jam-packed with people and livestock rescued from the floodwaters of the Hawkesbury River.

Aided by his crew and a couple of settlers, Justin had contrived a jury rig—a spar lashed to the masthead. It had held; the lashing was secure enough, despite the fact that he and Cookie Barnes had had to work in icy darkness, with the gale threatening to hurl the pair of them into the sea. He had brought his passengers safely into Sydney Cove, and as a result had been well nigh overwhelmed by their gratitude. Indeed, for all the state of penury in which so many of them existed, they had taken up a subscription for him, to cover the cost of a new mast. Justin would be only a few pounds out of pocket when Mr. Campbell's account for the mast was settled. But . . . His scowl deepened. He had wanted to be on his way back to the Hawkesbury as soon as the storm abated, for the work of rescue was not yet finished. The flooding had been unusually severe, and even in places where the banks were up to thirty feet high, the swollen river had risen above them . . . and in the course of a single night.

His mother's farm at Long Wrekin was on high ground, and although both arable land and some of the sheep pastures might be flooded, the farmhouse itself and most of the buildings should be in little danger. All the same, he had wanted to make sure, for the flood had come without warning—fed during the hours of darkness by swollen torrents from the Blue Mountain range—while not a drop of rain had fallen on Sydney until the day before yesterday, and the temperature had been in the high eighties.

The *Flinders* was not, of course, the only vessel engaged in rescuing endangered stock. Jed Burdock, with his ketch

Fanny, Andre Thompson, the Governor's bailiff at the Green Hills, and a score of oared-boat owners had rallied to the aid of isolated settlers in the area, as had the government sloop *Lady Nelson* and several others from Sydney. Most of the harvested wheat would be saved, if it was stored out of reach of the invading water, but the livestock, Justin thought regretfully, probably would not fare so well.

He turned, hearing his name called, and saw Sammy Mason crossing the wharf in his direction, a coat pulled over his head against the driving rain.

"You still there, Justin?" the shipwright shouted, cupping his hands about his mouth.

"Yes, I'm here." Justin hoisted himself from deck to wharf with the ease of long practice. "Have the men shown up?"

"No, and not likely to, lad. Here, let's get under shelter while I tell you who has . . ." Samuel Mason led the way into the carpenters' shed and, divesting himself of the coat, shook the worst of the dampness from it before thrusting his powerful arms back into the sleeves. This done, he eyed Justin appraisingly before going on. "I've the offer of a hiring for your *Flinders*."

"Oh, for mercy's sake, Sammy," Justin protested. "You know I can't accept a hiring until we get that new mast stepped! And when we have, I'm promised back up the Hawkesbury. Dammit, I—"

"Hold hard, lad," Mason enjoined him. "You've not heard who wants your boat and why. Maybe you'll change your mind when you have."

"Well, I'm all ears," Justin invited guardedly. "If it's a run to Parramatta, I daresay my jury rig would serve. But—"

"It'll serve to take you to the Heads, I reckon . . . and that's where Colonel Foveaux wants to go," Mason interrupted.

"Colonel Foveaux—the Lieutenant Governor in person?" Justin laughed. "Are you jesting, Sammy? He has his own official barge . . . what does he want with my *Flinders*? I've been carrying sheep from the Hawkesbury, and hogs and chickens too, and I've scarcely had time to clean up

after them. His Honor wouldn't like the stench, any more
than he'd fancy getting his uniform messed up."

"He's not bothered about that, Justin, or so he told me.
He has urgent business with the new Governor, and his
ship's lying off the South Head. As to the official
barge"—Mason's tone was undisguisedly malicious—"her
oaf of a cox'un neglected to secure her last night. She
broke free of her moorings when the wind got up and was
driven on shore, with half her bottom boards stove in. If
His Honor put out in her, she'd sink before she ever left
the cove!"

"Do you mean it? You're not jesting?"

"I'm not jesting. And the colonel isn't, neither. He's
waiting in my office." The shipwright jerked his head in
the direction from which he had come. "In a powerful
hurry, seemingly, 'cause he said I was to tell you he wants
to get under way at once."

"I ply for hire, Sammy," Justin reminded him. "What is
he offering?"

"Enough to pay for that new mainmast of yours, I
shouldn't wonder. But you'd best strike your own bargain
with him, lad. He's a rich man, don't forget . . . and the
Flinders is the only sailboat here right now. You can hold
him to ransom."

Justin grinned. "Some might—I won't. All right, Sammy,
my friend, tell him I'll take him out to South Head, but at
his risk for thirty shillings. To be paid when I put him
alongside the new Governor's ship . . . *if* I do! I'll rouse
Cookie Barnes and be ready to get under way as soon as
I've checked that lashing on the masthead. Say in half an
hour."

"Right, lad, I'll tell him."

Mason peeled off his coat and once again draped it over
his head and shoulders. Justin Broome was a fine young
fellow, he thought approvingly; a good example of the type
of youngster this colony could breed from its convict stock.
But then his father had been a prime seaman, who had
served as sailing master under Captain Flinders in the *Investigator*, and his mother, by all accounts, was a fine
woman. An emancipist, whose pardon, if his memory

served him right, had been granted by Governor Phillip, together with land on the Hawkesbury, and who had married, as her second husband, the late-Governor's aide, Captain Andrew Hawley of the Royal Marines.

Captain Hawley was in bad odor with the rebel administration, of course, and had been banished from Sydney because he had resolutely refused them his support; but he was a cut above the self-styled Lieutenant Governor, now waiting so impatiently in the wharf office. Samuel Mason spat, accurately and derisively into a puddle of rain, as he reached the office door. It did not do, as he was well aware, to offer criticism of those in power, and Colonel Joseph Foveaux *was* in power these days, although—thanks be to God—with the arrival of the new Governor, he was unlikely to be for very much longer.

And that, the shrewd old shipwright guessed, was—whether young Justin Broome realized it or not—the reason for his impelling desire to go out to the recently arrived convoy from England. By hook or by crook, Colonel Bloody Foveaux intended to be the first to gain the new Governor's ear and to give his own account of the overthrow of Governor Bligh and what had led up to it . . . and even if he had to lie his head off, he would endeavor to justify everything the rebel administration had done in the interim.

Well, bad cess to him! He would have his work cut out to explain the thousands of acres of prime farming land that he and his nominal superior, the drink-sodden commandant of the Corps, Colonel Paterson, had given so freely to their adherents during the past year. Over sixty thousand acres, if the rumors were to be believed . . . and Sam Mason for one *did* believe them. But maybe it would be as well if Justin's jury-rigged masthead would prove unequal to the strain he was about to subject it to—the wind was veering southwesterly and showed no signs of moderating. If the lad had any sense, he would come about and head back to the cove long before he came within hailing distance of the new Governor's ship . . . and be damned to Colonel Foveaux's thirty shillings!

Pausing by the door, Samuel Mason composed his leathery features into some semblance of an obliging smile, and then, wearing it as conspicuously as he could, he donned his dripping jacket and reentered the office.

Colonel Joseph Foveaux, who had been pacing up and down the length of the small wooden building, came to a halt at the sound of the opening door. He was a tall man, now in his mid-forties and inclining slightly to corpulence, with dark eyes and a deeply tanned skin which, despite the elegance of his impeccably cut uniform, gave him the appearance of having Romany blood . . . or at least of not being English. Indeed, Samuel Mason had heard it said that his mother had been French, and his father an aristocrat . . . probably, he thought unkindly, one of those the French revolutionaries had sent to the guillotine, before the advent of the dreaded Boney. It was a pity they had not sent his son with him. . . .

"Well, my good fellow?" the colonel demanded. "Have you succeeded in persuading young Broome to take me out to the King's ships?"

"Aye, sir, I have," Mason answered. "Not that he was eager, you understand." He explained about the *Flinder*'s mainmast head, taking particular care to emphasize the extent of the damage the cutter had sustained, but Colonel Foveaux waved him to silence.

"Yes, yes, I understand perfectly. But Broome's a good boat handler, is he not, and his vessel otherwise sound?"

"Oh, yes, indeed, sir."

"Well, then?" Foveaux snapped. "When will he be ready to receive me and how much will he charge?"

Samuel Mason, resenting his arrogant tone, continued nevertheless to smile up at him. "Just as soon as he's checked the mainmast lashings and roused up his crew, sir. Say twenty minutes, and . . . it'll be forty shillings for the hire, Your Honor, to be paid when Broome puts you alongside the *Dromedary*." He hesitated, hoping for a reward for his pains, but Colonel Foveaux showed no sign of reaching into his pocket.

"The *Dromedary*?" he echoed, frowning. "I thought His—ah—His Excellency would be on board the frigate. She's the *Hindostan,* is she not, of fifty guns?"

"Aye, sir, that was the signal. But His Excellency's on board the *Dromedary*, according to the master of a sealer that put into port ahead o' the convoy. He'd spoken the frigate, Your Honor, off Cape Pillar, Van Diemen's Land, a fortnight since. She'd carried away her main topmast and stuns'l boom and—"

Again the colonel cut him short. "Yes, yes, but that's of no matter now. Just so long as I know that Colonel Macquarie is on board the *Dromedary*." He glanced through the open doorway at the teeming rain and asked, with an abrupt change of tone, "Have you any oilskins, Mason, that I can borrow?"

"Oh, aye, sir, certainly." Samuel Mason went to rummage in one of the store cupboards, taking his time. "For yourself, sir, is it? You'll not be taking any other gentlemen with you?"

He knew the answer before it was given but was quite unprepared for the vehemence with which Foveaux spat out, "No, damn your eyes, I am not!" The oilskins in his hands, he backed away in alarm.

"No offense, Your Honor. It was just that . . . well, sir, seeing I was getting out the oilskins, I thought maybe you'd want more than one set and—"

"Don't speculate on matters that are none of your infernal business, Mr. Mason," Colonel Foveaux warned him wrathfully. "All right—away with you and tell Broome to make ready. I shall be out as soon as I have donned those oilskins, if you will kindly give them to me."

Ten minutes later, the *Flinders* cast off from the wharf, and the old shipwright muttered obscenities under his breath as he watched her go, only her headsails set as she drew away. Justin, he reflected moodily, had been wise to abandon the overambitious rig for which he had initially designed her. Under a gaff mainsail, a square-cut topsail, and two jibs, she was ideal for the work she did, but all the same he hoped that the lad would watch out for himself and his vessel when he reached the Heads. If he hadn't the sense to turn back . . .

On board the cutter, Colonel Foveaux stood by the weather rail until Justin had manuevered her out of the

shelter of the anchorage and cautiously run up the reefed
mainsail. Then, as the wind caught her and she heeled
over, he took himself below to the comparative comfort of
the cabin. There he remained, seemingly preoccupied with
his own thoughts until, after a rough but otherwise uneventful run down Sydney's rain-obscured harbor, the *Flinders*
neared three King's, lying under storm canvas off the Heads.

"Convoy's in sight, sir!" Justin sang out, but he received
no reply from the cabin. He stood on, running by the lee
and having to fight the wheel as the wind veered and the
Flinders started pitching wildly. "Stand by to tack," he
warned Cookie Barnes, his crewman. "The ship we want is
to loo'ard."

The *Dromedary*, although he had never seen her before,
was easily distinguishable from her consorts by her size.
The new Governor's ship was a bluff-bowed Indiaman,
with an elaborate figurehead and much gilded scrollwork
decorating her stern windows and galleries, her gunports—
like those of a ship of war—painted black.

As the distance between the two vessels lessened, Justin
saw that half a dozen of the *Dromedary*'s maintopmen were
aloft, struggling to take in a flapping storm trysail that had
split in the wind's relentless assault. More men were
scurrying up the shrouds to their aid, and all attention on
the transport's deck was concentrated on their efforts, an
officer bawling orders to them through his speaking trumpet.

No one saw or hailed him as he put his wheel over,
slipped a lashing on it, and went forward to help Cookie
Barnes lower the mainsail. Returning to the wheel, he ran
the *Flinders* under the *Dromedary*'s stern and skillfully
brought her alongside the lee quarter. Barnes hooked on to
the chains as the *Flinders* lost way, sheltered at last from
the wind by the transport's towering bulk, and between
them they took in the jibs.

After a perceptible delay, an officer hailed him, and by
the time Colonel Foveaux emerged from below, a rope ladder snaked down from the entryport and a seaman leaned
out, ready to assist his ascent.

Foveaux started to peel off his oilskins but then, glancing upward to the head of the rope ladder, changed his mind. He felt in his breeches pockets, brought out a half-guinea and some small silver coins and, realizing that together they did not amount to the hiring charge to which he had agreed, returned the silver to his pocket.

Thrusting the half-guinea into Justin's hand, in the manner of one offering largesse to a mendicant, he said, with lofty jocularity, " 'Pon my soul, Broome, I seem to be short of cash . . . and who isn't, in this infernal colony? But you did well to get me here. Present yourself to my clerk at the Corps barracks—he'll pay you the balance."

He grasped the rope ladder and, with Justin steadying its foot, made the ascent with some trepidation, to vanish into the darkness of the *Dromedary*'s lower deck as the ladder was hauled up and the entryport slammed shut behind him.

Justin looked at the single small coin in his palm, grinned ruefully at Cookie Barnes, and tossed it across to him. "Your share, Cookie, my friend . . . I doubt that I shall ever see mine."

"You earned it twice over," Cookie Barnes told him indignantly, but he grinned, tucking the coin into his own breeches pocket. "Are we waiting or do we get under way?"

"We get under way," Justin decided. "They're not offering us any hospitality, are they? Shove off and tail on to the weather head-braces. I'm going to take her out and tack when we're well clear of South Head."

They would have to beat back against the gusting wind, he knew, and it would take several hours of toil and effort to return from whence they had come, with the same wind behind them then. True, it was continuing to veer northerly a point or two, and he was familiar with every cove and inlet of the great harbor of Port Jackson, but . . . Cookie Barnes's shout of warning came a moment before a man's high-pitched, despairing cry reached him, coming from the ship they had just left astern of them.

Justin did not see the *Dromedary*'s topman come hurtling down from her mainmast shrouds, but he saw the body strike the angry, white-crested water in his own ves-

sel's wake, and out of the corner of his eye he glimpsed a
dark head break the surface a minute later.

"He's alive!" he yelled to Cookie Barnes. "Stand by to go
about!"

With a silent prayer that the mast would hold, Justin put
his helm hard down, as Cookie flung himself across the
deck, his hands clawing for the peak halyard. The *Flinders* shuddered, heeling almost onto her beam-ends as she
started to come about. He held her, easing the wheel to
bring her head to the wind and then bearing away, as
she buried her sharp-raked bow in a welter of gray-green
water and, still shuddering fearfully, rose above it, the
water she had shipped cascading from fo'c'sle to stern in
a flurry of icy spray.

For a tense moment, he was waist-deep in water, feeling
its power, clutching the wheel with both hands to keep
himself from being washed overboard; but he stuck grimly
to his task, and a second tack brought the cutter onto an
even keel long enough for him to glimpse the swimmer
again and steer toward him. Justin knew there were sharks
in the waters of Sydney's harbor, and he searched the
foaming water in the man's immediate vicinity for the
sight of a telltale fin—but he could see nothing. This did
not prove that sharks were not converging on their target,
but rather that he must make haste and reach the swimmer
before they did . . . whatever the risk to his jury-rigged
mast or even to the *Flinders* herself. He had seen the result
of a shark attack on too many human bodies to count the
risk to himself . . . and the *Flinders*'s hull was stoutly
built. She would retain her buoyancy and float, whatever
wind or sea did to her, of that he was certain.

The next few minutes were blurred in his mind; he acted
more from instinct than reason, screeching orders to
Cookie that the man neither needed nor heard, for he, too,
was guided by the instinctive awareness of what was
required of him and did not wait to be told.

Miraculously, they reached the *Dromedary*'s topman
while he was still afloat and able, somehow, to grasp the

end of the rope that Cookie threw to him. Buffeted by the wind and spray, they hauled the mainsail down between them and, as the *Flinders* momentarily lost way, between them dragged the half-drowned seaman onto the deck and from thence, careless of broken bones, let him slither down the cabin hatchway.

But then their previous good fortune deserted them. The cutter's head started to pay off, tons of water crashed over her from astern, the jibs filled, and a rogue gust of wind began to carry her toward the tall, menacing face of South Head. Breathless and once again almost waist-deep in water, Justin fought his kicking wheel as Cookie struggled to hoist the mainsail to enable him to bring her about. With the outer jib torn and spilling wind, and the mainsail up and drawing, they had come within an inch of setting her on the other tack when, with a crack like the sound of a musket's discharge, the lashings on the jury rig parted.

It was what he had feared might happen, and Justin now realized that there was no way he could ward off disaster. The weather stays parted; the mast itself did not come down, but it might have served them better if it had, for its weight and that of the sail robbed the cutter—already canted an impossible angle to leeward—of what little stability she had left. She turned over and, like a harpooned whale, lay on her side, incapable of righting herself, as wind and current carried her slowly but inexorably toward the line of angry surf breaking on the rocks at the foot of South Head.

Justin found himself in the choppy water, the wheel wrenched from his chilled fingers as he slithered helplessly across the canting deck. He was near enough to drag himself onto the *Flinders*'s waterlogged hull and made to do so, but a hoarse cry from his left caused him to change his mind. The man they had rescued was floundering some thirty feet from him—a white, terrified face met his gaze, the lips moving, but no sound coming from them now, as the angry sea washed over his head and the undertow dragged him down.

Justin was a strong swimmer. He struck out with power-

ful strokes, reached the drowning man and, grasping him
by the shoulders, contrived to tow him back to the *Flinders*.
Minutes later, with no conscious recollection of how he had
managed to get himself there, he was lying spread-eagled
on the half-submerged hull, the *Dromedary*'s topman beside him and Cookie a few yards off, clinging for dear life
to the trailing mainsail boom.

Boats had been lowered, he observed with relief, from
both the frigate *Hindostan* and the *Dromedary*, but with
their crews pulling frantically on their oars, they were still
a long way off. He found himself praying that they would
reach his helpless vessel before she was smashed to pieces
on the rocks. His *Flinders* was lost, he knew, and the
knowledge was bitter; he had built her himself at the end
of the apprenticeship he had served under old Tom Moore
at the shipyard, and she had been his first command. She
was also his livelihood, he thought wretchedly—or had
been, until now, and . . . Startled, he heard Cookie emit a
scream and, twisting around, saw to his horror that the little man was losing his hold on the boom. Like so many
seamen, Cookie Barnes could not swim; scared by the age-
old belief that sailors who knew how to swim would meet
a lingering death, he had always obstinately refused to
learn, and now, his hold on the boom weakening, there was
little chance that he would be able to climb back unaided
onto the *Flinders*'s rolling hull.

Justin hesitated for an instant. The man he had just
plucked from the sea was no youngster. He looked dazed
but he had some, at least, of his wits about him and had his
arms locked about the cutter's rail . . . he could be left to
fend for himself. The sharks were there, even if they were
not visible . . . they were always there. But perhaps the
fact that there had been no human blood spilled explained
their failure to attack up to now.

It was then that he glimpsed the shadowy gray shape in
the gray, wind-tossed water. It was barely visible, but a
split-second of shocked recognition and Justin then understood why Cookie had screamed.

"Hang on, Cookie!" he yelled. "I'm coming!"

The wind bore his words soundlessly away, but Cookie

saw him and made a last desperate effort to retain his hold
on the boom, and Justin grabbed him by his coat collar just
in time. Less than two feet away, the gray shape, thwarted
of its prey, rose to the surface of the water and then vanished in a swirl of spray. Cookie gasped out, "Thank
Gawd!" and Justin had to cling to him with aching arms or
they would have slid from their precarious, wind-lashed
perch. They were both near to drowning when the *Hindostan*'s longboat reached them and hauled them to safety, the
Dromedary's topman with them, now mumbling his gratitude in all but unintelligible words.

As they rowed back to the convoy, the longboat's midshipman observed regretfully, "She's going, sir!" and Justin, his heart breaking, dragged himself up to watch the
last he would ever see of the *Flinders*, as the great, white-
fringed rollers spewed her out onto the rocks like a discarded toy. In a matter of minutes the surf pounded her to
destruction, and all that was left were a few misshapen
timbers, floating aimlessly this way and that.

"Signal, sir, from the commodore," the midshipman
went on. "We're to put you on board the *Dromedary*. I
expect," he added consolingly, "that His Excellency Colonel Macquarie wishes to thank you in person."

From the porthole of her cabin on board the *Dromedary*,
Jessica Maclaine had seen the graceful cutter's approach,
and had watched with interest the arrival of the oilskin-
clad officer. The Governor's housekeeper, Mrs. Ovens, had
told her that he was one of the officers of the rebel New
South Wales Corps, who had governed the colony since the
deposition of Governor Bligh.

"Leastways," the plump, rosy-cheeked woman had qualified, "that is who Joseph Big says he is, and he usually
knows. Name of Foveaux, Colonel Foveaux, he said . . .
and Their Excellencies are receiving him in the great cabin,
so you'll not be wanted for a while."

Joseph Big was the new Governor's coachman; he, like
Mrs. Ovens and herself, Jessica knew, would be fully employed when they landed in Sydney Town. On board the
ship, Mr. Big's and Mrs. Ovens's duties had been lighter

than her own, but she did not begrudge them that; she enjoyed her work and had come to love and respect her pretty, copper-haired mistress, who was unfailingly kind to her.

She was about to question the plump housekeeper further when, from the deck above, came the cry they all dreaded and had heard, not infrequently, before.

"Man overboard! Off the larb'd beam, sir!"

"God help him," Mrs. Ovens whispered and crossed herself. "It's to be hoped he is more fortunate than that poor soul who fell from the *Hindostan*'s masthead, when we first sighted Van Dieman's Land. They say the ship sailed right over him."

"The sailboat is going to his aid," Jessica exclaimed excitedly. "The one that brought Colonel Foveaux out from Sydney Town." She watched the cutter's maneuvering until it vanished from her line of vision, and then snatched up her shawl, intent—for no reason that she could have explained—on witnessing the outcome of the rescue attempt. "The poor sailor is still afloat, Mrs. Ovens. I'm going to the sternwalk—there will be no one there, if Their Excellencies are receiving in the great cabin. Will you be coming with me?"

The housekeeper shook her head. "In this wind? It will be too cold for my liking."

And cold it was, Jessica soon discovered, when she reached her chosen vantage point. But, keeping out of sight of the windows of the great cabin, she drew her shawl over her flying hair and crouched in what shelter she could find to watch the drama unfold.

The sailboat, even to her untutored eyes, was being expertly handled. A young man, with a mop of unruly fair hair, stood at the wheel; a second—small and bent and clearly a good deal older—was busy in the forward part of the boat, hauling on a rope, which brought the sail over to its other side. Waves were washing over its deck, but neither man wore oilskins, as Colonel Foveaux had done . . . indeed, she realized, the young, fair-haired helmsman was clad only in breeches and a thin white shirt and must be soaked to the skin. And even from this distance, he looked very young—a midshipman, perhaps, from the colony's naval establishment.

She saw the boat change course, heading now for the poor seaman who had fallen from the *Dromedary*'s rigging, and drew in her breath in a gasp of relief as she watched him being plucked from the sea's clutches. From behind her, she heard a cheer go up and then, glancing down, glimpsed the oared boat, which the *Dromedary*'s master, Captain Pritchard, had ordered to be lowered. The *Hindostan,* too, had launched a boat, and it was already in the water, pulling after the cutter, with ten or a dozen men at the oars.

Wondering at their haste, Jessica turned her gaze once more to the sailboat and understanding came, with a sinking heart. The top of the mast had broken off and the whole mast was bent, the sail trailing in the wind-wracked water. It lasted only for a moment thus, and then, to her horror, the vessel heeled over, to float on its side, for all the world like a seabird with broken wings, soon to be overwhelmed by the waves against which it had pitted its feeble strength.

A voice said, from beside her, "Merciful heaven, they are lost!" She spun round, startled, having supposed herself to be alone, and recognized the heavily muffled figure as that of Mrs. Bent, the judge advocate's wife, and hastily dropped her a curtsy. Mrs. Ellis Bent was vivacious and charming when in the company of her social equals, but, Jessica had learned, where the lower classes were concerned, both she and her handsome barrister husband were careful to keep their distance. In her own case—probably because the Governor's lady had come to treat her more as friend and confidante than servant—Mrs. Bent displayed a generous condescension, from which Mrs. Ovens was, for some reason, excluded.

She responded, with her usual charm, to Jessica's curtsy, and then both, as if to a magnet, returned to their shocked contemplation of the foundering sailboat.

"It was the boat which brought Colonel Foveaux out to

us from Sydney Cove," Mrs. Bent said. "Poor souls—I hope they will not drown before our eyes! Can you see them, Jessica? I believe that one of them has managed to catch on to the mast. I can just see his head."

"Oh, yes, ma'am," Jessica asserted, her hopes rising. "And I can see a man climbing onto the hull now, I'm sure." And it was the fair-haired young helmsman, she was thankful to observe, the one she had supposed to be a midshipman.

"No, there are *two* men—he's pulling a man up behind him! I do declare, that is the bravest act I have ever seen!" Mrs. Bent exclaimed. "Look, it is the young man who was in command of the cutter, and now he is trying to save the unfortunate fellow still in the water!"

"Yes," Jessica managed, her voice not steady. The two oared boats were gaining on the waterlogged cutter, she saw, the boat from the *Hindostan* making the best headway. She saw first one man and then the other hauled bodily from what she had feared would be their watery grave and cried out eagerly, "They're saved, Mrs. Bent! All three of them are saved, thanks be to God!"

"So they are," Mrs. Bent agreed, with an audible sigh of relief. "And . . . His Excellency has seen it all, as well as ourselves." She gestured to the stern windows, at Jessica's back, and added ruefully, "To think that I might have watched everything from the great cabin in comfort, instead of risking my death of cold, standing here! But I was still in dishabille when Mr. Bent was summoned to meet Colonel Foveaux. My maid is, alas, not such an early riser as you are, Jessica." Her smile, if still condescending, was warm. "Remember, won't you, that should Mrs. Macquarie ever wish to dispense with your services, *I* should be more than delighted to give you employment."

Surprised but nonetheless pleased by the implied compliment, Jessica promised that she would remember, and Mrs. Bent, still smiling, took her leave, to reappear, a few minutes later, among those who had been watching the work of rescue from the Governor's day cabin.

Jessica, feeling the cold, waited only until the *Hindo-*

stan's boat came alongside and she saw that the fair-haired midshipman was safe and seemingly unharmed; then she, too, went shivering below to discard her damp shawl and don a warmer dress. December, she had been told, was midsummer in the antipodes, but today was as cold as any December day she had experienced in England or Scotland, and the rain rivaled the worst that an Indian monsoon could hurl down from the skies.

But perhaps, when the wind changed and enabled the convoy to enter the harbor of Port Jackson, the weather would improve and the sun come at last to shine on the new Governor.

It was not until New Year's Eve that the gale blew over, and with a light easterly breeze and in blazing sunshine, the fifty-gun frigate *Hindostan* led her two consorts into Sydney Cove and there dropped anchor, amid cheers and the firing of salutes from the shore.

Colonel Lachlan Macquarie took his first long and critical look at the colony he was to govern, and what he saw did not please him.

Joseph Foveaux had warned him of what he might expect, it was true, but from the *Dromedary*'s poop what he saw was worse than he had expected . . . even with Foveaux's cautiously worded warnings.

Foveaux had been of immense assistance to him during the days of waiting, the new Governor reflected . . . indeed, he had learned more, during those three days of enforced inactivity, than he had believed possible. He had been told the full, unvarnished story of the events that had led the colony's military garrison to rebel and place their Governor under arrest; he had heard, in precise detail, the shameful recital of Captain William Bligh's tyranny, his peculations, his arrogance, and his uncontrollable temper.

Colonel Foveaux, admittedly, had not been present or in command of the New South Wales Corps at the time of the rebellion. He had still been on sick leave in England, and Major George Johnston had been the regiment's acting commandant—the officer responsible for Bligh's deposition.

Johnston had perhaps acted unwisely, Foveaux had reluctantly conceded, but he had been under great provocation, and as a friend of John Macarthur, whose ruin Bligh had moved heaven and earth to encompass, poor Johnston had been left with scant alternative. With Macarthur in the felons' jail and his life almost certainly in jeopardy, and the people of Sydney ready to take the law into their own hands, raid the jailhouse to free him, and probably even to lay violent hands on Governor Bligh, the commandant had taken the action he had, with the full support of his officers and of the town's respectable inhabitants.

All had signed a petition to that effect—there were hundreds of names appended to it—and Johnston, poor fellow, was on his way home to face a court-martial, which might well condemn him to death as a traitor. Yet he had acted honorably and did not, God knew, deserve to die for it, Colonel Foveaux had asserted, with an emotion that, in the new Governor's opinion, did him credit.

In any event, what Foveaux had told him had borne out, in virtually every particular, the account he had been given in Rio by Dr. Jamieson and his colleague, Dr. Harris. And both had been present; both had, on their own admission, been signatories to the petition on which the unfortunate Johnston had acted. . . . Lachlan Macquarie gave vent to a deep and heartfelt sigh.

The return of Commodore Bligh from Hobart and his brief, temporary reinstatement as Governor would add immeasurably to the complexity of the problems he would face. For one thing, he himself could take no official action as Governor until after Bligh's restoration to office, and for another . . . He started to pace the deck, his gray eyes troubled.

New South Wales, Foveaux had told him, was on the verge of famine—and by no means for the first time in its short history. Agriculture was languishing; there had been a recent and very damaging flood in the Hawkesbury area, where most of the colony's grain was grown; and in Sydney, the public buildings—including Government House—were in a state of dilapidation and, as Foveaux had put it, "moldering into decay."

"The morals of the great mass of inhabitants are in the lowest state of debasement," the Corps's acting commandant had added censoriously. "Religious worship is almost totally neglected, and the people are depressed by poverty. The larger landowners contribute nobly to the colony's resources, sir, but they, of course, are all officers of my regiment or civilian officials. It is the onetime felons, now emancipated and given land grants, who have failed so dismally. They are drunken and idle—they sell their produce for liquor and allow their land to lie fallow or revert to jungle, their livestock to die of neglect. And, sir, the convicts allocated to public labor do not, by honest toil, even repay the cost of their sustenance."

He had said more, the new Governor reflected sadly, most of it calculated to dishearten him.

There were few roads or bridges, and even these had been allowed to fall into disrepair; the country forty miles from Sydney was impenetrable, hidden behind the great, unclimbable barrier of the Blue Mountain range. Blame for the present unhappy state of the colony's affairs rested squarely on William Bligh's shoulders, if Foveaux was to be believed . . . according to him, the so-called rebel administration had done all in its power to improve conditions.

"But our power was, you will understand, sir, very limited. We had no authority from the home government to act. I did all I could during the short period when I acted as Lieutenant Governor, but when my immediate superior, Colonel Paterson, returned at long last from Van Diemen's Land, such matters were allowed, once again, to lapse."

He had volunteered no more on the subject of Colonel Paterson, but the tight-lipped look of disapproval on his face had been enough. Pressed, he had eventually been compelled to confess that Paterson was a sick man, suffering from chronic alcoholism, who spent most of his time at the Governor's residence in Parramatta, drinking himself into a stupor and seldom bothering to sign even the most urgent administrative documents.

"Indeed, sir, the only papers he willingly dealt with were those which allocated grants of land to his friends and sup-

porters. He was, sir, most generous with all of them . . .
even the commander of Mr. Bligh's ship, Captain Porteous
of the *Porpoise,* was given a substantial grant."

Well, at least he could nullify Paterson's misplaced generosity, Lachlan Macquarie thought, with satisfaction. His
instructions from the Colonial Secretary specifically called
for him to do so, save in certain cases in which, at his
discretion, he might judge a grant to be deserved. And
perhaps Porteous, after a year spent with his ship under
Bligh's command, might be said to have deserved his land
grant, on the grounds of extreme hardship, if for no other
reason.

The new Governor crossed to the taffrail and stood,
shading his eyes with his hand, looking across to the town
that was to be his domain and to the white-painted, two-story
building that—moldering into decay or not—was to be his
official residence. Both looked pleasant enough from this
distance, and the great harbor of Port Jackson, through
which his ship had just passed, had seemed to him truly
magnificent, with its coves and islets, its tree-grown
heights, and its golden sandy beaches.

There were windmills on the skyline, two trading vessels
tied up at the commercial wharf, and another, half-
completed, on the stocks at the nearby shipyard. And the
rows of neat, white-painted houses, in which the majority
of Sydney's population seemingly lived, had an attraction
that the setting sun enhanced, gilding their sloping shingle
roofs and falling kindly on their small, fenced-in gardens.
The Government House lawn was well kept, the tall Norfolk pine and the flowering shrubs that grew there adding to
its peaceful charm . . . as a prospect, Colonel Macquarie
decided, it was not quite as grim and hopeless as Foveaux
had implied.

Roads could be constructed, under the supervision of his
officers and NCOs; the public buildings could be repaired—or pulled down and rebuilt, should they prove beyond repair; and the wealthier owners of land within the
boundaries of the town encouraged to set up houses worthy
of their positions and affluence.

Undoubtedly the New South Wales Corps—known, to their eternal shame, as the Rum Corps—must, for all Foveaux's defense of them, take a major share of the blame for the present run-down state of the colony. Their officers had failed to enforce discipline, preferring to line their own pockets to attending to their military duties . . . but his fine 73rd Highlanders would swiftly change all that. The 73rd was a fighting regiment, with a splendid tradition of service to the Crown; it had no convicts in its ranks, no tradesmen among its officers—it would not be corrupted or seduced by loose women and imported rum. By heaven, he would see to that and see, also, that respect for the Church and attendance at Christian services were revived!

Deeply engrossed in his own thoughts, Colonel Macquarie watched the sun go down; he continued to pace the deck, making his hopeful plans and considering what steps could be taken in order to set them in motion.

There must, he told himself, be reward and encouragement for all whose conduct deserved it, be they convict, emancipist, or free. Those who had come out originally as convicted felons and who had earned their freedom by servitude, pardon, or emancipation should in all respects be considered on an equal footing with everyone else in the colony, according to their rank in life and their character. This was a principle by which he was determined to abide and . . . A smile lit his lined, austere face, as he recalled the young man whose bravery had stirred him deeply, three days before.

Justin Broome was a product of the colony, the colonel reminded himself, and by George, he was a fine example of its youth! At eighteen, with a record behind him that any prime seaman in the convoy would envy, since it included service under Matthew Flinders's command, young Broome had risked life and limb to save the unfortunate fellow who had fallen from the *Dromedary*'s rigging. He had lost his cutter as a result—a vessel that, apparently, he had built himself—but he had asked for no reward, not even for compensation for the loss. Instead, after modestly accepting his own and Captain Pritchard's thanks, the boy had quietly returned to Sydney in the boat that had brought the harbormaster and pilot, Isaac Nichols, out to the anchored convoy.

He had left his convict crewman to be cared for in the *Dromedary*'s sick bay, but that was all. . . . The new Governor's smile widened. Through Justin Broome, he would initiate his policy of reward and encouragement for the deserving. The boy should have his patronage, and if he wished to make a career in the Royal Navy, Captain Pasco of the *Hindostan* should be asked to accept him as a midshipman.

John Pasco was a distinguished officer. He had served as Lord Nelson's signal lieutenant at Trafalgar, and it had been he who had hoisted the immortal signal, "England expects that every man will do his duty," as Nelson's flagship, *Victory,* closed with the enemy fleet. Broome could ask for no better mentor, and should he, in the fullness of time, be commissioned by Their Lordships of the Admiralty, he would serve as an excellent example of what the offspring of convict parents could achieve.

Well pleased with this decision, Colonel Macquarie descended to the quarterdeck. It was, he realized, New Year's Eve—Hogmanay—the last day of the year 1809. His soldiers, being Highlanders, would celebrate; they were to be issued an extra ration of grog to mark the occasion, while he himself, with his dear Elizabeth, would entertain Captain and Mrs. Pasco, Captain Pritchard, Colonel O'Connell, and one or two others at dinner in the great cabin. Two of the regiment's pipers would play the New Year in, kilted, as the 73rd should be.

It was a pity, Lachlan Macquarie reflected, with sincere regret, that the British Colonial Office had persuaded the Horse Guards to order the regiment to dress in trousers while they were stationed in New South Wales. But at least the pipers were exempt from this unpopular decree, and so, by heaven, was he! As he entered his night cabin, his smile returned, for Elizabeth, he saw, had anticipated his unspoken wish and, with her remarkable womanly intuition, had had his kilt laid out for him on his cot.

He called out to her, but only her pretty, raven-haired maid responded from the adjoining cabin. His lady, she told him, dropping a respectful curtsy, had preceded him to the great cabin, to ensure that all was in order for the dinner party.

"I am to say, Your Excellency," she added demurely, "that Colonel Foveaux has gone ashore and that he has sent a saddle and hindquarter of lamb, with his compliments, sir, for your Hogmanay celebration."

The new Governor of the colony of New South Wales was not, as a rule, prone to show his feelings, but after the wearisome diet of salt meat they had endured for close on six months at sea, the gift of fresh lamb was welcome indeed.

"Thank you, Jessica," he acknowledged, beaming his delight with almost boyish enthusiasm.

What an excellent fellow Foveaux was, he thought as the girl withdrew. An intelligent, well-informed, and reliable officer and one it would behoove him to keep at his side for as long as possible . . . particularly when the time came to deal with his predecessor, Commodore Bligh.

His instructions were to disband the Corps—now to be designated the 102nd Regiment—and to send its officers and men back to England, in what amounted to disgrace. But . . . perhaps he could retain Foveaux, in some official capacity, to play the role of counselor, since he himself had so little knowledge of the country and the people he was to govern.

Whistling tunelessly, Colonel Lachlan Macquarie stripped off his white knee-breeches and stockings and buckled his kilt about his waist.

In his mind, he composed a letter to the Horse Guards, requesting that Lieutenant Colonel Joseph Foveaux, of the 102nd Regiment, might be transferred to his own 73rd in his present rank and without loss of seniority. . . .

CHAPTER III

Jessica saw the New Year in with the regiment's women on the orlop deck.

With only a few exceptions—and those few predictable—they had not begrudged her the good fortune that had seen her appointed to the service of their colonel's lady. Most of the older women had known her since her birth; some even remembered her father, and all knew and respected her mother, so there had been little resentment, even when it was known that she had the privilege of a cabin to herself on the officers' deck.

Their own conditions, Jessica reflected, were cramped and uncomfortable, in spite of the reduction in their number made before leaving England. And each day, like the men, they had been mustered for inspection—very often by Colonel Macquarie in person—they and their children with them, under standing orders to show themselves cleanly and respectably clad, sober and free of sickness. They were army women, accustomed to almost as strict and unyielding a discipline as their menfolk, and during the long voyage, they had obeyed whatever orders they were given, in fair weather or foul, with little complaint.

But this evening—the last day of the year and the end of the passage—all were in a mood for celebration. The *Drom-*

edary's portly master, Captain Pritchard, who victualed his ship himself, had treated them kindly and had seen to it, throughout the passage, that they were as well fed as his means would permit. Tonight, although he was a Sassenach—an Englishman—to whom Hogmanay had little significance, he had donated a cask of Cape brandy to the regiment's women from his own private stores and—before dining with Colonel Macquarie's party in the great cabin—had made his way below to drink a toast with them.

The big, round-faced master received a warm welcome, and in addition to the toast he had proposed to the "future of the regiment," his own health was drunk, and the women clapped and cheered him with great enthusiasm.

Jessica had never tasted spirits before and she drank sparingly, but even so, as the evening wore on, she found her head in a whirl and became anxious, aware that her mistress would require her help when the time came for her to retire for the night. Seeking escape, she edged her way toward the companion hatch leading to the upper deck as unobtrusively as she could, but Mrs. Macrae—her mother's friend—called out to her to wait.

The woman was in tears, her once plump, rosy-cheeked face thin and wan and her voice slurred. She had been pregnant when she had boarded the *Dromedary*, but her baby, born prematurely during the passage out, had sickened and died—as so many of her children had—and the poor woman was heartbroken, Jessica knew.

"What is it, Mrs. Macrae?" she asked pityingly, dropping to her knees beside the bunk on which the older woman was slumped. "What ails you?"

Morag Macrae choked back her tears. Grasping Jessica's hand in hers, she said in a low, stricken voice, "It is on my conscience, Jessica India, that I have broken my word to your mam. I was promising her that I would care for you on this long voyage. But I did not."

"I was in no need of care, Mrs. Macrae," Jessica began. "You see, I—"

It was as if the woman had not heard her, for she interrupted fiercely, "No, no, lass, I am at fault. Oh, it is true that you have had it easy on board this ship and the mistress you serve is one of us, a good Highland lady, full of kindness and goodwill. But when you go ashore with her, Jessie, you will be finding it is very different. The people here will not be like those of the regiment, and when you go with your lady to Government House, you will be in a position to hear talk and to do favors. Some folk will be trying to take advantage of you and to seek favors from you. They will ask you to break confidences and to repeat what you are hearing."

"But I would not do anything of the kind!" Jessica protested indignantly. "I know my duty, Mrs. Macrae."

Morag Macrae's red-rimmed dark eyes searched her face. "Aye," she conceded at last. "I am not doubting that you do. All I am doing is offering you advice—or a warning, if you like it better and in plain words. And it is in my heart to tell you that, should you ever find you are wishing to leave your lady's service, there will be a home for you with Sergeant Macrae and myself. Remember that, lassie, and forgive me for my neglect of you. I was having . . . much to trouble me."

Jessica thanked her, oddly moved by her words, and when she finally contrived to slip away, Morag Macrae had reverted to her soundless, bitter weeping and had seemingly forgotten her.

Her encounter with her mother's oldest friend was not, however, the only surprise she was to receive that evening. On her way back to her cabin, a tall, uniformed figure came from the shadows to bar her way, but it was not until he spoke that she recognized him as the young recruit who had carried her bundles to the orlop at Captain Antill's behest, the day they had boarded the ship at Yarmouth.

She had seen him occasionally in the distance when he was on guard or fatigue duty and at muster, and her first impression of him now was that he had matured and bore himself with the disciplined assurance of a trained soldier, rather than as a confused recruit. He was kilted, wearing the plaid and feather bonnet of a piper, evidently having come from playing the New Year in for Governor Macquarie and his guests in the great cabin.

"Your pardon, mistress, but I was waiting here in the hope that I might see you." He addressed her in the Gaelic. "I am Fergus Mackinnon. It is likely that you will not be remembering me." Seeing Jessica's faint frown, he reverted to English. "I am sorry, perhaps you are not fluent in the Gaelic."

"I was brought up in India," Jessica said defensively, "and we no longer speak in Gaelic in the family." And on her stepfather's account, she thought, regretting the forced admission. As a child, on her own father's knee, she had spoken the language of her homeland fluently enough . . . and Hindustani, too, with the native children.

"I mean no offense," Fergus Mackinnon apologized, reddening.

"And I was taking none," Jessica assured him.

"I am thankful for that."

An awkward silence fell between them. The young soldier clearly had something he wished to say to her, but it seemed he was unable to find the words. Thinking to help him, Jessica asked if he had piped for the Governor's Hogmanay dinner, and he beamed at her proudly.

"Yes, indeed. Donald Macdonald and myself were the ones chosen."

"Has the party ended yet?"

He shook his head. "We were dismissed, but His Excellency is still talking with his guests. They will be a while yet, I am thinking. I . . ." His cheeks were again suffused with embarrassed color. "I was wanting to ask you . . . that is, you see, I . . ."

Jessica waited, anxious not to add to his embarrassment. Fergus Mackinnon cut a very fine figure in his tartan and piper's green jacket, but he was young—only a year or two older than herself, she judged—and his looks were homely rather than handsome, his face boyishly round and innocent. She found herself comparing him to the young man from Sydney, who had sailed his cutter so courageously to the rescue of the drowning seaman a few days before. His name, Mrs. Macquarie had told her, was Justin Broome, and he had been born here, in this land of exile, to convict parents.

She caught her breath on a sigh, and Fergus Mackinnon,

mistaking her sigh for an indication of impatience, stammered uncertainly, "I was brought up on the estate of Colonel Macquarie's mother—Torloisk, on the Isle of Mull. That is where I was learning the piping. I have some skill in it, but I was not expecting to be chosen this evening or, indeed, to be accepted as a piper when I was joining the regiment."

"Then you have reason to be proud, have you not?" Jessica suggested when he broke off, looking down at her gravely.

"Oh, yes, indeed I have," he agreed. She listened in attentive silence as he told her of his childhood and of the pride he had felt on joining the regiment, in which his father and two uncles had also served. Then, visibly nerving himself, he asked diffidently, "When we are landed and settled ashore, I was wondering whether you would permit me to keep company with you? Oh, I am knowing that your parents were left behind at Portsmouth and that it is their permission I should be seeking, but I—I should deem it an honor, Mistress Jessica, if you would allow me to pay court to you."

Jessica hesitated. It would do no harm, she thought; he was well mannered and personable, and being in the regiment, they would have that in common—the regiment was family to them both. And in an alien land, in which they were strangers, to keep company together would be an antidote to loneliness and, perhaps, a means by which they might both make friends with those who had come out here before them. Mrs. Macrae's warning could not, surely, apply to Fergus Mackinnon? He would be seeking no advantage from her position and would not be interested in any talk that she might overhear in her lady's bedchamber or elsewhere in Government House.

She had much to gain and little to lose, Jessica told herself, and yet she continued to hesitate, a vision of the young sailor, whose vessel had been driven onto the rocks, returning unbidden to her mind. She would probably never see him again, never be given the opportunity even to make his acquaintance . . . and yet, for all that, he had made other men seem somehow less desirable.

"Have I offended you?" Fergus Mackinnon questioned, worried by her silence. "I had not thought to do anything of the kind. Truly, I—"

"Oh, but you have not," Jessica hastened contritely to reassure him. She added, reddening in her turn, "I have never kept company with anyone before, Mr. Mackinnon. You have paid me a compliment and I thank you. But I shall need Mistress Macquarie's permission before I can give you an answer. I am in her employ and am expecting to remain so."

"I pray that she will be giving permission," Fergus Mackinnon said fervently. He reached for her hand, held it for a moment, and then, suddenly awkward and ill at ease, let it fall and hurriedly took his leave.

Jessica watched him until he was out of sight and then, with a new spring in her step, made her way to Mrs. Macquarie's sleeping cabin, to wait in readiness for the Hogmanay party to come to an end. Her stepfather had never permitted any young man to approach her in the past and, she knew, would not have allowed her to keep company with Piper Fergus Mackinnon, had he been consulted. But he was not here and therefore could not be consulted, and she hugged this knowledge to her, enjoying at long last the heady taste of freedom. . . .

Early on New Year's Day—January 1, 1810—the men of the 73rd Highlanders mustered for inspection in their new colonial uniforms. Boats from the *Hindostan* and the *Dromedary* rowed them to the government wharf, but when they stepped ashore, it was to find that the New South Wales Corps—now designated the 102nd Regiment—had arrived there before them.

Smartly accoutred, the regiment they had been sent out to replace was already occupying the available space at the pierhead. With their colors still furled and cased but their drums and fifes playing, they were evidently preparing to provide a guard of honor for the new Governor. The Highlanders did not hear the heated words that were exchanged between Colonel Foveaux of the 102nd and their own commanding officer, Colonel O'Connell, but the latter's red and angry face spoke more eloquently than any words when he barked out the order for them to line the route from the wharf to Government House.

The distance was short, and they stood shoulder to shoulder, their pipes silent, while the 102nd's band filled the air with a shrill rendering of "The British Grenadiers."

"I was thinking," the pipe major observed resentfully to the regimental sergeant major. "Indeed, Mr. Farquharson, I was led to believe that the Hundred and second was a regiment of mutineers and, as such, to be in disgrace. But it seems I was misinformed."

"You were not misinformed," the sergeant major snapped back wrathfully. "That is what they are. It is their commanding officer who is in error, and I shall speak with Colonel O'Connell whenever he will be giving me the opportunity."

As soon as she had broken her fast, the new Governor's lady ascended by herself to the *Dromedary*'s poop deck to watch, from behind the partial concealment of her parasol, the preparations for their landing.

Elizabeth Henrietta Macquarie had no experience of military pomp and ceremony, apart from the little she had gained during the seven-month voyage from England. As she followed the wheeling and marching of the troops and listened to the band, she was in blissful ignorance of the slight which had been inflicted on her husband's proud regiment, and she had no inkling of the angry emotions it had aroused.

The youngest daughter of an impoverished Scottish laird, Sir John Campbell of Airds, Elizabeth had spent her early youth on her father's small estate in Appin. Her family, if poor, were well connected, and hers had been a peaceful and uncomplicated life. Most of her time, until her father's death, had been occupied in caring for him and in outdoor pursuits. She was an expert horsewoman, a keen walker, and she had considerable skill with rod and line . . . not qualities to attract many suitors, and unlike her sisters, she

had not married at an early age. But this had been as
much from choice as for lack of opportunity; she had
been happy enough at Airds, and she had been quite cheerfully resigned to spinsterhood when, at the advanced age of
six-and-twenty, she had made the acquaintance of Colonel
Lachlan Macquarie, a distant relative, on leave from India.

Lowering her parasol to shield her eyes from the glare of
the sun, Elizabeth Macquarie smiled as she recalled that
first meeting. It had been unexpected, and had taken place
in London, at the home of an aunt, whither she had jour-
neyed from Edinburgh as escort to the two schoolboy sons
of the head of her mother's family, so that they might attend his deathbed.

A sad occasion for them all and not least for Lachlan
himself, to whom the old chief, Maclaine of Lochbuie, had
been patron and friend since boyhood . . . and Lachlan
had been genuinely grief-stricken. She had sought to comfort him, Elizabeth recalled, but entirely without ulterior
motive. He was forty-three and had served overseas, in
America and in India, for most of his life. And in Bombay,
he had married a beautiful young woman, with whom, he
had told her with praiseworthy frankness, he had been
deeply in love, and whose memory he still revered.

Jane Jarvis . . . She bit back a small, inaudible sigh.
Lachlan had married Jane Jarvis in September of the year
1793, when she herself had been a schoolgirl of barely fifteen, riding her shaggy pony through the morning mists to
the old wooden schoolhouse at Portnacroish. Or—
Elizabeth's sigh became audible as the memories flooded
back—or when school was over, casting a long line across
the Airds Pool on the Creran River or rowing, with blistered hands, along the reed-grown banks of Loch Fasna-
cloich as her father's line snaked out astern and he swore
when the reeds entangled it.

That was when Lachlan had lived with Jane as his wife;
in Bombay, where he had been major of brigade; in Cali-
cut, in the Madras command as paymaster to the 77th Regiment. A brief separation, when he had gone on active
service to Ceylon and aided in taking Pointe de Galle and

its fort from the Dutch; then back, once more, to Bombay and Jane.

He had found Jane very ill on his return. The doctors had told him that her illness was fatal; in a despairing attempt to save her, Lachlan had taken her on a sea voyage to Macao, and there, on July 15, 1796, she had died, after just three years of marriage.

He had told her all this, Elizabeth recalled, while he was courting her. After poor Lochbuie's funeral, he had persuaded her to travel back to Edinburgh with him, sharing their post chaise discreetly with the old chief's two sons. He had not proposed to her by the time they parted, but they had met again in December at her aunt's London house and she had known then that he would do so.

The proposal, when it came—on January 8, 1805, according to her diary—coincided with Lachlan's receipt of orders that required him to return to Bombay. And he intended to return, although not, as she had hoped, with her as his bride. . . . Elizabeth's lips tightened involuntarily, as she recalled the reason he had given her and which she had also recorded in her diary, on March 26.

Lachlan, it seemed, had vowed after Jane's heartbreakingly premature death that he would never marry again in India nor bring a wife to India. He had begged her to wait for him, promising that he would come back, if the good Lord should spare him, within four years. There was talk of war in India, where the French were stirring up trouble, and he was a soldier, with his duty to do and a regiment to command, and so . . . she had agreed to his terms and, with regret and no little apprehension, had let him go.

They had exchanged embraces and locks of hair before he had embarked in the Indiaman *City of London,* and she had waited, living her life as best she might on limited means, sustained by Lachlan's infrequent but lengthy letters and coming—for all her good intentions—bitterly to resent the woman who had been her predecessor.

She no longer went to Airds, save on brief visits, for her father had died in the interim and her brother—who had a wife and a large family—had inherited the estate, and much as she loved the place, it was not the same. She had stayed in Edinburgh with one sister, in London with another, and with her aunt, ever conscious that time was passing and the years taking their toll of her.

And then, miraculously, Lachlan had been appointed to the command of the 73rd, which was in Scotland, and he had written to say that he was coming home. They had married at last on November 3, 1807—and her diary had faithfully recorded that their wedding had been at the Church of Peter and Paul, in Holsworthy, Devonshire, where she had been visiting relations.

Contrary to her fears and expectations, Lachlan had proved an ardent and warmly affectionate husband, concerned for her happiness and well-being and eager for her to give him children . . . which Jane, for all her tenacious hold on his heart, had been unable to do. Eleven months after their wedding, Elizabeth had given him a daughter, but . . . Elizabeth's blue eyes misted. The baby had died, poor wee soul, and with its dying, had come perilously near to breaking her spirit and ending all hope of the fulfillment for which she had longed.

For she had fallen in love with her aging husband . . . deeply, irrevocably, and passionately in love, although, when she had promised to marry him, she had done so out of a sense of duty and because he had offered her what was undoubtedly her last chance to escape from a role she had come to hate: that of a poor relation, at the beck and call of married sisters and youthful kin merely because she was unmarried.

Elizabeth lowered her parasol, to study, with excited intensity, the scenes now being enacted ashore. She had not supposed, when she and Lachlan had taken up residence on the small estate he had purchased on the Isle of Mull, that her husband's future could possibly encompass all that it had—a governorship, an income of two thousand pounds a year, and the promise of a pension at the end of his term of office. And the power that his new responsibilities would confer on him . . . power to show favors, to make government appointments, to meet on equal terms eminent personages such as the Prince Regent of Portugal in Rio de

Janeiro, and the Governor of the Cape of Good Hope, Lord Caledon, who had charmingly played host to them in Capetown.

Lachlan, instead of being plain Colonel Macquarie, was now His Excellency, His Britannic Majesty's Captain General and Governor of New South Wales, to be promoted, surely very soon, to the rank of brigadier general. While she herself would be entitled to receive the bows and curtsies of the inhabitants of the colony—convict, emancipist, or free, officers and civilians alike. It was an incredible change from her previous existence as the unmarried youngest daughter of an impecunious Scottish laird, whose title—although he had continued to use it—of Baronet of Ardnamurchan had been stripped from the ancestor who had held it, for his support of the Stuart cause in the rebellion of 1745.

"Ma'am . . ." Elizabeth turned, hearing the soft, diffident voice of her little lady's maid behind her, and instantly a smile lit her face. Jessica India, despite her youth and inexperience, had proved a treasure on the long voyage out—always at hand when she was needed, and quiet and unobtrusive when she was not. And she, too, had reason to be grateful for the escape this journey had afforded her, for had not Henry Antill said that her stepfather, a senior sergeant in the regiment, had subjected her to a brutal beating on the day the families had boarded the *Dromedary*? The stepfather had been among those left behind in Portsmouth—providentially, or perhaps thanks to her husband's handsome young aide-de-camp, since it had been Henry who had recommended the girl to her as a maid.

"What is it, child?" she asked.

Jessica held out a shawl. "I heard the order for His Excellency's barge to be called, ma'am, and I was thinking that perhaps you would wish me to bring you your shawl. I have your bonnet also, ma'am. They are saying that it is hot on the wharf and that there is no shade."

Her tone held anxiety, as well as eagerness, and Elizabeth's smile widened, as she draped the shawl about her slender shoulders and held out a hand for the wide-

brimmed straw bonnet. Only Jessica knew of the hope she
now cherished that she was again pregnant. A few weeks
only, and as yet she had not dared to impart her news to
Lachlan, lest she arouse false hopes. . . . She adjusted the
bonnet over her shining bronze curls, turning to her maid
for approval.

"How do I look, Jessica?"

"You are looking lovely, my lady," Jessica assured her,
with truth. Yet she was thirty-two, Elizabeth reminded herself, letting her hand stray for a nervous moment to her
thickening body beneath the stomacher. She was approaching middle-age, when childbirth presented a danger, both to
herself and to her coming child . . . and Lachlan, her beloved Lachlan, was almost fifty, his health an added anxiety. He had been unwell since their first sighting of the
coast of Van Diemen's Land, and the *Dromedary*'s surgeon
had had to prescribe large doses of mercury and severe
purging.

"Where is His Excellency?" she asked, aware that he
had still been dressing when she had left their night cabin.
"Have you seen him?"

"I was seeing him with Captain Pritchard, ma'am," Jessica began, but at that moment, the Governor himself
emerged onto the quarterdeck and she broke off, realizing
that Elizabeth Macquarie had seen him, too. Besides the
Dromedary's corpulent master, both the Bents and Captain
Antill were with him, and as if their appearance had been
a signal for which he had been waiting, the officer of the
watch shouted an order through his speaking trumpet and
the seamen of both watches started to swarm up the rigging.

"Oh!" Elizabeth exclaimed, at once moved and excited.
"They are manning the yards!"

"The other ships are doing the same, ma'am," Jessica
told her, pointing.

The girl was right; first the *Hindostan,* as befitted the
crew of a ship of war, then the *Dromedary,* and finally the
transport they had escorted from Rio, the *Anne,* and the
colonial schooner *Lady Nelson* had their seamen aloft,
standing out along the yards. To the sound of their cheer-

ing, the *Hindostan*'s barge came alongside the *Dromedary*, and Elizabeth, conscious that her husband would be wondering where she was, drew her shawl about her and hurried down to join the party on the quarterdeck.

Lachlan gave her a faintly reproachful glance, and then, after acknowledging the cheers, he offered her his arm.

"It is time we went ashore, my dear," he said. "They are waiting to receive us."

To the booming of signal cannon, firing the traditional salute of fifteen guns from ships and shore, they were rowed to the wharf, where Colonel Foveaux was standing at the head of a short flight of stone steps, hat in hand. He greeted them effusively, as old friends, and Elizabeth found herself resenting his familiarity and the unnecessary solicitude he displayed, when assisting first her husband and then herself to ascend the steps.

The band of the 102nd struck up the national anthem, the guard of honor presented arms and stiffened to attention, and then a tall, stooping figure in a faded and ill-fitting scarlet uniform stepped forward to mumble a barely audible greeting.

"Colonel Paterson, Your Excellency," Foveaux announced, ranging himself beside the older officer, as if intent rather on hiding him from view than on making the required introductions. "Commandant of the Corps—ah, that is, sir, the Hundred and second Regiment. And . . . Mrs. Paterson."

The stooping figure contrived an awkward bow; he was pale, his cheeks damp with perspiration, Elizabeth observed, as she accepted his limp hand . . . clearly, the poor old gentleman was gravely ill, as Colonel Foveaux had told them. In this instance, he had not exaggerated.

Mrs. Paterson, whose hand she next took, was a small, homely person, with white hair and a lined, tired face. Nevertheless, Elizabeth joyfully recognized her accent and saw the warmest of smiles echo her own. She was Scottish, and there was an air of indomitability about her that had unexpected appeal. Elizabeth would have lingered, but Colonel Foveaux's hand on her arm propelled her forward.

"Captain Abbott, of my regiment, Mrs. Macquarie . . .

Captain Fenn Kemp . . . Lieutenant Lawson, Mrs. Lawson, Lieutenant Bayly, Mrs. Bayly . . . my wife, ma'am . . ."

The introductions came in bewildering succession, and they continued, with a young officer named Finucane taking Colonel Foveaux's place when he led the Governor away to inspect the guard of honor.

Elizabeth smiled, acknowledged polite curtsies, reciprocated greetings and good wishes, and tried vainly to remember names. Ellis Bent and his wife followed her, the young judge advocate, as always, making a good impression with his wit and charm, and his wife, as always, in a gown that outshone her own. The Pascos had come ashore from the *Hindostan,* the captain, with his wife on his arm, bowing and gallantly kissing the female hands that were extended to him, while his wife, as was her custom, reserved her favors for those she judged to be socially deserving of them . . . and this morning, there appeared to be singularly few of these.

And yet, Elizabeth thought, as she halted beside a very beautiful woman of about her own age, with perfect Celtic coloring and the most welcoming smile she had received, Mrs. Pasco's judgment was harsh. This woman, for instance, bore the unmistakable mark of good breeding, and so, too, did the two young girls who accompanied her, and she listened with particular care to Lieutenant Finucane's introduction.

"Mrs. Jasper Spence, ma'am . . . Mrs. Desmond O'Shea and Miss Lucy Tempest. And, at your pleasure, ma'am, Mr. Jasper Spence, who is a magistrate and justice of the peace . . . and Mr. Timothy Dawson, one of our most prominent agriculturalists. Mr. Dawson has bred some of the finest horses in the colony."

Elizabeth halted. It was becoming increasingly hot, as the sun rose higher—an extraordinary contrast to the cold they had experienced when the westerly gale had kept the convoy at anchor off the Port Jackson Heads. She silently blessed Jessica Maclaine for the forethought she had shown in choosing the wide-brimmed straw bonnet, since, with so many hands to shake, she had been compelled to close her parasol, and at least the brim shaded her face from the worst of the glare.

As if sensing her discomfiture, Mrs. Spence opened her own parasol and held it over her unobtrusively as they talked. Her husband, Elizabeth's mind registered, was considerably older than she—older, probably, by several years, than her own Lachlan—but he was fit and slim-hipped, his face healthily tanned. And the elder of the two girls—their daughters or stepdaughters, she supposed—whom Mrs. Spence addressed as Abigail, was truly lovely. An English—but no, her name was O'Shea, if she remembered rightly—an Irish rose, with vivid blue eyes and hair the color of molten gold . . . With regret, Elizabeth Macquarie moved on at Lieutenant Finucane's prompting, observing as she did so that Mrs. Bent and Mrs. Pasco passed the little group without exchanging a word. Both, however, seemed to have plenty to say to the tall, broad-shouldered Mr. Dawson. . . . Mrs. Bent, no doubt, was interested in the purchase of one of his riding animals and a pair for the curricle she and the young judge advocate had brought out with them.

"Mr. and Mrs. Blaxland, ma'am, Mr. Robert Fitz . . . Dr. Townson, the Reverend William Cowper . . ." The introductions went on, young Lieutenant Finucane never at a loss for a name and seemingly indefatigable as he led her on, the men doffing their headgear and bowing, the women dropping curtsies and eyeing her furtively as they rose to take her hand. Elizabeth, conscious that her face was scarlet from the heat and that she was perspiring profusely, was thankful when, at last, she saw Lachlan returning to her side, bearing himself stiffly as a soldier should but, for all that, looking tired.

Then, as the band of the 102nd fell silent, she heard the skirl of the pipes and her heart lifted when she recognized the tune—"The Red-Tartaned Army," the Macquaries' own tune. Led by the drum major, pipes and drums advanced to meet their colonel and commander in chief, a sight indeed to stir the heart as they halted before him, brave in their green and scarlet and tartan, the feather bon-

nets adding impressively to each man's height. They
wheeled, in perfect unison, rank by rank, the drums beating the step, and with the drum major's massive figure
again at their head, the tune changed to the regimental
march—"Hie'land Laddie"—and Lachlan gravely offered
her his arm.

Elizabeth took it proudly, and together they walked
along the short graveled road to the gates of Government
House, the way lined by men of the 73rd presenting arms,
the troops left behind at the pierhead cheering themselves
hoarse.

Behind the closely packed lines of the 73rd, the less respectable inhabitants of Sydney Town—drably clothed and
not considered worthy to be presented to the newly arrived
Governor—had gathered in their hundreds. Most of them
bowed or waved their hats in the air, some cheered, but
others stood sullenly motionless, evincing neither pleasure
nor interest and apparently deaf to the stirring music of the
Highlanders' pipes.

Reaching the front of the Government House, Elizabeth
found herself again deserted, as Colonel Foveaux and another officer bore Lachlan away, Ellis Bent, Henry Antill,
and his secretary, John Campbell, following at their heels.

Lieutenant Finucane led her, with Mrs. Bent, Mrs.
Pasco, and various other ladies, to chairs that had been set
out in readiness on the Government House veranda, and
she sank into one of them with a sigh of relief. The shade
and the tray of drinks on the table between them were both
equally welcome, and Elizabeth accepted a glass of wine
that a servant offered her, drinking it thirstily before surreptitiously mopping at her heated face.

Eliza Bent exclaimed excitedly, "My husband is about to
administer the oath of office to His Excellency, Mrs. Macquarie! And see . . . he has the great seal of the territory
in his hands. Oh, what a moment for pride and rejoicing!
Are you not elated, Mrs. Macquarie?"

Elizabeth murmured what she hoped was an appropriate
reply, but as she listened to the young judge advocate's
loud and confident voice reading her husband's commission

and then administering the oath of office, she was conscious of more anxiety than elation.

This was a strange place, where the military garrison could mutiny and depose the appointed Governor, and yet—with impunity, it appeared—form a guard of honor when his successor landed, and . . . yes, she was not mistaken: The 102nd's band had entered the grounds of Government House and, ranged behind the official party, was striking up "God Save the King"!

Her delicately arched brows met in a worried pucker, as she watched her husband mount the wooden rostrum that had been prepared for him, fumbling with the papers on which he had written out his speech. Lachlan's responsibilities were likely to be heavy, and initially, she was aware, they would be totally unfamiliar to him. He was a transparently honest and kindly man, but for all that, he was a simple soldier, whose only previous command had been that of a single regiment. True, he had proved his courage in battle on many occasions, and he had held appointments on the staff. He had served as deputy adjutant general in the Egyptian campaign, under General Baird, and he had been military secretary to the Governor of Bombay, General Duncan, but . . . Elizabeth tensed, sitting very still in her chair, as the 102nd's band lowered its instruments and lapsed into silence.

Colonel Foveaux, who had been much to the fore during the earlier part of the proceedings, stood aside, leaving the new Governor alone on the small, raised platform, an upright, soldierly figure who, in that moment, looked impressive, even to his wife's anxiously critical eyes.

"Fellow citizens and fellow soldiers!" Lachlan Macquarie's voice was strong and clear, and his audience listened attentively as he assured them that it was his firm intention to exercise the authority vested in him with strict justice and impartiality.

"But it is my painful duty," he went on, sternly now, the customary platitudes delivered, "publicly to announce His Majesty's high displeasure and disapprobation of the mutinous and outrageous conduct displayed in the forcible and unwarrantable removal of his late representative, Commodore William Bligh, and of the tumultuous proceedings connected therewith. . . ."

Elizabeth lost his next few words, her attention caught and held by the expression on Colonel Foveaux's saturnine face. Clearly, he had been taken by surprise at the forcefulness of the new Governor's condemnation of his regiment's part in the rebellion, and it had not pleased him.

She turned her gaze once more to her husband and heard him say, "I am, however, sanguine that all dissentions and jealousies which have unfortunately existed in the colony for some time past will now terminate forever, and harmony and union be restored. To this end, it is my hope that the higher classes will set an example of subordination, decorum, and morality—and that those of an inferior station will endeavor to distinguish themselves by their loyalty, their sobriety, and their industry. By these means alone can the welfare and happiness of the community be effectively promoted. . . ."

He went on to recommend all classes of the colony's inhabitants to a strict observance of their religious duties and a constant and regular attendance at divine worship.

"I trust that the magistrates and all other persons in authority will exert themselves to the utmost in checking and preventing all kinds of vice and immorality. And I need not, I hope, express my wish that the natives of the country, when they come in a peaceable manner, will not be molested in their persons and property by anyone. They should be treated at all times with kindness, so as to conciliate them as much as possible. . . ."

His sternest warning, delivered at the end of his speech, was addressed to the troops.

"From those in the King's service and under my command I shall expect a most vigilant discharge of every part of their duties. In this regard, it is my earnest hope that their steadiness, sobriety, and strict discipline will preclude the painful necessity of resorting, save rarely, to any punishment. And for the rest, may I assure you all, the honest, sober, and industrious inhabitants, whether free settler or convict, will ever find me both friend and protector. . . ."

"An excellent address," Mrs. Bent observed, when the speech came to its appointed end and the Governor stepped down from his rostrum, to the polite applause of those gathered about him. But her tone was condescending, and Elizabeth rose, conscious, as she so often was in Mrs. Bent's company, of a feeling of annoyance which, however justified, she knew that she must not express.

Lieutenant Finucane appeared attentively at her side and she said, in a flat, controlled voice, "I should be obliged, Mr. Finucane, if you would show me to His Excellency's rooms."

"Why, certainly, ma'am," the young officer responded. "But we have prepared a buffet for yourself and your guests. Perhaps you—"

"I shall be happy to attend," Elizabeth told him, asserting herself, "when I have had the opportunity to wash and change. Perhaps you will be so good as to send for my maid."

The guns were firing yet another thunderous salute as she mounted the wide staircase in Lieutenant Finucane's wake, feeling suddenly unbearably weary and disspirited. But perhaps, she told herself, hugging the thought to her, perhaps she was pregnant and this was the reason for her weariness.

"Please God I am," she prayed silently. "Please God, for Lachlan's sake, let me give him a son!"

CHAPTER IV

Andrew Hawley had not been among the privileged party of officials and prominent inhabitants who, with their wives, had been invited to receive the new Governor at the pierhead.

Nevertheless, as the former Governor's aide-de-camp, he had been ordered to present himself in Sydney Town, to await—as the order from Colonel Foveaux had put it— "His Excellency's pleasure." He had ridden from Parramatta with Colonel and Mrs. Paterson and now stood wedged in among the motley crowd of soldiers and civilians that had gathered on the Government House lawn to witness the swearing-in of the new Governor.

The speech—or, at all events, what he had heard of it— differed little from the speech that William Bligh had made when he had taken office four years ago. Perhaps it had been more placatory; Colonel Macquarie, save when he had censured the Rum Corps in somewhat general terms, had made no threats. Like Bligh, he had urged the colony's inhabitants to be diligent in their Christian worship, sober, and industrious; but where all too many of them were concerned, his injunctions would go unheeded, Andrew was only too well aware.

Sydney was a sinful town, peopled by corrupt officials,

publicans, whores, bawdy-house keepers, and all manner of
illicit traders . . . and by a military garrison that, until
Governor Macquarie's coming, had neither kept order nor
cared a whit for discipline. The rebel administration had
appointed the officials and the justices and had given land
and convict labor as freely as they had granted liquor licen-
ses to their supporters. Their officers owned the taverns
and market stalls; they fostered and took part in most of
the trading; and since the rebellion, with few exceptions,
they had sought only to line their own pockets while the
opportunity to do so still remained to them.

Yet, thanks to Joseph Foveaux's scheming, the mutinous
Rum Corps had paraded with the new Governor's own regiment . . . and, indeed, had been permitted to take precedence over the Highlanders throughout the ceremonial
reception, which had been carefully planned with that end
in view.

Andrew scowled, looking down at the faded scarlet cloth
of his uniform jacket. The last occasion when he had worn
a uniform had been almost a year ago, when he had
watched Governor Bligh's departure on board H.M.S. *Porpoise* . . . for England, as he had then supposed.

He himself had left Sydney after that, with his wife,
Jenny, to return to Long Wrekin, their farm on the Hawkesbury. They had been happy enough there, for they both
had farming in their blood, the land was good—save when
it was flooded—and the rebel administration had left them
in peace. Until now . . . Andrew glanced up at the new
Governor, who had come to the end of his address, and
found himself wondering what manner of man Colonel
Lachlan Macquarie would prove.

It was, he knew, widely rumored that the Colonial Office had given instructions for Governor Bligh to be restored to office for twenty-four hours, and he was expected
shortly to return so that these instructions could be put into
effect. His officials—the civil magistrates like Robert
Campbell and Dr. Arndell and poor William Gore, the ex-
provost marshal—were, it was said, to be reinstated. Their
support for their lawful Governor, when John Macarthur's
iniquitously mismanaged trial had taken place, had been

punished most cruelly by the rebel rulers of the colony, but now, thank heaven, justice was to be done to them . . . and he himself, presumably, would be reinstated with them. He had not resigned his captaincy in the Royal Marines, although it had been suggested to him that he should, and he had not gone with the deposed Governor to Van Diemen's Land, so that . . . Andrew turned his gaze to the crowd about him, looking for familiar faces but seeing none.

Simeon Lord was not there; neither were Commissary Palmer and his wife or the Arndells. The unfortunate Gore had been tried by the Corps's magistrates and sentenced to hard labor at Coal River . . . poor devil, he at least would be thankful for the new Governor's arrival, and the emancipist lawyer, Crossley, perhaps even more than he. His sentence had been harsher, and . . . Ranging over the crowd from his commanding height, Andrew's gaze lit on the ungainly, shambling figure of Richard Atkins, and he swore under his breath.

Judge Advocate Atkins's handling—his *mishandling*—of John Macarthur's trial had been in no small measure the cause of the late Governor's downfall. But . . . the drunken swine had turned his coat, after Bligh's departure. Foveaux had bought him, with promises and grants of land and with his restoration to the office he had been deprived of by Macarthur. For the past year, he had served the rebel administration—incompetently, it seemed, since he no longer had the benefit of Lawyer Crossley's legal expertise and experience which had so nearly resulted in Macarthur's conviction. But now he, too, was to be superseded, praise be. Governor Macquarie had brought his own judge advocate with him—a young barrister, the handsome fellow who had just administered the oath of office to him.

But . . . Andrew's jaw dropped, in ludicrous surprise. Although Foveaux had not seen fit to include Atkins in the official party he had assembled on the wharf, it was evident that the turncoat lawyer intended to introduce himself to the new Governor. He was thrusting a determined way through the press of spectators thronging the Government House garden, elbowing aside without apology those who impeded him, and for all the wrathful attention he attracted, he finally reached the group surrounding Governor Macquarie. Plump hand extended, he executed an awkward bow, and Colonel Macquarie—who clearly had no idea who he was—responded courteously, accepting the proffered hand.

Foveaux attempted to intervene but was too far away to do so, and the Governor, ignoring this urgent endeavor to catch his eye, started to move toward the crowd. A kindly smile on his lips, he exchanged greetings with all and sundry and then, catching sight of Andrew's tall, uniformed figure, indicated with a raised hand a desire to speak to him. The crowd parted to let him through, and Governor Macquarie, still smiling, acknowledged his salute.

"A captain in His Majesty's Royal Marine Corps!" the Governor said, brows raised in an unvoiced question. But before Andrew could make reply, Colonel Foveaux was beside them.

"Captain Hawley, sir," he announced, his tone deliberately cold and edged with malice. "The late Governor's aide-de-camp, to whom, you may recall, I drew Your Excellency's attention when we talked on board the *Dromedary* a few days ago. He's a farmer now, are you not, Hawley? Virtually retired to the Hawkesbury and did not welcome my summons to abandon his harvesting in order to attend this reception. But I supposed that, in view of Lord Castlereagh's instructions, Your Excellency would wish him to present himself, together with the rest of Mr. Bligh's following."

It was as damning an introduction as he had ever been given, Andrew thought, but he did not betray his feelings, remaining stiffly at attention, as the Governor studied him, brows still raised in polite inquiry.

"I take it that you still hold His Majesty's commission, Captain Hawley?" he suggested, after a short silence.

"I do, Your Excellency," Andrew confirmed. Foveaux shuffled his booted feet impatiently, but the Governor appeared not to be aware of his desire to terminate the interview.

"Did you serve with Commodore Bligh at sea?" Macquarie asked. Andrew had intended to answer with a brief affirmative, but pressed for details, he gave them, and saw the new Governor's eyes light with a gleam of approval.

"You have served your country with distinction, Captain Hawley," he observed. "And under the great Lord Nelson at Aboukir and Trafalgar . . . distinction indeed for any officer! I shall, I am sure, be able to avail myself of your military services, should you desire to offer them in the near future. Are you married?"

Once again Foveaux intervened. "Captain Hawley's wife is one of our first settlers, sir—she came out, I believe, with Admiral Phillip's fleet."

The implication was plain and Andrew reddened with anger. "My wife is an emancipist, Your Excellency," he stated flatly. "She has held a land grant since receiving her pardon twenty years ago. And, sir—"

"Hawley? *Hawley?*" the Governor put in, frowning in what appeared to be an effort to remember. "I have heard so many names today, I confess I am a mite confused. But . . . is not Mrs. Hawley the mother of the young sailor I had reason to commend for his courage and seamanship? The young man who brought you out to us, Colonel Foveaux, when the storm that kept us lying off the Heads was at its height, risking life and limb to do so . . . what was his name?" His expression relaxed. "Justin Broome—by George, that was his name, was it not?"

Foveaux made no attempt to hide his growing impatience. "Yes," he agreed shortly. "It was young Broome who brought me out in his cutter. We were fortunate to reach you, Your Excellency—the cutter was unseaworthy and in need of repair. Ah—forgive me, sir, but there are preparations being made for a banquet, and you—"

Governor Macquarie cut him short. He described the rescue of the *Dromedary*'s topman and the subsequent loss of the *Flinders,* and Andrew, who had known nothing of Justin's escapade, listened in stunned dismay. The poor lad would be heartbroken, he thought. He had seen that the *Flinders* was not at her usual anchorage in the cove, but fool

that he was, it had not occurred to him that she was lost.
Justin had been assisting with the salvage of flooded livestock
and crops on the Hawkesbury and—devil take it, he had assumed that the boy had returned there! Jenny had expected
him at Long Wrekin and had suggested that he might take
passage in the *Flinders* himself, if Justin had not already
left Sydney.

"Well, now, Captain Hawley . . ." The Governor was
about to move on. Andrew had not taken in all that he had
said, but he had heard enough to realize that his stepson
had made a very favorable impression on the colony's new
ruler, and he felt his flagging spirits lift. "I shall do whatever is in my power to assist your stepson to advance his
career, of that you may rest assured. I have some influence
with Captain Pasco of the *Hindostan,* and I intend to bring
the matter to his attention, in the hope that, perhaps, he
can be persuaded to give the young man his patronage."

"That is very good of Your Excellency," Andrew answered. He drew himself again to attention. "Thank you,
sir, on my stepson's behalf. And on my wife's, also."

"Ah, yes—the young man's mother. You will, I trust,
bring her to dine with Mrs. Macquarie and myself when
we are settled in. And"—the Governor extended his
hand—"give some thought to the possibility of returning to
military service, Captain Hawley. An officer of your caliber is wasted on a farm."

He wrung Andrew's hand, smiled, and passed on, with
Foveaux striding ill-temperedly after him.

Justin was on his way to Robert Campbell's yard when a
man who had been watching the landing of the new Governor—like himself, from the edge of the crowd—called on
him to wait.

With some surprise, for the man was one of the colony's
richest shipowners, Justin recognized Mr. Simeon Lord and
halted at once. Lord was an emancipist, but he had become
so wealthy that few people either recalled the fact or taxed
him with it. He owned one of Sydney's finest houses, built
his own ships on a scale that even Robert Campbell could

not match, and in addition to being appointed government auctioneer by the rebel administration, he had done Colonel Foveaux many favors, and in consequence wielded more influence than his office alone would ordinarily carry. Yet, Justin thought, puzzled, he had apparently not received an invitation to join the party at the pierhead or to the luncheon and reception that was about to be held at Government House.

A slight, whether intended or not, on Colonel Foveaux's part, surely . . . but, he decided prudently, one it was probably best not to mention.

"Mr. Lord, sir," he said and waited for the older man to make his wishes known.

Simeon Lord gestured to him to walk on and fell into step beside him. As always, he was well dressed, his silver-buttoned coat made of velvet and expertly tailored to his thin, slight frame, his linen and his white doeskin breeches spotless. He was well into his middle years, Justin knew, and his fair hair was turning white, but his energy and fitness were the envy of men half his age.

He walked briskly now, eyeing Justin covertly for a moment or two without speaking, and then said, with genuine sympathy, "They tell me the *Flinders* is lost."

"Yes, she is, sir, alas! She ran onto the rocks at South Head," Justin confirmed. Even now he hated to think of the cutter's fate and he hoped that Simeon Lord would not ask too many questions. His hope was not in vain; beyond a gruff "I'm sorry to hear it," the shipowner made no further direct reference to his loss . . . probably, Justin reflected cynically, because he already knew all there was to know. He employed a large number of seamen and shipwrights and was usually well informed on maritime happenings.

"Are you looking for work, my boy? A new command maybe? Or—" Lord hesitated, continuing to eye him pensively. "Or do you intend to build another vessel?"

"I should like to build another, Mr. Lord. But I can't afford to, at present." Justin sighed.

It was the truth. Rescue work, when the Hawkesbury

swept over its banks, was unpaid, and he had never asked a penny from any of the settlers, aware that their losses far exceeded his own. His charters had paid for the *Flinders*'s unkeep and Cookie Barnes's wages, but the cutter had been too small to carry much cargo, and during the past year, he had been given no mail charters. The Corps's two lieutenant governors—Paterson and Foveaux—had used sealers and an occasional whaling ship to carry local mail or to communicate with Hobart and Port Dalrymple, for which there was no hurry. Norfolk Island was now virtually evacuated, and the bulk of their mail had, in any case, been directed to England and consigned to returning transports, via India or China.

When he next built a vessel for himself, Justin thought, she would be brig-rigged and twice the *Flinders*'s size . . . and she would cost time and money. He said as much to Simeon Lord, and the shipowner nodded his understanding.

"Then you are seeking employment?" he suggested.

"Yes, sir, if any is offered, I'd consider it."

"You're young to be entrusted with a command," Lord told him. "But you've been well trained and I know your record. My first thought . . ." His thin lips twitched into a smile. "Indeed, until this morning I confess my only thought was to offer you employment in my yard. You served your apprenticeship under old Tom Moore, did you not?"

"Yes, Mr. Lord, I did," Justin answered, his hopes rising. Mr. Campbell had already offered him work as a shipwright but he had refused, aware that he could find a berth as a junior mate in almost any of the Indiamen or tea ships calling at the port. But that would mean leaving New South Wales and his family for several years, and in any case, a command of his own was infinitely more desirable. . . . He turned, breaking his stride, to search Simeon Lord's round, smiling face for some sign of his intentions.

"You know my schooner the *Dolphin*, I imagine?" Lord said.

Justin's heart leapt. "I know her well, sir." The *Dolphin*

was not a new vessel; she had seen fifteen years of service as a trader in the Pacific, but she was fleet and well designed, capable of going anywhere in the world if well fitted. She was careened in Mr. Lord's yard at the moment, he knew, having her bottom scraped and some caulking done to her aging timbers. Lord had purchased her fairly recently from her previous owners, the Hulletts of London . . . cheaply, it was said, because of her need for extensive refitting.

He added cautiously, "She's a fine ship."

"And she'll be ready for sea in a week or two," Lord stated. He listed the repairs he was making and his smile faded. "She's costing me a packet, needless to tell you, and as soon as we can get her back in the water, she'll have to start repaying me for the work I've had done on her."

"Yes, sir, of course," Justin said, and waited for the offer that, he was now certain, was coming.

"Her first mate, Toby Cockrell, is a man of forty or so, and he holds a master's ticket. But—" Simeon Lord shrugged his narrow, sloping shoulders. "I don't trust him, between you and me, Justin. He drinks and he's dishonest. Added to that, he's a poor navigator. It took him weeks longer than it should have done to bring her here from Otaheite—and that was either bad navigation or he embarked on some private trading for his own profit. Her master stayed in Otaheite, leaving Cockrell to deliver the ship to me—which he shouldn't have done, damn his eyes! But—" He repeated his shrug, somewhat resignedly. "That's water under the bridge now, is it not?"

"Yes, sir, I suppose so," Justin murmured, feeling that some response was required from him. Lord lapsed into a pensive silence, and they continued to walk in the direction of his imposing two-storied mansion, now less than fifty yards away on the far side of the Tank Stream. "Mr. Lord . . ." Justin hesitated, drawing a deep breath. But it was now or never, he told himself, and if the wealthy ship-owner was still undecided, he would have to aid him to make up his mind. "Sir, are you offering me command of the *Dolphin*?"

Simeon Lord inclined his head. "That's what I had in mind, Justin. There will be certain conditions, you understand. You've no master's ticket for a start, have you?"

"I have a colonial license and am rated a master's mate in the navy, sir. I—"

"And you served under Matthew Flinders's command in the *Investigator*," Lord put in. He laid a hand on Justin's arm and his smile returned. "I know all about you as a seaman and navigator, Justin lad, and I know that you're an honest young man. What I do *not* know is how you can command other men—men like Tobias Cockrell, who won't much fancy taking orders from you. The cargo manifests will have to be in his name, because you've only a colonial trading license and that might make difficulties for you."

"I can handle them, Mr. Lord," Justin asserted.

Simeon Lord's hesitation was brief. "All right," he said briskly. "The *Dolphin*'s yours, but you are on trial for your first round voyage with her present crew. And my offer's one I fancy will appeal to you, in the circumstances. You go to work on her in the yard from tomorrow, and when she's ready for sea, you carry whatever cargo I see fit to load in her. You'll not be paid for your services, in the yard or at sea. But if you bring her back to me safely, I'll make you free of my shipyard and the materials you'll need to build yourself another small trading vessel—and I'll provide two of my best men to work with you. What do you say?"

There was only one thing he could say, and Justin, his tanned young face wreathed in smiles, said it at once.

"I'll accept, Mr. Lord, and gladly. Thank you, sir."

He offered his hand but Lord shook his white head. "No, lad, not here in the street. We'll seal our bargain in my house, over a glass of ale. I've been standing for too long in the blasted sun, and I'm parched! Lead on, Captain Broome—you know the way."

Five minutes later, in the cool parlor, they shook hands and drank a solemn toast to the *Dolphin*. . . .

* * *

Dickon was crying when Abigail O'Shea reentered the Spences' large, luxuriously furnished residence on the corner of Mulgrave Street. She was hot and tired from her lengthy wait on government wharf, but recognizing, from the little boy's high-pitched, almost hysterical sobbing, that he must have wakened to find her gone, she ran up the stairs in panic, to arrive breathless in his nursery.

Mary Ryan, the Spences' parlormaid, who had been looking after Dickon in her absence, greeted her arrival with relief.

"Such a crying as the poor wee fellow set up, when he found you were not here, ma'am!" she exclaimed. "And dere was I, tryin' to make him understand that you were not gone forever. But I could not make him understand, whatever I said."

"He cannot," Abigail said, picking the child up and holding him to her in warm and loving arms. "You have to face him when you speak to him, so that he may see your lips moving. I did tell you that, Mary," she added, her tone reproachful. "And I'm sure Kate Lamerton did. Dickon is deaf. He cannot hear you or understand what you are telling him, poor mite."

She had, she thought ruefully, accepted the fact of her little son's deafness, but even now she found it hard to reconcile herself to it, particularly when it became necessary to explain his deficiencies to someone like Mary Ryan. Dickon was two years old, and unlike other children of his age, the sounds he emitted were virtually unintelligible to all who were not attuned to them. She and his nurse, Kate Lamerton, could usually converse with him, after a fashion, and he could make his wants known in a strange mixture of sign language and grunts, but . . . She dismissed Mary Ryan with a brief word of thanks, as the child's sobs ceased.

Dr. Redfern, who was a clever and knowledgeable physician, had examined him with exemplary care over a period of weeks, and his verdict, while not encouraging, had at least held out some hope. Dickon was of normal intelligence, he had insisted; he could be taught to speak, given time and a great deal of patience with his tuition, and . . .

Abigail held her son from her and, mouthing the words slowly, said, "I am back, darling. Mummy is here with you."

His smile lit his small, thin face to radiance. He made the sound that, she knew, meant "Mummy," and flinging his arms round her neck, he hugged her. She always referred to herself as "Mummy," feeling it to be an easier sound for him to echo than the more usual "Mama," and he tried harder with that word than with any other . . . and yet, for all his efforts, it was badly distorted as he said it.

Apart from his deafness—his congenital deafness, Dr. Redfern had labeled it—and his odd speech, Dickon was a lively, most attractive little boy. He was even tall for his age, and his dark hair and coloring were the image of his father's—the father, Abigail thought regretfully, who had not lived to see him. The father who . . . She thrust the thought from her, refusing on this day of hope, which the arrival of the new Governor had brought, to dwell on her regrets or allow herself to yield to grief.

The past was over; she was young and had no lack of friends and admirers, and Dickon was a source of great joy to her and her hostess, Frances Spence, the kindest and most charming woman she had ever known. And besides, there was her brother Rick's friend, David Fortescue, a lieutenant serving with him on board Governor Bligh's ship, H.M.S. *Porpoise*. David Fortescue had paid ardent court to her prior to his ship's departure, and now, everyone said, the *Porpoise* would be returning to Sydney in order that the deposed Governor might be reinstated for the formal twenty-four-hour period which the Colonial Secretary had decreed.

The ship was only in the Derwent, in Van Diemen's Land, so that it would not be long before she again dropped anchor in Sydney Cove and Rick and David were given shore leave. . . . Abigail smiled and, still holding Dickon in her arms, crossed to the wall mirror on the opposite side of the room, to subject her image to a critical scrutiny.

She was twenty years old now, but in spite of all that she had gone through since arriving in the colony—the beatings administered by her guardian, Caleb Boskenna, the loveless marriage he arranged for her with Desmond O'Shea, and so much more—the face that was reflected back to her now was still that of a young girl. There were no lines; her skin was smooth and supple, her coloring—which David Fortescue had once likened to that of an English rose—was as striking as it had always been. And Dickon's premature birth had not made any noticeable difference to the slender trimness of her body, save perhaps to enhance it. But her hair was in disarray, she noticed, and reached for a comb—there had been a lively onshore breeze on the wharf and they had all been kept standing there for an unconscionable time. Her fingers moving swiftly, she set the moist golden tendrils to rights, and Dickon, watching her in the mirror, gurgled with delight, putting up a small hand to grasp a lock that had strayed within his range.

"Bad boy," Abigail chided him indulgently. "Let go . . . Mummy wants to tidy her hair, not have it pulled. There, now, that's better, is it not, my darling?" she added, as he obediently relinquished his hold and slipped nimbly from her arms, to patter across to the door and stand there, head on one side, waiting expectantly.

He made the sound that meant "Kate" to him, and Abigail beamed at him approvingly. It always puzzled her that, despite his deafness, Dickon knew when his nurse might be expected—and knew it, usually, long before anyone else, herself included, had heard the faintest sound of her approach. But he was seldom wrong, and a few minutes later, Kate herself appeared, stout and red of face and perspiring freely, to gather the little boy into her embrace with her accustomed affection.

She, too, had watched the arrival of the new Governor and his entourage, and as Abigail completed her toilet by changing into a clean housedress, Kate regaled her with interesting gossip and remarks she had overheard in the crowd.

"Most folk seemed to like the look o' His Excellency, Miss Abigail. He's maybe a mite older than I expected, but

he has a kind and honest face, has he not? An' that's what
we need here, after them rogues o' the Rum Corps. There'll
not be many honest folk who'll be sorry when they go, an'
that's the God's truth!"

It probably was, Abigail thought, although since the majority of Sydney's inhabitants could scarcely be described as
honest, there were bound to be quite a number who would
regret the Corps's departure.

She had come straight back on Dickon's account and
had not heard the new Governor's address, but Kate had,
and with the little boy happily seated on her ample lap, she
repeated all she could remember of it.

"He's urgin' us all to attend church regular, Miss Abigail, like they all do when they first get here, but I don't
suppose Governor Macquarie knows as there's only half a
roof on the church an' the Reverend Mr. Fulton's been sent
to the Green Hills!" Kate's laugh was loud—almost a guf-
faw—but it was lacking in amusement. "Like you noticed,
I don't doubt, His Honor Colonel Foveaux was set on
playin' the host an' spent much o' his time whisperin' in
His Excellency's ear. 'Twill be a pity if all *he* said gains
credit, for he'll have been tellin' a right pack o' lies, if I
know anythin' about him. Featherin' his own nest, that's
what he's tryin' to do, I'd take my oath on it."

"Did the new Governor speak of Governor Bligh's return?" Abigail asked.

Kate Lamerton considered the question and then shook
her head uncertainly. "Not in so many words, Miss Abigail. I wasn't that close, so I didn't hear everythin' he said.
There was somethin' about the unwarrantable removal o'
Commodore Bligh an' mutinous conduct, by which he
meant the Rum Corps . . . but I didn't catch no more.
Folk in the crowd was sayin' as Governor Bligh would be
comin' back, though, an' I, for one, hope they're right.
When I think o' poor Mrs. Putland an' what she's had to
put up with these two years past, my blood boils, for if ever
there was a fine young lady, it's Mrs. Putland. An' her
widowed an' all . . . it don't bear thinkin' about, Miss Abigail."

"No," Abigail conceded. "It does not."

"I did see Mrs. Dawson drive up in her carriage," Kate went on, a faint hint of malice in her voice. "But she couldn't get up to the Government House gates for the crowd, an' in the end, she had to climb out an' walk."

Henrietta Dawson, Timothy's wife, had declined to join the party at the pierhead, Abigail recalled, making the excuse that she did not feel up to standing for a long time in the sun. "Merely for the doubtful privilege," as she had put it, "of shaking the hands of those I shall, in any event, meet socially very soon."

Her real reason was, however, a less worthy one . . . or so Abigail had suspected, and Kate, too, if her tone was anything to go by. Henrietta went nowhere in her stepmother's company, publicly at least. Frances Spence was her equal in breeding, but she had been deported to New South Wales as a seditionist and a supporter of Wolfe Tone's rebel Irish Defenders, and she was therefore—in Henrietta's eyes—a convict, whom only marriage to her father had freed.

Like all too many others in the colony, Henrietta Dawson clung arrogantly to her exclusive status as a free settler, and despite the warmhearted kindness Frances had always shown her, there was a gulf between them—of Henrietta's making—which she would not cross.

She made use of her father's second wife; accepted Frances's hospitality, sent her children to the Spences' Sydney house when the school they attended was in session, and even stayed there as a guest on occasions like this, when the town celebrated. But the gulf remained, hurtful to Frances and to Jasper Spence and evident to all who knew them.

Indeed, whoever had issued invitations to attend the official welcome to Governor Macquarie and his lady must also have been aware of it, for the luncheon invitation had been sent to the Dawsons, but—seemingly as an oversight—Jasper Spence and his wife did not receive one. Frances, with her accustomed tact, had made light of the omission, Abigail recalled, while Henrietta—Abigail sighed, indigna-

tion coloring the memory—Henrietta Dawson had lost no
opportunity to add to what she had supposed to be her
stepmother's humiliation by talking of it in Frances's presence . . . while at the same time accepting her aid in the
fashioning of her own and her two young daughters'
gowns, which had been specially made for the occasion.

"Did Mrs. Dawson look well, in the lilac silk, Kate?"
Abigail asked.

"Oh, yes, that she did," Kate confirmed. "Miss Julia and
Miss Dorothea, too . . . they were pictures, the two of
them. But for all that"—she chuckled—"our Miss Lucy
was the one that caught the eye! There were half a dozen
of the new young officers clustered round her, like bees
around a honeypot, the minute the parade was over, and
she was laughin' an' quizzin' them. We shall have to
watch her, Miss Abigail, an' see that all the attention does
not go to her head."

"Yes," Abigail agreed gravely. "We shall."

Her younger sister, Lucy, was now almost seventeen; a
strange, moody girl, possessed of dark good looks and considerable charm, when she chose to emerge from the protective shell of silence she had built about herself. The last
tragic days she had spent at Yarramundie, their property
on the Hawkesbury, had had their effect on Lucy. She had
witnessed the death of the Reverend Caleb Boskenna and
had been in danger of losing her own life at his hands, and
for months afterward she had been so deeply shocked by
this that even poor little Dickon had been more communi-
cative and easier to console than she had.

Henrietta had, however, exercised a strong influence
over her and, Abigail was forced to concede, had done
more than anyone else to restore the girl to her present
happy, less inhibited state of mind.

Lucy had finished with school, of course, and by rights
they should both have returned to Yarramundie long
since. She herself had done so, taking Dickon and Kate
with her, but Lucy had refused to accompany them, meeting every plea that she do so with outbursts of hysterical
tears and the contention that, so painful were the memories

Yarramundie held for her, she could not bear even to spend a single night there.

"You can have no notion what it was like, Abby," she had sobbed. "After all, Mr. Boskenna did not aim his musket at you, did he? And you did not see poor Mrs. Boskenna's grief, when those black men speared him and the unhappy soul realized that he was dead. She loved him, you know, whatever you may have thought of him, and I . . . I was fond of her, because she was always good to me. I can't go back there and I won't, as long as I live, so it's no use begging me to!"

She had ceased to beg, Abigail thought, realizing that nothing she could say would be of any avail. . . . Frances Spence, as she always did, had come to the rescue with an offer of hospitality. Lucy could help her with the Dawson children and could stay in Sydney for as long as she wished. She would be glad to have her, Frances had said, and should she want a change of scene, she could go to Upwey, the Dawsons' property, during the holidays, when the three young Dawsons normally returned there.

It had proved a beneficial arrangement, at least so far as Lucy was concerned. After a separation of almost six months, Abigail had seen a striking difference in her, when she herself had come to Sydney in order to consult Dr. Redfern concerning Dickon's deafness. Lucy was very much at home in the Spences' household, on excellent terms with Henrietta and the children, and clearly as settled and contented as could be hoped for. Only the mention of Yarramundie still upset her, precipitating the floods of tears and the reiterated refusal to consider making her home there. . . .

Abigail glanced uncertainly at Kate. Dear, faithful, kind-hearted Kate, who had served her so well and cared for all of them so deeply! But Kate was a shrewd observer and a very reliable judge of character; even Lucy was unable to pull the wool over her eyes, and her chuckle, although it had expressed amusement, had been followed by a warning . . . and Kate Lamerton did not issue warnings without good reason.

What had she said about Lucy? *We shall have to watch her, Miss Abigail, and see that all the attention does not go to her head.* . . .

But surely attention was what Lucy needed, to bring her out of the dark places in which her childish mind had wandered? Male attention, flattery, compliments . . . were these not what every young girl sought and treasured? Did she not yearn for such things herself, very often, when the isolation of Yarramundie shut her off from them? True, she had Dickon, and she had known Titus's love, but . . . Sydney en fête, as it was now, with the arrival of the new Governor, and a new regiment, was a gay, attractive place.

There would be receptions, luncheon and dinner parties, picnics, and excursions—perhaps even a ball—and dancing on board the King's ships now at the anchorage. There would be endless opportunities to don formal dress, to talk of home with the new arrivals, to make the acquaintance of those who had come in the Governor's train, and to hear news, at first hand, of what was happening in Europe and the progress of the war. Perhaps there would be victories to celebrate and . . .

"I am in no hurry to go back to Yarramundie," Abigail said, and realized, a moment later, that she had spoken her thoughts aloud.

"And why should you be, Miss Abigail?" Kate responded, beaming. " 'Tis a hard life for you out there, and lonely, too, at times, although you don't complain. Besides, the Governor's coming back soon, ain't he—Governor Bligh, I mean? They all say he is, an' Master Rick will be with him. Like I was tellin' you, folk in the crowd seemed pretty sure, even if His new Excellency didn't say nothin' for definite. An' Miss Lucy would benefit from a few weeks o' your company."

Lucy again, Abigail thought. "What did you mean, Kate," she asked, "when you said we should have to watch Miss Lucy?"

Kate shrugged her plump shoulders. Dickon had fallen asleep in her arms, and she shifted his weight from one shoulder to the other before replying. "Just that she might go from one—what's the word I want? *Extreme,* that's it—

one extreme to t'other. 'Twould be as well, maybe, if you was to keep her under your eye for a while, Miss Abigail. An' 'taint as if you're forced to go back to Yarramundie right away, is it? I mean, you can trust Jethro to look after the place."

Indeed she could, Abigail reflected. Jethro Crowan—the shepherd her father had chosen to come out with them to Sydney—was as trustworthy and reliable as Kate herself. It was he, rather than she, who ran the farm; she was learning, but it was with Jethro as her teacher, and the fact that Yarramundie was prospering was to his credit, more than it was to hers. She kept the books, and with the gold she had inherited from her late husband, she had paid for stock and seed and the keep of the convict laborers, but it was Jethro who told her what to purchase and he who gave the laborers their orders.

She sighed, her thoughts again returning to Lucy. The girl had absorbed many of Henrietta's prejudices—she had noticed that very soon after seeing and talking to her again. Her attitude toward convicts and emancipists was the echo of Henrietta's, and so, too, was her view of Sydney society . . . and, on occasions, her manner where Frances Spence was concerned. But all the same . . .

"Miss Lucy acts a mite wild, with the young gentlemen these days," Kate suggested diffidently. "Meanin' no offense, Miss Abigail. An' she's a mite discourteous, sometimes, to Mrs. Spence."

Her own conclusions, Abigail realized, expressed in different words but the same, save for Kate's reference to Lucy's behavior in male company. She had not observed that or . . . perhaps she had not wanted to, perhaps she had shut her eyes to it, feeling herself in no position either to judge or to condemn her sister on that account.

Her gaze went to the sleeping face of her little son. Dickon bore the name of O'Shea, her late husband's name, as she did herself—he was Richard Edmund O'Shea on Sydney's register of births—but Desmond O'Shea had not fathered him. Titus Penhaligon had been Dickon's father— Titus, whom she had loved when she was little older than Lucy was now—and with each day that passed, the resemblance between them was becoming more evident, to her eyes, at all events. And, perhaps, to Kate's, although the good soul had never so much as hinted that she knew. . . .

"I reckon I'd best put Master Dickon into his cot," Kate said, rising cumbrously to her feet. "He'll sleep through till dinner time, an' then I'll take him out so's he can look at the ships, Miss Abigail. They make a rare sight, don't they—three King's ships, lyin' there in the cove. 'Tain't often we see that many, an' when the *Porpoise* comes back, why then I'll ask your leave to go an' cheer her in." She laid the sleeping child in his cot. He did not stir, and she turned, smiling, to Abigail. "Good as gold, ain't he, the precious lamb? 'Twas a pity you missed the new Governor's grand luncheon, Miss Abigail. I told you I wouldn't be gone long an' Mary could've managed."

Abigail made no reply. Kate was right, she knew, but—while she might leave Yarramundie without compunction in Jethro's care—she never left Dickon for long, even when Kate was in charge of him. He was too vulnerable, too dependent to be left. Besides, he—

A bell jangled from the front door below, and Kate crossed to the window to peer down.

"Why," she exclaimed, " 'tis young Mr. Broome—Justin Broome, Miss Abigail! Will it be Mrs. Spence he's wantin' or the master? Shall I go down an' tell him they're lunchin' with Mr. and Mrs. Robert Campbell?"

"No." Abigail's conscience pricked her. She had arranged to charter Justin Broome's *Flinders* cutter in a week's time for the return journey to Yarramundie, but . . . she would have to cancel the charter now—or, at all events, postpone it. "I think he has come to see me," she told Kate. "I'll go down and speak to him."

When she reached the door it was to find Justin still standing there, almost as if he were being held at bay by Mary Ryan. He was clad in blue knee-breeches and a spotless white shirt, but had not donned a jacket, and Mary— with the social discrimination many convict servants displayed when employed by wealthy Sydney citizens—had clearly decided that he was not a visitor whom her mistress would expect her to usher into her withdrawing room. Unless, that was to say, he explained whatever business had brought him to the house . . . Abigail smiled and waved to her to stand aside.

"It's all right, Mary," she said. "This is Mr. Justin Broome, master of the *Flinders,* and he has called on me. Come in, Justin, if you please." She led the way and, entering the cool, shuttered withdrawing room, with the beautiful, hand-carved furniture Frances Spence had brought back from voyages to India and China, invited him to be seated.

"I'm glad you've come," she added, "because I have been wanting to talk to you about my charter. I should like to postpone it for a few weeks, if that would not inconvenience you."

Justin eyed her soberly, his blue eyes oddly lackluster. "It will have to be postponed indefinitely, Miss Abigail," he told her. "I no longer have a vessel I can charter to you. The *Flinders* is lost."

"Lost?" Abigail echoed incredulously. "Do you—oh, Justin, do you mean that she is wrecked?"

"Yes," he confirmed. "She was smashed to pieces on South Head four days ago. But I've had a word with Jed Burdock, and he says he will take you back to Yarramundie in the *Fanny,* with whatever stock you're buying here, if you can give him reasonable notice. He'll charge you less than I should have had to. He has the regular mail charter, you see, so he can afford to ask less for his freight."

"That doesn't matter," Abigail assured him gently. "I mean, I will ask Mr. Burdock when the time comes, and thank you for mentioning me to him. I . . . I shall stay here until Governor Bligh returns, with the *Porpoise.* My brother, as you may remember, is one of her officers—Rick Tempest."

"Yes, I remember him well, Miss Abigail."

"I . . . ." He sounded so constrained and bitter that Abigail was concerned. Justin Broome was a fine young man, who had once delivered a letter to Titus at Coal River, simply because she had pleaded with him to do so, she reminded herself. And it had been he who had first taken her and Lucy to Yarramundie, along with Caleb Boskenna and his troublesome horse. "I am so sorry that you have lost your beautiful *Flinders,* Justin," she added, with genuine sympathy. "Truly, truly sorry. I . . . What will you do now? Have you made any plans?"

He inclined his head, his face still gravely set and unsmiling, and Abigail wondered whether she had offended him. But he answered readily enough, "I've accepted a command—Mr. Lord has offered me one of his trading schooners, the *Dolphin.* We're fitting her for sea now, and I shall sail for Hobart next week."

"You are not going to build another *Flinders?*" Abigail suggested.

"Not yet, Miss Abigail." Justin rose, smiling for the first time since he had entered the house. "I intend to, but it will take time—and money, of course. The days are gone when a vessel like my *Flinders* could be built for next to nothing, with government-supplied timber and as much free labor as anyone could want." He bowed over her hand, a trifle stiffly and clearly not at ease. "If there's ever any way that I can serve you, Miss Abigail, you have only to ask."

Abigail went with him to the door. Thinking to put him at ease, she said lightly, "Well, who knows? By the time you have built your new ship, I may be married and I shall call on you to convey the new master to Yarramundie, as well as Kate and Dickon and myself."

Justin halted and turned to face her, frowning. "Married?" he questioned, in a low, choked voice.

"Why, yes," Abigail answered, continuing to make light of it. "One of my brother's shipmates, Lieutenant Fortescue, intends to settle here when the *Porpoise* returns. Did I not tell you that he had asked me to marry him? I'm sure that I did."

Justin's expression did not relax. He laid both hands on her shoulders, and Abigail felt as if they were burning her skin through the thin silk of her dress. Taken by surprise, she retreated a pace and said, forcing a laugh, "Oh, Justin, did you think me so old and passé that no man would look at me? Or that I should be content with widowhood and loneliness at Yarramundie? Come—that is churlish of you! I am only a year or so older than you are, truly."

"I know that," Justin admitted. He reddened and let his hands fall limply to his sides. Avoiding her gaze, he added quietly, "Do not be in too great a hurry to wed, Miss Abigail, I beg you. I . . . Before heaven, I am not churlish where you are concerned! I have long cherished a—a very warm admiration for you. And I . . . Miss Abigail, things change, and one day I shall have my own ship again. But she will be a trader, oceangoing, not like the *Flinders,* and then I shall be in a position to pay my addresses to you. Or I might enter the Royal Navy . . . the new Governor spoke of the possibility, and I—"

Abigail cut him short with a stifled exclamation. "Please, don't say any more. I—"

She had never thought of Justin Broome as a prospective suitor, and his words, for all they were so quietly and earnestly spoken, shocked her more than they pleased her. They were flattering, of course. He was an attractive young man, tall and personable, with his slim, lithe body, his brilliant blue eyes—the eyes of a seaman—and his gentlemanly manners. But he was of convict stock; his mother was an emancipist—widely respected, it was true, and now the wife of Captain Andrew Hawley, the former Governor's aide—yet even so . . . Her teeth closed swiftly over her lower lip, biting back the rejection she had been about to voice. Had Henrietta's prejudices begun to influence her? she wondered, uneasy in her turn and reluctant to hurt him . . . was she, too, an elitist at heart, unable to cross the gulf between those who had come willingly to this country and those who had come in chains?

Not that Justin had; he had been born here. Yet it did not make much difference, Abigail thought—the stigma remained. He was—what was the derisory term for it? He was a "currency kid," and whatever he achieved, that label would continue to adhere to him, as that of emancipist ad-

hered even to wealthy and successful men like Simeon
Lord and, despite his title and his aristocratic background,
to Sir Henry Brown Hayes.

Had not John Macarthur, the son of a tradesman if rumor were to be believed, caused poor Sir Henry to be sent
to Coal River, where conditions were so appalling that few
survived its rigors? She shivered involuntarily, remembering Titus's dismay when he had been posted there, in
charge of the hospital, and then, recalled to the present by
Justin's stammered apology, managed a smile.

"I am promised to David Fortescue," she explained, hoping that her excuse would be accepted, and that Justin
would read no more into it than a natural desire to keep
her word, since she had given it. "He asked me to wait for
him, and I assured him I would. He is a good friend of my
brother's, and Rick speaks most highly of him."

"And he is an officer and a gentleman, as your father
was," Justin returned flatly. "I understand, Miss Abigail.
Forgive me, I beg you, for speaking out of turn."

She might as well have spoken her thoughts aloud, Abigail thought ruefully as he bowed and took his leave. He
had read them as clearly as if she had done so. Aware that
she had wounded him, she closed the door on his tall, retreating figure, conscious of regret.

Mary Ryan, hovering in the darkened hall, came to remind her that her luncheon was ready.

"It has been ready this half hour past, Mrs. O'Shea,
ma'am," the girl added, her tone faintly reproachful. "The
mistress was saying that you—"

"I don't want anything," Abigail said, with unaccustomed tartness. The thought of food was suddenly abhorrent
to her, but relenting, she said in a placatory tone, "Thank
you, Mary. I would like some tea, though. Perhaps you'd
be so good as to serve it in the nursery."

"In the nursery, yes, ma'am. But—" The maid's sharp
ears caught the sound of approaching carriage wheels before Abigail's did, and she broke off, to smooth her apron
and hasten to the door as the carriage drew up before it.
" 'Tis the master and mistress back, ma'am. You'll be

wanting to take tea with them in the drawing room, will you not?"

"Yes," Abigail acknowledged. "Yes, of course." The Campbells, she saw, had come with them.

With Frances Spence pouring from the fine Indian silver teapot and exercising her usual warm and hospitable charm, the events of the day were discussed at length and the room gradually filled. Lucy returned, with the Dawsons and their children; visitors called, and in a mood of fresh optimism, approbation of the new Governor and his lady was freely expressed.

"Governor Macquarie's arrival heralds a new era for this colony, I truly believe," Timothy Dawson said. "I had the honor of talking with him after the luncheon, and he told me of his plans to embark on an extensive building program in the town. He's already heard that it is falling down and seen for himself that Government House is in imminent danger of collapsing about his ears. He talked of establishing a bank and of clearing and resurfacing our streets and building roads to the settlements—this last with the aid of his troops, which will be a surprise for those idlers of the Rum Corps, will it not?" He laughed shortly, without amusement, and then added, grave again, "And he wants to name our whole continent as Matthew Flinders wanted to name it—Australia."

There was a short silence as what he had just said sank in, and then a concerted murmur of approval.

"That will require the consent of the home government," Commissary Palmer observed thoughtfully. "And perhaps an act of Parliament."

"But it will give us dignity," Jasper Spence suggested. "And the hope of better things for all our people, convict and free. So long as His Excellency can enjoy the full support of the Colonial Office."

"He appeared to suppose that he would, sir," Timothy Dawson put in. "He's been promised a free hand to make what reforms he deems necessary."

"Then let us pray," Robert Campbell said, his tone a trifle skeptical, "let us pray most earnestly that the home government will permit him sufficient money to effect those reforms!"

"Amen to that," Jasper Spence applauded.

Henrietta, who had remained in moody silence during what had been a largely male exchange of views, said suddenly, "*I* talked at some length with Mr. and Mrs. Ellis Bent and found them both most charming. But Mrs. Bent told me that the new Governor has some dangerously radical notions. He intends, she said, to appoint emancipists to the magistrates' bench and even to invite them to dine at Government House! Can you imagine what effect *that* will have on this community?"

No one answered her. Frances, Abigail saw, flushed scarlet, her eyes rimmed with tears. Abigail half rose, wanting to go to her, but Jasper Spence was before her. He crossed to his wife's side and, his arm about her, said in a low, controlled voice that was yet redolent of feeling, "I agree wholeheartedly with the Governor. When a man—or a woman—has served whatever sentence was imposed or has received a pardon, that should suffice. You cannot, in justice, punish for the rest of their lives those convicted of quite minor offenses and who have paid in full the penalty demanded by the law."

To Abigail's astonishment, Timothy Dawson joined in with what, in effect, amounted to a condemnation of his own wife's attitude. Looking directly at Frances, he stated with conviction, "Neither is it justice to ostracize those whose offenses were crimes only in British eyes. We may call them rebels—their own people call them patriots!"

His meaning was clear enough, even to Henrietta. She glanced resentfully from her husband to her father and rose, with dignity, to her feet.

"I must ask you to excuse me," she said, addressing no one in particular. "I have a headache . . . I shall lie down. Come, children—such talk as this is not for your ears."

She swept out, her two daughters obediently at her heels, her young son, Alexander—who had been seated on the arm of his father's chair—following more slowly.

Timothy said, with a wry smile, to his father-in-law,

"That had to be said, sir, if there is to be a new era in this colony. His new Excellency will, I fear, need all the support we can give him, if he is to bring it about."

"Even from the Irish, Tim?" Frances quipped, recovering her composure, although her beautiful eyes were still filled with tears. "Would you have support from rebels?"

"If they accept that Australia is their country now," Tim answered, without hesitation.

"Let us drink to that," Jasper Spence invited. He crossed to the sideboard and swiftly filled the glasses that stood there. "I give you a toast," he added, when the glasses had been passed round. "To the future of a new Australia!"

"And an end to Colonial Office parsimony!" Commissary Palmer put in, with a tight smile. "May God bless and aid Governor Macquarie!"

Frances Spence, Abigail observed, was among the first to raise a glass to her lips.

CHAPTER V

The new young stallion was called Sirius, and Jenny Hawley was proud of having bred him out of her aging mare, Grasshopper. The sire was Timothy Dawson's fine animal, Sinbad II, which she had sold to him—reluctantly—the previous year.

But well-bred stallions were a luxury in the Hawkesbury settlements. Only she and Timothy bred horses; most of the settlers ran sheep, hogs, and cattle on a fairly small scale, reserving the bulk of their land for wheat and maize and following the usual Hawkesbury practice of sowing maize in the wheat stubble as soon as the crop was harvested.

This year, however, the wheat harvest had been poor, and because of the silt left behind by the recent floods, the maize crop seemed likely to be even poorer. This, at least, might have the effect of raising the price of grain. However, there was talk of the government being forced to import grain from Bengal to ward off a food shortage, and should this become necessary, Jenny knew from past experience, the prices for her own crops would plummet.

In consequence, she regarded her horse-breeding as a good, long-term investment. There was a growing need for riding and carriage horses throughout the colony, and they fetched good prices at the Sydney and Parramatta markets—provided that they could be offered for sale as broken to saddle and harness. And that made it essential that the young stallion be taught to carry a saddle and a rider on his proud chestnut back; she could not keep him solely for breeding purposes, since few of the neighboring farmers could afford to pay stud fees, even if they wanted to breed from their own working mares.

Aided by her ten-year-old son, William, and the Bediagal boy Kupali, Jenny had been working to this end for the past few weeks. Using a lunge rein, as she could remember her father had done, years ago, on their Yorkshire smallholding, she had begun the lessons, patiently coaxing the young horse to accept and answer to bit and bridle and to move in obedience to her vocal commands.

Sirius had been a wild, almost unmanageable creature initially, fighting for freedom and lashing out with his heels at any human being who approached or attempted to lay a hand on him. Ears back and teeth bared, he had resisted even the rope head-collar by means of which she had first led him round the yard or paddocks; but slowly, with gentle insistence, she had won his trust. He now was accustomed to carrying the felt saddle that her late husband, Johnny Broome, had fashioned for her—more years ago than she cared to count—and he did not snap at her when its girths were tightened. He had let her add leathers and stirrups to it and had stood rock-still when she had hoisted her light body into the saddle, with William holding his head.

Today, Jenny had decided, she must teach him the final lesson and ride him. The days were passing all too swiftly, and she had given all the time to Sirius's breaking-in that she could afford. The work of the farm was heavy. She had no convict labor, and with Andrew away in Sydney, there remained only Tom Jardine, the foreman, and his wife, Nancy, with herself and William and the two aborigine boys, Nanbaree and Kupali, to cope with the farm's incessant demands.

To add to her sense of urgency, both the native boys had been absent for over a week—off on what they called walkabout, she could only suppose. And William, whose main interest was in sheep, had lately been complaining that he had tasks of more importance than horse-breaking that required his attention.

"That stallion may be your pride and joy, Mam," he had told her reproachfully, "but it will be a long while before he repays all the work you've put into him. Unless you sell him to one of the officers in Sydney or to the new Governor, perhaps, to ride on the parade ground . . . though I can't see you parting with the creature in a hurry. Not unless you're offered his weight in gold!"

William was right, Jenny was forced to concede, as she carried her saddle and the rest of the tack out behind the farm buildings to the paddock in which Sirius was kept. He came to her, whinnying softly, when she called to him, and fondling his gleaming neck, she was conscious of the upsurge of pride that the sight of him always engendered. In all the years that she had toiled to build up her grant of land, to stock and crop it and wring a living from its soil, this beautiful chestnut stallion, with his two white socks and his splendid head, represented the height of her achievement—in her eyes, at all events.

His dam had been ordinary enough—a good Cape mare, well-mannered and docile; but his sire had Arab blood—far back, it was true, but Sirius had inherited it in full measure. It was manifested in his gracefully arched neck, his clean and slender legs, the way he carried himself and, when he lifted his head, in the flaring nostrils and the liquid dark eyes.

She took an apple from her pocket and, while the horse was crunching it, slipped the saddle onto his back. He submitted to bit and bridle, when the apple was finished, first curling his long tongue round the bit, as if to tease her, and then letting her push it gently into place and ease his ears under the headband.

Tom Jardine came from the milking shed, driving the three house cows before him. He hustled them into the paddock they shared with a sow and her litter and came striding across to Jenny's side, a stocky, gray-haired man, his broad shoulders bowed a little now and the tanned skin of his face deeply lined.

"You aimin' ter take a ride on that horse, Mrs. Hawley?" he asked anxiously.

"Yes, Tom," Jenny confirmed. "He's ready, I think. I'll give him a lunge first and then try him."

"Alone?" Tom challenged. "Don't you want me or young Willie ter help you?"

She shook her head. "Willie's busy with the ewes in the river paddock. He fears that some of them have got foot rot . . . and you know what he's like with his breeding stock! *I* saw no signs of foot rot."

"No more did I, missus." Tom grinned. "But seein' as it'll be back to school for him and Rachel in a week or so, I guess the lad wants ter make sure. Don't trust either o' us with them sheep o' his, do he?"

"No, I'm afraid he doesn't." Jenny attached the long lunge-rein to Sirius's noseband and, clicking her tongue, set the chestnut stallion to circle round them at a leisurely trot. She went on ruefully, "I'll have trouble persuading Willie to go back to school this year, Tom. He says he's learnt all he needs to know, as a sheep farmer, and insists that he'd use his time better staying here."

"And so he would," Tom said. "With them two Indian lads off on their travels, we could do with him here. I'm not gettin' any younger, Mrs. Hawley."

Jenny stifled a sigh. Neither was she, she reminded herself; she was only two years from her fortieth birthday. Her daughter, Rachel, a year younger than William, liked school and was eager to join the Dawson children at their highly respected seat of learning in Sydney . . . and Frances Spence had repeatedly invited her to do so. Mrs. Jones's new academy for young ladies had already acquired an excellent reputation, but . . . there would inevitably be objections from Henrietta Dawson if she were to accept Frances's invitation. In any event, Jenny thought, she did not fancy taking favors that she had not the means to repay, least of all when they involved Timothy Dawson's wife. Henrietta had long resented her friendship with Timothy and the regard they had for each other; the woman made no secret of her feelings . . . and probably would not do so in Rachel's presence.

Apart from that, the school Rachel and William now attended was probably better scholastically than any in Sydney Town. The Reverend Henry Fulton had started it, when the rebel administration had banished him to the Green Hills, suspecting his loyalty to Governor Bligh . . . and he was a good and kindly man. William and Rachel boarded in his house in term time, and Rachel had seemed to be quite happy there—until now, when Timothy had again suggested that she should join his two daughters at the academy.

"I'll think about keeping Willie here," Jenny said, repeating her sigh. She shortened the lunge rein and called out a crisp "Whoa!" to Sirius, and the big chestnut obediently pulled up.

"You're set on backin' that animal, then?" Tom said resignedly.

"Yes. I'll ride him down to the river, to Nanbaree's old hut—I want to see if he's come back." With the stallion nosing her, in the hope of a second apple, Jenny tightened the girths before giving him what he wanted. "Give me a leg up, will you, Tom?"

"Sure. But I wish you'd let me come with you," the foreman persisted. "I can saddle old Baneelon in a brace o' shakes, and—"

"No, Tom. You have more than enough to do and it's not necessary. Sirius is as quiet as a lamb with me now." Jenny put a foot onto Tom Jardine's work-roughened palm and swung herself lightly onto the stallion's back. He did not move, and she smiled down into the foreman's apprehensive eyes, savoring her small triumph. "You see? He's ready for it, is he not?"

"You done a fine job on him," Tom conceded. "But you'd best take this, Mrs. Hawley, if you're goin' looking for Nanbaree." He took a pistol—which he always carried—from the pocket of his coat and, holding it by the barrel, handed it up to her. "It's loaded but not primed, so take the powder horn as well. You've not forgotten how ter use a pistol, have you?"

"No, I haven't," Jenny assured him. Andrew had made a point of teaching her how to handle both a musket and a pistol, after the raid on the farm, three years ago, by Governor Bligh's would-be assassins, but she still disliked carrying weapons of any kind, and she hesitated to take the pistol. "I don't need it, truly, Tom. I'm on my own land, and the blacks have never troubled us since Nanbaree and Kupali came to work here. You know they have not."

"They ain't here now, missus," Tom pointed out unanswerably. "Neither of 'em. And there's word that some o' the young Bediagal have come across the river lookin' for trouble. Best take the pistol, just in case you should run into any of 'em."

"Oh, all right. But I shall need both hands for Sirius." And all her concentration, Jenny thought, accepting the heavy pistol with reluctance. In the absence of a safer or more convenient hiding place, she slipped it into the bosom of her dress, where it bulged uncomfortably, its metal barrel cold against her skin. She hung the powder horn—which had a sling—around her neck, then half stood in the stirrups to arrange her voluminous skirts.

She rode sidesaddle now, more often than not. It was a fashion set by the officers' wives in Sydney and followed, even on the farm, by those who, like Henrietta Dawson, set great store by their gentility. The light felt saddle she was using for Sirius, however, made no provision for gentility, and for this initial attempt to ride her mettlesome young stallion—skirts or no—she felt more confident astride. Besides, there was little danger of an encounter with any critical strangers.

"You can let his head go now," she instructed, and Tom Jardine nodded and let his restraining hand fall from the rein.

"Have a care, Mrs. Hawley," he advised, and stood aside.

Sirius, responding to the voice he knew, moved forward quietly at Jenny's command. Then, as if only just aware of the burden he was carrying, he arched his neck and let fly with his hind legs in an attempt to dislodge his rider's light but unaccustomed weight. It failed and he resorted to rearing, pawing the air with his forelegs, coming down onto them stiffly and rearing again. But Jenny sat him easily, and finally, in panic, the big horse tried to bolt. The bit between his teeth and his head down, he tore off across the paddock, to be brought to a snorting halt by the stout wooden fence by which it was surrounded.

"There, boy, there," Jenny soothed him. She did not raise her voice and her hand moved gently along his sweat-damp neck. "Easy . . . no one is going to hurt you. Walk on now, that's a good fellow!"

Tom stood by the paddock gate, waiting to open it. He said admiringly, when she walked the stallion slowly over to him, "Well done, Mrs. Hawley! I reckon that horse'll do all you ask him to now."

"As long as nothing scares him," Jenny qualified. She went through the gate and, keeping to the edge of the culti-vated land, where the first green tips of maize were start-ing to show, put Sirius into a canter. The maize, her mind registered, was poor—patchy, rather than thin—but at least this part of her land was high and had remained clear of the floodwaters and the aftermath of silt. Lower down, she knew, despite all the hard work Andrew had put in, ridging and turning the wheat stubble over with a plow, the yield would be barely worth the cost and toil of harvesting . . . and would certainly not repay the charges made for transport to Sydney.

It might, in the long run, be better used to feed stock. Pigs, in particular, thrived on it, and if Justin could pur-chase a dozen or so sows, their litters would be ready by the time the maize grew. He could deliver them in the *Flinders* during the next month or so and . . . Sirius came abruply to a halt, punishing her for her momentary lapse of attention by almost precipitating her over his head.

He stood, ears pricked and nervously twitching, as if something had alarmed him. Following the direction in which his pricked ears were pointing, Jenny noticed that a thin wisp of grayish-white smoke was rising from midway up a tree-grown slope, about half a mile to her left.

The land was not part of the Long Wrekin holding. It was a twenty-five acre grant belonging to a settler named Adam Brown—an emancipist, with no experience of farm-ing and a reputed partiality for strong liquor—who had lost so much stock, because of his own ineptitude and the recent floods, that he had abandoned the place and gone back to Sydney some weeks ago. Latterly, he had been on bad terms with the Bediagal, whom he had accused of stealing the few emaciated sheep he had left, and it was rumored that he had shot at and wounded an old man of the tribe, claiming to have caught him red-handed with his booty.

Jenny watched anxiously, as the smoke grew from a wisp to a thick, flame-tinged cloud. Could it be, she wondered, that the young blacks, of whose presence Tom had warned her, had decided to raid the property, seeking revenge? In all probability they would not know that Adam Brown had gone. After the manner of their kind, they would have approached warily, setting light to the trees and brushwood above the farmhouse in the hope of enticing Brown out into the open to investigate the cause of the blaze . . . knowing that, under a cover of choking smoke, their spears would be a match for any settler's musket.

Sirius snorted and tried to back away, but Jenny, still undecided on what course of action to take, held him steady. The wind was blowing in the direction of the river, she realized, and the fire—if it were confined to Adam Brown's property—would do scant harm, since apart from the tumbledown wattle-and-daub house at the foot of the slope, there was little to be destroyed. As long as the wind did not change, there would be no danger to her own property and the fire would burn itself out when it reached the river, having done nothing worse than reduce an isolated clump of gum trees to charred trunks on its way.

There was always a risk that the wind might change, of course, but . . . Jenny glanced skyward at the clouds. They were moving very slowly; the wind was light and westerly, usual for this time of year. There was only a small risk of its changing. . . . She touched Sirius's sides with her heels and rode on toward Nanbaree's hut. If the young Bediagal warriors had crossed the river the previous evening, there was a chance that Nanbaree or Kupali—or both of them—might have crossed also, if for no better reason than to protect their own property from the avenging party's depredations.

To her relief, this supposition proved to be correct. Kupali called out a greeting and came to meet her as she cantered up to the edge of the clearing, and his elder brother was standing at the entrance to the first of the bark huts, the one they had built when he married. His wife, Murruba, with her two young children, was dimly discernible within its dark interior, and she, too, held up a small brown hand in greeting.

Both young men carried throwing sticks and spears, but neither had painted his face as indication of warlike intent, and they seemed, to Jenny's anxious eyes, as serene and untroubled as they usually were when at work on the farm. No explanation of their prolonged absence was offered and neither apologized for it, although the fact that they had been away was tacitly acknowledged by the eagerness of their inquiries concerning William and Rachel and the Jardines. Kupali, whose close friendship with William had resulted in his speaking English with more fluency than Nanbaree, expressed astonishment at Jenny's seemingly easy mastery of Sirius, and it was several minutes before she could induce either of them to listen to her questions concerning the fire on Adam Brown's holding.

"Him bad man," Kupali stated, with conviction. "Old feller Narona go his place ask food—*tulani* take muss-kit, shoot him dead!"

"But surely Mr. Brown did not kill him?" Jenny protested.

"He die *kurrara*—" The boy gestured toward the distant foothills, indicating an aborigine camping ground. "Many days hurt him bad. Him *aranga*, missus." The brown hands described the shape of a beard, as if one were growing, long and white, from his own hairless chin. The word, Jenny knew, meant that the old man, Narona, had been a grandfather, venerated by his tribe because of his age.

"So the Bediagal make *gwee-un*—fire—and burn the house?" she said accusingly.

Both natives shook their heads. "They *iliara*," Nanbaree

explained, his tone indulgent. "Boys! Not burn house
. . . make *burringi*."

"Smoke, missus," Kupali interpreted. "Make bad man
come out."

"But he's not in the house, Kupali," Jenny told him. "He
left, long time ago."

"He come back. Bring woman alonga him."

"A woman—*dee-in?*" Jenny was startled. "A *white*
woman?" The two dark heads inclined in unison in answer
to her question, and she drew in her breath sharply, conscious of a chilling fear. If Adam Brown had indeed returned, it was quite possible that he had brought a woman
with him, although previously he had lived and worked the
farm alone. And if he had, the woman could expect no
mercy; the aborigines' treatment of their own women was
brutal in the extreme, and if it was their intention to
avenge the killing of Narona in blood, they would shed that
of Brown's woman without compunction, should she be un-
wise enough to show herself.

But would they, Jenny wondered, listen to her, if she
went there and attempted to dissuade them? They would
offer her no violence; over the years, all her dealings with
the Bediagal had been friendly, and she would be in no
danger from them, particularly if Nanbaree and Kupali
came with her. But whether or not the young Bediagal
would listen to her was another matter. . . . She glanced
again at the rising cloud of smoke, brows knit in frowning
indecision. She wished that Andrew had accompanied her
or that she had permitted Tom Jardine to do so. But she
had not, and it was too late now for regrets.

"Him very bad man," Kupali asserted, as if sensing her
thoughts. "Stay here, missus."

The warning was plain, and Jenny knew that she would
have heeded it, without any qualms of conscience, had
Adam Brown been alone. He had never been the kind of
neighbor she wanted, and she had not welcomed his arrival
on the land bordering Long Wrekin; but if he *had* brought
a woman with him from Sydney, she could not remain
here, not lifting a finger to help either of them. She had to
do what she could, in common humanity, and . . . she

had Tom's pistol. With its aid, she might induce the young
Bediagal to spare the white woman.

Her decision reached, she shook her head at Kupali, to
indicate that she could not take his advice. "I go there, help
white woman. You come with me?"

Kupali hesitated, looking at his elder brother, but Nanbaree's headshake was as emphatic as her own had been,
and he put out a hand to grasp Sirius's bridle, seeking to
dissuade her. The stallion backed away, jerking his head
free, and Jenny waited no longer. She dug her heels into
his sides and the big horse bounded off, carrying her
swiftly toward the trees and the thickening column of
smoke that floated above them.

Left to themselves, Nanbaree and Kupali again exchanged uncertain glances; then, without a word, they set
off after her with long, loping strides, covering the ground
less swiftly than the galloping horse but with grim purpose-
fulness, their bare feet making no sound as they ran.

Adam Brown was standing by the open door of his ramshackle farmhouse when Jenny came in sight of it. The
trees within fifty yards of the building were blazing
fiercely, the wind blowing smoke and flames toward it, but
she could see no sign of the young blacks who had started
the conflagration, and the emancipist, his musket threaten-
ingly raised, clearly had no target at which to aim.

He was swaying from side to side, screaming in a loud,
angry voice at his assailants to show themelves, and receiving no answer, he resorted to obscenities, his fury and frustration growing. Sirius, alarmed by the burning trees, came
to a trembling halt, and it took all Jenny's skill and resolution to hold him still. Talking to him quietly, patting his
sweat-streaked neck, she managed to induce him to move
near enough to the wattle-and-daub house for her voice to
be heard by its occupant, and she called out to him by
name.

"Mr. Brown—Adam Brown, have you a woman with
you?"

The big man spun round, startled. He had neither seen
nor heard her approach up the tree-grown slope, it was
evident. It was also evident to Jenny, when he answered

her, that he was by no means sober, for his voice was slurred and he stumbled and almost fell as he moved away from the support of the wall against which he had been leaning.

"Who in hell wants to know?" he demanded thickly, a hand raised to shade his eyes as he peered at her through the swirling smoke. "Who are you?"

Before Jenny could reply, the woman herself came to the door, crouching there unsteadily, her frightened sobs audible above the crackling of the burning timber. "I'm here—here in the house! Help me, for God's sake, whoever you be!"

"Make a run for it!" Jenny urged her. "This way . . . run this way!"

"Come nearer . . . oh, please!" the woman begged. "I can't see you an' I'm scared. They're out there with their spears—I dursn't come out."

But Jenny could coax Sirius no nearer; the stallion was fighting for his head, snorting and whinnying in his attempts to get away, his ears laid back. She considered dismounting but dismissed the thought, aware that on foot she would not have the strength to hold him.

"Run!" she besought the sobbing woman, seeing her dimly as the smoke billowed in a dense black cloud between them. "I'm on a horse. I—"

A spear, thrown from somewhere among the trees at her back, came hurtling through the air, to bury its barbed point in the ground a scant two yards from her, and she was forced to break off as Sirius reared in terror. She managed somehow to control him and heard the woman shriek that she was coming.

"Wait for me! Wait till I—" But the poor soul's cries were cut short by a roar from Adam Brown.

"I told you not to show yourself, you bitch! Get back in the house!"

He must have flung her bodily into the house, for her shadowy form vanished from Jenny's sight, and an instant later the emancipist himself came pounding through the smoke toward her, clutching his musket and swearing angrily as he tripped on the uneven ground. Taken by surprise, she did not at first guess his intention, and it was only when his big hand came out to seize her rein that she had any inkling of it.

"Off with you!" he yelled at her. "And give me the horse. Damn your eyes, woman, it's me those bloody savages are after, not you! Get off or I'll pull you off!"

He did not wait for her to obey him. The butt of his musket was rammed into her stomach; Sirius reared, his forelegs threshing the air in front of him, and Jenny was sent crashing to the ground. She fell heavily, the breath knocked out of her, and Tom's pistol, for which she had been belatedly reaching, dropped uselessly into the churned-up dust beside her.

Adam Brown made two attempts to vault into her saddle, and at the third attempt he succeeded. But he was encumbered by the musket, and even his brute strength did not suffice to bring the wildly struggling stallion under control. Head down, the horse bolted with him, and at the edge of the small clearing where his stockyard had been, three dark-skinned naked figures emerged from their concealment, spears and throwing sticks poised.

Jenny scrambled to her feet and, giddy and badly shaken, tried vainly to draw the breath back into her lungs. She wanted to beg the young Bediagal to spare Sirius, to aim their spears at the man, not the horse, if throw them they must, but her cry was too faint to carry to where they were standing. Even to utter it caused her intense agony from what, she supposed dully, were broken ribs.

Yet, it seemed, Sirius had heard her . . . or perhaps it was mere coincidence that he halted his headlong flight and pitched the man who had stolen him off his back, before cantering down the slope, away from the smoldering blaze, heading unerringly in the direction of home.

Watching him go, Jenny prayed that he would not stumble, that he would make his way to safety. . . .

From the door of the farmhouse, the woman called out fearfully, but Jenny ignored the call and, oblivious to any danger she herself might be in from the young Bediagal, stood where she was, all her attention concentrated on Adam Brown. The big emancipist had not fallen as heavily as she had, and he was on his feet seconds later, apparently unhurt and still holding his musket . . . and, once again, his reaction took her by surprise.

He put the musket to his shoulder and, as if he did not see the three aborigines advancing on him from the clearing, aimed it at the fleeing horse. It was a long shot; Sirius was seventy or eighty yards away and gathering speed with every yard he covered, but Brown had loaded his musket with buckshot, and because of its wide spread, he did not entirely miss his target. Sirius was hit on the rump— probably, Jenny thought sadly afterward, causing him no more pain than the bite of a horsefly, since the shot must have been spent. But it added to the poor animal's terror; he stumbled and then went crashing down the hillside, somersaulting in a welter of flying legs and, coming at last to rest, lay motionless . . . his neck, Jenny knew, even at that distance, broken and the life gone from him.

"Bad cess to the plaguey brute!" Adam Brown yelled, waving his musket drunkenly in the air. "That'll teach him to throw me! That'll show who's master here and—" The words died in a strangled gasp, as a spear struck him and sent him sprawling.

It was thrown by Nanbaree. He and Kupali ranged themselves at Jenny's side, breathing hard from their long, uphill run, and as two more of the young blacks came to hurl their spears, Nanbaree uttered a stern warning. The Bediagal retrieved their weapons and took their silent leave, vanishing as swiftly as they had appeared, only one of them pausing to turn Adam Brown's limp body over with his foot to make sure that he was dead.

Flames were licking at the roof and walls of the house now, and the woman came staggering out, choking in the smoke, her face badly bruised and discolored from the blows Brown had rained on her. But she showed no signs of distress at the sight of his body and, quickly sizing up the situation, ran toward Jenny and the two Bediagal, who stood safely out of the path of the fire.

As they all watched the house go up in flames, Jenny, feeling it incumbent on her, offered the woman shelter for the night. The woman shrugged and accepted without thanks or any expression of gratitude.

"It'll just be for the night," the woman said offhandedly. "I'll go back to town tomorrow, if there's a boat. Or to the Green Hills maybe—I've a feller there."

Jenny said nothing. Her heart heavy, she looked again down the slope to where Sirius was lying, hoping to see some movement . . . but there was none. Nanbaree touched her arm gently and shook his head.

"Home," he said, in careful English. "Go home, missus, alonga Kupali."

There was little else she could do, Jenny thought bitterly. The fire would burn itself out when it had consumed Adam Brown's ill-constructed buildings and reached the river; his death would have to be reported, his body buried, and his woman sent on her way. For this she had sacrificed the finest horse she had ever bred . . . Sirius, her golden stallion. She crossed unsteadily to where he lay, but all hope faded when she reached him and saw, beyond shadow of doubt, that his neck was indeed broken, just as she had feared when she had watched him fall. She knelt there, the handsome chestnut head cradled in her arms, feeling as if her heart would break; but when the tears came, she brushed them resolutely away. Tom Jardine could attend to Brown's burial, she told herself, but Sirius . . . The dingoes would come, scavengers in the night, and that realization hurt her more than the pain in her chest.

"Make *gwee-un*," Nanbaree promised, reading her thoughts. "Burn 'im like Bediagal *beeyung* . . . father of sons."

Jenny inclined her head in assent, her throat tight. Sirius had sired no progeny; only one young mare had ever stood to him, and that had been unintentional, the result still uncertain. "Good," she managed. *"Bud-ye-ree."* There were no words that she knew in the native tongue to signify gratitude, but Nanbaree took her brief smile as his reward and smiled back at her.

"Go home," he urged again. "Longa Kupali, missus."

She needed Kupali's arm and the support of a stick he cut for her before she reached Long Wrekin, Adam Brown's woman trailing reluctantly in her wake, offering only whining complaints concerning the distance she was compelled to walk, and her desire to seek other company.

Weary and disspirited, Jenny shut her ears to the shrill, unpleasant voice, with its seemingly insatiable demands on her attention and, for no reason that she could understand, on her pity. She felt no pity, save for Sirius, and . . . Again the tears came, but again she stemmed them, with the back of a smoke-grimed hand, refusing to make a display of her grief.

Her heart lifted, however, when William came running from the fold yard to call out excitedly that he had sighted Jed Burdock's *Fanny* coming upriver and that he was sure that he had recognized Andrew standing on deck. "I'll take a horse and go and meet him at the wharf, shall I, Mam?" the boy offered, with touching eagerness, when she told him, in a few brief and bitter words, what had happened. "Maybe you'll feel better when Andrew's back here with you."

And probably she would, Jenny told herself. Andrew was a good husband, staunch and loyal, and she loved him deeply.

It was only after William had ridden off and Nancy Jardine had taken Adam Brown's woman to the kitchen for a meal that, at last, she gave in to her grief and let the tears come. But she fought down her weakness, and was composed and dry-eyed when Andrew came striding into the house. He inquired anxiously as to her injuries, and then, after she had given him a restrained account of the day's events, she pointedly changed the subject and drew him on to a discussion of the new Governor's arrival and of the hopes he had expressed for the colony's future.

CHAPTER VI

Within a few days of taking up residence in Sydney's Government House, Mrs. Macquarie suffered a miscarriage.

They had been hectic days for the new Governor and his wife, marked by scenes of wild rejoicing throughout the town. There were speeches, signed addresses of welcome, bonfires, a fireworks display, and on the part of the self-styled respectable inhabitants, a succession of receptions and dinner parties, the most lavish being hosted by officers of the 102nd Regiment.

Elizabeth Macquarie, seemingly indefatigable, had taken part in all of these, but now, Jessica thought sadly as she carried a laden tray to her mistress's bedroom, the poor, sweet soul was paying the penalty . . . she had lost the child she wanted so much.

Dr. William Redfern had attended her, and he had done all that medical skill and compassion could do, but it had not been enough. He had prescribed bed rest, purging, and an end to all social activities for at least the next ten days, and he had impressed on Jessica that she must do all in her power to ensure that the patient adhered strictly to his instructions.

But this was easier said than done, the girl reflected. She set down her tray on the bedside table, but her attempt to pour tea was forestalled by the invalid herself, who sat up and firmly took the teapot from her.

"I am not ill, Jessica . . . I am a perfectly strong, fit woman. A woman with obligations and duties to perform, in her husband's support! For mercy's sake, child, do not coddle me!"

"No, ma'am," Jessica responded submissively. "But Dr. Redfern did say that you—"

Her mistress impatiently cut her short. "I know what Dr. Redfern said. But I have been here for a week, scarcely stirring hand or foot, eating the slops you bring me and swallowing a succession of the most nauseating potions . . . and that is long enough!"

"They will restore your strength, ma'am. They—"

"Fiddlesticks!" Elizabeth Macquarie exclaimed. "The good young doctor admits himself that I am as strong as any woman my age—stronger than most, in fact—and that there is no reason of which he is aware that precludes me from bearing a child to its full term. With certain precautions, of course, including bed rest . . . and those I shall take more than gladly, should I become pregnant again. God grant I may! But in the meantime . . . Ah, child, I am speaking above your head, am I not? And of matters you cannot be expected to comprehend. I forget sometimes how young you are and let my tongue run away with me."

Jessica flushed. "I have some experience of such matters," she asserted, thinking of her mother's friend, Morag Macrae, who had openly bewailed the succession of miscarriages and stillbirths that she, poor woman, had also been fated to endure. And besides, had not her mother given birth to wee Flora prematurely and required her assistance, prior to the arrival of the midwife? She added, with conscious pride, "I am a woman grown now, Mrs. Macquarie. In less than three months' time I shall be eighteen."

"That is a great age indeed, Jessica India," Mrs. Macquarie said indulgently. "An age when many girls dream of marriage." She tasted a spoonful of the steaming bowl of bread and milk on the tray and pushed it from her with an expression of distaste. "Ugh! That is quite uneatable."

Mindful of Dr. Redfern's injunctions, Jessica added sugar to the bobbing lumps of bread floating in the crested silver bowl and eyed her mistress pleadingly. "I am thinking it will taste better now. Please, ma'am, will you not be trying it, at least? Dr. Redfern said that he would hold me to blame if you did not eat."

"Then for your sake, I will endeavor to swallow it." The spoon was plied halfheartedly, and Elizabeth Macquarie's expression did not change, but she managed to finish most of the bowl's contents before again pushing it from her. "Did Dr. Redfern not advocate porridge? I should find that more to my taste and more sustaining, I dare swear."

"I could make porridge for you, ma'am," Jessica offered eagerly.

"Then do so, for my breakfast, if you please. I have had enough of Dr. Redfern's pap. And tomorrow morning, Jessica—" The invalid sat right up, thrusting the bedclothes aside with the same disdain as she had displayed when ridding herself of the unpalatable bread and milk. "Immediately I have broken my fast, you will be so good as to lay out my green taffeta gown and assist me to don it. I intend to get up and to greet Dr. Redfern on my own two feet when he calls. But do not mention this to anyone else, child—least of all to His Excellency."

"No, ma'am, of course not. But you—"

"I have told you, I am now quite recovered. And I cannot continue to lie here in idleness when His Excellency needs me at his side. All of these functions he has to attend . . . poor soul, they are endless! And . . ." Elizabeth Macquarie's firm mouth tightened. "Before we know it, the late Governor, Commodore Bligh, and his daughter will be arriving here, and I must certainly be on hand to assist in receiving them. Tell me . . . have you heard any word as to when they are expected?"

Jessica hesitated. A ship called the *Estramina* had, she knew, been dispatched to Van Diemen's Land to convey the late Governor and his party back to Sydney, but she had heard nothing else, save speculation on the part of one of the old Government House servants, who had insisted that Commodore Bligh would return in his own King's ship . . . or not at all.

"Regular stickler for what's right and proper is His late Excellency," the man had said. "Colonel Foveaux offered him the *Estramina* before, but he took His Majesty's ship *Porpoise* and insisted on it. She's a ship of war, see, and armed, and they do say as he was going to open fire on Sydney Town before he left, only her captain wouldn't do it."

Wisely mistrusting the credibility of this piece of gossip, Jessica did not repeat it. "They all say that it will be very soon, ma'am," she evaded.

"Then I must indeed hasten my recovery. His Excellency is anxious to show the commodore all the honors to which he is entitled, and of course there must be a dinner to bid him welcome. I am especially eager to make the acquaintance of Mrs. Putland, for I have heard so much about her." Mrs. Macquarie sipped her tea, and Jessica, who had been expecting her dismissal, waited with the patience the past few months had taught her, as her mistress talked on. "His Excellency told me yesterday that he intends that the Seventy-third shall form the guard of honor and that they shall parade wearing the kilt." There was pride in the soft voice and in the smile that lit Elizabeth Macquarie's pale, oval face. "I have not been with the regiment for as long as you have, Jessica, but I think the soldiers will be pleased, don't you?"

"Oh, yes, I am sure they will, ma'am," Jessica spoke with conviction, aware that very few in the regiment had welcomed the order—from the Horse Guards, she could only suppose—to change their traditional Highland uniform to that of the English line. There had been resentment, too, at the manner in which the 102nd had taken precedence and pride of place on the day that Colonel Macquarie had landed as Governor . . . she had heard Captain Antill speaking of it to the Governor's nephew, Mr. John Maclaine, who was an ensign in the 73rd, and both had sounded angry.

"They are damned mutineers, ordered to be sent home in disgrace!" Captain Antill had complained indignantly. "And they have felons in their ranks—felons and deserters, shipped out here as convicts. Yet they were permitted to parade with their colors and their infernal band and to play the national anthem into the bargain! That was Foveaux's doing, of course. He sprang it on His Excellency without asking permission."

Colonel Foveaux, Jessica reflected, was now a frequent visitor to Government House in spite of this, seemingly trusted and on the most friendly terms with Governor Macquarie . . . and the more so, since his wife's illness. Mrs. Macquarie, she recalled, had admitted that she did not much care for the smooth-tongued colonel, and the Governor's two aides-de-camp appeared to share her opinion.

But at least reparation was to be made, on the occasion of Commodore Bligh's return to Sydney. The regiment that had arrested and deposed him would be kept in barracks, their colonel no doubt with them, and the 73rd would muster in their tartan and scarlet, with their pipes and drums at their head, playing the marches and tunes to which they had in the past gone so bravely into battle.

Jessica's heart swelled with the pride that had been fostered in her since her earliest childhood, as she visualized the scene and imagined Fergus Mackinnon striding out in the tartan ranks. She had not seen him since the landing, almost three weeks ago—the regiment was quartered two miles from Sydney Town, and he had not been among the pipers selected to play at any of the Government House dinners as yet. And . . . she had not sought permission to keep company with him, but in light of Mrs. Macquarie's illness and her disappointment at the loss of her unborn child, it would have seemed heartless, at such a time, to have intruded on her mistress's grief. There had been much to do, and she had been needed in both sickroom and kitchen.

Mrs. Macquarie set down her cup with an air of finality but still did not dismiss Jessica. She said pensively, "It is always believed that a woman is only fulfilled when she has a husband and children, and I waited long enough for fulfillment, the good Lord knows! But marriage, to the right husband, is worth waiting for, Jessica India . . . remember that, will you not?"

A trifle taken aback by this sudden change of subject, Jessica dutifully inclined her head. "Oh, yes, ma'am, I will," she managed, and wondered uneasily whether her mistress had read her thoughts or had guessed that she had been thinking of the young soldier who had invited her to keep company with him.

Perhaps she had: Elizabeth Macquarie had an uncanny habit of reading the minds of those about her. The housekeeper, Mrs. Ovens, had observed this and warned her about it, Jessica recalled.

"She is a Highland lady and fey, child. You will have to take care when you are with her. She will talk to you freely, but she will listen, too . . . often to things you have not uttered aloud!"

Feeling the telltale color rushing to her cheeks, Jessica turned away, to busy herself about the room. In any case, she reflected with conscious bitterness, her mother's second marriage to Sergeant Major Duncan Campbell was a more than sufficient warning to her not to enter the bonds of matrimony lightly or in haste. . . .

"It was your own father who had you christened India, was it not?" Mrs. Macquarie asked, again with her uncanny perception, seemingly as if she had read the trend of Jessica's thoughts.

"Yes, ma'am, it was."

"And he was killed in action, at the siege of Seringapatam, I believe?" Jessica nodded in wordless assent, and Mrs. Macquarie went on, "You see, I am learning something of the regiment's history. Captain Antill has been telling me about Seringapatam, and he mentioned, quite recently, that he owed his life to the heroism of a corporal named Murdoch Maclaine—but I had not, until he spoke of it, realized that Corporal Maclaine was your father. You know the story, I imagine?"

"Oh, yes, I do," Jessica confirmed eagerly. Her mother had retold it many times, her eyes always brimming with tears when she described, to herself and Murdo, how their father had carried the wounded Captain Antill to safety and then gone back, into the thick of the savage, hand-to-hand battle only to meet his death at the hands of one of Tipoo Sultan's turbaned swordsmen.

She repeated the story, in her mother's brief, sad words and then broke off in mid-sentence, fearing that she had let herself be carried away and forgotten her place. The kindly Mrs. Ovens, for years in domestic service and seeking to train her, had reiterated often that good servants knew how to keep their place in the presence of their betters.

But, to her relief, she saw that her mistress was smiling at her, evidently not in the least put out. "That explains why Captain Antill has such a soft spot for you, Jessica. I had wondered why."

"A . . . soft spot, ma'am? I do not think he has. That is, he—"

"He hid you, did he not, when the ship was about to sail from Portsmouth and your mother and stepfather were put ashore?"

This time Jessica could not hide her confusion. She colored more deeply than before, uncertain whether to deny or admit to the truth, and finally took refuge in apprehensive silence. Elizabeth Macquarie reached for her hand and patted it reassuringly.

"He told me himself, child, so do not concern yourself. In any event, it is past history now and you have nothing to fear. Even when your stepfather rejoins the regiment, it will be my wish that you should continue in my service. You have looked after me well, Jessica India, particularly during the past week when I . . . when I know that I have made many demands on you. Now . . ." She released Jessica's hand and gestured to the tray. "Take that away, if you please, and see to it that everything is ready for tomorrow. The green taffeta and fresh linen and a pair of low-heeled shoes. I am leaving my bed and putting my—my disappointment behind me."

"Very good, ma'am." Jessica picked up the tray and moved toward the door of the sickroom. It was opened before she reached it, and she stood aside as the Governor himself came in.

He paused for a moment, frowning, and then said, addressing his wife with unusual testiness, "Commodore Bligh's ship has been sighted off the Heads, my dear. The wind's in his favor and he's expected to make port before dark . . . and come ashore tomorrow morning. Damme, he's come sooner than I anticipated, and I'm not ready for him! I'm sending Maurice O'Connell out to meet him, but with you laid up and Bligh's daughter with him, my plans for their reception are likely to go sadly awry. Joseph Foveaux has said that his wife is willing to stand in for you, but I cannot possibly accept *that* offer, can I? The commodore would take it as a personal affront. There's Mrs. Paterson, I suppose, or Mrs. Bent, but—"

"No!" Elizabeth Macquarie's response was swift and vehement. "*I* shall receive Mrs. Putland and be at your side throughout the proceedings. Oh, do not worry about me, Lachlan . . . I have already resolved to leave my bed tomorrow morning. Instead, I shall leave it now—I am perfectly all right, I do assure you. Jessica, fetch me my robe and slippers, if you please."

She put the bedclothes from her, and as Jessica helped her to don her robe, she was smiling, her blue eyes bright with determination. She came a trifle unsteadily to her feet but added, in a tone that precluded any objections her husband might make, "Be so good as to inform Mrs. Ovens that I shall be dining with His Excellency this evening, child. And then come back and assist me to dress. As for tomorrow . . . clearly, the green taffeta will not do. We shall have to think again and devise something more appropriate."

"The tarlatan, ma'am, with the tartan shawl and underskirt?" Jessica suggested, greatly daring.

Mrs. Macquarie steadied herself carefully and then clapped her hands in delight. "Of course, child . . . what could be more in keeping with the occasion?" She glanced amusedly at her husband's solemn face and challenged, with gentle mockery, "Dearest Lachlan, why so unhappy? Commodore Bligh will come, but he cannot stay here . . . *you* are the Governor! You will receive him with the Seventy-third at your back and your wife at your side, both sporting the tartan. And when it is over and what is necessary has been done, we shall speed him on his way, and he will leave us in peace. It is *you* the people want, not Bligh . . . only think how warmly they have welcomed you!"

"Aye, they have been kind," the Governor conceded. "Indeed, I believe that I am well received."

"Of course you are, my dear," his wife assured him. "And when the Rum Corps also go, there will be nothing to stand in the way of the peace and prosperity of this colony under your command."

"I pray God you are right," the Governor said gravely. "But I shall be thankful to have you with me tomorrow." He reached for his wife's hand and bore it to his lips. "You are a fine, brave woman, Elizabeth, and I appreciate your loyalty. But you will need to take care not to overtax your strength—I'd never forgive myself if any harm came to you."

Jessica slipped away unnoticed, leaving them together.

On January 17, 1810—two years after the commandant of the New South Wales Corps had deposed him by force of arms—Governor Bligh returned to Sydney.

As the brig *Porpoise* entered the cove, wallowing under her dingy headsails, her pumps creaking, the signal guns boomed the same traditional salute that, barely two weeks before, had marked Governor Macquarie's landing. The ships at the anchorage—their number now augmented by the trader *Marian*, recently arrived with a cargo of wheat from Bengal—manned their yards and cheered as the *Porpoise* dropped anchor.

On the government wharf, the troops paraded with their colors flying, and to the skirl of the pipes, Governor Macquarie took post with his officers at their head. The guard of honor formed up, the strong sunlight glinting on their bayonets, the shouted orders of the guard commander carrying across the intervening distance between ship and shore. They made a brave sight in their tartan and scarlet, but Commodore Bligh watched them unmoved. He stood on the brig's cramped quarterdeck, hands clasped behind his back, maintaining an ominous silence that even Mary Putland dared not break.

She watched as the Governor's barge, smartly manned by seamen from the *Hindostan,* put off with the 73rd's commanding officer, Colonel Maurice O'Connell, in the sternsheets. O'Connell had, in fact, gone out to meet the *Porpoise* the previous day, in order to inform Governor Bligh of details of the reception being prepared for him, and standing in self-imposed silence at her father's side, Mary was conscious of a fluttering of the heart as the tall, good-looking colonel once more saluted her father and bowed over her hand.

"All is in readiness, Your Excellency," he announced, with impeccable courtesy. "If you and Mrs. Putland would care to come ashore, His Excellency Colonel Macquarie and his lady are eager to bid you welcome."

"Where, sir," Bligh asked, when they were seated in the barge, "are we to be accommodated?"

He had become accustomed to slights from officialdom during the past weary months, Mary thought pityingly. Colonel Collins, since the flogging of his son, had become even more hostile than he had been before the boy's foolish drunken escapade. He had refused the facilities of the port—primitive enough, heaven knew—to the *Porpoise* and her company, rejected appeals for urgent repairs to be made to her leaking hull, and had gone so far as to hang a wretched colonist who had gone counter to his orders and supplied the ship with water and fresh meat.

Even when the sealer *Albion* had brought news of the Colonial Secretary's decision to reinstate her father as Governor for the twenty-four-hour term that would redeem his honor, Colonel Collins had not relented, Mary recalled. The *Porpoise* had had to leave the Derwent and put to sea in so bad a state that it was little short of a miracle—and thanks to a spell of unusually mild weather—that she had reached Sydney at all.

But they were here; reparation was about to be made and justice done to her father at last, the two-year nightmare he had been forced to endure finally over—his contention that he could not abandon his post without orders from His Majesty's government fully justified. Mary looked proudly at her father and then waited, with a certain anxiety still, for Colonel O'Connell's answer to the question he had asked. Clearly they could not expect to return to Government House. The new Governor had arrived in the colony on January first, and it was now the seventeenth; he and his wife would already be installed there and could hardly be asked to remove elsewhere for a mere twenty-four hours.

Maurice O'Connell met her apprehensive gaze and smiled at her warmly, with clear admiration.

"A house has been made ready in Pitt Street to accommodate Your Excellency," he said. "I hope and believe, sir, that you will find it comfortable and adequate for Your Excellency's requirements. A guard has been detailed and servants engaged. And, sir, His Excellency Colonel Macquarie would esteem it an honor if you and your daughter would take dinner with his wife and himself this evening, at Government House."

Her father's acknowledgment was, Mary knew, from long experience of him, noncommittal, but Colonel O'Connell appeared to notice nothing amiss.

"We shall be near neighbors," he told her, with satisfaction. "And, my dear Mrs. Putland, if there is any way in which I can serve you, then I assure you, you have only to ask."

For no reason that she could have explained, Mary flushed under his scrutiny. For much of the past year, she had lived on board the *Porpoise* in an exclusively male environment, and she found herself wondering why, in Maurice O'Connell's company, she should feel so strong an inclination to behave, if not quite in the manner of a young girl, then scarcely in that expected of a widow in her twenty-seventh year.

His looks were striking, it was true, and he had all the charm for which the Irish were renowned, coupled with a ready wit and an impressive military bearing. It was undeniably pleasant to be the object of so handsome an officer's interest and admiration, and she thanked him, with sincerity, for his offer to serve her. Indeed, she reflected, with remembered bitterness, his attitude was in marked contrast to Captain Porteous's thinly veiled hostility toward both her father and herself, which had never been more apparent than during the short passage back to Sydney.

And there was Lieutenant Kent, still officially under arrest pending his court-martial, with whom, she was quite certain, the *Porpoise*'s commander had planned and executed the supposed accident that had left poor young Lieutenant Fortescue behind in Hobart on the day the ship had sailed. . . . Mary sighed. David Fortescue had been loyal to her father—too loyal, perhaps, to suit his captain. John Porteous had known, as they all had, that the young man had a lady love waiting for him in Sydney, whom he had hoped to wed on his return there. A girl called Abigail O'Shea, a young widow like herself, whose husband—an officer in the New South Wales Corps—had died in tragic circumstances very soon after their marriage, leaving her with a prematurely born child and a large property on the Hawkesbury.

David and young Rick Tempest, who was Mrs. O'Shea's brother, had talked of her often, but now . . . Mary braced herself, as the barge came alongside the familiar government wharf. Now she must forget the *Porpoise* and the past unhappy year and give all her attention to her father, for whom today would be an ordeal . . . the most testing, perhaps, that he had ever faced, even in battle at sea. His temper, always unpredictable, had not improved. It was, on his own admission, on a very short fuse, and any insult—whether deliberate or unintentional—was liable to provoke an outburst.

Her father had not asked for her support; he was too proud to ask, but . . . Mary put out a hand to touch his and received a tight-lipped smile in acknowledgment. He looked older, she thought regretfully, stouter and less assured, and his uniform, like the sails of the leaking ship that had brought him here, was shabby and salt-stained, the gold braid on the cuffs and turn-back of his full dress coat badly tarnished. The waiting crowd would mark a difference in him, for all the studied dignity of his bearing and the veneer of rocklike calm he had assumed to enable him

to face them again . . . and to greet his successor publicly, without rancor.

The crew of the barge tossed oars smartly, and the band
of the new Governor's regiment struck up the music of
"God Save the King" on fifes and drums, as the guard of
honor came to attention and presented arms.

Governor Lachlan Macquarie stood at their head, his
plumed hat in hand, his thinning reddish hair ruffled by
the breeze, his square, somewhat austere face wreathed in
smiles. William Bligh, in the act of advancing to accept his
extended hand, halted suddenly, as if taken aback, and
Mary, following behind him on Colonel O'Connell's arm,
came abruptly to a standstill, seeking the cause of her father's evident discomfiture.

She had not far to look. At Governor Macquarie's side
stood the two rebel officers who had used her father so
ill—Colonel Paterson and Colonel Foveaux—both, it appeared, now ready to join in the expressions of welcome.

Her father kept his hands at his sides. He bowed stiffly
to the man appointed to supersede him and, pointedly ignoring Paterson and Foveaux, strode past them to greet,
with great affability, the *Hindostan*'s commander, Captain
Pasco, and his wife.

Colonel Macquarie's smile faded. "He has not changed
one whit, sir," Mary heard Foveaux observe, his remark
clearly intended to be audible, not only to the Governor but
also to those about him. "Damn his arrogance!"

She tensed, but Maurice O'Connell's fingers closed gently about her arm and her momentary anger cooled, as she
saw her father recover his composure and fall into step
with Captain Antill, the Governor's aide. The pipes skirled
and she watched him walk, with head high and his face
impassive, to inspect the guard of honor of kilted soldiers
of the King's 73rd.

"Henry Antill is, I understand, your cousin, Mrs. Putland—or so he claims," Colonel O'Connell said, having to
bend close in order to make himself heard. "He's most anxious to pay his respects to you, but in the meantime . . .
permit me to introduce you to Mrs. Macquarie, who is also
all eagerness to make your acquaintance."

His gesture indicated a tall, slim woman, wearing a silk tartan shawl over a ruffed white dress, who had tactfully separated herself from the little group of officers' ladies of which she had been part. The group, Mary realized, included Mrs. Paterson and Mrs. Foveaux, and her heart went out in gratitude to the unknown Mrs. Macquarie, who had spared her the embarrassment her father had suffered when faced by their husbands.

"Elizabeth Macquarie is the most delightful person," her escort confided, as he led her on. "She is intelligent, kindly, and possessed of a wonderful sense of humor . . . I am sure that you will take to each other, Mrs. Putland. But she has been ill, poor lady, and though I know she would not want me to tell you this, she has risen from her sickbed to receive you."

"Oh, dear!" Mary exclaimed, turning to look at him in anxious question. "What should I . . . that is, my father—"

Colonel O'Connell smiled at her in reassurance. "May I suggest, perhaps," he offered diffidently, "that you and Commodore Bligh dine with *me* this evening, instead of at Government House? As I mentioned to you earlier, we are near neighbors—I, too, have a house in Pitt Street, and I should be more than honored to entertain you and His Excellency your father." He saw Mary's frown, and added, still smiling, "I intend no affront to the Macquaries, believe me, my dear Mrs. Putland. But as Colonel Foveaux is likely to be present at Government House, it occurred to me that . . . well, that my company and that of Henry Antill, your cousin, might in the circumstances be preferable."

"It would," Mary answered, without hesitation. "Oh, yes, indeed it would!"

"Then I shall explain to Elizabeth Macquarie that you have a prior engagement," O'Connell said. "She will understand, believe me." He released her arm, as they drew level with the solitary figure of the new Governor's wife, and Mary, as they exchanged courtesies, found herself—as he had prophesied—taking a warm and instant liking to the slim, blue-eyed woman in the tartan shawl.

"Let us walk a little," Elizabeth Macquarie invited, holding out her hand, "while the military continue with their ceremonial, which I feel sure they can contrive to do without us." She turned her back on the group she had been with earlier, first giving them a dignified bow and then, her parasol held so as to shelter them both from the strong sunlight, led Mary away from the wharf.

They passed through the Government House gates, the sentries springing to attention at their approach, and Mrs. Macquarie led the way, with an apologetic, "Permit me, if you please," to the shadowed veranda which Mary knew so well. To a pretty, dark-haired maidservant waiting there, she gave the order for tea to be served and then seated herself, with a sigh of relief, gesturing her guest to a chair opposite her own.

The tea came at once, and as she poured out, Elizabeth Macquarie said, still sounding apologetic, "I thought that a talk might be advantageous to us both to . . . well, to overcome any difficulties, social difficulties, which might arise. But if you would rather I did not speak of them, Mrs. Putland, then of course I will not."

Mary shook her head, appreciating the older woman's directness and liking her the more for it, and she went on, after a short silence, "I do not know the whys and wherefores of your father's situation, I am bound to confess. I have heard only one side, so I am in no position even to comment, still less to judge. In any event, the matter is for my husband and Commodore Bligh to settle officially between them, is it not?"

"Yes," Mary agreed. "No doubt it is, Mrs. Macquarie. But I—" She broke off, uncertain of how much she dared say, even to this well-meaning, obviously sympathetic woman. "You have recently been ill, Colonel O'Connell told me. I do not want to trouble you if you are not yet recovered."

"It is nothing. I am a trifle weak, that is all . . . and I could not have stood for much longer on the wharf, with the sun blazing down on me!" Elizabeth Macquarie sipped her tea and then added, smiling, "Maurice O'Connell is the soul of tact . . . he warned me that there are certain persons here whom you would prefer not to meet socially. Including some of those who are our guests here tonight."

"Yes, that is so." Mary spoke flatly.

"So you and the commodore will not be dining with us?" Mrs. Macquarie suggested.

"No, I . . . Colonel O'Connell has invited us, and I accepted his invitation. He assured me that you would understand."

"Oh, I do . . . dear Mrs. Putland, I do! Although—". Elizabeth Macquarie was eyeing her expectantly, Mary sensed, and she quickly looked away, not wanting to offend her, yet determined not to respond to the appeal in the frank blue eyes. "My husband is hoping for a reconciliation, for a mutual agreement to bury the past. He is willing, I know, to act as mediator, if there is any possibility of such an outcome."

A reconciliation, Mary thought, with an upsurge of anger—a reconciliation between her father and the men who had schemed so treacherously to bring about his downfall? The men who had taken up arms against him, and those who had held him—here, in this very house—a prisoner for over a year, subjected to every kind of torment and humiliation they could devise? True, Major Johnston and the arch-traitor, John Macarthur, had fled to England, but the two self-styled Lieutenant Governors, Paterson and Foveaux, were still here . . . busy, it seemed, ingratiating themselves with Colonel Macquarie and, there could be little doubt, poisoning his mind by lying about her father's administration. Had not they done so where Colonel Collins was concerned?

She looked about her, as the bitter memories came flooding back once more. In the room immediately behind her hung the portraits of the King and Queen, which her father had veiled so that they might not look down on members of the rebel administration when he had been compelled to negotiate with them. And . . . her throat tightened. From this very veranda, on which she was seated drinking tea, Major Johnston and Captain Abbott had laid violent hands on their lawful Governor and dragged him forcibly out into the street—and she had run after them, right to the door of the Corps's barracks, where they were seeking to confine him.

She drew a deep, shuddering breath and said stiffly, "There is no possibility of a reconciliation, Mrs. Macquarie. The officers of the Corps are traitors, and my father is quite determined that they must be brought to trial, together with their commandant and Mr. Macarthur and those civil officials who supported them in their rebellion."

"I see," Mrs. Macquarie acknowledged, with evident disappointment. "Is there not the smallest chance that your father might be persuaded to change his mind? Could you not persuade him to do so?"

"There is no chance," Mary answered, without hesitation. "And I would not even attempt to persuade him." She set down her cup, her hand shaking visibly. "I—I am sorry. Perhaps I should go, Mrs. Macquarie. I had supposed," she added, anger getting the better of her, "that you and Colonel Macquarie were fully conversant with the reasons for the Colonial Office's decision to order my father's reinstatement as Governor and his return here. But if all you have heard has been from Colonel Foveaux, and if you have believed what he has told you, then there is little I can say to convince you otherwise. Save perhaps—" She rose, still indignant. "Save that my father considers him equally guilty of treason with those who will be tried and condemned for what they did. Colonel Foveaux countenanced their actions, Mrs. Macquarie. He—"

"Please sit down, Mrs. Putland," Elizabeth Macquarie begged. "There is no reason why you and I cannot be friends, surely? I should value your friendship, in all sincerity—I have heard so much about you and have been eager to meet you in person from the moment I first heard your name." She gestured to the chair Mary had vacated and picked up the teapot. "Let me pour you another cup of tea. We can talk of other matters and leave what they are pleased to call politics to the menfolk, can we not?"

It would have been churlish to reject so disarming a plea. Instantly contrite and regretting her loss of temper, Mary resumed her seat and held out her hand for the replenished cup.

"I like this veranda," the new Governor's wife observed pleasantly. "It commands a splendid view of the cove and the anchorage, and I enjoy sitting here and watching the ships come and go. See—there is one setting sail now from Mr. Lord's wharf. A trading schooner, is she not?"

Mary turned to follow the direction of her hostess's gaze. "Yes," she confirmed. "That is the *Dolphin*, Mrs. Macquarie—she belongs to Mr. Lord. I have seen her often enough in the Derwent during the past year."

The *Dolphin* was one of Simeon Lord's rum traders, she thought wryly, permitted to run her illicit cargoes without let or hindrance by Fouveaux's rebel administration, since Lord himself was one of their supporters, and the rum he shipped to Coal River and Van Diemen's Land was purchased from the Corps syndicate, at a handsome profit to both.

She was about to say so but hastily changed her mind when Elizabeth Macquarie remarked innocently, "My husband is most impressed by Mr. Lord. He holds him up as an example of what a man who came out here as a convict can achieve when he has earned his freedom. He has the finest house in all of Sydney Town, has he not? And the *Dolphin* is not the only ship he owns." She laid a hand on Mary's across the table and added, smiling at her, "Lachlan is very anxious to put an end to the discrimination that precludes any emancipist, however wealthy and hardworking, from regaining his place in society. Or from exercising authority. He is thinking of recommending that men of Mr. Lord's caliber should be appointed to the bench, as civil magistrates."

Feeling suddenly sickened, Mary remained silent, hearing little as Elizabeth Macquarie talked on.

Colonel Lachlan Macquarie would have to learn the lesson her father had learned, she reflected with infinite sadness, and found herself praying that, in the learning, he would not suffer the same consequences. Probably he was a good man, kindly and well-intentioned, as his wife undoubtedly was . . . and at least he would have a loyal regiment at his back, to enforce his authority and guard his life.

It was with relief that, when Colonel O'Connell called to escort her to Pitt Street, ten minutes later, she took her leave of Mrs. Macquarie. They parted as friends, both lingering over their farewells, and as Mary walked at his side to the gate and the now dispersing crowd, Maurice O'Connell said approvingly, "You liked Elizabeth and she very evidently took you to her heart, Mrs. Putland. I am so glad."

Mary glanced at him a trifle uncertainly, very conscious of his proximity and of the warm pressure of his fingers on her arm. He was not only handsome, she decided, he was an exceedingly attractive man, in whose company she could relax a little, forget the guard that, with most of the others, she had to place on her tongue, and perhaps even laugh again without caring what people thought.

She smiled up at him, her eyes bright, and said truthfully, "Yes, Colonel O'Connell, I liked her very much indeed. We had, inevitably, to agree to disagree on certain matters, but our future relationship need not suffer on that account."

"Would that I could say the same of His Excellency your father and His Excellency my commanding officer," O'Connell observed, his tone unexpectedly cynical.

Mary's smile instantly faded. "Are they not in accord?" she questioned, dismayed.

He shook his head. "Alas, no. I can only compare them to two puglists, shaping up for a bare-knuckled fight. Foveaux did not help, of course, but I hardly think he intended to . . . and even poor old Paterson contrived to add fuel to the flames. Not, perhaps, intentionally. Mrs. Putland—" The tall young colonel came to a halt and stood looking down at her gravely. "May I propose that we form an alliance—you, Elizabeth Macquarie, and myself—with the object of keeping the peace?"

Mary's eyes widened in astonishment. "An alliance, sir? I—I don't quite understand."

Heedless of the watching sentries, Maurice O'Connell took both her hands in his. "You exercise considerable influence over your father, and Lachlan, although he may affect not to, listens to his wife. If I act as—what shall we call it?—liaison officer between you, I think it is possible that we may see that full justice is done to your father, without any loss of dignity to my esteemed superior. What do you say?"

Mary's hesitation was brief. "I say yes, Colonel O'Connell," she answered gladly. "And thank you!"

He raised each of her hands, in turn, to his lips and said softly, "May our alliance bear fruit, dear lady!"

CHAPTER VII

Justin took his new command to sea under a cloudless blue sky, running out of Port Jackson before a light westerly breeze, which freshened and backed round to the southwest as he tacked to weather South Head.

Despite her age and the fact that her refit in Simeon Lord's yard had not been quite as thorough as he had wanted, the *Dolphin* was a beautiful vessel to handle and Justin had become deeply enamored of her by the time the towering cliffs at the harbor mouth had faded into the heat haze astern.

He was less enamored of her crew. With the exception of the boatswain—a quietly spoken, gray-haired man known as Dutch Holland—they were either time-expired convicts whom Lord had signed on in Sydney, or deserters from other ships, going under any names but their own.

The mate, Tobias Cockrell, had served in the Royal Navy and had jumped ship in Calcutta in order, as he cynically expressed it, to better himself by transferring to an Indiaman. He had worked his way up from A.B. to fourth mate on his first voyage in his new ship, and he was, Justin recognized, a prime seaman, with fifteen years of varied experience behind him.

A husky, black-browed, taciturn man, he had made it clear from the outset that he resented Justin's appointment as master of the *Dolphin,* and his resentment took the form of sullenness and a willful refusal to obey the orders he was given. The crew were with him; he had previously been in command of the ship, and they gave him what loyalty they were capable of on this account—but, it soon became evident, they did not respect him. Something, Justin suspected, must have occurred on the passage from Otaheite to arouse their mistrust.

His own youth, he was unhappily aware, told against him, in the men's eyes as well as in Cockrell's; he was a beardless boy, put in command of those who were twice his age by some inexplicable whim of the *Dolphin*'s owner. He possessed but one advantage, in their opinion, and this was his long familiarity with coastal waters that, to Tobias Cockrell in particular, were virtually unknown. The mate had only once entered Port Jackson; he had never sailed any vessel out of the harbor, and as they had boxed about off Pinchgut Island, waiting for the breeze to freshen, he had shown his ignorance, yelling a string of contradictory orders and cursing angrily when these could not be obeyed.

Justin had waited his chance and then taken the wheel, using breeze and current with the skill of long practice to get the ship under way and . . . He smiled to himself. Dutch Holland had, perhaps, been the only one who was seaman enough to realize that Cockrell's bluster could have lost them several hours and—as a result of one of his ill-timed orders—the best bower and most of its cable.

The boatswain came to him now, and Justin's smile widened when the man offered to relieve him of the wheel.

"Thanks, Mr. Holland," he acknowledged. "But it's not really your job, is it?"

"Nor the master's neither, Mr. Broome . . . according to the mate, that is."

Justin met his dark, inscrutable gaze but ignored the implication of his words. "Have we a competent helmsman in the crew?"

Holland shook his head. "Lucas and Fane are well enough in fair weather, sir. But I'd not trust either of 'em if it should turn foul."

"As I fear it's going to." Justin gestured to the southern sky, now gray and filled with lowering clouds.

"Aye, I noticed the glass was falling before we weighed," the boatswain confirmed. "But she's a weatherly ship, is the old *Dolphin*. I've made a few bad passages in her with Cap'n Mason. . . ." He went into remembered details, with a brief but graphic description of a typhoon in the China Sea and a gale among the coral reefs of Tonga Tabu, his lined face unexpectedly expressive as he spoke of the schooner's former master with something resembling awe. "Knew her like the back o' his hand, did old Taffy Mason, and always got the best out of her. Oh, he carried away a few spars and scraped her bottom a time or two on the coral—never would use a pilot, in the islands, see, because he reckoned he knew better than any of 'em. And he mostly did." Holland's grin was wry. "He loved the *Dolphin*, Mr. Broome, as if she was his own. Which she was, for twelve years . . . and before that, he was her mate. Only in them days, she was called the *Dragon*. Bin the *Dolphin* for fifteen years and *Dragon* for another nine or ten."

Which made the ship even older than he had been led to believe, Justin thought, and explained some of the defects he had found when she had been careened. But Mr. Lord had pooh-poohed them. . . .

"Why did Captain Mason quit?" he asked curiously.

It was as if Dutch Holland had pulled a mask over his craggy, weatherbeaten countenance.

"He had his reasons," he said warily.

"Was Mr. Cockrell one of them?" Justin suggested.

"He could've bin. But Taffy Mason wasn't young, and he had a wife and kids in Tonga . . . figured it was time to retire there with 'em, I reckon."

"That was all, Mr. Holland?"

"Well . . ." The boatswain's strong brown fingers tightened about the spokes of the wheel. "Maybe not, Mr. Broome. Didn't fancy the new owner overmuch. Made two voyages for him and that was enough. Different kind o' trade, see—different way o' going about things." He hesitated and then, encouraged by Justin's silence, asked quietly, "What made *you* sign on as master?"

"I was made an offer I couldn't refuse."

"Going to replace the cutter you lost, is he?" It was a

shrewd guess and Justin nodded. "I figured as much," Holland observed. "It'd have to be a pretty good offer, to make you take on the *Dolphin*, 'cause you'll have a job on your hands. But I s'pose you know that."

"Yes, I know," Justin admitted, thinking again of Tobias Cockrell and the sullen, ruffianly crew Mr. Lord had given him to command. There was the skimped, overhurried refit, too, with Lord complaining of the expense and reiterating his desire for the schooner to put to sea and start earning her keep.

"I mostly try to keep out o' trouble," Holland said. He moved the plug of tobacco he was chewing from one side of his mouth to the other and spat expertly in the direction of the lee scuppers. "Do me job and leave it at that. But you can count on me, if you should need me to lend a hand, Mr. Broome. Wouldn't want to see a fine young feller like you get too far out o' his depth, you understand."

"Thank you, Mr. Holland," Justin answered with sincerity, taking this to mean any future threat to his authority that Cockrell might decide to offer. The wind, he could feel, was freshening, and the cloud banks to the south held the promise of rain—heavy, perhaps, if they sank any lower—but the ship was running free and making good progress, and Dutch Holland was quite evidently capable of handling her at present.

"I've got some work to do on my charts," he added, wishing, not for the first time that day, that Cookie Barnes had been fit enough to sign on with him. But the little man had not recovered from his lengthy immersion in the South Head surf; although out of the hospital, he could barely walk, and a broken collarbone, added to severe bruising and lacerations, had left him virtually crippled. "Lucas is watch below—he can relieve you."

"Aye, aye," the boatswain acknowledged. "Until that westerly blows up—wind's veered a point while we've been talking. Still, I don't reckon we'll have much to worry about before morning. The mate's taking the gravy-eye, ain't he, Mr. Broome?"

He had rostered Tobias Cockrell for the middle watch, Justin recalled and frowned, the mate's sullen reaction still rankling. "Yes," he said. "I told him to." He glanced at the binnacle and from it to the mist-shrouded land to leeward, from which, on her present course, the *Dolphin* was drawing away . . . and better so, he thought, if they did strike a westerly gale. "Very well thus," he told Holland. "Call me if you sight a squall."

Sounds of revelry and drunken laughter assailed his ears as he descended to the lower deck. The sounds came from the mate's berth and they increased in volume, as if Tobias Cockrell had sensed his presence when, suddenly angry, he came to a halt outside the curtained doorway. But, after a momentary hesitation, Justin moved on; there was no point in provoking the man, he decided. It was his watch below; he was not on duty until midnight, and so long as he was sober when he relieved the deck, he was within his rights to take a drink in his own cabin. Less so, perhaps, when—as he evidently had—he chose to share his liquor with some of the off-duty seamen.

"A scurvy convict's brat, that's what he is." Cockrell's voice was raised and the curtain twitched, bringing Justin once again to a halt, but only in time to see the edge of the curtain fall back into place, the hand that had raised it barely glimpsed. "A sodding currency kid . . . that's what they call his kind in the colony o' New South Wales, and it ain't meant to be a compliment! Cabin boy in Flinders's *Investigator*, I was told . . . and on the strength o' *that*, our bloody owner gives him command of my ship, damn his eyes! Well, we'll see what sort o' master he makes, by God!"

"Convict stock ain't all bad," one of the men objected. "Hell's teeth, Mr. Cockrell, I copped a seven-year stretch just on suspicion o' smugglin' a few kegs o' French brandy! 'Twasn't never proved, and anyways I—"

The mate cut him short. "Maybe we'll find a use for your talents, Billy boy." He laughed, with what sounded like genuine amusement. "Maybe that's why you were signed on. All right, lads, drink up—there's another bottle where this one came from. Fetch it out of my locker, Zac."

Justin waited to hear no more. Seething with barely suppressed fury, he went into the master's stern cabin. It was commodious, and the *Dolphin*'s previous master had left most of his furnishings to be inherited by his successor; his cot, two shabby but comfortable armchairs, a clothes press, and a dining table and chairs, together with a chart table, set just in front of the stern windows.

Before going on deck, Justin had spread his charts out on the table, placing quill, ink, and navigational instruments with them, ready to hand, but as he strode across the cabin he saw, to his intense dismay, that the inkstand had been tipped over and the topmost charts were covered with a mixture of red and blue ink, which rendered them well-nigh indecipherable.

It was impossible that the inkwell could have been upset accidentally—there was a hollowed-out space on the table, designed to hold it in place in the roughest of weather conditions—and he swore aloud as he surveyed the damage. The two ruined charts had been Matthew Flinders's parting gift to him, when Flinders had sailed on his last, ill-fated homeward voyage. As such—quite apart from their practical use—he had valued them highly, and this malicious destruction hurt almost as much as it enraged him. Still swearing angrily to himself, Justin attempted to mop up the ink but with little result.

He had duplicate charts of the area—copies he had made himself—and these were untouched. He plotted his course, brought his log and journal up to date, and gradually overcame the sense of outrage that had filled him. He had no proof and therefore could make no accusations, though he had little doubt as to whom to attribute the blame. But . . . he would bide his time, he decided. Sooner or later, Tobias Cockrell's malice would cause him to go too far, and when that happened, devil take the swine, he would be ready to take action.

The cook, a slovenly, shifty-eyed man of uncertain age, responded to an impatient demand for food with a watery stew, heavily spiced and, as far as Justin was concerned, inedible. Wishing once again that Cookie Barnes had been in charge of the galley, he forced himself to swallow a few mouthfuls, washed down with a beaker of his mother's homemade cider, and still hungry, returned to the deck.

The storm struck just before midnight, heralded by thunder, lightning, and torrential rain. Warned well in advance of its arrival by the falling glass and a shift of wind, Justin prudently took in sail. Under double-reefed topsails and a single jib, the *Dolphin* remained buoyant and manageable, for all the ominous creaking of her ancient timbers. The westerly gale whipped the sea into a flurry of white-crested water, lit by almost continuous flashes of lightning; the rain beat down on the unprotected deck, and thunder rumbled and echoed overhead.

At the wheel, Justin was soon soaked to the skin and increasingly conscious of his chilled body and aching limbs, as the ship heaved and plunged beneath his feet and he fought to hold her against the buffeting of the wind. But, under Bo'sun Holland's urging, the men of the watch worked well, obeying every order he gave them without question or hesitation, and even the cook came staggering up on deck with a lidded pannikin of cocoa, liberally laced with rum, which he proffered with an ingratiating smile.

The mate, however, did not appear. The watch below turned out, muffled in oilskins, punctually at eight bells, but one of the men—the relief helmsman, Lucas—was plainly too drunk to be of any use. Justin cursed him roundly and sent him below, with a stern injunction to report when he was sober. He did not send for Tobias Cockrell, and Holland, without being asked, remained on deck in his place.

"You going to log him, Mr. Broome?" he inquired, cupping his hands about his mouth in order to make himself heard above the thunderous roar of the storm.

"That I am!" Justin shouted back furiously. "And he's not sailing with me again. I'll put him ashore at Hobart and he can whistle for another job!"

The night passed, and although the rain abated, the wind did not, and a mass of heavy dark clouds all but obscured the pale watery glow of the newly risen sun.

Justin remained at the wheel throughout the day, trusting no one save Holland to relieve him. The course he had plotted kept the *Dolphin* well away from the land—he had made sure of that before the storm broke, well aware of the dangers the desolate rocky shoreline presented with the wind in this quarter. George Bass and even the experienced Matthew Flinders had both come near to disaster when they had searched for the strait that now bore Bass's name; and he himself, he recalled, had almost lost the *Flinders* after sailing out of Storm Bay into a gale, three years ago.

Well, she was lost now, well and truly lost, but that did not mean that he was going to take any risk of losing the *Dolphin*. Simeon Lord had set him no time limit and had not specified a date by which he must make port in Hobart, so . . . if a passage that normally took under a week had, of necessity, to take twice that time, he would not have to accept the blame for it.

Justin shifted his weight from one leg to the other, seeking to give his weary muscles some relief, but looking out across the gray waste of tossing water by which his ship was surrounded, he knew that, for him, there could be no rest. Tobias Cockrell—the only qualified navigator, apart from himself—continued to keep to his cabin, sending a message by Fane that he was unwell. It was insolently couched, and, Justin was quite certain, the mate had decided to remain below with the intention of causing him the maximum of inconvenience. That he was drinking heavily was in no doubt: Holland had reported that he was, and Fane, when questioned, had admitted it, offering the lame excuse that Mr. Cockrell was in pain, and only brandy could assuage the agony he was enduring.

He could not be logged for it, of course. His illness might be genuine, and there was no proof that it was not, but . . . Justin remembered the damaged charts and scowled up at the darkening sky. When they reached Hobart, Tobias Cockrell should be given short shrift. As he had told Dutch Holland, he would not sail with the man again, in any capacity, and least of all as mate of the *Dolphin*, whatever the schooner's owner might say on her return to Sydney.

He straightened up, both legs firmly braced, as the *Dolphin* heeled suddenly, plunging into the trough of a towering whitecap, her bluff bows and most of her forecastle vanishing momentarily into its depths and then, as he spun the wheel, emerging from beneath a curtain of spray to climb slowly and almost reluctantly up to its crest. It was going to be a long night, he thought wearily, but despite his fears concerning the ship's all-too-brief refit, she was sound and was holding her own . . . and, please God, the storm could not last forever.

It lasted, in fact, for another forty-eight hours. Then the wind backed to the south and the sea subsided to an oily swell, in which the *Dolphin* wallowed like a stricken whale, her pumps clanking dismally and her 'tween decks awash. So exhausted that he could barely stand upright, Justin altered course and crammed on sail, heading at last for Storm Bay and the mouth of the Derwent River.

Cape Pillar was sighted just before dusk on the following day, and after lying at anchor in the bay during the hours of darkness, at first light Justin ordered sail set once more and, under a light southwesterly breeze, worked his battered vessel upriver to the anchorage off Hobart Town.

Only then did he divest himself of his seaboots and oilskins and climb stiffly into the cot that had been Captain Mason's, leaving Bo'sun Holland in charge, with instructions to postpone the landing of cargo until the following morning.

"I'll have caught up on my lost sleep by then, Dutch," he said, "and we'll warp her into the inner harbor. In the meantime, Cockrell has our manifests—better get them from him. I'll see about putting him ashore first thing tomorrow. Provided he's recovered from his recent malaise, that is."

"Shall I tell him?" Holland asked, his smile unashamedly malicious.

"If you want to." Justin smothered a yawn. "I can't keep my eyes open any longer, so let me sleep, will you?"

"Aye, aye, Cap'n Broome," the boatswain acknowledged. It was, Justin realized with a small glow of pleasure, the first time any member of the *Dolphin*'s crew had addressed him as captain. "Mr. Broome" had been respectful enough, but . . . His heavy lids fell and he slept.

His awakening was sudden, and at first as he responded sluggishly to an unknown voice calling his name, he thought that he must be dreaming, for there were two scarlet-coated marines standing guard at the door of his cabin, and the man who was bending over him was an officer of the Corps.

"For the Lord's sake!" he exclaimed, struggling to sit up. "What do you want of me?"

"Is your name Broome?" the officer demanded. "And are you the master of this vessel?"

"Yes," Justin confirmed. Still stupefied by sleep, he repeated his question. "What do you want of me, sir? Has there been some—some irregularity?"

"There has indeed," the marine officer told him icily. "You are under arrest, Mr. Broome, and I am taking you ashore to answer charges of a grave nature. Be so good as to attire yourself, if you please."

Justin stumbled to his feet, reaching for shirt and breeches but too dazed to recall where he had put them and finding only a single seaboot. The officer picked up the damp, discarded garments from the floor of the cabin and, an expression of distaste on his good-looking young face, offered them for his inspection.

"You may expect to be held in jail for some time, Mr. Broome," he observed, letting them fall again. "Dry clothing and a clean shirt would, perhaps, be advisable."

Justin acted on this advice, still uncertain as to whether he was awake or dreaming. It was dark, he realized—one of the marines was holding a lantern—so he must have slept for five or six hours and possibly even longer.

He asked, as his numb fingers struggled with the buttons of his blue pea jacket, "With what am I to be charged? Are you at liberty to tell me? I only made port in the early hours of this morning, and I'm not aware of having committed any crime—certainly not one that would require me to be held in your jail, sir. The devil take it, I've unloaded no cargo, I—"

The marine officer held up a hand to silence him. He answered, his tone colder than ever, "You will be informed of the charges in due course by the deputy judge advocate.

My orders are to place you in arrest and escort you ashore. If you have completed your dressing, pray accompany me to my boat."

Justin bit back the indignant words to which he was tempted to give voice. Nothing would be gained, he thought bitterly, if he attempted to argue with the officious young ensign, who had two armed men at his back and who seemed to be convinced that he had been sent to arrest a villain of the deepest dye, whose lengthy incarceration in Hobart's jail was a foregone conclusion. In all probability there had been some mistake on the part of the port officials which, as soon as the judge advocate questioned him, he could quite easily clear up. He might unwittingly have contravened the quarantine regulations—which were always being altered—or perhaps Tobias Cockrell had failed to produce the cargo manifests when Bo'sun Holland had asked for them.

Justin rolled up a fresh shirt and stuffed it, with a change of underwear and his razor, into his canvas kit bag and bowed stiffly.

"I am at your service, sir," he announced, with what dignity he could muster. "But you will, I trust, permit me to hand over command to my bo'sun before I leave the ship."

The officer gave him an oddly startled look, but did not reply to his request. Led by the marine carrying the lantern, and with his comrade, musket at the ready, bringing up the rear, they made their way to the *Dolphin*'s entry-port, and there Justin found a fresh shock awaiting him. Lying, half-covered by a blood-soaked blanket, was what, at first sight, appeared to be the dead body of Dutch Holland.

In the dim light it was difficult to make out the precise nature of his injuries, but Justin's horrified gaze took in the fact that he had sustained a severe head wound, from which the blood was still oozing, and that his face was so badly bruised and swollen as to be scarcely recognizable. The boatswain's eyes flickered open and stared up at him in what, for a stunned moment, he interpreted as reproach.

"God in heaven!" he exclaimed, dropping instinctively to

his knees beside the prostrate form. "He's alive! Look, his eyes are open!"

"Does that surprise you, Mr. Broome?" the marine officer challenged, a harsh edge to his voice. "Had you left him for dead?"

"It surprises me that you haven't seen fit to call a surgeon to care for him," Justin returned hotly. "Or sent him ashore to the hospital—for mercy's sake, man, he could die lying here! He's in need of skilled help."

"The surgeon from the port authority pronounced the poor fellow dead an hour ago," the ensign claimed, less sure of himself now. He eyed Justin from beneath frowning brows, in evident bewilderment, and then came to bend over Dutch Holland, listening intently. "He's still breathing . . . we'd better take him ashore in my boat." He rapped an order to his men, and visibly startled, both slung their muskets and prepared to lower the injured Holland into the boat that was tied up alongside.

"Have a care with him," Justin pleaded. "Here, let me bear a hand. You—"

The ensign's arm came out to detain him. "No!" he snapped. "Stand back, Mr. Broome."

"Oh, for God's sake!" Justin protested. He turned, looking about him, but his own crew had, it seemed, disappeared. Which of them, he wondered bitterly, had been responsible for poor Dutch's injuries? Or . . . His mouth tightened. Had they all had a hand in it?

The young marine officer drew him to one side. "You are showing strange concern for the unfortunate fellow," he said accusingly. "But it is somewhat late in the day for that, Mr. Broome, since you yourself beat him within an inch of his life, did you not?"

"*I* beat him?" Justin could scarcely believe the evidence of his own ears. "You think *I*—oh, in heaven's name, are you out of your mind? Dutch Holland's the best man I have, the only one I could trust in my whole rapscallion crew!" The unpleasant truth dawned on him suddenly and he rounded on the ensign, cold fury in his eyes. "Is *that* what I'm to be charged with—you're accusing *me* of trying to kill my bo'sun?"

The ensign faced him, his expression withdrawn and disdainful. "Certainly," he stated, with conviction. "There are a dozen witnesses—including the mate, Mr. Cockrell—who are willing to swear on oath that you did. They saw you, Mr. Broome! Cockrell sent word to the port authority, he summoned the surgeon, and I was sent out, as a result, to effect your arrest. And the charge, since you are so anxious to know its nature . . . the charge is likely to be murder, if your unhappy victim does die. And attempted murder, if he does not. So, if you please"—he gestured to the waiting boat, into which Dutch Holland had now been lowered—"step into the boat. We've wasted enough time, and I'm anxious to lodge you in the jail before the head jailer goes for his evening meal."

In rebellious silence, Justin did as he had been asked. There was a bloodstained marlinespike lying on the bow thwart, he saw, with one of the boat's crew guarding it, and anger rose in his throat, threatening to choke him. Cockrell had even supplied the weapon, to be used as evidence in support of his foul lies . . . plague take him, the cunning swine had thought of everything! If they accepted his account, backed by a dozen others all telling the same story, the Hobart magistrates would be presented with a cut-and-dried case . . . unless Dutch lived long enough to refute their perjured accusations. From the look of him, poor devil, it seemed unlikely that he would survive the long pull across the outer harbor to the shore, but . . . Justin tensed, as the bowman cast off and the boat pulled away.

Gazing down at him from the *Dolphin*'s deck were the leering faces of her crew, white blurs in the gathering darkness, with Tobias Cockrell to the fore, a speaking trumpet to his lips.

"You'll get your just deserts, *Captain* Broome!" the mate yelled at him, in ugly triumph. "I'll see you hang for what you did, bad cess to you!"

Justin controlled the impulse to reply and, fists clenched at his sides, affected not to have heard the taunt, for all it set his heart plummeting. Did Cockrell really want his death, as well as Bo'sun Holland's? Were they all without conscience—even those who had worked so well during the storm? Those who had taken his orders, while the mate had been skulking in his cabin, swilling his liquor and not standing his watch or his trick at the wheel? Did they not see Cockrell for the unprincipled villain he was?

Justin smothered a sigh. Beside him in the sternsheets, the marine officer observed loftily, gesturing toward the *Dolphin*'s deck, "You were not, it would seem, a popular master, Mr. Broome."

"No," Justin conceded, tight-lipped. "I don't court popularity with rogues. Their charges are a tissue of lies, sir, I give you my word. I was asleep in my berth when the bo'sun was set upon."

"It will be your word against theirs," the ensign reminded him dryly. "Unless the bo'sun lives long enough to testify on your behalf."

Justin looked back at the ship, his taut nerves perilously near to breaking point. She had been his first real command, and now, thanks to the pack of scoundrels Simeon Lord had engaged to crew her, she was lost to him. Cockrell had her; he could take her wherever he wished, he . . . Struck by a sudden flash of insight, he turned to the officer at his side.

"May I offer you a suggestion, sir?" he asked, with studied restraint.

"If it is valid—then certainly, Mr. Broome." The ensign eyed him curiously. "What is it that you wish to suggest?"

"That you should place a guard on my ship, sir, whilst I am held in your jail," Justin told him.

"And why should I do that? *You* are the one we have to guard, surely?"

The young officer's tone was so supercilious that Justin lost his temper. "Because, damme," he retorted with asperity, "those villains will probably steal her if you do not! For the Lord's sake, man, you must believe me! You—"

"I will report your suggestion to my commanding officer, Lieutenant Lord," the ensign promised. "For what it's worth. But since those villains, as you are pleased to call them, will be required to make sworn testimony at your trial . . . well, frankly, Mr. Broome, I don't anticipate their leaving port until you have received what *they* were pleased to call your just deserts. For which reason I hardly think a guard will be necessary."

Justin lapsed into glum silence, and the young marine officer made no attempt to break it until the boat came alongside the main wharf. Then, quite courteously, he said, "Be good enough to step ashore, Mr. Broome. If you will give me your parole, I will escort you to the jail, and my men can convey your bo'sun to the hospital without delay."

They lifted Dutch Holland onto the wharf as carefully as they could, but one of the marines, bending over him, exclaimed ruefully, "He's gone, sir, I reckon. Leastways, he ain't breathin', and—" He applied his ear to the boatswain's chest, listened for a moment, and then shook his head. "Can't hear no heartbeat, Mr. Finch, sir."

Ensign Finch shrugged. "Then the charge is murder, I fear," he said to Justin. He gave instructions to his men as to the disposal of the body and turned back to Justin. "Be so good as to accompany me, Mr. Broome. The surgeons will report on the cause of death in due course, I imagine."

Justin walked with him along the familiar road to the little township without protest, torn by conflicting emotions. Dutch Holland had been a good man and a first-rate seaman, and he regretted his passing, and, in particular, he regretted the manner of it, for Dutch's sake. For his own sake, too . . . He frowned, wondering how he could refute the charges Cockrell had laid against him, now that Dutch was dead and could not name his killers. But perhaps, if the mate was not aware that his victim had died, he would take the *Dolphin* to sea before Hobart's judge advocate could start to ask any awkward questions. Or before any of his crew lost their nerve and ran . . . Justin sighed in frustration, as his escort halted in front of the jailhouse. It had been added to and improved since the last time he had seen it, but like most of Hobart's ramshackle wooden buildings, it was a makeshift place, distinguished only by its fenced exercise yard and by the armed constable pacing at its entrance.

The formalities were quickly and cursorily completed, and he found himself locked in a small cell, of which, to his relief, he was the sole occupant. No food was offered to him, but to his surprise, he had barely had time to accustom himself to his new surroundings when the jailer announced that there was a visitor for him. By the light of the single flickering candle that was all the illumination his cell provided, the visitor was revealed as a tall, fair-haired man of perhaps three-and-twenty, pleasant-faced and dressed in naval uniform. He came in smiling and with hand outheld.

"Justin Broome? I've just heard that they brought you here. . . . I'm David Fortescue. Abigail O'Shea has spoken of you in very appreciative terms, so I thought I should come along at once and ascertain whether there is any way in which I can be of assistance to you." He waved a proprietary hand about the dismal confines of Justin's prison and smiled a trifle wryly. "I occupied this cell until quite recently. Now I'm paroled and I share a quarter with Enoch Finch—with whom, I gather, you are already acquainted."

Justin stared at him in bewilderment. He knew who his visitor was, of course—David Fortescue was the man whom Abigail purposed to marry. But . . . He asked uncertainly, "Do you mean that *you* were arrested? Surely you're one of the *Porpoise*'s officers? How could they dare arrest an officer from a King's ship?"

David Fortescue lowered his tall body onto an upturned sea chest, which served as a table.

"His Majesty's ship *Porpoise* was regarded as an enemy vessel during the latter part of her all-too-lengthy stay here," he explained. "She was refused supplies, even of water, by Colonel Collins—acting, one can only presume, on the instructions of the rebel administration in Sydney. We were all, every man jack of us, threatened with arrest if we set foot ashore."

"But you did?" Justin hazarded. "And were duly placed in arrest?"

"I landed, with three seamen, on the orders of Captain Porteous," Fortescue answered, his voice clipped and resentful. "To replenish the last of our water casks, prior to sailing for Sydney. The ship was at anchor in D'Entrecasteaux's Channel, and normally we met with no trouble when we landed for water. But it was my infernal bad luck to find an armed party lying in wait for us at the watering place. They must have been there all night, because I didn't see hide nor hair of them, until, damn their eyes, they jumped us!" He shrugged his broad shoulders. "The *Porpoise* weighed—Porteous made no attempt to take us off. It was up anchor, make sail, and away, curses rain upon him for a scurvy swine!"

"Did he know you'd been taken?" Justin questioned, still puzzled.

"He was on deck, watching us through his glass, my dear fellow," Lieutenant Fortescue asserted. "Oh, I knew the commodore was in an almighty hurry to return to Sydney, but even so, I don't believe *he* gave the order to weigh."

"How did you get on with him?"

"With Commodore Bligh, you mean? Oh, exceedingly well." Fortescue laughed, without amusement. "And Mrs. Putland, of course, who is the bravest and noblest of women. But the *Porpoise* was not a happy ship, Broome. If you got on with Bligh, Porteous and Kent had no use for you. I don't think I ever spent a more miserable year at sea than this last one. But . . ." He eyed Justin apologetically. "Damme, I'm talking of my troubles, to the exclusion of yours! Finch said your people have charged you with murdering your bo'sun. For God's sake, Broome, you didn't, did you?"

"No, I did not," Justin assured him. Under David Fortescue's prompting, he described the events leading up to his arrest and saw his visitor's blue eyes narrow as he came to the end of his brief recital.

"It sounds to me like a put-up job, if ever there was one!" he exclaimed indignantly.

"I'm pretty sure it was."

"But with what object? The *Dolphin* belongs to Simeon Lord, does she not?"

"Yes, he bought her quite recently." Again Justin went into detail. "Cockrell resented the fact that Mr. Lord gave

me the command. He's years older than I am and he has a
master's ticket, and I can understand his resenting me. But
in heaven's name, that cannot justify what he's done!
Dutch Holland was a decent fellow." He drew in his
breath sharply, as the memory of Dutch Holland's bruised
and bleeding face flashed into his mind. "I can only suppose," he went on flatly, "that it's Cockrell's intention to
steal the ship. He may take her back to Sydney, of course,
but I don't fancy he will—because Lord won't give him the
command. He'd have given it to him instead of to me, if
that had ever been his intention."

"That is a reasonable supposition," David Fortescue
agreed. He smiled suddenly. "And to think—I'd planned to
ask you to give me passage to Sydney in the *Dolphin,* when
I saw you bring her in!"

Justin eyed him ruefully. "Can they convict me, on the
evidence of a man like Cockrell?"

"I fear they can, if Cockrell plays his infernal cards
right. But if he does make off with your ship . . ." The
older man rose, still smiling, and laid a consoling hand on
Justin's shoulder. "Your troubles would be over, would they
not?"

"Yes, perhaps they would."

David Fortescue moved toward the door of the cell. "I'll
do all I possibly can to help," he promised. "And I'll have a
meal sent down to you. Eat and try to get some
sleep. . . . I'll be back in the morning, to let you know
what's going on. Finch will keep me posted. And—I imagine the judge advocate will be along to get a statement
from you tomorrow sometime." He shouted to the jailer,
who came grumbling to unlock the door of the cell, and
Justin saw a coin change hands.

A few minutes later, the jailer was back, a beaker filled
with rum in his hand and the assurance that a meal would
be forthcoming within half an hour. Despite these attentions, Justin spent a restless and uncomfortable night, his
anxiety too acute to permit him to sleep.

But soon after he had broken his fast next morning,
Lieutenant Fortescue was back.

"I bring you the best possible news, my young friend,"

he announced, beaming. "The crew of your ship spirited her away in the night! But better still, the cook ran . . . and he substantiated *your* account of what occurred to cause the bo'sun's untimely death. Your troubles are over, my dear Broome—only a few formalities have to be completed and then you'll be released, without a stain on your character."

Justin's heart leaped. He stammered his thanks, unable at first to believe what had happened. A nightmare had ended, but . . . He met Lieutenant Fortescue's smiling gaze and said gravely, "Fortescue, I have to get my ship back. I have to go after them."

David Fortescue's smile faded. "I rather supposed that might be your reaction," he answered, with equal gravity. "You'll have to see the Governor. We shall need some help."

"We?" Justin echoed. "But you are under no obligation. It's good of you, but you've already done more than I have any right to ask, and—"

"I want passage to Sydney in the *Dolphin*," Fortescue reminded him. "Devil take it, I have no desire to rot in this inhospitable place any longer, and besides . . . I have the most adorable young lady waiting for me in Sydney Town. We are to be wed, you know."

Abigail, Justin thought, with a twinge of jealousy. His beautiful, unattainable Miss Abigail . . . But his resentment vanished when David Fortescue went on eagerly, "We've the makings of a boarding party already—my boat and my seamen. The boat carries a lug sail. If Colonel Collins will let us take half a dozen of his marines, we'll bring that rogue—what's his name?—Cockrell to justice, and his scum of a ship's company with him. What do you say, Master Broome—will you permit me to earn my passage?"

"What can I say?" Justin answered. "Except thank you and yes, Mr. Fortescue."

"Good," Fortescue approved. "I'll have a word with the marine commandant and arrange for you to see His Honor the Lieutenant Governor as soon as you're released. We should not be more than—what? Ten or twelve hours behind those scoundrels. And," he added, grinning, "no one knows this estuary better than I do. There will be no place for them to hide! Can you use a cutlass?"

"I never have," Justin admitted, but he, too, was grinning. "I can learn, though, can I not?"

The last vestige of his resentment faded. David Fortescue, he decided, was a very fine fellow indeed—a man truly after his own heart—and he deserved a wife of Abigail O'Shea's caliber. In any event, he was the one Abigail had chosen, and the choice was hers to make, hers and hers alone. No one, least of all himself, had any right to question it. . . .

A little over three hours later, the *Porpoise*'s longboat was making good headway downriver, the lug sail set, and Ensign Enoch Finch, a surprise volunteer, in command of five marines and a sergeant who, with Colonel Collins's permission, had joined the search party.

"Wind's sou'easterly," Lieutenant Fortescue observed, "and veering." He put the tiller over, at the end of their tack, which brought them within hailing distance of the Front Cove shore. "What do you say, Broome? Shall we take a look into North Bay?"

Justin nodded assent. "Cockrell will anchor overnight," he said, with conviction. "We might just catch him there."

Luck was with them, as well as a brisk following wind, once they emerged from the river mouth; and although a swift inspection of North Bay proved fruitless, they sighted their quarry, just as dusk was falling, on the northeast side of the bay beyond. She had her topsails set and appeared in no hurry, and Fortescue, studying her through his glass, announced triumphantly, "She's heading for Gull Island! There's a tidy little anchorage nor'east of the island which some of the sealers use, in four to five fathoms . . . that'll be where she's making for. She must have picked up a man who is well acquainted with this area, because it's as snug a hiding place as you could find."

It was indeed fortunate that they had seen her before the darkness swallowed her up, Justin thought. He glanced skyward, estimating that nightfall would come within less than half an hour, and then turned to David Fortescue, brows lifted in mute question.

The *Porpoise*'s lieutenant grinned back at him in high good humor. "We'll give them time to settle down, I think . . . a couple of hours or maybe three. They're drinkers, you said?"

Justin nodded. "Most of them are, when they're given the chance. And if they imagine they're well hidden, I can't see Tobias Cockrell forgoing his evening drink."

"Good," Fortescue approved. He raised his telescope again to his eye. "There's another small islet off the anchorage—Southmouth, they call it. We can lie up there, while we're waiting, and then row in."

"Muffled oars and over her stern?" young Finch suggested eagerly. He grasped the hilt of his sword, his eyes bright with anticipation. "I've served in the Royal Marines for over two years, and the one thing I've always longed to take part in is a cutting-out action. Damme, David, I'm glad you invited me to come along! I'd begun to despair of ever seeing action, after all the dreary months I've had to spend in Hobart, guarding scurvy convicts and killing blackfellows." He hesitated, looking at Justin. "I suppose Cockrell and his people will be armed, will they not?"

"The *Dolphin* carries half a dozen muskets in her arms chest," Justin told him. "I have the key still, but—" He shrugged. "It wouldn't take much to break it open. And Cockrell has a pistol."

"Then we must take it that they're likely to be armed," David Fortescue observed soberly, "and make our plans accordingly." He clapped a friendly hand on Ensign Finch's scarlet-clad shoulder and added quietly, "Despite your longing to see action, Enoch, I confess that *I* hope they won't have broken into the arms chest, and that they'll submit without bloodshed. But we are dealing with men who have countenanced the murder of a shipmate and who have committed an act of piracy by stealing the *Dolphin*, so . . ." He sighed. "We board her and invite them to surrender, but if they decide to make a fight of it, then it's their decision and we oblige them."

Lying under the lee of the tiny islet he had chosen, they

ate the provisions they had brought with them and agreed on their plan of action. Justin, claiming the privilege as master of the *Dolphin*, and because of his familiarity with her crew, was to lead the boarding party and call on Cockrell to yield up his stolen prize; David Fortescue was to follow him, Finch and his marines bringing up the rear.

"Do not open fire unless they do," Fortescue warned. "I said before and I say again—we want no bloodshed, unless it's unavoidable."

The approach to the anchored *Dolphin* was made in virtual silence, the seamen pulling on their muffled oars with a will and the darkness effectively hiding them from any save the most vigilant lookout. By the time the moon rose, the *Porpoise*'s longboat was within pistol shot of the schooner's stern, apparently unobserved, and sounds of singing and ribald laughter, coming from below, suggested that her crew were, as Justin had expected, engaged in drunken celebration of what they deemed to be a successful escape.

Nevertheless, the men in the longboat were tense, and Justin, crouching in the bow, felt his stomach churning as David Fortescue brought her deftly alongside. There were lights in the stern cabin above his head, throwing reflections onto the dark water, but no sign that they had been observed. The oarsmen shipped their oars, and leaning forward, Justin used the boathook to propel the heavy boat under the *Dolphin*'s counter and along her larboard side. After what seemed to him an interminable delay, he was able to hook onto the larboard chains, and giving his boathook to the marine sergeant, he started to haul himself up to the deck, hand over hand in the darkness.

It was only when he reached it that he realized, to his dismay, that he had forgotten to bring the cutlass with which he had been provided, and he cursed under his breath, shocked by his own stupidity. But there was no going back for the weapon now—Fortescue had followed close on his heels and . . . yes, the devil take it! There *was* a man on watch, though fortunately he was on the opposite side of the deck and was only now becoming aware of the fact that the ship had been boarded.

"Who in hell . . ." the shadowy figure exclaimed. "What do you—" Recognizing the voice as that of Fane, one of the two helmsmen and a particular crony of the mate's, Justin flung himself across the deck, hoping to silence him before he could give the alarm. But the seaman eluded him, fending him off with a powerful arm, and his shout echoed the length of the ship before, renewing his efforts, Justin managed to bring him down with a shoulder charge.

He knelt on the prostrate figure and, regaining his breath, yelled out the warning that they had agreed should be given.

"Cockrell—this is Captain Broome! I am here with an armed party, and I call on you in the King's name to yield up this ship. D'you hear me? Come on deck with your hands raised above your heads, all of you, or we shall open fire!"

There was no response, save for some shouted oaths and the low murmur of voices coming from below. As Ensign Finch and his marines gained the deck and spread out across it, with muskets at the ready, Justin repeated his summons, and the white blur of a face appeared over the after hatchway coaming. The owner peered about him, startled and seemingly doubting the evidence of his own eyes; then, as the truth of it slowly dawned on him, he called out in a slurred voice, "Hell's teeth, Toby, it's Broome all right! An' he's got soldiers wiv' him, dozens o' the bastards!" He made to duck below again, but changed his mind. "I declare to God I ain't fightin' soldiers, whatever you say. I'm givin' meself up."

He scrambled out onto the deck, arms held stiffly above his head, and at a nod from Fortescue, one of the marines seized him. There was a loud, angry altercation below, and Justin rose to his feet, recognizing Cockrell's voice. He thrust his own prisoner toward the line of marines and strode across to the hatchway.

"Give yourself up, Cockrell," he ordered harshly. "It'll do you no good if you resist. My party is armed. You've no chance of getting away."

Cockrell cursed him with barely contained fury and the argument went on, the mate clearly endeavoring to persuade his companions to put up a fight. "The swine will hang us if they take us back to Hobart Town," Justin heard him threaten. "Back me up, you lily-livered scum!"

" 'Tis you they'll hang, not us!" another voice retorted. "An' them sojers have muskets—we've only got our bare hands."

David Fortescue joined Justin at his vantage point. "So they didn't break into the arms chest after all," he observed with satisfaction and leaned forward to snap a brusque order to the men to give themselves up.

Two of them obeyed it, followed more reluctantly by the crouching figure of a small, bearded man whom Justin did not recognize.

"An escaped convict," Fortescue said, pointing to the man's scarred wrists as he raised them above his head. "Damme, I wonder how many more of the wretches they smuggled aboard!"

From the cabin below came the ominous sound of heavy blows and the splintering of wood. They were breaking out the muskets in the arms chest, Justin realized, and David Fortescue, coming to the same conclusion, stood back and drew his cutlass.

"We'll have to rush them," he decided. "Mr. Finch, leave one of your fellows to guard the prisoners, and let's have the rest of you here!"

Finch responded with alacrity, his marines' booted feet thudding on the deck planking as they came pounding after him. Fortescue attempted to lead the rush, but Justin was ahead of him.

"This is my ship, sir, and these are my men. So if you please . . ." He thrust in front of the *Porpoise*'s lieutenant without waiting for him to reply and, descending the companionway at a run, made for the captain's cabin. In the dim light of the lantern suspended from the deck beam above their heads, he made out a group of ten or twelve men milling about the shattered arms chest, from which, even as he burst in upon them, they were taking the weapons intended for the ship's defense.

But they had had no time to prime and load the muskets, and Justin hurled himself into their midst, laying about him with his fists and, with a well-aimed kick, knocking away the clubbed musket butt that one of the men raised against him. The sight of the scarlet coats of the marines at his back put an end to the crew's brief attempt at resistance; they let the useless muskets fall and, one by one, held up their arms in token of surrender.

"Don't shoot! For the love of God don't shoot—we're givin' in!"

The voice was Cockrell's, bereft of its earlier defiance. The mate stepped forward, and an instant too late, Justin realized that he had not made the anticipated gesture of surrender and that, belying his words, he had a pistol in his hand, cocked and aimed straight at him.

"If I'm to hang," he spat out venomously, "I'll make sure I take you to hell with me, *Captain* Broome!"

"Look out, Broome!" Fortescue exclaimed. "The swine's armed—let me at him!"

The pistol exploded in Cockrell's hand, the sound reverberating in the confined space of the cabin, but the ball missed its mark, as Justin tripped over David Fortescue's outstretched foot and measured his length on the deck planking. Fortescue came crashing down on top of him; there was a second shot and a scream of agony from Cockrell, and then, as Justin managed to drag himself up on one knee, he saw that blood was welling from Fortescue's chest.

Dear God, he thought, sick with horror, the *Porpoise*'s lieutenant had taken the shot that had been intended for himself. He bent over the slumped form, feeling desperately for a heartbeat and brought his hand away, sticky with blood.

"It's all right," Fortescue gasped. "I . . . don't think . . . I'm badly hit."

At least he was alive . . . Justin gestured to Enoch Finch to help him, and together they lifted the injured man onto the cot.

"Get those blackguards out of here, Sar'nt," Finch ordered, his young voice harsh with shock. "And that carrion who fired the pistol. He's dead, isn't he?"

"You hit him between the eyes, Mr. Finch," the sergeant answered grimly. "He's dead all right."

When the cabin had been cleared, Justin took down the lantern and, holding it over the cot, endeavored by its flickering light to ascertain the extent of David Fortescue's injuries. Although not as serious as he had initially feared—the ball had entered well above the heart—the wound was bleeding copiously, and Fortescue, for all his stoicism, appeared to be in considerable pain.

"I'll try to stanch the bleeding," Justin said, keeping his voice low. "But we've got to get him to a surgeon as quickly as we can." He set the lantern down. Poor young Finch was retching his heart out behind him, and he added, with intentional brusqueness, "Fetch me a shirt from that closet over there—jump to it, lad! We've no time to waste."

Finch gulped and went in search of the shirt.

"David is a good friend of mine," he stammered brokenly. "I let him down, I . . . Oh, the devil take it, Broome, I should have fired sooner than I did! But I believed that rogue Cockrell when he pleaded with us not to shoot."

"So did I," Justin confirmed, tight-lipped. He ripped the shirt into strips and, working swiftly, fashioned a bandage. "Help me to ease him up, will you?"

Between them, they contrived to bandage the ugly wound and stop the flow of blood, but David Fortescue had lapsed into unconsciousness long before they had finished.

"He's in a bad way, is he not?" Finch suggested wretchedly.

"Not if we can get him to a surgeon tonight," Justin said. "But the wind's foul—it'll take us all our time to make it back to the river."

"In this ship, d'you mean?" Finch questioned. "Would it not be quicker to take him in the longboat?"

Justin considered the suggestion, his brain racing as he weighed up the possibilities open to them. Poor Fortescue would rest more easily in the comparative comfort of the *Dolphin*'s cabin, he knew, and to attempt, however carefully, to lower him into the longboat might cause his bleeding to start afresh.

The wind had backed almost due south while they had waited in the lee of Southmouth Island, he reminded himself. He could use it to run up to Point Record, on the northern curve of the bay, and then—then, devil take them, his erstwhile crew and the convict escapers they had smuggled aboard could man the longboat and the *Dolphin*'s jollyboat and take her in tow. With a pair of Finch's marines in each boat, they would give no trouble, and off Betsey's Island, he could call the boats in and run by the lee into the river mouth.

After that, if the wind held, it would be plain sailing, and the *Dolphin* would come into her own. Justin frowned, visualizing the chart, and assessing the distance to be covered, under sail and under tow. The men would have to sweat at the oars; they would have a pull of eleven or twelve miles, unless the wind changed, and that did not seem probable.

But he had no sympathy to waste on these men, even if they had allowed Tobias Cockrell to dupe them. They could sweat, and with David Fortescue's life at stake, it would only be justice if they did.

He turned to Enoch Finch, his mind made up.

"*This* ship, Mr. Finch," he said. "And God willing, we'll have Lieutenant Fortescue back in Hobart Town and in the surgeon's hands by first light. I think, though," he added, "we had better both be armed."

Ensign Finch watched him as he picked up Cockrell's discarded pistol, loaded it, and tucked it into his jacket pocket. "You weren't armed when you boarded this ship, were you?" he accused.

"No," Justin admitted ruefully. "I left my cutlass in the longboat. I'm not accustomed to bearing arms. Or perhaps the truth is I'm not a fighting man, Mr. Finch."

"Oh, you're a fighting man all right," Finch assured him gravely. "What I don't understand is how I ever took you for a murderer. It was, after all, *I* who took a man's life tonight, was it not? Even if I did so belatedly, I killed him."

"You saved the hangman his work," Justin asserted gruffly. He bent once more over the unconscious Fortescue and, satisfied that he was breathing more easily, gestured to the curtained doorway. "Let us get back on deck, Mr. Finch."

"I await your orders, Captain Broome," the marine officer said, and stood aside to permit Justin to precede him.

CHAPTER VIII

The mist of early morning was beginning to disperse when, on February 27, the transport *Anne II*—a stout vessel, of 627 tons burden—came to anchor in Sydney Cove preparatory to landing her cargo of male convicts, trade goods, and West Indian rum.

On that portion of her spacious deck reserved for fare-paying passengers, the Reverend Samuel Marsden, senior chaplain to the colony, a tall, somewhat corpulent figure in his clerical black suit, waited with foot-tapping impatience for the arrival of the boat he had ordered to take him ashore.

There were a number of changes, he saw, visible to the naked eye—more windmills on the skyline, several brick and stone buildings, and a new wharf under construction, with the familiar working parties of fettered convicts shuffling out to their daily toil, sullen and resentful as they always were.

The chaplain sighed, as memory returned. It was over three years since he had left Sydney with his wife and family, on home leave, in the company of the late Governor King and his staff on board H.M.S. *Buffalo,* but despite his prolonged absence, he had kept abreast of the colony's affairs. He had been in frequent contact with all three of the previous governors—and with Captain King right up to the time of his death, two years ago—and he had corresponded regularly with friends and associates in Sydney. But three years was a long time to be away. . . . Samuel Marsden repeated his sigh. He had been granted audiences by the King and the Archbishop of Canterbury, yet his efforts to raise money and support for his missionary work—in both New South Wales and among the warlike Maoris of New Zealand—had not been as successful as he had wished. The Society for the Propagation of the Gospel, in particular, had disappointed him, despite representations made on his behalf by Mr. William Wilberforce. Nevertheless, he had returned with promises of aid and some charitable funds which, God willing, he could put to good use . . . always provided that the new Governor gave him a free hand.

The chaplain's thick, reddish brows met in a pensive frown. The appointment of Colonel Lachlan Macquarie, in place of the deposed Commodore Bligh, had disconcerted him, for he had expected the appointment to go to Admiral Hunter's nephew, Captain William Kent . . . and, indeed, he had done his best to aid Kent's candidacy. But the Colonial Office, in its wisdom, had decided to eschew naval post captains and had chosen an army officer instead and, by sending him out in command of his own regiment, had given him more power than any of his predecessors had wielded.

Which was as it should be, of course; the Governor of so remote a colony had need of loyal troops at his back, and Samuel Marsden could not but applaud Lord Castlereagh's decision, since it was one he himself had long advocated. But Colonel Macquarie was an unknown quantity, Marsden had reminded himself, and it would be prudent for him to make his first call on one who he was confident would be in a position to enlighten him. Then he could present himself at Government House, and . . .

"Your boat's alongside, your reverence," a passing seaman informed him, and Marsden's expression relaxed. He settled his hat more firmly on his now balding pate and climbed down to the waiting boat with the agility of long practice.

There was also a horse waiting for him when he stepped

ashore, held by a wizened old convict groom, who grinned at him in half-recognition and gave him a leg up when he requested it. The note he had sent by the pilot boat had been acted upon, he thought, and with the discretion for which he had asked . . . since it was best that his visit to an emancipist—even one as respectable as Esther Abrahams—should not be the subject of gossip or speculation.

He rode the four miles to Major Johnston's opulent house at Annandale at an easy pace, arriving there just as its mistress was sitting down to her luncheon. She greeted him with astonishment but also with pleasure and, as the chaplain had expected, invited him to join her at the table. In the presence of the servant who waited on them, she confined her questions to generalities, and Marsden studied her covertly as he replied to them.

Esther Abrahams was a handsome woman, now gray of hair and a trifle stouter than she had been when, twenty-two years earlier, she had been sentenced to seven years' transportation for a trivial theft. Sent on board the *Prince of Wales* of Governor Phillip's First Fleet, she had caught the eye of George Johnston—then a lieutenant of marines—and, transferred to his ship, the *Lady Penrhyn,* had become his mistress.

Samuel Marsden had held no brief for Johnston, but the man's relationship with Esther had been a long and happy one, and although the late commandant of the Rum Corps had never married her, she had borne him seven children, including an elder son in whom he took inordinate pride.

Tactfully, as he ate with enjoyment, Marsden inquired for the family and was brought up to date with news of their doings, but as soon as the serving maid withdrew, Esther Abrahams asked anxiously, "Mr. Marsden, had George reached England before you left?"

The chaplain shook his head. Privately, as a committed supporter of the deposed Governor, he had been thankful that neither Johnston nor John Macarthur had made their appearance in London prior to his own departure. No one knew better than he what dire consequences might be expected to result, should Macarthur learn of the partisan championing of Bligh's cause in which he had indulged . . .

John Macarthur's enmity, once incurred, was implacable and greatly to be feared.

But the unfortunate George Johnston had been made the scapegoat; it was he, not Macarthur, who was to be tried by court-martial, and Samuel Marsden, despite his own deep feelings concerning the Rum Corps rebellion and the treatment meted out to the Governor they had overthrown, could still find it in his heart to pity George Johnston. *That Turnip-head Fool*, the Sydney rhymesters had dubbed him, *Jack Boddice's Tool . . . stepped into Bligh's station—he dare not oppose.*

As a serving officer and holder of a King's commission, Johnston was subject to military law which, because he was a civilian, Macarthur was not. It was a parody of justice, but . . . The chaplain looked into the troubled eyes of Johnston's faithful mistress and sought for what words of consolation he could offer.

"I heard that he and John Macarthur had reached Cork," he said, "and that the major intended to wait on His Grace of Northumberland at the first opportunity. With the duke's influence exerted on his behalf, it is possible that a court-martial may deal with him leniently."

"But they will still try him," Esther argued, her voice low.

"They are bound to," Marsden confirmed. Commodore Bligh would insist on a trial, he was well aware, and the charges would be serious ones—Johnston would be arraigned for mutiny and sedition, for which the penalty might well be a firing squad. Rumor had it that George Johnston was the illegitimate son of the Duke of Northumberland, and the duke did possess considerable influence, but even so . . . He looked down at his empty plate, suddenly reluctant to meet Esther's searching gaze.

"Commodore Bligh is here, you know," she observed bitterly. "Reinstated for twenty-four hours, by order of His Majesty's government, and now engaged in seeking witnesses and documents to take back to England with him for the trial. Governor Macquarie has been ordered to afford him every facility, and he is doing so . . . all the letters and papers in the government files have been made available to him. And, besides that, he is accorded all honors, Mr. Marsden! He has a military guard of the Seventy-third to accompany him and sentries posted outside the house he is occupying in Pitt Street. They pipe him aboard the King's ships in harbor and salutes are fired, just as if he were still Governor! Whilst my poor George . . ." She broke off, and tears welled into her fine dark eyes. "He is promoted to lieutenant colonel, he told me, in a letter I received from Rio. But . . . they could still sentence him to death, could they not, if Bligh is able to prove the charges against him?"

It was as if she had read his earlier thoughts, Marsden told himself uneasily. He attempted to prevaricate, but Esther waved him almost contemptuously to silence. "It is Macarthur they should hang, not George," she asserted. "He took his two younger sons, James and William, home with him to be educated privately. Edward has been procured a commission in the Thirty-ninth, and John is reading for the law . . . but my boys, George's boys, remain here with no one to train *them* for a profession or procure them military advancement. And if their father is found guilty and condemned, what is to become of them?"

The interview was not proceeding along the lines he had intended, Samuel Marsden thought. Esther Abrahams's bitterness, if not unexpected in the circumstances, went deeper than he had imagined it would, and her distress was greater than he had anticipated, even allowing for the perilous situation in which George Johnston had now found himself. But she was a sensible, down-to-earth, and above all, well-informed woman, and he devoted the ensuing ten minutes to an attempt to raise her spirits, reaching across the table to take one of her hands sympathetically in his own.

The tactic succeeded; Esther became more cheerful and eager, under his careful prompting, to speak of those matters concerning which he wished to be informed. The new Governor, she told him, was universally popular.

"He is a good, well-intentioned Christian gentleman, Mr. Marsden, and he seems determined to restore this whole colony to godliness. Church attendance is again compulsory for the troops and the convicts, and most of the settlers and emancipists follow His Excellency's example and are regular worshippers. And St. Philip's has a roof now!" Esther smiled. "It produces an echo you will relish, when you come to deliver your sermons there."

"Good!" Marsden applauded, returning her smile. Well aware of the booming quality of his voice and its strong Yorkshire accent, he was not offended by the implications of her remark or by the faint mockery that underlined it.

"His Excellency is demanding other reforms," his hostess went on. "There is to be no Sabbath breaking, under the threat of arrest. And he recently issued a public statement, expressing his determination to end—and I am quoting his words from memory—'the scandalous and pernicious custom so generally and shamelessly adopted throughout this territory of persons of different sexes cohabiting and living together, unsanctioned by the legal ties of matrimony.' Such proceedings he described as 'a scandal to religion, to decency, and to all good government.' It is a pity," she added, with a flash of sardonic humor, "that George is not here to take cognizance of that forthright statement, is it not, seeing that he has cohabited with me for over twenty years, unsanctioned by the ties of matrimony."

There was no answer to her remark that would not smack of condescension or censure, and since he himself had supplied the Colonial Office with a list he had compiled of those women who had cohabited thus without the blessing of the established Church, Marsden wisely let it pass unanswered.

"How are the troops behaving?" he asked, changing the subject quickly, in the hope that Esther did not know that she had figured on his list as Johnston's concubine.

"Ours or the Governor's?" Esther shrugged, seemingly amused. "Ours are careful to give no offense. Many of the rank and file are most reluctant to leave the colony, and His Excellency has offered to form up to three hundred of them into a veterans' company . . . and I fancy more than that number will volunteer. Some of the officers, too; although by order of the Colonial Office, land granted during what is now to be termed 'the rebel administration' is to

be declared Crown property again. We may lose ours at Ca-
bramatta, and if George is found guilty—" She broke off
abruptly, turning her head away, to continue with admirable restraint, "The Seventy-third is a regiment of Highlanders, well disciplined and religiously inclined. The behavior
of the rank and file has been exemplary . . . but that of
some of the younger officers somewhat less than exemplary, I am afraid."

Marsden's heavy brows rose in surprise. "How so?"

"His new Excellency's policy toward emancipists does
not please them. It is, to say the least, liberal, and I, for
one, thank God for it!" Esther quoted from the Governor's
official proclamation, eyeing Samuel Marsden with a
faintly derisive smile. " 'Those who have earned their freedom by servitude, pardon, or emancipation shall in all respects, be considered on an equal footing with everyone
else in the colony, according to their rank in life . . .' His
Excellency's own words, Mr. Marsden. And they are no
idle words, I do assure you. Emancipists are entertained to
dinner at Government House by Colonel Macquarie and
his lady, and there is talk of appointing the more respectable of them to the magistrates' bench!"

Samuel Marsden was unable to hide the shock her words
had induced. His florid cheeks became even redder than
their wont, and he bit back an exclamation of mingled dismay and disbelief, but undeterred, Esther Abrahams went
on smoothly, "One of the Seventy-third's young officers—
an Ensign MacNaughton, I believe—left His Excellency's
table in high dudgeon, refusing to sit down with the emancipists who were his fellow guests! They included Simeon
Lord and Thomas Reibie, as well as Surgeon Redfern."

"And what," Marsden managed, in a choked voice, "was
the outcome of the ensign's action?"

"The young gentleman was given a severe dressing down
by the Governor," Esther told him, with satisfaction.
"Things are changing here, Mr. Marsden. No doubt you will
have observed that the roads are greatly improved. Colonel
Macquarie has his soldiers working on them, as well as the
convict gangs, and he plans to build a turnpike road from
Sydney to the Hawkesbury. Already it is halfway to Parra-

matta, and you will hardly know the township now—the roots have been grubbed up, brick houses are to be erected, and the wooden shacks pulled down to make room for them. There is talk of banishing the domestic animals from the main streets, and His Excellency has reduced the number of licensed houses in the Rocks to a mere twenty!"

Marsden let her talk on, his brain reeling. He could not but approve of the majority of the new Governor's measures, of course; they were in the nature of measures he had long advocated, particularly the keeping of the Sabbath and the compulsory church services. And the Rocks had harbored too many bawdy houses and grog shops under the lax rule of the Rum Corps, whose officers had, in any event, owned many of them, their servants or their women nominated as license-holders.

"Another of the young gentlemen got himself into the Governor's bad books," Esther was saying, "but for a different reason. Mrs. Macquarie has a young lady's maid she's very attached to—she brought the girl out from England with her. Jessica India, they call her, although for the life of me I don't know why, because she's as white as you or me, Mr. Marsden."

"Is she a convict?" Marsden asked, without much interest.

Esther shook her neatly capped head. "No—she's the daughter of a sergeant of the Seventy-third, I heard, and as I mentioned, the Governor's lady sets great store by her. Very anxious to preserve her innocence because both her parents had to be left behind in Portsmouth. But"—her tone was dry—"that's easier said than done out here, is it not?"

"Alas, it is," the chaplain confirmed, with a heavy sigh. "And presumably the young gentleman had other notions?"

"He did indeed—and he was caught red-handed by the Governor's aide, Captain Antill. The word is that the young rip is facing a court-martial, charged with conduct unbecoming to an officer and a gentleman. Most folk think he'll be cashiered and sent home."

Samuel Marsden considered the story pensively. The

new Governor, if Esther Abrahams's account of him was to be believed, was most certainly a Christian gentleman and, furthermore, one who was prepared to exercise his reforming zeal in a manner the colony sorely needed. He would no doubt welcome support from the Church, as personified by its senior chaplain, and, by heaven, he should have it! Poor Captain King had cherished similar ideas when he had first assumed the governorship, but he had had Macarthur's malign influence to cope with, and, sadly, he had weakened and permitted matters to slide. Commodore Bligh, too, had attempted reform, but . . . Marsden frowned, tugging at his long red whiskers.

"You said that Governor Bligh is still here, Esther?"

"Yes—and there's no word of his leaving, that I've heard. The two King's ships are kept here, waiting his pleasure, and the Corps is to return with him to England. I don't envy them—Bligh is a vengeful man. He will make sure they're made to suffer every humiliation and discomfort he can devise during the passage." Esther spread her plump hands in a gesture that was half of pity and half of resignation. "I am thankful on that account that George left here when he did—Bligh would have sent him home in chains! But . . ." She smiled suddenly, her eyes dancing. "One happy event I forgot to mention—Mrs. Putland is being courted most ardently by Colonel O'Connell, who commands the Seventy-third. We all think they will make a match of it, and I am pleased for her sake. She is a fine young lady, who scarcely deserved the father the good Lord wished on her, but for all that, she stood by him loyally through all his trials and tribulations. George admired her, you know—he told me so more than once—and I do confess, so do I."

It was a generous tribute, Samuel Marsden thought, coming from Major—no, he was now Lieutenant Colonel— George Johnston's mistress, but no doubt Mary Putland deserved it, and he nodded his approval. She would be an asset to the colony if she stayed, and might, perhaps, be more successful than Ensign MacNaughton had been in stemming the flood of emancipist guests at the new Governor's table. Although her father had drawn most of his support from among the emancipist landowners and smallholders in the Hawkesbury settlements, he had never, as far as the chaplain knew, invited any of them to dine with him.

"Does Governor Macquarie encourage the match?" he inquired curiously.

"Mrs. Macquarie does," Esther answered, without hesitation. "And it is said that His Excellency listens to her."

So the Governor was influenced by his wife, Samuel Marsden told himself. "What manner of woman is the Governor's lady?" he asked.

"I have not met her socially, of course." The statement was made without bitterness; a statement of fact, rather than an expression of regret. "But everyone who has seems greatly to like her. She is kindly and well disposed, they tell me—a Scottish lady of breeding and very well connected. I can only say, from what I have seen of her, that she is comely, but not beautiful, and"—Esther's smile was indulgent—"her taste in hats leaves much to be desired!"

Marsden echoed her smile. Esther Abrahams, he recalled, had been a milliner before her conviction and sentence, and indeed, if his memory was to be trusted, her crime had been the theft of trimmings for a hat. He let her talk on, once more busy with his own thoughts, and then, conscious that time was passing and there was still much to be learned, he cut her short.

"What of the others?" he demanded, realizing that she had made no mention of them. "Colonel Paterson and Colonel Foveaux?"

Esther flashed him an oddly resentful glance. "You can discount Colonel Paterson," she said flatly. "He is drinking himself into the grave. He has scarcely ever been sober since his return from Van Diemen's Land."

"And Foveaux?"

"Joseph Foveaux is a most unprincipled person," Esther returned. "He is all things to all men, caring only for his own advancement. He has duped the new Governor into supposing him to be honest and trustworthy and is constantly at his side, counseling and advising. He and the unspeakable Nanny Sherwin, whom he claims to have married"—her tone became acid—"are always at Government House, and they are guests at every dinner. Nobody, it would seem, has had the courage to tell His Excellency what Foveaux countenanced, when he wielded power in this colony, after George relinquished it. For years he purported to be George's friend, but now he has basely betrayed him and John Macarthur, too. Why . . ." She was waxing so indignant that Marsden again interrupted her.

"Both Paterson and Foveaux are ordered back to England with their regiment, Esther," he reminded her, in a placatory tone. "They will have no choice but to obey."

He did not add that he had heard Lord Castlereagh speak on the subject in the House and privately, and in anything but placatory tones. The Colonial Secretary, when he had time to spare from prosecuting the war against Bonaparte and the French, was grimly determined to bring the colony to heel. All who had played any part in the recent rebellion were to be removed from New South Wales, including Governor Bligh . . . and they would ignore the noble lord's instructions at their peril. Even Macarthur, for all his wealth and the influence he commanded, would not escape scot-free.

A chill little smile played about Samuel Marsden's thick lips. Had he not seen to it himself, when the Colonial Office had sought his opinion? Had he not told Castlereagh and Undersecretary Cooke the truth about Macarthur in the confident belief that—whatever the outcome of George Johnston's trial—they would find a means to ensure that the infamous Jack Boddice did not return to his vast acres and his opulent life in New South Wales? That might not be retribution enough to satisfy Esther Abrahams, admittedly, but for Macarthur himself it would undoubtedly be painful. . . . Marsden heaved himself to his feet, going through the motions of consulting his pocket watch and offering thanks for the hospitality he had received.

Esther accompanied him to the door. She said, as they waited together for his horse to be brought from the stables, "You will call on the Governor, I suppose?"

He eyed her with raised brows, surprised by the question. "Why, of course. His Excellency will expect the civility."

"Call also, once you are settled in again, on Mr. and Mrs. Ellis Bent," Esther suggested. "He is the new judge advocate, a barrister of Lincoln's Inn." Without waiting for Marsden's anticipated question, she added, with a tight smile, "I fancy you will find the young gentleman congenial. And the Wentworths enjoy the viceregal favor at present."

Was there, Samuel Marsden wondered, a hint of malice in her observation? Dr. D'Arcy Wentworth had come out under a cloud, if not precisely as a convict, and he had married a convict girl, about twenty years ago, when he had been doing duty at Norfolk Island. Their eldest son, William Charles, had—like John Macarthur's boys—been sent to England to complete his education, and . . .

Once again Esther Abrahams anticipated his unvoiced question. "There is talk of an official position for young William Wentworth when he returns here," she volunteered. "That of provost marshal, I believe, since poor Mr. Gore is to go to England as one of Bligh's witnesses. And it's said that Dr. Wentworth is angling for a contract to build a new hospital, with Alexander Riley and Garnham Blaxcell in partnership with him, and Simeon Lord sniffing at their heels." She waited, clearly expecting him to betray some sign of disapprobation, but he simply grunted.

A groom appeared with his horse, and having achieved the object of his visit, the stout chaplain scrambled awkwardly onto the animal's back and, regaining his breath, repeated his thanks. He was stiff and saddlesore, he realized, after the long months he had spent at sea, so that perhaps a return to the ship and a few hours' rest in his comfortable cabin might be advisable, before he called to pay his respects to the new Governor.

Esther had, as he had expected, given him food for thought. He would mull over all she had told him, he decided, and make his call next day, with his future course of action clear in his mind.

The good Christian colonel should have his support, but he would be given advice, also, on the manner in which emancipated felons might best be treated. Wining and dining the more wealthy at Government House might conceivably pay dividends, but if Macquarie was thinking of elevating any of them to the magistrates' bench, he would have to be warned of the dangers of such an action . . . and of the adverse effect it would have on the respectable members of the community.

But . . . Samuel Marsden dug his heels into his horse's sides and set his face toward the town. Perhaps the warning would more tactfully be delivered in the form of a sermon, prefaced by an appropriate text. He had always been noted for the power and eloquence of his sermons, and . . . today was Tuesday. That would give him almost a week to settle in, land his family and his household goods, and make arrangements for the disposal of the merchandise he had brought with him.

He would preach at the newly roofed Church of St. Philip next Sunday—provided that the new Governor and his lady were certain to be in the congregation, and . . . His lips pursed, he considered what text he would choose. St. Matthew, perhaps: *It must needs be that offenses come but woe to that man by whom the offense cometh.* Or St. Paul to the Romans: *For ye have not received the spirit of bondage again to fear but ye have received the spirit of adoption* . . . No, that was too obscure, its meaning hidden. Something more straightforward was required, from which he could launch directly into his warning dissertation.

Paul to the Galatians . . . *Ye are fallen from grace,* or better still: *God is not mocked, for whatsoever a man soweth, that also shall he reap.* That would serve his purpose admirably, the colony's senior chaplain decided. He rode slowly on, composing his sermon as he went.

* * *

A buffet luncheon had been set out on the lawn at Government House, the rows of trestle tables shaded from the sun beneath a canvas awning. The repast—thickly sliced bread, cheese, cold meats, and flagons of ale—was scarcely of the kind normally served to the Governor's guests, but he had himself drawn up the menu, and Jessica, hurrying from table to table with cutlery and platters, decided that the choice was likely to please those who, today, had been invited to partake of it.

For they were convicts—building workers and road menders from the chain gangs, with their overseers—and the luncheon was in the nature of a reward for the manner in which the repairs to Government House, its stables, and the surrounding roads and walks had been carried out. The gardeners and boatmen and men from the brickfields had also been included in the Governor's invitation—in all, some fifty-eight or sixty workers were expected, and as Mrs. Ovens had assured her, they would, Jessica knew, without exception be hungry. Convict rations were meager and their hours of work long and arduous; few, if any, of them, would have seen such plenty since the transports had landed in Sydney Town.

She set down the last of her pile of thick earthenware platters on the table at which Mrs. Ovens was preparing to preside, and the plump housekeeper thanked her abstractedly.

"You've not seen my carvers, have you?" she asked. "The ones with the deer-antler handles? I've hunted high and low, but for the life of me I don't know where I can have put them."

"They're still in the kitchen, Mrs. Ovens," Jessica told her. "I'll run and fetch them for you."

She started back toward the big, rambling house, skirting its wide veranda on which, she saw, her lady and the Governor were seated, and made for the kitchen premises at the rear, unable to suppress a reminiscent shiver as she did so.

It was broad daylight now, of course, and she had nothing to fear, with the sun blazing down from a cloudless blue sky and a small host of servants bustling about, both inside and outside the house. But the night when Ensign MacAlpine had stumbled drunkenly from the Governor's dining table and accosted her was still a vivid and distressing memory, his flushed face and the naked desire in his dark eyes a recurring nightmare when she slept.

And she had done nothing to provoke his assault; indeed, until that moment when she had encountered him in the darkness of the garden, she could not recall ever having set eyes on him before. He had joined the regiment only a few weeks prior to its departure from the Isle of Wight, and had come out in H.M.S. *Hindostan*, whereas she herself had been on board the *Dromedary* with the Governor and his staff and servants, so that he could not have known who she was.

Yet he had known her name; he had called her by it and had made demands that, even now, brought a blush of shame to her cheeks. Had it not been for Captain Antill's providential arrival . . . Jessica shivered anew, fearing to follow that thought to its logical conclusion but hearing in memory the hateful, arrogant voice. "Jessica—Jessica India, come here, I want you!"

True, she had struck out at him. She had kicked and struggled like a mad thing and had even managed to break free of him and take to her heels, but that, seemingly, had only served to inflame her assailant the more. He had pursued and brought her down, reminding her of her stepfather in one of his passions and as deaf as Duncan Campbell had always been to her pleas to be let alone.

She must have cried out because it had been then that Captain Antill had appeared. He had given the young officer short shrift, and—Jessica caught her breath. She had fled, shocked and sickened, to the kitchen and the motherly arms of Mrs. Ovens, dreading her mistress's reaction when the unhappy incident should be reported to her, and afraid—yes, actually afraid—that Mrs. Macquarie might decide to dispense with her services, holding her to blame for what had occurred.

But, as it had turned out, Mrs. Macquarie had done no such thing. She had been very kind and understanding, her anger directed solely against Ensign MacAlpine, and the

Governor had shared her view of his conduct. The Honorable James Carlisle MacAlpine—who was the younger son of an earl—was suspended from duty and would, in all probability, be sent home in one of Commodore Bligh's ships and transferred to another regiment.

But for all that, Jessica reflected sadly, tongues had wagged, and among those who had listened to the rumors was, it seemed, Piper Fergus Mackinnon, for he had made no attempt to see or seek her out . . . not even when summoned, as he had been recently, to pipe at a Government House dinner. She had recognized him, of course, but he had walked past as if he were unaware of her existence, his expression blank and unsmiling. And he was here today, with the regimental guard and the escort of mounted troopers detailed to accompany Governor Macquarie to Parramatta, as soon as his convict guests had eaten their fill and departed. She had seen him march up to the guardhouse, but . . .

"Lookin' for these, are you?" the cook greeted, as Jessica entered the dark, low-ceilinged kitchen. He held up Mrs. Ovens's precious carvers, grinning good-naturedly. "I reckoned it'd not be long afore Mistress O. missed 'em. I'd have sent 'em to her, if I'd had anybody to send, but they're all out on the lawn, waitin' ter hobnob with their old shipmates in the chain gangs!" His grin faded. "Rum do, ain't it, His Excellency givin' luncheon to convicts?"

"Yes, I—I suppose it is," Jessica confirmed uncertainly. The Government House cook was a onetime merchant seaman, who was said to have jumped ship in Sydney several years before, and, she sensed, his attitude to the convicts was similar to that of the majority of the town's free inhabitants . . . even a deserter considered himself a cut above them, for no better reason than because he had not come out in chains. She took the carvers, not wanting to give voice to her own feelings, and was about to leave when he called her back.

"There was a young feller in here a few minutes since, askin' for you."

"A young fellow, Mr. Dawkins?"

"Aye—a sojer," the cook said. "One o' His Excellency's catawaulin' bagpipers."

Fergus Mackinnon, Jessica thought, and despite her earlier misgivings concerning him, her heart lifted. Perhaps he had not meant to pass her by; he had been on duty, which might account for his having done so. She started to thank her informant but broke off as the sound of pipe music reached her, coming from the front of the house.

"Won't be able to hobnob with you now, will he?" the cook observed, his tone faintly mocking. "Seems like the guests are arrivin' on the dot, don't it? Gawd, I wonder if His Excellency knows what he's doing! 'Cause this'll make a stir an' no mistake—convicts eatin' their dinners on the lawn at Gov'ment House! He could've fed a mob o' blackfellers here on the fat o' the land and folks would just have said he was obeyin' orders from His Majesty the King to get on friendly terms with 'em. But convicts . . . that's another matter altogether. Fairly set the cat among the pigeons, that will, when word o' it gets out, I can tell you!"

"His Excellency is only rewarding them for the hard work they've done, repairing this house," Jessica defended. "And they *have* worked hard, Mr. Dawkins. Some of the walls were ready to fall down when we first moved in, you know they were."

"That's what convicts are for, to work hard," Dawkins retorted tartly. "They get bloody backs, if they don't, so what's the sense in rewardin' 'em?" He sniffed disparagingly. "You mark my words, Miss Maclaine . . . that old Bible-thumper, the Reverend Marsden, will give us a sermon next Sunday that'll make his last one seem like kiddies' prattle or a meetin' o' the Church Ladies' Guild! He can hand it out, can Samuel Marsden . . . and he don't care who he hands it out to. Why, I've heard him preach agin' Mister Almighty John Macarthur hisself an' him sittin' there in the front pew, as large as life."

Jessica made her escape before he could say any more. She had glimpsed the Reverend Marsden a few days ago, when he had called to pay his respects to the Governor, and, for no reason that she could have explained, she had been repelled by the sight of him. The Governor, on the other hand, had accorded him a cordial reception, and Mrs. Macquarie had expressed the view that he was a good man if, perhaps, a trifle coarse in voice and manner.

But at least today he was not here, either to condemn or to praise His Excellency's magnanimity toward the convicts, Jessica thought. She slipped through the rear entrance to the marquee and, breathless from the speed with which she had come, handed over the precious carvers to Mrs. Ovens. Already the first of a hungry multitude were being marshaled into line by their overseers; subdued and for the most part silent, they differed in no respect that Jessica could see from Sydney's free citizens. Almost all wore their own clothes; a few—newly arrived in the colony—were attired somewhat oddly in a prison issue of old army uniforms, from which the badges and buttons had been removed.

She was kept busy, helping to serve them, but had time to observe that they were mannerly and grateful, each man accepting his piled platter with a nod or a word of thanks. Joseph Big, the Governor's coachman, who was in charge of the barrels of locally brewed ale, grinned mightily as he doled out brimming beakers of the frothy liquid, clearly to the astonishment of the recipients, who had not anticipated such largesse.

At the entrance to the marquee, His Excellency received the incoming line, bowing graciously in response to the doffed caps, and speaking personally to any he recognized as men who had assisted with the repairs made to his official residence. From the lawn outside, Jessica could hear the lively skirl of Fergus Mackinnon's piping, but she caught only an occasional sight of him, when he passed in front of the entrance to the marquee, and even that was partially blocked by the Governor's stooped figure and the taller, burlier ones of his two uniformed aides.

After about an hour, when most of the guests had been served, Mrs. Ovens sent her to attend her mistress, who had remained on the Government House veranda to watch the proceedings.

"I'll manage fine now, with the girls I have," the housekeeper said. She was privy to Jessica's interest in the young piper, and smiling, she gestured in his direction as he played the last, poignant notes of "The Green Hills of Tirol" and let the mouthpiece of his chanter fall from his lips. His face was red and glistening with perspiration from his exertions in the hot sun, and Mrs. Ovens added in a confidential whisper, "I don't doubt His Excellency would give his approval, were you to take the poor young fellow a beaker of ale, on your way out."

Jessica felt the awkward, embarrassed color come flooding into her own cheeks. But Fergus Mackinnon *had* asked for her—the cook had said so—therefore he could not take it amiss or deem her unduly forward, surely, if she brought him some liquid refreshment of which, by the look of him, he was sorely in need?

She carried the beaker out to him, receiving the expected nod of approval from the Governor, and offered it shyly. "Mistress Ovens was thinking that you would wish to slake your thirst, Piper Mackinnon," she told him.

"Ah, now, indeed I do!" he agreed. But his tone was stiff, the look he gave her lacking in warmth, and Jessica's spirits sank as she watched him tuck his pipes under one arm and lift the beaker to his lips with the other. He was very much the soldier on parade, she thought, but perhaps, under the eyes of the Governor and two of his officers, it was necessary that he should behave thus . . . as it had been on the night of the Governor's dinner party. Her stepfather always acted in similar fashion, when officers were present, his manners impeccable, whereas in his own home, with her mother and herself as audience, it was difficult to realize that he was the same man. He . . .

"Thank you," Fergus Mackinnon said, returning the now empty beaker. But he made no move to take up his piping again, and Jessica suggested uncertainly, "Mr. Dawkins said that you were coming to his kitchen, asking for me."

"Aye," he admitted. "So I did. I was wanting to speak with you."

"I am here," she reminded him.

"We cannot talk here!" he objected.

"I am going back to the house now, to wait on my lady. Could you not walk with me?"

He hesitated, frowning. The Governor had gone into the marquee, his two aides with him, and there seemed no reason why he should not accede to her suggestion, yet he continued to hesitate, and Jessica, losing patience with him, challenged bitterly, "You were asking me to keep company with you, Piper Mackinnon, were you not? Are you fearing now to be seen in my company, lest His Excellency might observe us?"

Fergus Mackinnon's color deepened and spread. "You do not understand," he protested. "I beg you to permit me to explain."

"I am listening," Jessica assured him quietly. He took her arm and led her with nervous haste to the rear of the marquee where, out of sight save from the servants' quarters and the kitchen, he came abruptly to a halt, still very red of face and inexplicably silent.

Jessica freed her arm from his grasp and turned to look at him, her lower lip trembling a little. "Now," she urged. "We cannot be observed, unless it is by Mr. Dawkins. Pray give me your explanation, Piper Mackinnon . . . and do not concern yourself with my feelings. Have you, perhaps, heard some talk of me that did not please you?"

"Aye," the young soldier admitted. He shuffled his feet awkwardly, avoiding her gaze. "Of you and one of our officers."

"And you were believing what was said?"

His headshake lacked conviction. "I know Ensign Mac-Alpine; he is in my company, and he is not an officer I can admire. But that is not the reason I sought to speak with you, mistress."

"Then what *is* the reason?" Jessica demanded, again out of patience. He was truly a fine figure of a man, she had to concede, tall and well proportioned, setting off his splendid uniform to perfection, and yet . . . She smothered a sign of mingled regret and disillusionment, seeing him suddenly with new eyes as, perhaps, her stepfather had been in his youth. Straitlaced and puritan, hidebound by the strict religious upbringing he had received, and prone to judge others by his own bigoted standards—to judge and find them wanting, as, from the expression on his face, it seemed that Fergus Mackinnon had judged her.

He was not a brutal, violent bully, such as Duncan Campbell had become; indeed, he was gentle and kindly, but . . . had not Duncan Campbell appeared kindly enough, when her mother had first married him? And had he not accused her of wantonness, when she had been too young even to comprehend the meaning of the word . . . and with as little proof on which to base his accusation as Fergus Mackinnon had now?

Jessica's head came up and her voice had a sharp edge to it as she repeated her question.

"Well, what reason have you?"

He continued to avoid her gaze, his own fixed on the highly polished toecaps of his boots.

"His Excellency Colonel Macquarie is to select a personal piper from our ranks," he managed at last. "And there is a chance—a good chance—that I may be the man chosen. It would be a great honor if I were, as you will be knowing well. But . . ." He looked up to meet Jessica's gaze with disconcerting suddenness. "The pipe major is saying that he could not recommend me if I . . . that is to say if I were to be keeping company with a member of His Excellency's household."

And one concerning whom there was talk, Jessica thought. But her brief bitterness faded; she had been brought up in the army and was well aware of the harsh discipline imposed on the rank and file, and of the behavior expected of any soldier appointed to a position of privilege in an officer's household. The Governor's personal piper would be in a position of privilege, but if he were seen to be taking advantage of it, his appointment would undoubtedly be short-lived.

"I understand," she said, quite gently. "If that is your reason, you are under no—no obligation to me."

Fergus Mackinnon smiled his relief. "There is no other reason, only that; I give you my word, mistress. I was hoping that if I could see you and tell you of it myself you *would* understand, for I am not one to break my word.

I . . . as to the matter of Ensign MacAlpine, I had no thought of it. He is a high-spirited young gentleman, and when he is taking too much drink there is no knowing what he will do."

It was, Jessica told herself, the most she could expect, and although it still seemed to her a trifle lacking in conviction, she wanted to believe his assurance. He must know, surely, if he knew anything of her stepfather, how harsh a disciplinarian he was and how strictly she had been brought up?

She echoed his smile uncertainly, but since there was nothing to gain by prolonging their brief meeting, she excused herself. "I have my duties also, Mr. Mackinnon. My lady will be expecting me to attend her, so if you will pardon me, I will go to her."

"Oh, aye." Fergus Mackinnon stood aside and she ran from him, smoothing her apron as she reached the steps to the veranda.

Mrs. Macquarie was still sitting there, a tray of virtually untouched food in front of her and a pensive frown creasing her smooth white brow. The food, Jessica saw, was the same as that served to the convicts, save that the bread was more thinly sliced, and she said, after dropping the customary curtsy, "Ma'am, do you wish me to take this away and bring you something you would like better?"

The Governor's wife shook her head. "No, do not trouble, Jessica—I am not hungry." She gestured in the direction of the marquee. "Are His Excellency's guests enjoying themselves, do you think?"

"Oh, yes, indeed, ma'am, I am sure they are." There were flies clustering hungrily about the tray, and Jessica picked up a napkin with which to cover it, worried by her mistress's lack of appetite. "I could make you tea, ma'am, if you would fancy it. Mr. Dawkins is in the kitchen, and—"

"No, child, thank you. I truly do not want anything. It is the heat, I suppose. It is so—so relentless. I . . ." Mrs. Macquarie broke off, clicking her tongue in sudden agitation. "Oh, dear, I do believe that we have callers! See, there is a carriage at the gate, with two ladies seated in it.

They could scarcely have come at a more inopportune moment. I . . . Jessica, go quickly, if you please, and see who they are. If it is Mrs. Putland, I will most gladly receive her, but if it is anyone else, say that I am not at home. Do you understand?"

"Yes, ma'am," Jessica assured her. She sped off on her errand and, reaching the gate, recognized the younger occupant of the carriage as Mrs. O'Shea, a friendly, charming young lady and a not infrequent caller at Government House. Her companion was older and less familiar, dark-haired and more than usually good-looking, but with a thin, petulant mouth and an air of conscious superiority that was accentuated when she spoke.

Ignoring Jessica's curtsy and her polite greeting, she waved a disparaging hand in the direction of the lawn beside her, onto which a number of the convicts had now emerged, and asked sharply, "Who are those men?"

"They . . . why, they are laborers, ma'am, who have been working on repairs to the house. They—" Jessica hesitated, uncertain of how much more it would be prudent to tell her. "They have finished the work, and—"

The dark-haired lady cut her short. "You mean they are *convicts*? Is His Excellency the Governor entertaining convicted felons on his lawn?" She sounded shocked and incredulous, her slim, dark brows lifted in astonishment. "Good heavens, Abigail!" She turned to the girl seated beside her. "What are things coming to? My father told me that the Macquaries frequently invite emancipists to dine with them, but this . . . oh, it is past belief! I declare we are more conscious of social distinctions on the Hawkesbury than our new Governor appears to be. And you've been trying to tell me what a fine gentleman he is!"

Her tone was scornful and she made no attempt to lower her voice. The lovely, blue-eyed Abigail O'Shea met Jessica's embarrassed gaze and said pleadingly, "Oh, hush, Henrietta, I beg you! Do you want His Excellency to hear you?"

"I care not a whit if he does," the lady she had addressed as Henrietta retorted. "And I am certainly not calling on Mrs. Macquarie when Government House is crawling with convicts." To Jessica, she said icily, "Be good enough to inform your mistress that Mrs. Dawson and Mrs. O'Shea came here in error, not realizing that Their Excellencies had guests. Tell Jonas to drive on, Abigail."

Mrs. O'Shea leaned forward reluctantly to give the order to the coachman. She gave Jessica an apologetic smile and the carriage pulled away from the gate.

Jessica hesitated, wishing that Mrs. Ovens or even the Governor would summon her, but neither did so and she walked slowly back to the veranda.

"And that, I think, was Mrs. Timothy Dawson of Upwey Farm on the Hawkesbury, was it not?" Mrs. Macquarie said, before Jessica could speak. "And little Abigail O'Shea with her? Oh, do not fret, child, or endeavor to phrase the message you were given so as not to cause me offense . . . I can guess with what critical scorn it was worded!" She gave vent to a tired sigh. "They do not understand, any of them, what His Excellency is trying to do here. They imagine, in their ignorance, that it will strike at the foundations of their privileged existence if convicts are treated as human beings. Our young officers are beginning to think along the same lines, alas . . . yet they do not hesitate to invite Sir Henry Browne Hayes to dine in their mess, whilst refusing to sit down at *my* table with men like Dr. Redfern and Mr. Lord. Does being a baronet remove the emancipist stigma?"

Her outburst was unexpected and, to Jessica, out of character, for her mistress seldom expressed such views in her hearing. Wisely she made no reply, and Mrs. Macquarie, recovering from her momentary anger, gave her a weary smile. She said, with a swift change of tone, "I will take tea now, Jessica, if you please . . . and bring two cups. I am sure His Excellency will join me, before he leaves for Parramatta."

"Very good, ma'am." Jessica picked up the cloth-covered luncheon tray and was on her way into the house when Mrs. Macquarie called out to her to wait.

"Look," she requested, pointing. "Your eyes are younger

than mine. That ship, the one that is just coming into the cove . . . is it not Mr. Lord's schooner the *Dolphin*?"

Jessica set down the tray and, obediently, a hand shading her eyes, followed the direction of her mistress's pointing finger.

"Yes, ma'am," she confirmed. "I think so. And I can see redcoats on the deck—marines, they look like."

"Mr. Lord had word by a whaling ship's master that the crew of the *Dolphin* had stolen her," Mrs. Macquarie said thoughtfully. "I was concerned because that very brave young man, who saved the life of one of our seamen when he fell from the *Dromedary*'s masthead, was in command of the *Dolphin*. What was his name, Jessica, do you remember? Was it not Brown?"

"It was Broome, ma'am," Jessica supplied. "Justin Broome." She had a swift vision of the tall young sailor with the mop of unruly fair hair who had battled so manfully to drag the *Dromedary*'s topman from the raging seas off South Head. He had lost his own vessel, she had recalled—she and Mrs. Ellis Bent had watched the frail craft being dashed to pieces on the rocks in stunned dismay. And then . . .

"I hope young Mr. Broome is safe and on board his command," Mrs. Macquarie went on. "Because His Excellency has made arrangements with Captain Pasco for him to serve as a midshipman in the *Hindostan,* when she sails for home. He felt it to be a fitting reward for the young man's heroism. It would be a salutary lesson for the doubters, would it not, were the son of emancipist parents to gain his commission and make a career in the Royal Navy?"

It would indeed, Jessica thought, as she went to the kitchen with her tray. It would be even more of an honor than being appointed as personal piper to His Excellency the Governor, and for no reason that she could have explained, she felt suddenly elated.

CHAPTER IX

Justin left Simeon Lord's waterfront office with the praises of the *Dolphin*'s owner still ringing in his ears.

Praise from Simeon Lord was not lightly earned; neither was the offer of further employment, yet, for all that, he had hesitated and then refused it, preferring to keep to their original agreement.

The wealthy merchant had eyed him in surprise and asked, a hint of annoyance in his voice, "You want to go back to plying for charter on the Hawkesbury, do you, when I'm ready to give you command of the *Dolphin* on a permanent basis? Think on it, lad—don't make up your mind now. If you use my yard to build your own vessel, she'll be no bigger than the *Flinders* . . . that was what we agreed, was it not?"

And, of course, it had been, Justin reminded himself, although he had planned more ambitiously in his own mind. Lord's offer had been for a replacement for his lost cutter, and he could insist on no more.

"Why?" the older man had persisted. "Lost your nerve, have you, because I gave you a tough crew to handle?"

Justin was silent, keeping his thoughts to himself. They had been worse than that, with the exception of poor, dead Dutch Holland and, perhaps, the cook, who had been scared of his own shadow, but Justin knew that he could not admit that they—and Tobias Cockrell—had bested him. After all, he had brought the *Dolphin* back, with Simeon Lord's cargo of sealskins and whale oil intact. And Cockrell was dead, and Ensign Finch's marines had marched the rest of them to the Sydney jail, to await trial by the colony's justices. . . .

He had also brought news of two other deaths, but Lord could have no complaint on that score and was not entitled to any explanation, either, so Justin had evaded the question, answering it with a statement that at least had the merit of being true.

"I want to be my own master, Mr. Lord. I'll settle for building a new cutter in your yard."

With that, knowing that he must seek out Abigail O'Shea as soon as he could and break the sad tidings of David Fortescue's death to her, he had taken his leave, indifferent to the fact that, in so doing, he had incurred the wealthy Mr. Lord's disapprobation.

As he strode along the crowded street, past warehouses and market stalls, he endeavored to rehearse the words he would say to Abigail, seeking to soften the blow . . . if there was any way in which it could be softened.

They had brought her betrothed safely back to Hobart Town—that at least they had done, Justin reflected unhappily. David Fortescue had been conscious, had made light of his wound, and had seemed in little danger. He had again expressed his desire to be given passage back to Sydney in the *Dolphin* and had even made jest of it, begging Justin to postpone her sailing until he should be out of the surgeons' hands.

"Whatever excuses you have to make—wait for me. I'll not keep you overlong. Once they've dug the infernal bullet out, I'll be as fit as a flea and able to stand my trick at the wheel. So give me your word, like a good fellow, will you? Swear you'll not sail without me."

He had given his word, of course, Justin recalled, and they had brought him ashore, manning the longboat within minutes of coming to anchor. But they had found Hobart's inhabitants in a state of shock, stunned by the sudden and unexpected death of Colonel Collins, the Lieutenant Governor. He had died sitting in his armchair—it was presumed his heart had failed—and both duty surgeons were at Government House, an orderly at the hospital had informed them sourly.

"And you won't get 'em back here, not till Lieutenant Lord's ready to give the word," the man had added. "Set on giving His Honor the finest funeral Hobart Town has ever seen. The surgeons have to lay him out, so he can lie in state, if you please!"

It had taken two hours and all the powers of persuasion he possessed, Justin reflected bitterly, to ensure that the junior of the two assistant surgeons abandoned the corpse of the late Lieutenant Governor and the grandiose plans for his funeral for long enough to give poor David Fortescue the treatment he needed. But the young doctor had come at last, had probed for the pistol ball and expressed himself confident that his patient would live . . . he had even shrugged off any suggestion that the delay in removing the ball could complicate recovery to the smallest degree.

And, two days later, David had died. Justin felt his eyes fill with unmanly tears, as he recalled the last time he had seen Abigail O'Shea's betrothed. Aware that he was dying, his cheeks flushed with the fever that was consuming him, he had talked sadly of his love.

"I had such dreams, Justin—such splendid plans. Once I had wed Abigail, I had made up my mind to quit the navy and become a settler. We were to have made our home on the Tempest grant, with Rick Tempest's full approval, and farmed it for our mutual benefit—Rick's and little Lucy's as well as Abby's and mine. And I would have been a father to that poor little deaf and dumb boy of hers, I'd promised her I would, for she holds him very dear. But now . . ."

David Fortescue had faced death bravely, sustained by his faith and his prayers; he had not railed at his fate. He had known what was to come, but not for an instant had he flinched from it.

"Go to her, Justin," he had begged, as his strength and his voice slowly weakened. "Go to my sweet Abigail and tell her that her name was on my lips to the last. And . . . if she will have you in my place, it would be with my blessing, for I know that you care for her almost as deeply as I do."

He had not asked how his friend had known this, Justin recalled; perhaps he had revealed his feelings inadvertently, or perhaps it was given to the dying to see all things with a clarity the living did not possess. But . . . again he had given his promise, and now, God willing, he must endeavor to keep it. He smothered a sigh and strode on, deaf to the sounds about him and indifferent to those who passed him by, save when a boat put off from the King's ship *Hindostan* and, seeing the side manned, he recognized Commodore Bligh in the sternsheets and Rick Tempest as the boat commander.

He reached the town house of Mr. Jasper Spence ten minutes later and waited for a further ten minutes at the gate, in the hope that Rick might be coming ashore to call on his sisters. But there was no sign of him, and unable to put off his call any longer lest he should be tempted not to make it at all, Justin braced himself and, marching purposefully up to the ornate front door, rang an echoing summons on the bell.

A maid answered it, and on his requesting that Mrs. O'Shea should receive him, he was shown into a small, book-lined room and invited to make himself at home.

"They've been out in the carriage, Mistress O'Shea and Mistress Dawson, and they're not long back," the girl volunteered, eyeing him curiously. "Who shall I say is calling?"

Justin gave her his name, and cap held nervously in his two hands, he seated himself on a gilded chair that looked too frail to hold his weight and, feeling more ill at ease than ever, began again to rehearse what he should say to Abigail O'Shea.

"I regret exceedingly that I am the bearer of bad news, Miss Abigail . . ." No, she was Mrs. O'Shea and he must lead up more carefully to the tidings he had brought, lest he shock her too much. And, of course—whatever David Fortescue had divined concerning his own feelings for the beautiful girl who now owned Yarramundie—he could say nothing of them now. It would be premature and tactless in the extreme; besides, when he had attempted to do so, on the last occasion that he had called on her here, she had rebuffed him, and . . .

The door opened and he jumped to his feet, dropping his cap in his haste, his hands damp with perspiration. "Miss Abigail, I . . ." But it was not, he saw when he turned, Abigail O'Shea. Instead, a slender, dark-haired girl of about seventeen or eighteen confronted him, eyeing him with the same curiosity that the maid had displayed, an amused, faintly mocking smile curving her lips.

Justin stared at her for a moment without recognition, and then, astonished by the change in her, he realized that this was Abigail's sister, Lucy Tempest . . . a child, a schoolgirl, grown almost overnight to womanhood, and very conscious of her own charms.

Sensing that he had recognized her, Lucy smiled more brightly. "Why, good afternoon, Justin—or should I address you as Captain Broome? You are master of Mr. Lord's ship the *Dolphin* now, are you not?"

"I was, Miss Lucy," Justin acknowledged.

"And you brought her back, after she had been stolen?" Lucy suggested. "Oh, don't look so surprised—word is out, all over town, concerning your exploits. You will be the hero of the hour!" Her laugh was infectious, for all its underlying mockery, and she held out both hands to him, offering congratulations. "Tell me—you have come from Van Diemen's Land, from Hobart Town, have you not?"

"Aye, I have. But—"

She cut him short. "Did you bring my sister's affianced husband with you? Truth to tell, it was he I was expecting to see, when Mary Ryan informed us that there was a caller waiting in the study. She is a feckless girl and had already forgotten the name she was supposed to announce—she just told Abby that it was a seafaring gentleman, who was asking to see her. And since poor Lieutenant Fortescue was stranded in Hobart after the *Porpoise* sailed without him, we both thought that he might have taken passage with you."

"N-no," Justin stammered. "No, Miss Lucy. That is, he

. . ." Scarlet with embarrassment, he bit back the words he had been about to say. It was to Abigail that he must say them, not to her sister, who might repeat them in such a manner as to give offense, or even—his eyes narrowed, as he studied Lucy Tempest's pert and provocatively upturned face—even with the deliberate intention of wounding. He drew back, shaking his head. "I have to see Miss Abigail—Mrs. O'Shea, I mean. My news is for her."

Lucy was unabashed. "Oh, then you *do* have news of Abby's errant lover, Mr. Broome?"

"I . . . yes, I have news. But—"

"But he is not yet back in Sydney?"

Justin was compelled to concede that this was so. Lucy clasped her hands together in simulated dismay. "Oh, dear, poor Abby will be upset! She is changing, ready to receive him and convinced that he is here at last. I had better tell her, had I not, that *you* are her caller and she need not raise her hopes?"

Her malice was so evident that Justin rounded on her indignantly, but before he could give voice to his anger, she had gone, skipping gracefully away from him and only half-closing the door behind her. Justin heard her calling upstairs to her sister and caught the words, "It's only Justin Broome, Abby, but he has news," and then, before he could properly recover his composure, Abigail came into the room.

She looked downcast, but she greeted him pleasantly, as she always had—and without the hint of condescension he remembered from their last meeting—and asked expectantly, "Lucy says that you have news of Lieutenant Fortescue—is that so? I received a letter from him, a few weeks ago, and I . . . that is, I had hoped he might have come back with you, Justin. Is he still held in arrest in Hobart?"

All Justin's carefully rehearsed words went out of his head. He began carefully enough, with the preamble he had planned, but she saw through the empty phrases and cut in quickly, "Oh, Justin—is he ill? Is that what you are trying to tell me? Is that why he hasn't come back?" Her eyes searched his face, and reading the truth in it, she whispered brokenly, "Oh surely—he can't be *dead*?"

He told her then, as gently as he could, and she listened, white-faced and silent, her hands clasped tightly in front of her and the tears running unrestrained down her cheeks. She asked no questions until he came to the end of his recital, but after a lengthy silence when, Justin sensed, she was fighting to control her emotions, she questioned quietly, "Were you with David at the—at the end?"

"Yes, for as long as he was conscious I was with him."

"And he—he spoke of me?"

"He spoke of no one else, Miss Abigail." Reminded of the bequests David Fortescue had entrusted to him, Justin added, "He left you all his possessions. Most of them are still on board the *Porpoise*, but I have his sword and his Bible and a letter he dictated to me, setting out what he wanted you to have. I . . . that is, with your consent, I thought I would collect his sea chest from the *Porpoise* and deliver everything to you here tomorrow."

Abigail thanked him abstractedly. "What of his funeral, Justin—his grave?"

"He was buried in the military cemetery in Hobart," Justin told her. "And we arranged for a headstone to mark his grave." Not for Lieutenant David Fortescue the elaborate military pomp that had marked the late Governor's interment, however, he recalled with bitterness, with the flags at half-mast and the whole of Hobart Town in mourning. Edward Lord, the commandant of marines and for years Colonel Collins's friend and deputy, had organized a truly impressive ceremony for his old chief's passing, but when it was over, he had displayed scant concern for that of the *Porpoise*'s abandoned lieutenant, whom, it seemed, he still regarded as one of Commodore Bligh's officers and therefore an enemy.

David Fortescue had gone to his grave attended by the crew of his longboat and Ensign Finch and his five marines, with the surprise addition of the late Colonel Collins's son, who had, for a short time, served as a midshipman on board the *Porpoise*. . . . Justin bit back a sigh. It would be best, he decided, to tell Abigail nothing of this; they had paid her affianced husband the requisite military honors.

The marines had carried his coffin, draped with the Union flag; his boat's crew had stood, with heads bowed in grief; and volleys had been fired over the grave as the coffin was lowered into its last resting place.

Abigail inclined her head, seemingly satisfied by the account he gave her of the ceremony.

"What of the man who shot—who *murdered* him?" she asked.

"He was killed when we cut out the *Dolphin*."

"And the others—your crew. What of them?"

"I brought them back," Justin said flatly. "There is no authority for a trial on capital charges in Hobart, Miss Abigail. They will be put on trial here, with the necessary witnesses—David's seamen and the marines we took with us—to substantiate the charges. There's no doubt they will be convicted. They murdered my bo'sun, who was a good man, before they seized the ship."

"You are fortunate that you escaped with your life," Abigail said. Her voice was flat, devoid of feeling, but Justin reddened, sensing her condemnation of him.

"Go to her," David Forestcue had urged him. *"Go to my sweet Abigail, and if she will have you in my place, it would be with my blessing. . . ."* But she would not have him now, if he were the last man left alive on earth, he told himself. It had been his ship that had been seized, his crew that had committed murder—and the *Dolphin* had been recovered at the cost of David Fortescue's life. So far as Abigail O'Shea was concerned, that had been too high a price to pay.

He bent to pick up his cap, which had unaccountably slipped from his grasp, and said wretchedly, "Miss Abigail, it breaks my heart to be the bearer of such tragic tidings as these. I know how you must feel, and I—"

"Do you?" she challenged, a catch in her voice. "How can you know how I feel?"

Justin let the challenge pass. His had been a thoughtless remark, and he cursed himself silently for having made it. "I beg you to believe that I would gladly have died if, by doing so, I could have spared you David's loss and preserved his life. He was a fine gentleman, Miss Abigail, and a most courageous one. I . . . Forgive me. Perhaps I should take my leave. You will want to be alone."

Abigail inclined her head in constrained silence, and he stumped awkwardly to the door, aware that once again he had been clumsy. He had failed to convey to her the deep feeling he had for David Fortescue or the grief that still tormented him on that account.

Lucy Tempest was waiting for him in the hall. He would have avoided her, had this been possible, but she put out a hand to detain him.

"I heard," she confided, in a tense whisper. "I heard all you told poor Abby, and I am truly sorry. I hope you did not misunderstand my—oh, my jesting, but I had no idea that David Fortescue was dead."

"I did not misunderstand you," Justin returned stiffly.

"Oh, I expect you did—most people do, and they imagine I'm jealous of Abby. I'm not, I—it's just that she plays the elder sister and tries constantly to make me behave in accordance with her somewhat restrictive ideas. I'm very fond of her, if the truth were known, Justin."

Justin freed his arm from her grasp. He said, with intentional brusqueness, "*If* you are fond of her, then I would venture to suggest that you endeavor to comfort her. She is deeply distressed by the news I had to bring her, and since you were listening, you know what it was."

"I'll fetch Mrs. Spence," Lucy said. "Abby won't listen to me, I fear." But she had the grace to look ashamed, and Justin left her with a curt nod and let himself out into the street.

Cookie Barnes was waiting for him when he returned to the *Dolphin* in a single-handed dinghy borrowed from Simeon Lord's yard. Spry as ever, for all his hospital pallor, the little man stood at the foot of the boat ladder and, as Justin disembarked, deftly secured the dinghy's painter and, grinning widely, held out his hand in friendly greeting.

"Yer old bad penny turnin' up again, Mr. Broome," he offered. "Heard you was back."

"It's good to see you, Cookie lad," Justin answered, with genuine warmth. He led the way to the deck, pleased to see that, in his absence, his scratch crew had not been idle. David Forestcue's seamen would have to be returned to the *Porpoise,* he knew, but until her captain sent for them, he was in no hurry to see them go—they were good men, and the schooner's deck was as spotless as that of any King's ship, thanks to their efforts, sheets neatly coiled and dingy sails drying in the light onshore breeze.

Cookie looked about him and nodded approvingly. "The word is that Mr. Lord's lettin' you keep her. I come to sign on if you'll 'ave me, Mr. Broome."

"I'd have you," Justin assured him, "if I were still master of the *Dolphin,* but I'm not."

"You mean the word was duff—you wasn't offered 'er?" Cookie looked crestfallen.

"I was and I refused," Justin answered shortly. He lowered his voice and, leaning over the taffrail, gave Cookie a brief account of the happenings which led to Tobias Cockrell's attempt to steal his command. "I did wonder why Mr. Lord kept him on as mate—Cockrell was a rogue, and Simeon Lord knew it only too well. But he was useful when there was any dirty job to be done, and there was an illicit cargo of rum stowed aboard the *Dolphin* before I took command of her." He shrugged. "This is strictly between you and me, Cookie, you understand?"

"I knows 'ow ter keep me mouth shut, Mr. Broome," Cookie asserted.

"Right, so long as you do, I'll tell you why I said no to Mr. Lord's offer. It's because I'm pretty sure he intends to use the *Dolphin* as a rum trafficker. And . . ." Justin smiled. "That last cargo never reached its destination—I found it, after Cockrell was killed, and I brought the whole lot back here. Lord's liable to be very put out when he finds it's still on board. Mind, I couldn't unload the stuff in Hobart because I'd no idea who it was consigned to— only Cockrell knew that, and he never told me."

"Well, then, Mr. Lord can't blame you, can he?" Cookie argued.

"No. But he won't be pleased, all the same."

"You could still take the command. She's a real fine ship, this 'un."

"I know she is," Justin agreed. "And I'd give a lot to keep her, Cookie, believe me."

"What's a little rum trafficking on the side?" Cookie looked up at him, puzzled. "They're all at it, even Mr. Campbell an 'is brother-in-law the Commissary—what's 'is name?—Palmer, or so I've heard tell often enough."

"You can't believe all you hear," Justin retorted. "And I don't believe *that*! No, Cookie . . . I've never traded in rum, and I don't intend to start now, even to get the *Dolphin*."

"What're you goin' ter do, then?" Cookie demanded, a trifle sullenly. "An' what about me, come ter that? We ain't got the *Flinders* now, 'ave we?"

"No," Justin conceded. "But I struck a bargain with Mr. Lord. I'm going to build another small trading vessel in his yard. She'll be a mite larger than the *Flinders*, with more cargo space . . ." He went into details, and Cookie Barnes listened skeptically.

"That'll take you months, Mr. Broome, an' I can't 'elp you. I'm a seaman, not a soddin' carpenter's mate."

"Mr. Lord would sign you on for this ship, if you wish," Justin suggested. "He's going to need a crew for her, and if you've no objection to rum trading, you could do worse."

"I got ter earn me livin', Mr. Broome," the little man defended.

"Yes, of course you have." Justin put an arm round the thin, bowed shoulders and smiled, his momentary animosity forgotten. Cookie had served him loyally and well, he told himself; he had no right to expect him to wait—or to work as a roustabout in the yard—until he had built the *Flinders*'s successor, a task that would, as Cookie had pointed out, take months. "I'll put in a word for you with Mr. Lord tomorrow."

"Thank yer kindly, Mr. Broome," Cookie acknowledged. "I'll come back," he added, "an' ask for me old berth, when you've got that new cutter o' yours built an' ready for sea . . . six months from now, eh?"

"Maybe less than that, if I can get a couple of skilled men to help me."

"Oh-ah . . . *if!* Skilled men are hard to come by in this town. Well . . ." Cookie touched his battered old seaman's cap. "I'll be off, then. Want me ter take that dinghy back to the yard for yer? I come out in a lighter, but it'll be a while before she's ready to pick me up—she's waterin' the *Porpoise*." Receiving a nod of assent, he grinned. "No errands you want runnin' on shore, are there? I've got time on me hands."

"No, I . . ." Justin hesitated. It might be best if he let Cookie deliver David Fortescue's effects, he thought, instead of calling again at the Spences' himself. Abigail would feel bound to receive him, and he was suddenly reluctant to intrude on her grief. "Yes, come to think of it, there's one. I've a sizable package for Mrs. O'Shea. She's staying at Mr. Jasper Spence's house in Mulgrave Street—d'you know it?"

"Yes, that I do. Big two-story house on the corner, ain't it, with a garden that's a picture? Owns the Indiaman *Kelso,* don't he, Mr. Spence?"

"That's right, he does," Justin confirmed. "I'll get the package, if you'll deliver it for me."

Cookie was waiting by the gangway when he returned. "Expectin' a visit from His Majesty's ship *Hindostan,* are yer, Mr. Broome? 'Cos 'er cap'n's gig seems ter be headin' this way—look!" The little man pointed excitedly to the approaching boat, manned by six seamen in striped jerseys and spotless white duck trousers, with two uniformed officers seated in the sternsheets. "Cor!" he exclaimed, shading his eyes with his hand. "Looks like 'er cap'n's comin' in person, don't it? Cap'n Pasco . . . 'im that was signal officer in Lord Nelson's *Victory* at Trafalgar, or so they say. Made that there signal 'England expects every man ter do 'is duty' or summat like that. Hell's teeth, Mr. Broome, what've you done to 'ave Cap'n Pasco call on you?"

"I don't know," Justin confessed. "Perhaps he's making for the *Porpoise,* Cookie. Or—"

"Nah, he ain't," Cookie asserted. "He's comin' here, to your *Dolphin*. I'd best make meself scarce. Take care o' yourself, Mr. Broome."

Grasping the heavy package firmly, he descended to the dinghy and had pulled away a few minutes before the *Hindostan*'s gig came alongside. David Fortescue's seamen had seen and recognized the frigate's commander and, with admirable presence of mind, formed themselves into a side party in readiness to receive him, the young boatswain's mate, Justin saw, with his silver call to his lips.

Captain Pasco smiled appreciatively as he stepped onto the *Dolphin*'s deck to the shrill twittering of the pipe. He said, fingers to the brim of his cocked hat, "You run your ship naval fashion, Mr. Broome. Admirable!"

"These are naval seamen, sir," Justin confessed. "And only lent to me for the passage from Hobart." He explained the circumstances, and Pasco nodded his understanding.

"I will inform Captain Porteous, and he can send a boat for them. But now, Mr. Broome, I'm anxious to have a word with you. Can we go below?"

"Certainly, sir." Still at a loss to understand the reason for his visit, Justin led the *Hindostan*'s commander to his cabin, relieved when his offer of hospitality was refused. Pasco was a tall, slim man of about thirty-six or seven, with a fine-boned face and a pair of alert blue eyes which, ranging about the shabbily furnished cabin, appeared to miss little.

"You're snug enough, are you not?" he observed. "May I be seated?"

"Of course, sir." Justin pulled out one of Captain Mason's armchairs but remained standing, until his guest said crisply, "Don't stand on ceremony, Mr. Broome. Take a seat yourself. I've a few questions I'd like to ask you. No——" He held up a hand, as Justin started to speak. "I'm not seeking an account of your last voyage. Ensign Finch has been on board my ship for most of the day, and he's given me all the information I need concerning that and, of course, poor young David Fortescue's death. From what Finch has told me, you would seem to have acquitted yourself pretty creditably. You displayed courage and resource-fulness—fine qualities in a young sea officer. And you are young, are you not?"

"I'm eighteen, sir," Justin supplied.

"And the *Dolphin* was your first command? Apart, that is to say, from the cutter you so unfortunately lost off the Heads on the day of our arrival?"

"Yes, sir."

"The loss was most unfortunate," Captain Pasco said. "But nevertheless, it brought you to the favorable notice of His Excellency the Governor, and he is disposed to assist you in any way he can to advance your career. That is to say, your career as a seagoing officer. I take it you wish to make a career at sea?"

"Oh, yes, sir," Justin assured him, without hesitation. He waited, sitting nervously on the edge of his chair, at a loss to understand what Captain Pasco's questions were leading up to and for what purpose he was asking them. But he answered readily enough when asked about his seagoing experience and saw the older man's brow lift when he mentioned his voyage under Matthew Flinders's command in the *Investigator*.

"Ah, I heard that you were a good navigator, and no wonder, with so able and distinguished a mentor. Did Captain Flinders instruct you in cartography also?" Justin inclined his head, and the *Hindostan*'s commander expelled his breath in a silent whistle. He asked a number of questions about the *Investigator*'s last voyage and the officers and men, as well as the scientists, who had served her, and then said, with a sudden change of tone, "Had you ever considered making a career in the Royal Navy?"

"I did consider it, sir. Captain Flinders offered to take me with him when he left Sydney. But I—that is, sir, my parents needed me, so I—"

"So you did not accept his offer?" Pasco put in. "A wise decision, as it turned out, was it not? Poor Flinders was held prisoner by the French in Port Louis, Ile de France, on his way home, I believe. But you know that, I imagine?"

"I heard of it, sir." Justin's throat tightened, as the memories came surging back. Matthew Flinders had taken the small, Norfolk Island–built sloop *Cumberland* for his voyage home, after he and most of the *Investigator*'s company had been wrecked on the Barrier Reef six—no, seven—years ago, and for a long time nothing had been heard of him. Then news had come that the Governor of the Ile de France, General Decaen, had seized him and impounded the *Cumberland* when he had called at Port Louis for supplies, supposing himself to be protected by the passport with which the French explorer, Captain Baudin, had provided him. Since then, there had been no word of his having been exchanged or released, and Captain Pasco confirmed this, in reply to Justin's diffident question.

"No, not as far as I'm aware. Representations were made, but the poor devil's still rotting on that godforsaken island, I fear. As you might also have been, had you gone with him . . . eh, Mr. Broome?" Pasco was eyeing him searchingly, and Justin reddened under his scrutiny. "What did Captain Flinders offer you, as a matter of interest?"

"A midshipman's berth aboard his next command and his patronage, sir. He was confident that he would be made post when he reached home."

"As undoubtedly he would have been, poor fellow. A fine man and a peerless navigator . . . to whom this colony owes much. It's a damnable pity. But to revert to the reason for my call on you—which, I admit, was made because I wanted to meet and judge you for myself. Suppose *I* were to make you the same offer—" Captain Pasco's blue eyes seemed to be boring into his, and Justin stared back at him in astonishment. "What would you say? A mid's berth in the *Hindostan* and my patronage, with the promise of a recommendation to Their Lordships to commission you, when you've sat and passed your examination in navigation and seamanship?"

"I have passed the examination, sir," Justin managed, containing his astonishment. "I sat before a board of captains in Hobart Town, sir." He supplied details, in response to Pasco's prompting, and again saw his brows lift.

"Well, damn my eyes! At the age of . . . what?"

"Fourteen, sir. I have a certificate signed by the captain of His Majesty's ship *Calcutta*. I'd thought of entering the masters' branch, like my father, sir."

"Your father was in the navy? Was he a master?"

Justin nodded proudly. "He was Captain Flinders's master in the *Investigator,* after Mr. Thistle was drowned in Spencer Gulf. And he was given command of the *Cumberland* when she was first built and then of the *Phillip*—she was built here, sir, and classed as a colonial sloop of forty tons burden. My father served in the navy, sir. Under Captain Pellow in the *Nymphe* frigate, and—"

"In her engagement with the Frenchman, off Start Point in ninety-three?" Captain Pasco asked, with rekindled interest.

"Yes, sir. But—" Honesty compelled the admission. "He was a convict when he first came out here, like my mother."

"But your mother is married to Captain Hawley, is she not? I thought His Excellency told me she was."

"Yes, sir." Justin's tone was guarded. "My father lost his life in the Hawkesbury floods four years ago."

"I see." There was a brief silence, and then Pasco rose to his feet. "My offer is made at the Governor's behest, Mr. Broome, and now I'm ready and willing to make it on my own account. Think it over—consult your mother and Captain Hawley before you decide. It's evident that your prospects here are good, and you may not want a career in His Majesty's Navy. But if you do, I'll be more than pleased to have you under my command in the *Hindostan* when we sail for England—which will probably be in a few weeks' time." He smiled and held out his hand. "Early in May, I anticipate, when Commodore Bligh is satisfied that he has all the evidence he will require to bring charges against the officers who deposed him."

Justin thanked him and, still feeling a trifle confused, accompanied him to the gangway. He had, he knew, been offered a splendid opportunity and one that, since Captain Flinders's departure, he had never dreamed would be repeated. The prospect of being commissioned in the Royal Navy was a dazzling one for a "currency kid" like himself, and . . . He drew in his breath sharply.

Abigail O'Shea could no longer look askance at him, if he returned to Sydney with the same rank and status as David Fortescue had enjoyed. He would have to consult his mother, of course, as Captain Pasco had advised, but once he had handed over the *Dolphin* and her cargo manifests to Simeon Lord, there would be nothing to hinder him from paying a visit—a long overdue visit—to Long Wrekin Farm.

Indeed, it would be good to see and talk to his mother again, and granted a modicum of luck, he would be able to catch Jed Burdock's *Fanny* before she sailed for the Hawkesbury.

Whistling cheerfully, Justin made for the after hatchway, pausing for a moment to look across at the *Hindostan* and seeing her suddenly with new eyes. She made a brave sight, he thought, with her distinctive figurehead and the black and yellow paintwork that was known now as the Nelson checker . . . a fine, fifty-gun King's ship, commanded by an officer who had served under the greatest of England's admirals at Trafalgar.

And in a few weeks, God willing, he himself would be one of her company. Still whistling, he went below to check the *Dolphin*'s cargo manifests.

CHAPTER X

Jenny Hawley stood at the open door of the Long Wrekin farmhouse and watched, with relief, as Commodore Bligh's coach and his mounted escort vanished behind a cloud of choking dust in the direction of the river.

For the past three days and nights, the deposed Governor had occupied the bedroom which normally she shared with Andrew. He had contracted a fever, as a result of having left the coach in order to ride the last twenty miles to the Green Hills, where he had called a public meeting, and pale and barely conscious, he had been brought to Long Wrekin to recover.

She and Nancy Jardine had done their skilled best to nurse him, but . . . Jenny sighed. The commodore had proved an irascible and most difficult patient, and even the good Dr. Arndell, hurriedly summoned from his property nearby, had been able to do little to calm him.

"Plague take it, I've urgent matters to attend to!" he had growled at them. "That unmitigated blackguard Macarthur stole the papers I need as evidence against him, and those he did not carry off to England with him, Johnston contrived to destroy. My files, my letter books, copies of my instructions from the Colonial Office were all burnt by those villains, damn their souls to perdition! I need affidavits from the loyal settlers—that's why I'm here. I *must* go to the Green Hills without delay—the meeting must be reconvened."

It had been reconvened, of course, Jenny thought; the deposed Governor had no more loyal supporters than the Hawkesbury settlers, and they would all be there when he reached the Green Hills this evening. Andrew, pressed once again into his patron's service, had ridden ahead, with Justin, to ensure that they were. And Commodore Bligh had hobbled out to his coach, his stocky, now increasingly corpulent body bent double and his legs still painfully swollen, with a belated word of thanks to herself and Nancy but nothing but abuse for poor Thomas Arndell, on whose frail arm he leaned.

From behind her, Nancy Jardine said, as if reading her thoughts, "Well, that's one visitor I'll be in no hurry to see again—such a temper, an' such language!"

"His Excellency has had much to provoke him, Nan," Jenny felt bound to offer.

"Oh, aye, I know that—he talked o' little else," the foreman's wife returned tartly. "An' like most folks here, I want to see them rebel Rum Corps officers get their just deserts . . . an' Mr. Macarthur with 'em. But you ain't any too well yourself, are you, Mrs. Hawley? And he'd no consideration—ran you nigh off your feet, he did, with his 'Fetch me this' and 'Bring me the other' an' hardly a word o' thanks."

It was true, Jenny was compelled to concede. The ribs she had fractured when she had fallen from Sirius had been slow to heal, and she still experienced considerable pain as a result of the injury. But it was healing and . . . She smiled, recalling Dr. Arndell's well-intentioned advice to rest as much as she could and not to venture out on horseback, save as a matter of inescapable urgency. There were always matters of urgency to be dealt with on the farm, and with Andrew absent on military duty in Sydney for most of the time, only she and Tom and William were available to deal with them. And William, she knew, ought by rights to be at school with Rachel. . . .

"I've made a cup o' tea," Nan Jardine told her. "Why don't you come in an' sit down for a while? There's that parcel Mrs. Spence sent, with the dress an' all them fripperies—you've not hardly looked at 'em, have you?"

She had not, Jenny thought, her conscience reproaching her, as she followed Nan into the house. Frances Spence had made the dress for her, of exquisite Chinese silk, and what her foreman's wife was pleased to call "them fripperies" included a pair of elbow-length white gloves, stockings, a cashmere shawl, and Indian-made lizardskin shoes.

Frances's letter, delivered with the parcel, had come with Justin on board the *Fanny*, and it explained the reason for the lovingly assembled gifts. While Nan went to fetch the tea tray, Jenny took out the letter and, seated in an armchair, reread it.

There is to be a ball at Government House to bid our late Governor farewell. No one as yet knows when it will be, since Commodore Bligh has not yet intimated the precise date of his departure. But Mrs. Macquarie has already begun to make preparations for it, and on an unprecedented scale.

You and Andrew will certainly receive an invitation to attend, and needless to tell you, dear Jenny, Jasper and I will be delighted to offer you accommodation.

Living out on the Hawkesbury as you do, I anticipate that you will say that your wardrobe is deficient and contains no ball gown, so—to ensure your acceptance of Their Excellencies' invitation—I am taking steps to repair that deficiency.

It is many years since I first played the seamstress and fashioned Justin's first long trousers, but I hope that I have not lost my skill entirely, and that this dress may fit as well and give you as much pleasure as did Justin's nether garments, all those years ago.

Jenny sighed ruefully. The dress delighted her, but she had lost weight during the past year or so, and it would have to be taken in, while the gloves unfortunately were

too small for her rough, work-hardened hands, and the
shoes fitted Rachel better than they fitted her. But it had
been a kindly thought on Frances Spence's part, and she
was both touched and grateful.

She read on:

> Henrietta has at last prevailed on Timothy to buy
> her a house in town. They have found a suitable estab-
> lishment in Pitt Street, next door to Captain Hous-
> ton's, and Henrietta and the children will shortly re-
> move there.
>
> Abigail talks of returning to Yarramundie with little
> Dickon and the faithful Kate. Poor child, she is heart-
> broken by the tragic death of Lieutenant Fortescue, as
> no doubt Justin will have told you. Lucy is very loath
> to go with her—she is having too good a time here—
> but, even if she decides to remain, I shall have ample
> room for you and Andrew.
>
> Please come. I yearn to see and talk to you again,
> and it is so long since I last enjoyed the pleasure of
> your company. Make it a long visit, if you can. This
> would not only please me—it would give Timothy the
> opportunity, which I know he wants, to endeavor to
> persuade you to sell Long Wrekin to him. . . .

Jenny let the letter fall, frowning as the import of the
last words sank in. Tim Dawson had long wanted her land;
he would, she knew, husband it a great deal more efficiently than she could. He was a rich man; he could afford
to employ more labor, to stock it as it should be stocked,
and he had promised, when he had first sought to buy the
property, that he would continue to employ Tom Jardine as
foreman. Latterly, Andrew had urged her to reconsider the
offer he had made, and . . . She stirred restlessly in her
chair. Andrew had set his heart on accepting a transfer to
the veteran company of the 73rd, now in the process of
formation, and if he were to do so, he would have little
time to spend on farm work and would, in any case, have
to accept whatever posting he was given. And that might
just as easily be to Coal River or Parramatta as to Sydney

or even the Green Hills, and since she was his wife, he had a right to expect her to accompany him. With Justin going to England and William's education sadly neglected, selling Long Wrekin was clearly what she ought to do, but . . .

Nancy Jardine came bustling in from the kitchen with a laden tray, which she set down with a cheerful clatter at Jenny's side.

"There," she exclaimed approvingly. "I'm right glad to see you sitting down, Mrs. Hawley. 'Tis high time you took things a mite easier—we'm none o' us gettin' any younger, an' Dr. Arndell did tell you you was to rest, didn't he?"

Jenny did not answer her. She poured tea for them both and waved Nan to the chair opposite her own. "Did Tom tell you what time he expected to be back?" she asked, thinking of the evening chores, the brood mares to be watered and fed, and the house cows milked. There was a sow due to farrow, and the usual hunt for eggs from the free-ranging hens. . . . She suddenly felt very tired, and it was with relief that she heard Nan say, "Tom didn't go to the settlers' meetin'."

"He did not go? But I thought—"

"I told him he was needed here," Nan said, with a tight smile. "All they do at them meetings is talk, an' there'll be more'n enough o' them to do that, without Tom addin' his piece." She thrust a plate in Jenny's direction and added pointedly, "That's fresh baked bread, Mrs. Hawley, spread with apple jelly. I baked while you was runnin' round after His Excellency Governor Bligh first thing. An' I fetched in the eggs when you was helpin' him into his carriage."

And Tom would do the milking, Jenny thought, and attend to the sow if it were needed; William would water the brood mares, as soon as he returned from the far paddock with Nanbaree. . . . She echoed Nan's smile and accepted a slice of the newly baked bread, a pleasant sensation of lassitude creeping over her.

"So you haven't nothin' to do, 'cept drink your tea an' maybe do a bit o' stitching on that dress," the foreman's wife finished triumphantly. "An' I can help you with that. 'Tis a rare handsome dress, Mrs. Hawley."

"Yes," Jenny agreed. "It is, Nan. A beautiful dress."

"You'm goin' to wear it at the Governor's ball, ain't you?"

"I . . . well, yes, I suppose so. If I *am* invited." It was a far cry from the days when she had been a convict, Jenny reflected, when the only time she had entered Government House had been . . . oh, goodness, over twenty years ago, after a night of punishment spent on Pinchgut Island. Governor Phillip had lectured her severely concerning her conduct on that occasion and had advised her to marry a good steady man.

"A convict, Your Excellency?" she had asked with bitterness, hating him, in that moment, because it had been he who had ordered Andrew back to England to prevent their marriage. And the Governor, blind to her resentment and, no doubt, forgetful of its cause, Governor *Phillip* had inclined his bewigged head in assent and told her icily that she should choose a convict with only a short sentence to run.

"Then I could make a grant of land to both of you," he had said. "And if your conduct merited my favorable consideration, you could both gain remission and become free settlers. That would be a goal to work for, would it not?"

Well, she had worked for and achieved that goal, Jenny told herself; she had remembered it, as she had remembered Governor Phillip's advice and his prophetic promises for the future prosperity of the harsh, inhospitable land of her exile: *"Here are fertile plains, needing only the labors of the husbandman to produce in abundance the fairest and richest fruits. Here are interminable pastures, the future home of flocks and herds innumerable. . . ."*

As yet the fertile plains and the interminable pastures had not materialized—perhaps they lay on the other side of the hitherto impassable barrier of the Blue Mountains—but she had her land, she was a free settler, and the new Governor was about to invite her to a ball at Government House.

Feeling her eyes fill with tears, Jenny picked up her cup and hurriedly drained it. Nancy Jardine, seemingly noticing nothing amiss, said confidently, "Oh, you'll be invited sure enough, Mrs. Hawley, so we'd best get to work takin' in that there dress. And Tom can stretch the shoes. You'd not want to miss a grand occasion like that, would you now? 'Specially with Justin sailin' in a King's ship an' like to become an officer in the Royal Navy . . . sailin' to England, too! You've a right to be proud of him."

And she had, Jenny knew. Not that Justin had not deserved it. . . . Once again her throat tightened and tears burned in her eyes. Justin's unexpected arrival with his momentous news had filled her heart with pride, and she had hastened to assure him that there was nothing, on her account, to stand in his way. Captain Pasco's offer was one he must not even think of refusing—both she and Andrew had told him so, half a hundred times, and even the irascible Commodore Bligh, when he had learned of it, had ceased complaining of the pain of his swollen legs for long enough, at least, to echo their words. To Justin he had said, without condescension, "You may count on my patronage, Mr. Broome. If you can prove you've the right stuff in you, I shall do all in my power to assist you in your career."

Nancy Jardine reached for the teapot and refilled both their cups. "I can't say, though," she qualified bluntly, "I can't honestly say as I envy the lad havin' to serve under the likes o' Commodore Bligh. If the way His Excellency conducted hisself here is awt to go by, poor young Justin won't have no easy passage."

Jenny started to observe that the late Governor had had much to provoke him, and then, realizing that she had said the same thing earlier, she broke off with a wry smile.

"I don't doubt Justin will hold his own, Nan. He always has, since he was a little boy. And he's never wanted to do anything but go to sea."

"Like his pa," Nan stated shrewdly. "Not cut out for farmin' neither, was he?"

"No," Jenny acknowledged. She had a fleeting mental vision of Johnny Broome's tanned, smiling face and blue seaman's eyes, and felt her heart contract. Johnny—with the lash marks burned indelibly into the flesh of his back and the scars left by his convict fetters on wrists and ankles—Johnny had found his freedom at sea. He, too, would have been proud of his son. . . .

"Young William, though," Nan said, her plump, honest face suddenly wreathed in smiles, "he's born to it, Mrs. Hawley. I think you'll be makin' a mistake if'n you make him go back to school. His heart's here and he'll just fret if he's sent away for another year."

"He's only ten," Jenny reminded her.

"Aye, I know that. But I . . ." Nan hesitated, her expression suddenly serious and concerned. "Mrs. Hawley, Tom says you're thinkin' o' sellin' this land to Mr. Dawson. He says you told him so, not long since."

"Yes," Jenny confessed. "I did think about it—I'm still thinking about it, Nan. You and Tom would be all right, of course. Mr. Dawson would keep you on and pay you better than I can, I imagine." She went carefully into the whys and wherefores, and Nan listened in stolid silence, offering no comment until she had done. Then the foreman's wife said quietly, "I'd be saddened if I'd to see you go, an' I'll not pretend otherwise. But for *your* sake—yours and Captain Hawley's—it might be for the best. The work's too much for you, Mrs. Hawley, an' that's a God's fact."

"It's only since my accident, Nan," Jenny protested.

"Aye, that's true," Nan conceded. "But it weren't only them broken ribs—'twas losin' that stallion you put such store by. I got eyes in my head and I've seen. Losin' Sirius has taken the heart out o' you, hasn't it?"

Perhaps it had, Jenny reflected sadly. Sirius had been the key to her breeding plans, apart from the love and pride she had felt for the fine young animal. She had suffered losses before, of course, many of them more costly, but . . . Nan was right in one respect. The loss of Sirius had touched her heart.

"Seein' as Captain Hawley's wantin' to get back to his soldiering," Nan went on gravely, "an' with the new Governor makin' it plain that bein' an emancipist don't make decent folk into outcasts, you could go to Sydney, Mrs. Hawley. You could live like gentry, you an' him, 'stead o' slavin' away out here. You could have a real fine house, with servants to wait on you, an' go to dinner at Government House with the other officers' ladies."

In fact, she could become respectable, Jenny thought, following Nan's last suggestion to its logical conclusion. Her lips twitched into a grim smile as she pictured Henrietta Dawson's inevitable reaction, should they chance to come face to face with each other at the Governor's dinner table. Henrietta bitterly resented her stepmother, and Frances Spence had been gently born, whereas she herself . . . Her smile widened involuntarily. An upbringing in a poor cottage on a nobleman's estate in Yorkshire and a childhood spent at the Three Fools tavern in London—in the company of highway robbers and suchlike rogues—could scarcely qualify her for respectability, and yet . . . Nan saw her smile and put out a hand to take hers.

"If you're frettin' about William, Mrs. Hawley," she said, misreading Jenny's thoughts, "he can stay here along o' Tom an' me. You can trust us to care for the lad as if he were our own."

Jenny returned her handclasp warmly. "I know I can," she answered. "Thank you, Nan. I'm truly grateful, and . . . I *will* think about selling to Mr. Dawson. Perhaps the time has come for me to do so."

"That it has," Nan asserted. She started to pile up the crockery on her tray. "I'll just get this put away, an' then I'll be back to help you take in that dress for the Governor's ball."

She whisked away to the kitchen. When she returned to the living room, Jenny had donned the dress, holding the loose, shimmering silk folds about her, and Nan halted in the doorway, suddenly awed.

"Why, Mrs. Hawley!" she exclaimed. "You look beautiful, my oath you do! There'll not be anyone to hold a candle to you—not even the Governor's lady herself!"

Surprised but gratified, Jenny turned toward the doorway and saw that her son William was standing behind Nan's ample back. The expression on the boy's dust-grimed face was one of stupefaction, and his astonished, "Mam, I never knew you were a lady!" brought Jenny to her knees beside him, uncertain whether to laugh or cry.

"I'm just your mother, Willie," she managed. "But maybe I will play the lady for a little while."

* * *

Seated at his desk in the small rented house on the corner of Bridge and Pitt Streets, Commodore Bligh studied the documents he had brought back with him from the settlers' meeting at the Green Hills.

Admittedly the attendance had been small, due to his unfortunate indisposition and the fact that the meeting had had to be postponed, but that most loyal of his supporters, George Suttor, had organized an address of congratulation on the honorable termination of his "confinement and persecution," to which over four hundred signatures had been subscribed.

A similar meeting, held in Sydney and with the newly restored provost marshal, William Gore, in the chair, had yielded a less desirable result. Gore had done his valiant best, but strongly opposed by a hard core of Macarthur's supporters—including Simeon Lord, D'Arcy Wentworth, and John Blaxland—the resolutions condemning Colonel George Johnston's conduct had been carried by a very small majority.

Nevertheless, they had been carried, and a public statement, in the form of an address, had been presented to him. The signatories, having expressed their rejoicing in his reinstatement to viceregal office and the vindication of his character and conduct, went on to condemn Johnston's claim, in his initial dispatch to the Colonial Secretary, Lord Castlereagh, that he had "seized and imprisoned the colony's lawful Governor" in order to prevent his being massacred by the inflamed populace of Sydney. The deposed Governor frowned as he read:

> We jointly and severally disavow this false, illiberal, and treacherous charge, by which Colonel Johnston endeavored to stab our reputation in the dark and to transfer his own guilt, and that of his associate, John Macarthur, upon us.

His eyes moved down the page, to reread again the last sentence:

". . . this grateful tribute from persons who have been witnesses of Your Excellency's meritorious administration, will descend with the name of Bligh to posterity, as a token of the veneration and esteem in which we have ever held your character . . ."

Posterity, William Bligh thought grimly, could make of these words what it wanted. What now concerned him was whether they would suffice to see George Johnston condemned as a traitor and hanged. The trial of the archfiend Macarthur would, according to the new judge advocate, Ellis Bent, have to take place in the colony, but if Johnston were found guilty of treason at his court-martial, then undoubtedly no other verdict could be returned against Macarthur in Sydney. He must either remain in England as a fugitive from justice or take ship back to New South Wales and face the accusations made against him here. Whichever choice he elected to make, he would—a pox on him—be compelled to suffer for his crimes.

Bligh's firm mouth compressed into a tight, hard line as he folded the address carefully and placed it in his bulging file. There were the affidavits he had sought from the Hawkesbury settlers, signed and sealed; statements, duly witnessed, from a number of Sydney's most respectable citizens—merchants, as well as officials. And . . . He picked up the list he had compiled. Nine of the most loyal and reliable would accompany him to England on board the *Hindostan*. Commissary Palmer; Robert Campbell; William Gore; the Reverend Henry Fulton; Deputy Commissary Williamson; the two settlers, Sutter and Mason; Parramatta's chief constable, Oakes—who had arrested John Macarthur, prior to his trial three years before—and Superintendent of Convicts Devine. Richard Atkins and Lawyer Crossley would also sail, although Atkins, the former judge advocate, had given Foveaux's rebel administration his treacherous, turncoat support.

Joseph Foveaux himself, praise be to heaven, had left the colony six weeks ago, in the brig *Experiment*, hell-bent, William Bligh did not doubt, on influencing public opinion against him in England as, unprincipled blackguard that he was, the Rum Corps's late commander had endeavored to do here. That he had succeeded where Colonel Lachlan Macquarie was concerned had, of late, become increasingly evident. Macquarie was aloof, unhelpful, and at times barely civil to him . . . due almost entirely, Bligh was convinced, to the false impression Foveaux had gone to such pains to create, and to the malicious and unsubstantiated accusations he had poured into the new Governor's unsuspecting ear.

It was even said that Macquarie had wanted to retain his services—that he had offered Foveaux command of the new veterans' company or, alternatively, the lieutenant governorship of Van Diemen's Land, following Colonel Collins's sudden death. But Foveaux had elected to go home and . . . Bligh scowled down at the papers scattered about his desk. There could be only one reason for that decision—the scoundrel intended to oppose him, when Johnston was brought to trial. More with a view to his own advancement than to Johnston's salvation, in all probability . . . Joseph Foveaux was an opportunist, without scruples or loyalty, and he had influence in high places. They all had, the devil take them! Johnston through the Duke of Northumberland, Macarthur through Lord Camden and the infernal Board of Trade—which wanted his wool. Whereas he himself might only be able to count on Sir Joseph Banks . . . Bligh's scowl deepened. Banks's power was considerable; he was widely regarded as the foremost authority on the colony of New South Wales, and he had never wavered in his support. Indeed, if his beloved wife, Betsy, were to be believed, Sir Joseph had intervened most actively on his behalf, with the Prime Minister as well as the Colonial Secretary. He—

There was a soft tap on the door, and William Bligh's expression relaxed as he recognized the author of it.

What, he asked himself, would he have done without the loyalty and companionship of his daughter Mary during the past few troubled years? Mary, bless her warm heart, had never failed to hearten and console him. Griefstricken by the tragic death of her husband, poor Charles Putland, three years before, she had yet found the moral—yes, and the physical—courage to battle in his defense, and without complaint she had shared his incarceration after the Rum Corps rebellion and his exile in Van Diemen's Land.

"Dearest child!" William Bligh accepted her dutiful kiss and smiled up at her, thrusting the jumble of papers to one side, so as to make room for her to perch on the side of his desk. "All this will soon be over, thank God! I went on board the *Hindostan* this afternoon, and John Pasco showed me the preparations for your accommodation, which are almost complete. You will be on the same flat as his wife, Rebecca, and I've no doubt that you will find Pasco's officers more congenial company than Porteous's wretches."

"Yes, Papa, but I—"

He did not let her finish. "As soon as repairs to the *Dromedary* are complete, we can sail—we can leave this miserable place behind us, Mary! And I am confident that once Colonel Johnston's court-martial is over and I am wholly and publicly vindicated, Their Lordships will see to it that I am given my flag. Your dear mama shall have her house in Southampton or, if she prefers it, one in London—in Lambeth, perhaps, which she has always fancied. On a rear admiral's pay, I shall be well able to afford it."

Mary again attempted to interrupt him, the color draining from her lovely, oval face, but her father talked on, seemingly oblivious to her agitation and her pallor.

"I am due for promotion, you know," he observed. "Damme, I have held post rank for over twenty years! John Pasco, although he's in command of the *Hindostan*, has not yet been given his step, which he should have had after Trafalgar. That was the most damnable injustice, Mary—he was only telling me of the circumstances this afternoon. The late lamented Lord Nelson had a strange quirk. When his ship went into battle, he made the officer first on his list for promotion do duty as signal officer, and the junior that of first lieutenant. Poor Pasco, although he was senior of the *Victory* in the action, was given only a commander's commission . . . the sixth lieutenant, a boy named Quilliam, was advanced to post rank! And Pasco was severely wounded at Trafalgar, too—so severely that he was awarded a wound pension of two hundred and fifty pounds."

"Papa, please—I beg you to listen, to give me your attention." Mary's voice was strained and high-pitched, and at last her father broke off to eye her with concern.

"My beloved girl—are you ill? You are as white as a ghost. It is this infernal climate." Bligh reached for her hand and patted it gently. "A few weeks at sea, my dear, and you will be fully restored to your normal health and good spirits."

Mary shook her head and he saw, with alarm, that she was weeping. "Mary, what is the matter? Have I upset you?"

"No, dearest Papa." She repeated her headshake. "I . . . oh, God help me, I cannot! Please, Papa, Colonel O'Connell is waiting to see you. He will tell you, if you will receive him."

"Receive him? Of course I will receive him, Mary, and gladly—although I confess I am mystified. Are you sure that you are not ill?"

"Quite sure," Mary managed. She almost ran from the room, and a few minutes later, the 73rd's tall, good-looking commanding officer presented himself.

"Colonel O'Connell!" Bligh greeted him affably and without suspicion. They were near neighbors, and indeed, the deposed Governor reminded himself, socially he and Mary had seen considerably more of Maurice O'Connell than they had of the Macquaries. He had wined and dined them with lavish hospitality and, during his own recent absence at the Hawkesbury settlements, had squired Mary to a number of functions which, it seemed, she had enjoyed.

But, despite these favorable reflections, William Bligh was taken aback when, asked the reason for his visit, Colonel O'Connell answered without preamble, "I am come to request your daughter's hand in marriage, sir."

"Marriage? God in heaven, man, what are you saying? Mrs. Putland—Mary—is returning with me to England. Damme, her cabin's prepared!" Bligh's temper, never easily controlled, erupted in a succession of bitter oaths, but Maurice O'Connell held his ground, waiting for it to subside. "My daughter told me nothing of this . . . a plague on it, this sudden notion!"

"It is not sudden, Commodore Bligh," O'Connell assured him earnestly. "I have had a high regard for Mrs. Putland from the moment I had the honor to make her acquaintance. And, sir, I am the most fortunate of men, since she has told me that she reciprocates my feelings."

"She told you that, eh?" Slowly Bligh's fury ebbed, leaving him stricken with despair. It had never occurred to him that Mary—his loyal, devoted Mary, on whom he had always depended—might desert him, and his sense of loss was such that he could not bring himself even to look at the man who, it seemed, had stolen her from him. God help him, what would Betsy say, how would *she* feel if he returned to England without their daughter? "My daughter said nothing to me, Colonel O'Connell," he repeated bitterly.

"She felt it more fitting that I should do so, sir. I think—" O'Connell took pity on him. "Indeed, I know, sir, that she could not bring herself to hurt you, as she is aware that it must. But I love her truly, and it is my most heartfelt desire to make her my wife. I—my prospects are good, sir. I am, as you are no doubt cognizant, appointed Lieutenant Governor of this colony, and I have been advanced to the rank of full colonel, whilst I command His Majesty's Seventy-third Regiment. I am heir to a baronetcy, and—"

William Bligh, recovering his control, cut him short. "Yes, yes, I know all that. But before I can give my approval to the match, I must hear from my daughter's own lips that . . ." He had been about to say "that she intends to desert me," but quickly changed this to a more tactful "that it is her considered wish that I should do so."

"I will summon her, sir," Maurice O'Connell offered,

248   WILLIAM STUART LONG

with a complacency that rekindled her father's ire. "She
will, I assure you, bear me out."

He went to the door, and Mary, with suspicious alacrity,
came to join him. Her hand grasping his, she met her father's reproachful gaze with a warm and happy smile.

"Maurice has told you? Oh, please, dearest Papa, I beg
you to give us your blessing. The thought of parting from
you grieves me more than I can find words to express, but
I . . . Papa, Maurice and I are in such joyful accord.
Truly it is my considered and heartfelt wish that you
should give your consent to our marriage."

Standing there beside her handsome soldier, she looked
so radiant that William Bligh knew that, cost him what it
might, he could not refuse her plea. She was still young, he
reflected, still with her life before her, while he himself
. . . morosely, he was compelled to admit that his prospects could not match O'Connell's. True, he would probably
and Johnston condemned. But . . . would Their Lordships
send him to sea again, would they permit him to hoist his
flag? Or would the Rum Corps's dastardly mutiny be held—
in part, if not wholly—against him, just as the *Bounty*
mutiny had been?

He sighed and demanded gruffly, to conceal his emotion, "When have you it in mind to wed?"

Maurice O'Connell answered without hesitation, "Before
you sail, sir. Mary is most anxious that Your Excellency
should attend the nuptial service and give her away. It—"
He glanced down at Mary, his expression tender. "It would
be held at Government House, and the reception precede
the Governor's ball, with your agreement, sir. We thought,
since it would be an occasion for rejoicing, that the two
functions might happily be combined."

"And Mr. Marsden will marry us, Papa," Mary added.

So they had made their decisions, put their plans in train
without consulting him, William Bligh thought dully.
Mary—although, on her own admission, aware of the pain
their parting would inflict on him—Mary had taken his
acquiescence for granted. He felt suddenly weary of it all,
wanting only to board his ship and put to sea, leaving the
formalities behind him. The formalities and the heartbreak,

the veiled insults and the attempts to discredit him . . .
His mouth tightened.

Colonel Macquarie had sworn himself in as Governor,
had taken up occupation of his official residence and pro-
mulgated orders and edicts without waiting for his own return and reinstatement . . . let *him* stand sponsor for
Mary! Let him give her in marriage to his second-in-
command, since clearly he and his sly Scottish wife must
have encouraged the match clandestinely. Mary had spent
much of her time at Government House, while the difficult task of obtaining evidence for Johnston's trial had engaged his own attention. Perhaps he had neglected her; in
that regard, devil take it, perhaps he had been remiss or, at
best, thoughtless. If this were so, then no blame could be
attached to Mary, only to himself and the thrice-damned
Macquaries!

Bowed by the weight of what he recognized as his aging
and too corpulent body, William Bligh rose to his feet.
Mary's vivid blue eyes, which were the echo of his own,
met his gaze pleadingly, as if—as so often in the past—she
feared an outburst of ungovernable fury and was seeking,
as she always had, to prevent it.

"Papa," she began, in a tense whisper. "Dearest Papa, I
have given Maurice my word. I—"

Her father contrived to force his stiff lips into a smile.
He owed it to her to give her away at her wedding, he told
himself. She had made her choice, and his last act before
leaving the colony of New South Wales should be a gra-
cious one, in accordance with his adored child's wishes.
There should be no outburst, no bitterness, not even a word
of reproach, for she had chosen well. Maurice O'Connell
was held in high esteem by all who knew him, and Mary's
joy in him was evident.

"If you are sure, Mary, my dear," he managed, "then so
be it."

"I am quite sure, Papa," Mary answered, with quiet conviction.

The deposed Governor held out his hand to his would-be
son-in-law. "Then you have my consent, Colonel O'Con-

nell, although I confess that it breaks my heart to give it. This sweet child of mine is dearer to me than my own life! But I know you for a man of honor and high character, and if I must lose her, I can only rejoice that the loss is on your account. My sole concern is for Mary's happiness and continued well-being."

"And that will ever be mine, sir, you may rest assured." O'Connell wrung the extended hand warmly. "I shall give a dinner party tomorrow in order to announce our betrothal, and I trust that Your Excellency will honor me with your presence. At eight of the clock, sir, if that is convenient?"

"Certainly," Bligh returned, aware that he still sounded a trifle testy but unable to hold himself in check. Mary came quickly round the corner of the desk, and her kiss, affectionate and grateful, tore at his heartstrings.

When they had gone, he took up his quill and, pulling a sheet of paper toward him, started to write a letter to his wife, beginning it, as he invariably did, "My Dearest Love."

> Providence has ordained certain things which we cannot account for, and so it has happened with Mary.
>
> In the midst of most paternal affections and conflicting passions of adoration for so good and admired a child, I at the last have found what I had least expected—Lieutenant Colonel O'Connell, commanding the 73rd Regiment has, unknown to me, won her affections.
>
> What will you not, my dear Betsy, feel for my situation at this time, when I tell you that nothing I could say has had any effect? At last, overwhelmed by a loss which I cannot retrieve, I can only make the best of it and, having no alternative, consent to their marriage.
>
> Nothing can exceed the esteem and high character Colonel O'Connell has. He is likewise Lieutenant Governor of the territory, and I have many proofs of his honor, goodness, and sense . . .

The letter got no further. After several more vain attempts to put his thoughts and feelings into coherent words, William Bligh let his quill fall and tore the scattered sheets of paper into shreds.

Not for almost as long as he could remember had he wept, but the tears came now, the harsh, reluctant tears of a courageous man, who had endured much adversity and faced death in battle without flinching and always with dignity.

Now he was facing an unbearable hurt that must, somehow, be hidden from friends and enemies alike and hidden, most important of all, from the one who had caused it. Nothing must mar Mary's wedding day. . . .

It was almost dawn, and the Governor's ball was still in glittering progress. Kilted officers of the 73rd, scarlet-jacketed marines, naval officers in knee breeches and gold-braided full-dress uniforms, civilian gentlemen in velvet cutaway tailcoats danced with ladies in silks and satins and taffetas of every imaginable hue.

It was the most brilliant scene ever witnessed in the colony of New South Wales, and few guests showed any inclination to retire in search of rest.

Jessica watched, from a secluded corner of the gallery, her eyes heavy with sleep. She was close to exhaustion, for it had been a very long day, with all the last minute preparations for the festivities to be attended to. There had been great masses of flowers and native flowering shrubs to arrange, lanterns to be hung—in the trees outside, as well as in the ballroom and in the marquee erected for Colonel and Mrs. O'Connell's wedding breakfast—and food and drink, in unparalleled quantities, to be served.

Like the rest of the Government House staff, Jessica had been on her feet since the previous dawn. Gradually the house had filled with convict gardeners and kitchen workers, mess waiters and orderlies from the regiment, bearing crested silver with which to deck the tables, and an army of women cleaners and serving girls, recruited from among the 73rd's married families.

Mrs. Macquarie, with seemingly indefatigable energy, had directed the influx, bringing order to what, initially, had appeared to be chaos. The Governor's aides, his secretary, Mr. Campbell, and some of the officers' wives had been drafted into service and . . . Jessica smiled. A memory that would long remain with her was of Captain Antill and the Governor's young nephew, Ensign John Maclaine, aided by Piper Fergus Mackinnon and two orderlies, balanced on ladders in order to hang from the ceiling a festoon of flowers and greenery. In its center, picked out in silver lace, were the initials of Colonel O'Connell and his bride.

Their wedding service, performed by the Reverend Samuel Marsden, had been the highlight of the day. Jessica had only glimpsed it, from the vantage point she now occupied, for there had been her mistress's ball gown to lay out in readiness in the bedroom and half a dozen errands to run. But she had seen Mrs. Putland cross the floor of the newly built ballroom on her father's epauletted arm and had observed, with momentary envy, the joy in her face as her bridegroom stepped forward to take his place at her side.

After the service, there had been a reception in the marquee and endless toasts and speeches, followed by a truly splendid meal and yet more speeches, the only one of which Jessica could now recall being that of Governor Macquarie. In this, with what seemed genuine pleasure and affection, Colonel Macquarie had announced his official gift to the couple of two thousand five hundred acres of farming land at a place called Riverstone, on the Hawkesbury.

The announcement had been greeted by loud and prolonged applause, and . . . Jessica's head dropped, her heavy lids closed, and she slept, too tired to watch or to search her memory any longer.

An amused male voice awakened her, and she looked up in dazed astonishment to find Captain Antill bending over her, a glass in his hand.

"I saw you, hiding here, Jessica India," he said, smiling down at her. "And I brought you this, to refresh you." He

gave her the glass. "Go on, my child—drink it, for I'm sure
you have earned it a hundred times over. This is the first
time I have seen you sitting still all day."

"It has been a busy day, sir," Jessica admitted, "but a
memorable one." Shyly, she sipped the contents of the glass
he had brought her. It was a rum punch, heady and stimu-
lating, dispelling the mists of sleep.

"Hark!" the Governor's aide exclaimed. "It would seem
that we are to have some real dancing at last, and, by
George, not before time! They're bringing the pipes on."

Jessica looked down and saw that he was right. Two of
the 73rd's pipers—one of them Fergus Mackinnon, now
the Governor's personal piper—had taken the place of the
military string band on the dais. Grouped about them,
clapping and shouting enthusiastically, were a number of
kilted officers and some youngsters from the King's ships.

Captain Antill's smile widened. "I'll warrant that you
dance as fine a reel as any down there, my little India.
Come—" He took the glass from her and held out a hand
to assist her to her feet. "I lack a partner, and I am sure
that Mrs. Macquarie would not mind if I were to invite you
to tread a measure with me. In any event, she and the
Governor have gone to bed."

Jessica hesitated, but the invitation was irresistible, and
she let him lead her down to the ballroom. Numbers had
thinned; most of the older guests had, like the Governor
and his lady, long since departed to sleep for what remained of the night. There were calls from groups endeavoring to make up sets for an eightsome, their feet tapping
in time to the music, and with a delighted chuckle, her
partner guided her toward one in the center of the room,
pausing only to whisk off the frilled apron she had been
wearing. Beneath it, Jessica was very conscious, was the
dress her mistress had supplied her for the occasion, and by
no stretch of the imagination was it a ball gown. But it was
of dove-gray silk and fitted her slim figure well, and in
any case, with the music of the pipes in her ears and her
tall, kilted partner bowing to her, it was too late for her to
make her escape.

The set they had joined consisted of young people; no one questioned her presence in their midst, and . . . she was a good dancer and this was the music and the dancing to which, since her childhood, she had been accustomed. Her feet moved with practiced skill; she set to her partner and was whirled round on his arm, to find herself facing a fair-haired young naval officer, with midshipman's white patches on what appeared to be a very new uniform. It was not until he had linked arms with her that she recognized him as the young man who had rescued the *Dromedary*'s drowning topman, on the day of their arrival off the Sydney Heads, and recalled what Mrs. Macquarie had told her of the Governor's intention to reward his heroism with the offer of a naval career. And that his name was Justin Broome.

He slipped, almost losing his balance as they went into the figure of eight, and exclaimed ruefully, as Jessica reached out a hand to steady him, "Forgive me—the only dance I know is the hornpipe, and I'd hoped it would see me through."

His own partner, whom Jessica recognized as Lucy Tempest, gave him a scornful glance as she, in her turn, skipped into the center of the circle, to tread her heel and toe with natural grace. Jessica, next now to Midshipman Broome, gave him her hand and whispered consolingly, "Don't worry—it is quite a simple reel, Mr. Broome. To your right, eight steps, then eight to your left. Now set to your partner and swing her. That's it," as he returned, breathless but triumphant, to her side. "When Captain Antill has set to her, the three of you do the figure of eight, and it is all repeated with the other two couples."

He grinned. "Thank you—I'll get the hang of it soon."

And he did, Jessica observed with interest, but not, it soon became clear, quickly enough to satisfy Miss Lucy Tempest. "Let us exchange partners," she suggested, laying a proprietary, white-gloved hand on Captain Antill's arm and looking up at him engagingly, as the 73rd's two pipers broke into a fresh tune. "This will be a foursome, will it not? I've been practicing the foursome with Archibald MacNaughton and John Maclaine, and dear Captain Antill,

I *do* so want to show my teachers how well I can dance it . . . with an expert partner. You do not mind, do you?"

"If Jessica India has no objection?" Henry Antill, as always courteous, bowed and released Jessica's hand. "I had supposed," he added, addressing Lucy Tempest, "that you intended to accompany your sister, Mrs. O'Shea, to the Hawkesbury."

"Oh, *no!*" the girl retorted. "Abigail has gone, but I am staying in Sydney. There is no social life on a dreary Hawkesbury farm . . . I couldn't bear to go back to Yarramundie. Least of all with poor Abby in mourning. Oh, do pray come on, Captain Antill—" Her tone became impatient. "The dance is beginning, and I want to find John Maclaine."

They drifted away into the crowd of dancers, and Justin Broome said uncertainly, "I fear you have had the worst of the exchange, for I am totally unversed in—what did Miss Tempest call it? The foursome reel, was it not?"

"Yes," Jessica confirmed. "The foursome."

"Then with your permission, we will sit it out, Miss . . . Forgive me, but did I hear Captain Antill address you as Jessica India? It is an unusual name—are you Miss India?"

Jessica shook her head. "My name is Jessica India Maclaine, Mr. Broome."

He bowed and offered his arm. When they were seated, he asked, puzzled, "You know my name? How is that, since I cannot recall that we have met before tonight? And I *would* recall having met you, Miss Maclaine."

She reddened under the admiration in his eyes.

"I was on board the *Dromedary* when you went to the rescue of one of the sailors. I watched it all from the sternwalk, and I saw your boat driven on shore."

"My poor *Flinders!*" A flicker of pain succeeded the admiration in the blue eyes, but then Justin shrugged, losing his earlier stiffness. "But it's an ill wind that blows nobody any good, or so they say. As you may know, I owe my appointment to a King's ship to that unhappy accident— His Excellency the Governor witnessed it, and it is thanks to him that I now wear the King's uniform."

"Yes, I did know that, Mr. Broome. I heard Mrs. Macquarie speak of it not very long ago. And I was pleased, I . . ." Jessica looked up at him, smiling. "When I was watching I was fearful that you would be drowned—you and the little man who was with you, as well as the poor sailor. I prayed for you, I think we all did. Even Mrs. Ellis Bent, who was with me on the sternwalk, was full of admiration. She said it was the bravest thing she had ever seen."

"So you are an intimate of the Governor's lady and the judge advocate's also, Miss Maclaine?" Justin Broome's earlier stiffness had returned, like a defensive barrier between them, and Jessica eyed him in surprise. "I take it your father is a serving officer in His Excellency's regiment?" Before she could reply, he added forcefully, "I am here tonight very much on sufferance, and that fact has been made clear to me by certain gentlemen of the Seventy-third. This uniform, which I am now privileged to wear, does not change what I am—and it is what they are pleased to style a 'currency kid.' I am native born, Miss Maclaine, of emancipist stock—or convict stock, if you prefer it. Perhaps your father would not approve of your sitting here with me."

Momentarily robbed of words by the sheer unexpectedness of his bitter outburst, Jessica continued to stare at him, and then, struck by the absurdity of their situation, she started to laugh.

"If anyone is here on sufferance, it is I, Mr. Broome," she managed at last. "I am a stowaway on board the *Dromedary,* and thanks to Captain Antill's good offices, I obtained employment as Mrs. Macquarie's personal maid. My intimacy with Mrs. Bent goes no deeper than her desire to employ me in that capacity, should Her Excellency no longer require my services."

"Good heavens!" Justin exclaimed incredulously. Then he, too, was laughing. "You cannot mean it!"

"Oh, yes I do—and it is true, I assure you." Jessica gestured toward the gallery above their heads. "Half an hour ago I was up there—I had been watching the dancing, you see, and I fell asleep. Captain Antill found me, and—oh, I am knowing him since I was a child and he a young ensign with the regiment in Mysore. He has always been specially kind to me, never forgetting that my father gave me the name of India. He made me put off my apron and come down to dance with him, which perhaps I ought not to have done. But my lady has gone to her bed, and most of the guests are away—I did not think there would be any harm in it."

"There is not," Justin assured her. "For after all, it has enabled me to make your acquaintance, has it not? Jessica India Maclaine . . ." he repeated thoughtfully. "It is a name to conjure with, and one I shall remember. You say your father gave it to you—is he still with the regiment?"

"No, he is dead—he was killed at the siege and capture of Tipoo Sultan's fortress at Seringapatam, eleven years ago. His Excellency Colonel Macquarie was there, and Captain Antill carried the regimental color and was wounded. Seringapatam is one of the Seventy-third's battle honors. . . ." Encouraged by his evident interest, Jessica talked on, giving details of the battle and its aftermath, learned years ago at her mother's knee.

"So you were orphaned?" Justin suggested, when she came to the end of her recital.

"No. My mother married again. I have a stepfather, who is a company sergeant major in the regiment. Duncan Campbell is his name."

"And he is here?"

She shook her head. "No, neither he nor my mother. I—ran away from him. That was how I came to be a stowaway aboard the *Dromedary,* you see." Under his gentle probing, Jessica told him the story of her flight from her brutal stepfather, and Justin listened, his blue eyes fixed intently on her face.

"I, too, have a stepfather," he confided. "But I am more fortunate in that respect than you have been. My father was drowned in the Hawkesbury flood of eighteen-six, and my mother married her first love, who is one of the finest men I have ever known—Captain Andrew Hawley of the Royal Marines. I should like to introduce you to my family, Jessica India, but—" He shrugged despondently.

"There is so little time. We are ready to sail, as soon as Commodore Bligh gives the word. The troops are embarked, and I doubt whether any of us will be given shore leave, after tonight. His Excellency has seen his daughter married—he'll not want to linger now."

"But you will come back, will you not?" Jessica asked, conscious of a pang at the realization that she might never see him again. "This is your homeland."

Justin smiled. "God willing, yes, I shall come back. But it may be years before I'm given the chance—if the war continues and I'm appointed to one of the King's ships." He reached for her hand and bore it diffidently to his lips. "The party's over, alas, and I must go. But I shall not forget you, Jessica India."

The party, Jessica observed, was indeed over, the ballroom floor now almost deserted, and the pipes silent. She saw Piper Mackinnon staring in her direction, a disapproving scowl creasing his brow, but he made no attempt to speak to her and, a moment later, marched away with his fellow, receiving Captain Antill's thanks as they passed him. She saw Mrs. Ovens also, and found herself returning, in confusion, to her accustomed role and looking about her almost in panic for her lost apron. Miraculously, after Justin Broome had taken leave of her, she found and donned the square of linen, with its frilled bib, and with the strings tied neatly about her waist, summoned the courage to join the stout housekeeper at the foot of the stairs.

"Were you wanting me, Mrs. Ovens?" she inquired nervously. "I am afraid I was . . . that is, I—"

"You were where you'd no business to be, were you not?" Mrs. Ovens put in with asperity. But then, to Jessica's relief, her expression relaxed and she smiled. "Off to bed with you, my lass. What the eye don't see, the heart won't grieve about, and that's a fact. Just so long as you're up in time to take your lady her cup of tea I'll not say a word . . . and I don't suppose Her Excellency will either. But—that young officer you were with. Was he not the one that saved one of our sailors from drowning, when we first got here?"

"Yes, that's who he was, Mrs. Ovens." Jessica hesitated. "His name is Justin Broome."

"Then you were in good company, child," Mrs. Ovens asserted.

"I am thinking I was," Jessica agreed. She slipped away, and for all her earlier weariness, her step was light as she mounted the stairs that led to her room.

CHAPTER XI

Since early morning on Saturday, May 12, 1810, crowds had been gathering at every vantage point between the observatory and South Head to witness the departure of Commodore Bligh's three homeward-bound ships.

Divided between the *Hindostan* and the *Dromedary* were the officers and 345 other ranks of the regiment that —although now designated the 102nd—had long been known to the colony's inhabitants as the Rum Corps. With them were over two hundred women and children, most of whom had been in tears when the order came for them to embark. Their muted cries and their waving handkerchiefs brought a feverish response from those on shore, and Jenny, standing with Frances Spence among the packed crowd of watchers, felt her own eyes fill as she waited.

H.M.S. *Hindostan*, wearing the commodore's broad pennant at the main, was the first to get under way, her signal guns booming in response to the salute fired from Dawes Battery and her seamen manning the yards. It was impossible to identify Justin among the press on deck, but when the frigate worked out of the anchorage and started to make sail, she saw him—or imagined she saw him—go racing up to the foremast head and raise a hand in salute.

"They say," Frances Spence observed, thinking to distract her, "that they will make a fast passage, Jenny . . .

under five months, Captain Pasco told my husband. But I doubt whether even that will be fast enough for Colonel Paterson. I saw him when he went on board the *Dromedary*. He was a shadow of himself and so lame that his wife had to support him. I confess I felt sorry for him and wished that he might have been left here to end his days in peace. After all, he had no part in the Rum Corps's rebellion, had he?"

Jenny turned to look at her. Frances, she thought, seldom had a bad word to say of anyone, and like so many of her countrymen, she was the soul of kindness and generosity.

"Andrew always liked Colonel Paterson," she said thoughtfully. "But he was a broken man after that duel he fought with Mr. Macarthur. That was why he took to drink. . . . Andrew says he was never free of pain."

"God grant he may reach England safely. Although—" Frances sighed, her blue eyes troubled, "what evidence he can contribute to Colonel Johnston's trial passes my comprehension. And indeed I am unable to understand why only Colonel Johnston is to stand trial and Macarthur—who we all know was the real instigator of the rebellion—goes scot-free."

"Andrew said His Excellency told him that Mr. Macarthur would certainly be put on trial here, if he returned," Jenny supplied. She smiled without amusement. "And Commodore Bligh, during his enforced sojourn at Long Wrekin, made it quite abundantly clear that he intends to bring *all* the rebel officers to trial if he can, once he reaches England. I believe he consulted the new advocate general, Mr. Bent, as to the legal position—particularly in regard to Mr. Macarthur—and was told that it was a matter for the Colonial Office."

"Have you met the Ellis Bents, Jenny?" Frances asked curiously.

"Only at the Governor's ball, when you pointed them out to me. I've never spoken to either of them." Jenny turned again to watch the departing ships, as first the small *Porpoise* and then the lumbering *Dromedary* weighed anchor. On the wharf, the pipes and drums of the 73rd played them away, and the guard of honor presented arms. Andrew was in attendance on the Governor, and she recognized his tall figure among the group of officers surrounding the viceregal couple. Mrs. Macquarie, she saw, was talking to Mrs. Bent, and . . . yes, her eyes had not deceived her. Henrietta Dawson was with them, and Lucy Tempest stood a few yards behind her, twirling a frilled parasol and seemingly engrossed in conversation with one of the Governor's young aides.

"Henrietta is very friendly with Mrs. Bent," Frances said, following the direction of Jenny's gaze. "They are birds of the same feather, I think . . . certainly they are united in their disapproval of Their Excellencies' attitude toward those who did not come out here of their own free will!"

"Then they must have found the Governor's ball somewhat distasteful," Jenny suggested.

"Indeed they did," Frances agreed. "But I confess I enjoyed it immensely."

"So did I . . . entirely thanks to you, Frances. If you had not made me that lovely dress, I should never have found the courage to attend, despite Andrew's urging."

"My dearest Jenny!" Frances put an arm affectionately about Jenny's slim waist and hugged her. "I am only too delighted that I had the wit to think of it. You spend far too much time and work much too hard on that farm of yours . . . why do you not let Tim buy the place from you? You could come and live here. I declare to God, life is, from now on, going to be a joyous thing in Sydney . . . and the emancipists like ourselves will be permitted to enjoy it on an equal footing with the officials and the free settlers, according to our rank in life and our character. The new Governor has decreed it publicly."

"Yes, I know he has. But—" Jenny sighed.

Frances ignored the interruption. "There will be a spate of marriages," she predicted. "Men who have lived for twenty years with the poor souls whom the Reverend Marsden has designated their concubines will, for a paltry fee of three pounds, give them respectability. And they say that His Excellency intends to make Simeon Lord a magistrate.

You'll see, Jenny, that will be the thin end of the wedge—even the poor Irish will soon have priests and a church of their own."

"That would make you very happy, would it not?" Jenny hazarded.

Frances inclined her shining dark head. "It would restore my faith in God and in all humanity," she admitted gravely. "Not," she added, with a taut little smile, "not that I hold any brief for Mr. Lord, save as the thin end of the proverbial wedge. The source of his wealth would not bear too close an inspection, as we all know, but he has used his money well and greatly to the benefit of this colony. I'd not begrudge him his reward for that."

Jenny said nothing. Justin had spoken of Simeon Lord to her, had described him as a rum trafficker, but . . . how many of the colony's respectable citizens could plead innocence of some involvement in the liquor trade? Even Mr. Campbell and Commissary Palmer were said to have imported illicit cargoes on occasion; Frances's own husband had held shares in the Corps officers' syndicate, and had not Tim Dawson once owned and operated a whisky still?

Below her she saw the three ships moving swiftly now as the brisk westerly wind filled their sails. The *Hindostan* had her forecourse set and men aloft, loosing the main and mizzen. Soon Justin would be gone, and . . .

As if reading her thoughts, Frances said, "Shall we take the phaeton and drive out to South Head to watch them go, Jenny? The Governor's new road is excellent—we could be there before them."

"I . . ." Would it just be prolonging the agony she felt, Jenny wondered, or would the sight of her, waving him farewell from the cliff top, offer her son encouragement and a memory to hold during the long voyage? She was conscious of a nagging pain in her side as she turned to look at Frances; the pain was intermittent, but she had spun round too sharply, and a jolting ride behind Jasper Spence's spirited trotters would probably make it more acute, yet . . . "I'd like that," she said. "If it is not giving you too much trouble."

"We have servants to spare us trouble," Frances answered dryly. "Come on, Jenny, my dear."

Seated beside Jenny in the elegant phaeton, Frances returned to the subject of selling Long Wrekin. Clasping one of Jenny's hands, she said with gentle insistence, "You are not well, are you? Oh"—before Jenny could deny it—"I know, I've been watching you. Those broken ribs of yours haven't healed properly, have they?"

"It takes time," Jenny protested lamely.

"Have you thought about selling the farm—thought seriously, I mean?"

"Yes, I have, truly, Frances. And I've talked about the possibility to Tom and Nancy Jardine."

"Tim would buy you out tomorrow," Frances asserted. "And he would keep on the Jardines—he always promised he would. Would they mind?"

"Not if I sold the place to Tim. And William could stay there, if he wanted to."

"And Rachel attend school here, with Julia and Dodie," Frances said. "Jenny, Andrew wants you with him, does he not? If he transfers to the veteran company, you will have to give up the farm."

Andrew *did* want her to give up Long Wrekin, Jenny thought—for her own sake, as much as for his. He liked the new Governor and was anxious to serve under him; Justin also had sought to persuade her before he left . . . why then, she asked herself guiltily, did she vacillate? William was the only member of her family who might object, and his objections could easily be overcome, if he were permitted to stay on the farm. And the Jardines, she knew, could be trusted to care for him.

She glanced round at Frances, who said, again uncannily, as if she had spoken her thoughts aloud, "Jenny, I am not thinking of Tim Dawson's interests, only of yours, believe me. Oh, I will not deny that I should enjoy your company if you were here in Sydney—I should, and the more so, now that Abigail has gone back to Yarramundie. I miss her and little Dickon very much. But you . . . Jenny, you are my oldest friend! Indeed, you were my only friend when I first came out here, and I cannot bear to see you looking so thin and tired. What has Long Wrekin to offer that you are so reluctant to leave?"

Jenny sighed. "I suppose . . . oh, independence, the life I know."

"Life in Sydney has much to offer now," Frances reminded her. Jenny flushed unhappily.

"I am not accustomed to leading a social life. I'd be . . . out of place. What have I in common with ladies like Mrs. Macquarie and Mrs. Bent? Dinner parties, balls . . . Frances, it is different for you. You were bred to such things, I was not. Do you not know that the Governor's ball was the first I ever attended in my life? And the dress you made for me was the first ball gown I ever saw, much less owned and wore!"

"You will have more in common with Mrs. Macquarie than you realize," Frances said. "She is truly a charming, kindly, and most warmhearted person, and like you, she spent all her early years in the country. Think about it, Jenny. Sydney will not offer only dinner parties and balls—the Governor talks of encouraging horse breeding by setting up a racecourse. He has plans for aborigine schools, country fairs, new settlements, roads . . . a new hospital, and even a botanical garden, open to all."

"I cannot but applaud such plans," Jenny conceded. "Only . . ." She caught her breath, thinking of Long Wrekin, of the breeding stock and the rich acres of grassland where she could wander at will; of the great flowing river she had come to know so well, and of the native people living by its banks, many of whom had become her friends.

True, working the land was hard, but it was rewarding; true, the Hawkesbury might flood and spread destruction in its wake; crops might fail, prices fall, the livestock might die, as Sirius had died, and a year's toil yield little or no profit. But it was her life, she thought obstinately; the only life she had known for over twenty years, and it had given her contentment and a generous measure of freedom. And besides, the dream she had cherished, inspired so long ago by Governor Phillip, was at yet unfulfilled . . . the dream of those interminable pastures that must, she was convinced, lie beyond the Blue Mountains, if only a way could be found to scale and cross their formidable, unmapped peaks.

"I want one day to drive my flocks and herds over the mountains," she said, and realized that she had spoken the wish aloud only when she saw Frances eyeing her in surprise.

"There is no way over the Blue Mountains, Jenny. Perhaps there never will be."

"Governor Macquarie is building roads," Jenny said. "He'll not rest content with the colony as it is, hemmed in between the Blue Mountains and the sea. He will send people to find a way."

"Yes, I daresay he will," Frances agreed. "But think of all those who made the attempt and failed. Governor Phillip, Governor Hunter, Dr. Bass—even poor Colonel Paterson, in his youth—Surgeon White, and any number of the marine and Corps officers and men. Captain Tench, Colonel Collins, Lieutenant Dawes, the young engineer—what was his name? Bunyan? Banner?"

"Lieutenant Barailler," Jenny supplied. Frances was right, she reflected; there had indeed been many brave attempts to cross the tree-clad, trackless mountain barrier, and all had been compelled to admit defeat. Tim Dawson had gone partway with one expedition, after the discovery of Governor Phillip's missing wild cattle by Henry Hacking, a onetime petty officer of H.M.S. *Sirius*. Hacking had succeeded in penetrating further than most until he, too, had consumed all his provisions and been forced to turn back. But he had named the fertile valley, where he had traced the wild breeding herd, the Cow Pastures.

"I do not think," Frances said, "that the mountains will be crossed in our lifetime, Jenny. And you should think of yourself—even a few months' rest would improve your health, I feel sure. You owe it to Andrew to take better care of yourself . . . and to Justin."

Undoubtedly she did, Jenny knew. They were nearing the end of the new carriage road, and the coachman reined in his horses. On the cliff top a small crowd had already

collected, and several horse-drawn vehicles were drawn up
by the roadside, their passengers descending to join those
who had come on foot or on horseback. Jenny smiled.

"I'll think seriously about selling Long Wrekin to Tim,"
she told Frances as they, in turn, alighted. "But even if I
do sell, I truly do not want to live in Sydney—much as I
should like to see more of you, my dear Frances."

Wisely, Frances Spence did not press her. Linking arms,
they made their way to the edge of the crowd, which, as
soon as the convoy was sighted, became a forest of waving
handkerchiefs, the cheers and shouts mingling with the
crash of surf on the rocks below. All manner of people had
come to see the three ships on their way, Jenny observed, a
number of them soldiers of the Corps, now wearing the
dark-blue facings of the veteran company in place of their
old, distinctive yellow. There were women and children
with them, many of the women in tears, and seeing them,
Frances said pityingly, "More of Mr. Marsden's concubines, I fear, whose men did not seek the blessing of the
Church on their union."

And now abandoned, Jenny thought, to exist and bring
up their children as best they might without the support
their departing soldiers had provided . . . small wonder
the poor souls were weeping. She looked at them sadly, and
then her attention was distracted by a party of mounted
officers of the Governor's regiment, who came cantering
up, scattering the folk on foot as they made for the best
vantage point on the summit. There was a girl with them,
riding sidesaddle, and it was she who, with complete disre-
gard for those standing in her way, led what almost
amounted to a cavalry charge to the gates of the signal
station. She was laughing aloud as she did so, urging her
escort to follow her reckless progress, and Frances drew in
her breath sharply.

"Glory be to God!" she exclaimed, in a shocked voice.
"That is Lucy Tempest! What can Henrietta have been
thinking of, to permit her to come out here with those
young men?" She added, when Jenny stared at her in mute
bewilderment, "Since Abigail left, I found Lucy too much
for me, and I confess I was relieved when Henrietta moved

to the new house in Pitt Street and invited Lucy to go with her. But she is not a bit like Abigail, and lately, I am afraid, she has become very headstrong and concerned only with her own pleasure. Henrietta was full of complaints because of her behavior at the Governor's ball. Perhaps you noticed it? She was the toast of the Seventy-third's young officers and, to my mind, made quite a spectacle of herself on their account."

As she appeared to be doing now, Jenny thought and wondered, a trifle cynically, for how long Henrietta Dawson would tolerate the girl. Doubtless, as she had done when Abigail O'Shea had been her guest at Upwey, Tim Dawson's wife had supposed she was enlisting the services of an unpaid nursemaid, who would relieve her of the care of her three young children when they were not at school.

"Come on," Frances urged, grasping her arm. "The ships are here—we shall have a splendid view of them if we move over to the left."

Jenny went with her and forgot Lucy Tempest and the unfortunate women and children the Rum Corps was leaving behind. The three ships of the convoy were clearly visible in the blue waters of the harbor below them, skimming like white-winged seabirds across its ruffled surface, with all sail set. Then they wore in succession, the *Hindostan* majestically in the van, to bear away from the headland, and with the wind astern, all three headed for the open sea.

For the open sea and the great Pacific Ocean, for the perilous passage round the Horn to Rio de Janeiro and thence to England . . . Jenny waved and cheered with the rest, but she felt as if the departing ships were taking her heart with them, her vision blurred by unshed tears and her hand trembling as she waved.

What would Justin find when he landed in England, she wondered desolately. England was a country still at war, and Justin, if the Royal Navy accepted him, would go to war in one of the King's ships—as his father had done before him, and Andrew, too. Had she been wrong to let him go—to encourage him to go? Would he ever come back, would she see him again, or was he lost to her, as so many others were lost?

A signal hoist was run up to the *Hindostan*'s masthead and greeted by a roar from the watchers on the cliff top. "Farewell!" they chorused. "Farewell and a safe passage!"

Frances took Jenny's arm. "They've gone," she said gently. "They've gone, Jenny."

Lucy Tempest sat in sullen and rebellious silence as the Dawsons' swaying coach bore her toward the Hawkesbury and what she deemed to be exile at Yarramundie.

Seated opposite her—for the greater part of the long, tedious journey, and also in silence—Henrietta Dawson fanned herself vigorously and stared out, with lackluster eyes, at the passing countryside. The Governor's fine post road had progressed as far as the Parramatta settlement, but after leaving the township, the way was by bush track, potholed and dusty, over which even the well-sprung and elegantly appointed carriage was slowed to a snail's pace. Its lurching and bumping made Lucy feel physically sick; she longed to ask Henrietta Dawson to call a brief halt, to enable her to recover, but in the circumstances, she could not bring herself to ask even so small a favor.

Henrietta had, she told herself bitterly, treated her with great injustice. Previously, when they had both been under Frances Spence's hospitable roof, nothing had been said concerning her conduct or her friendship with the Governor's young aide, John Maclaine, and his brother officers. True, she had been discreet—or perhaps careful would be a more apt description—and the kindly, tolerant Frances had not criticized or attempted to rebuke her. But . . . Lucy gave vent to a petulant sigh. Because the Spences' household had seemed dull after Abigail had gone, she had eagerly accepted the invitation from Henrietta to remove to the new house in Pitt Street.

The house was large; it was only fifty yards from that occupied, in some state, by Commodore Bligh prior to his departure, and the Dawsons—at least when Timothy was there—entertained lavishly. She had supposed, quite incorrectly as it had turned out, that Henrietta would permit her as much freedom as she desired. Instead, within a week of moving to the Pitt Street establishment, Timothy Dawson had gone back to his farm at Upwey and his wife had retired to bed, suffering from some imagined malaise.

The parties had ceased, and she—Lucy flashed her erstwhile hostess a venomous glance—*she* had been expected to undertake the domestic management of the house, to play the part of governess to Henrietta's three spoiled children and virtually to withdraw from the social scene, at a time when dinner parties, picnics, and balls were suddenly much in vogue.

Of course, looking back, she was forced to admit that she had been foolish to accept Archie MacNaughton's invitation to dine and play cards in his quarters. She had known that his bosom friend, Philip Connor, would be there, and that Philip was a wild young man and a bad influence on both Archie and John Maclaine. All three had been reprimanded for riding into the crowd at the South Head, when they had gone to watch the sailing of Commodore Bligh's convoy . . . some malicious person had reported the incident, and His Excellency had lectured them severely. They had intended no harm, Lucy recalled. Certainly she had not—all they had wanted to do was to give poor Jamie MacAlpine a rousing farewell, because after the trouble he had brought on himself with Mrs. Macquarie's maid, the Governor had ordered him home in disgrace.

But, as always, a wretched spoilsport had taken exception to their youthful high spirits and made an official complaint, and like Jamie, they had found themselves in trouble. They had even been warned that they might share Jamie's fate and be sent home, and in view of that, Archie MacNaughton should have known better than to let his card party degenerate into a brawl.

Yet it had started innocently enough. They had enjoyed a splendid buffet supper and had played several hands of whist, in good but not boisterous spirits. She was the only girl, and . . . Lucy glanced again at Henrietta Dawson's shuttered, unresponsive face and repeated her sigh. She had tried to explain, but Henrietta had refused to listen.

"You are a deceitful little wanton, Lucy," she had ac-

cused, "and an evil influence, from which I must protect
Julia and Dodie. I shall take you to Upwey, and your sister
can send someone from Yarramundie to escort you there as
soon as possible. Let Abigail control you, for I cannot!"

But she was *not* a wanton, Lucy thought glumly. She
had not known—for how could she have known?—that
Philip would behave in the manner he had. It was true
that he had drunk more than he usually did and that he
had been intoxicated when he had suggested to Archie
MacNaughton that they should invite two more ladies to
join the party. She had endeavored to dissuade them, and
so had John Maclaine, and . . . perhaps they had not
tried very hard. Mainly because, of course, they had supposed that Philip meant that the invitation would be re-
stricted to ladies. It was probably his original intention, but
clearly he had not realized the lateness of the hour or
paused to ask himself how many ladies were likely to be
abroad so long after darkness had fallen.

Afterward, shocked into sobriety, he had admitted that
he had knocked and rung bells at the doors of several officers' homes and, receiving no response, had gone further
afield and, unfortunately for them all, had encountered an
elderly emancipist and the young woman with whom he
cohabited on their way home.

And . . . Lucy's mouth tightened, as she relived the
unhappy scene that had followed. Philip had invited the
young woman, Elizabeth Winch, to his quarters; she had
refused and run from him in terror, and Archie had gone
in pursuit of her, armed with a paling that he had
wrenched off an adjacent fence. The frightened girl had
taken refuge in the house of a man named Holness, who, in
his nightclothes and with his wife at his back, had attempted to bar the way to her pursuers. Archie and Philip
had promptly set upon him with their paling, and . . .
Lucy shuddered. By the time she and John Maclaine caught
up with them, the wretched Holness was lying in a pool of
blood, with his wife on her knees beside him, screaming
hysterically that he was dead and that the officers had
murdered him.

Inevitably, the affair had caused an appalling scandal.

Archie and Philip had been placed under arrest and were now awaiting trial in the Criminal Court, and although both they and John Maclaine had done all in their power to keep her name out of it, the fact that she had been present could not be hidden from Henrietta. And, Lucy thought bitterly, Henrietta's reaction had been equally inevitable. Having endured a veritable spate of reproachful criticism and wildly exaggerated accusations, she had been informed of her impending banishment to Yarramundie, and now, for all her pleas and tearful promises of more circumspect behavior in the future, she was on the first stage of the journey back to the place which, above all others, she hated.

And it *was* unjust. She had not killed old William Holness; she had not incited or encouraged Archie MacNaughton and Philip Connor to attack him—quite the reverse, in fact, since she had done all she possibly could to stop them. Her only crime, if such it could be called, had been that she had dined in Archie's quarters without first seeking her hostess's permission to do so.

"You crept out, without so much as a word," Henrietta had railed at her. "Yet you must have been aware that I would never have consented to your dining unchaperoned in Lieutenant MacNaughton's quarters, had you told me of your intentions."

That was true, admittedly, Lucy had to concede. But, on the other hand, she would not have been tempted to do anything of the kind had Henrietta continued to entertain in the new Pitt Street house, instead of pretending to be ill and spending all her days and nights in bed. It had been so unbearably boring, cut off from the society of her friends and with only the Dawson children for company, day after endless day, without even the prospect of a picnic or a drive in the carriage to break the monotony.

But . . . Lucy stifled a sob. It would be infinitely more boring at Yarramundie, isolated, cut off from civilization, with Abigail giving her lectures and the hateful Kate Lamerton openly disapproving and both of them caring only for the wretched little Dickon, who could neither speak nor hear a single word. At least Julia and Dorothea and Alexander, the Dawson children, could talk. . . . She sniffed audibly, and risked another covert glance at Henrietta, annoyed to see that the older woman was sitting with closed eyes, feigning sleep.

There was Luke Cahill, of course—as far as she knew, he was still working at Yarramundie. Lucy brightened. Luke was a handsome fellow, and when she had been with the Boskennas on the property, she had found him attractive and good company. They had both been very young, though, and Luke was a ticket-of-leave man, which—despite his good looks and his education—meant that there was an unbridgeable social gulf between them. He . . .

The carriage lurched into a pothole, jolting both its passengers from their seats. Henrietta called out angrily to the coachman and resumed her seat, looking ruffled and resentful. But her eyes were open; she could not go on pretending to be asleep, and Lucy launched into another attempt to gain her sympathy.

"Mrs. Dawson, please will you not consider letting me return with you to Sydney? I give you my word of honor that I will do everything you ask of me. I truly am sorry for what happened, and I—"

Henrietta did not let her finish. She said icily, "We have been into all this before, Lucy, and I see no reason whatsoever to change my mind. You have abused my hospitality and betrayed the trust I reposed in you. You are to go to your sister at Yarramundie, and there is no more to be said on the subject."

"But Mrs. Dawson, I *can't* go to Yarramundie!" Lucy exclaimed. "I . . . it will kill me to go back!"

"Why should it?"

"I . . . I have nightmares about it. Mr. Boskenna tried to shoot me, you know. He aimed his musket at me, and—" The ready tears, always a potent weapon where Frances and her husband and even Abigail were concerned, came welling into Lucy's dark eyes. The Reverend Caleb Boskenna had indeed sought to take her life; he had been appointed as their guardian when they had first come out to the colony, and wicked man that he was, he had gone to horrifying lengths in his endeavor to wrest their inheritance from them. Lucy started to recount the sorry tale, but once again Henrietta cut her short.

"I know what the Boskennas did. But it was all a long time ago, and you should forget it, as Abigail has done."

"Abigail wasn't there when Mr. Boskenna tried to shoot me—it's easy for her to forget. But I cannot. . . . Oh, please, Mrs. Dawson, I beg you not to send me back! If you don't want me with you in Sydney, would you not permit me to stay at Upwey? I'd work, I'd keep house for Mr. Dawson, I'd do anything, just so long as I don't have to go back to Yarramundie."

"I could not trust you at Upwey," Henrietta returned acidly. "You have lied and you have deceived me and you have behaved quite shamelessly. You will be permitted to stay at Upwey only until Abigail sends for you . . . and I trust she will do so with all possible speed."

"Oh, *please* . . . you do not understand. I—"

"On the contrary, I understand only too well." Henrietta's tone was repressive, her eyes cold. "I want to hear no more, so be silent and allow me to rest. You know I am not well."

She closed her eyes, to Lucy's chagrin, and settled back in her seat, affecting sleep. Angrily, the girl turned her gaze to the carriage window, but there was nothing to see, save an endless succession of gum trees, which bordered the track on one side, and the river, behind its precipitous bank, on the other. And even the river was lost to sight, as it curved and the track ceased to follow it but instead, rougher and dustier than ever, took a more direct line. The sun was sinking, the shadows beginning to deepen; in less than two hours, they would arrive at the Dawsons' property at Upwey and there would be no escape. Henrietta would tell her husband what had led up to this cruel banishment from Sydney, and she would be held a virtual prisoner until Abigail sent for her. How could fate be so unkind?

Lucy started to sob, her small, piquant face buried in her hands as the coachman, finding what appeared to be a comparatively smooth stretch of track, whipped his horses into a canter. The carriage rolled sickeningly, and once again she was hard put to it to control her rising nausea.

"Oh God," she prayed, in a tense whisper. "Please God, let there be an end to this torment! Let me go free. . . ."

The end, when it came, was not what she had anticipated and certainly not the outcome for which she had been praying. The right rear wheel struck some unseen obstacle, the spokes shattered, and the cumbersome carriage came crashing down onto its axle-ends, as the right front wheel buckled under the strain and the horses panicked.

Beyond Lucy's line of vision, the coachman was sent flying from his box, and the four horses, no longer under any restraint, bolted in terror. For about sixty or seventy yards they contrived to drag the carriage in their fleeing wake; then the heavy vehicle turned over, bringing the two hindmost horses down with it, and Lucy found herself flung violently against the splintered wood and smashed glass of what had once been the right-side door.

Bruised, bleeding, and badly shaken, she picked herself up, her ears assailed by a terrible, high-pitched screaming. At first she supposed it to be coming from one of the horses trapped by the traces beneath the wreckage, but when she managed to lever herself across to the opposite door and peer out, she saw that the two lead horses had broken free and were galloping away down the track. The other two lay silent and motionless; one, as nearly as she could judge in that first, frightened glance, with its neck broken, the other with what was left of the central carriage shaft impaled in its side.

And the screaming went on. . . . Weeping and choking from the dust, Lucy lost her grip on the windowsill. She slithered back into the interior of the carriage, and then horror was piled on horror when her gaze lit on the twisted form of Henrietta Dawson pinned down, as in a vise, by the shattered floorboards and by one of the heavy metal springs that had once cushioned the body of the carriage from the worst shocks of the ill-kept roads.

It was Henrietta who was screaming, the bemused girl realized, her mouth open and gaping, her eyes dark with agony.

"I'll get you out," she promised wildly, tearing at the

boards. "But please don't scream—I can't bear it. I'll get you out if you'll just stop screaming . . . oh, please, *listen* to me!"

But Henrietta did not hear her, and to Lucy's dismay, the coachman did not come in response to her own feeble cries for help. He, too, she supposed dully, had been killed or was too badly hurt to move from wherever he had fallen. In the dust-obscured interior of the overturned carriage, she could not see the extent of Henrietta's injuries, but she knew that they must be severe when, withdrawing her hands, she saw that they were heavily bloodstained, as were the floorboards she had been vainly trying to drag aside.

"Help!" she sobbed. "Please, won't somebody help me! Won't somebody come!"

But, as before, there was no response, and Henrietta's screams went on and on, beating on her brain and driving her to hysterical despair. She managed at last to prize loose one of the floorboards, but the rest defied her puny efforts, and try as she might, she could not shift the metal spring that, she was able to ascertain, had fallen across the injured woman's thighs.

It was impossible to free her; she had not the strength, Lucy recognized, and Henrietta Dawson would die if aid were not soon forthcoming. Perhaps, instead of continuing the abortive struggle, she should climb out of the wrecked carriage and go in search of help. This appeared to be an isolated spot, but . . . Upwey Farm could not be more than five or six miles away, and there was a chance that one or even both of the lead horses might still be in the vicinity. And on horseback, five or six miles would be nothing.

Lucy scrambled unsteadily to her feet. One of the padded seat cushions lay on the floor of the carriage; she had not noticed it before, but . . . with something like this to break her fall, there would be less risk of a sprained ankle or more bruises when she clambered out through the window and attempted to lower herself to the ground. She picked it up, surprised by its weight, and was endeavoring to maneuver it to the aperture above her head when Henrietta's screams were redoubled, and . . . Lucy turned, tried beyond endurance, when she realized that the injured woman was screaming accusations. They were hurtful, unjust accusations, and they were leveled at her.

"This is *your* fault! You are . . . deserting me when I need you! In God's name, Lucy . . . you cannot leave me like this! I should not . . . have been here if it had not been for your wanton behavior, your excesses! And now you are running away!"

"I am going to fetch help," Lucy cried indignantly. "I'm going to find Mr. Dawson."

But the flow of accusation, of reproach, could not be halted. Henrietta put out a hand to grasp Lucy's skirt, dragging her back.

"You shall not escape! If you try to run away, you will be caught . . . I shall see to it that you are. And you will be sent to Yarramundie, do you hear, Lucy? You are a wicked, wanton girl, and I will not have you in my house. Let Abigail have you, let her punish you! She is your sister. It is for her to control you. . . ."

Lucy's control snapped. In a swift surge of pent-up anger and resentment, she thrust the heavy cushion into Henrietta's face and, with all her remaining strength, held it there, choking with sobs.

The screams abruptly ceased. Henrietta did not struggle. She released her hold on Lucy's skirt, brought her hand up to tug weakly at the cushion, and then her hand fell, and a terrible, brooding silence seemed suddenly to envelop the interior of the wrecked carriage.

Horrified at the realization of what she had done, Lucy pulled the cushion away, frantically calling Henrietta's name. But there was no response; a white face and slowly glazing eyes looked back at her, and she knew that her tormentor was dead.

Bile rose sickeningly in her throat. Somehow, she managed to choke it back and clamber out through the shattered glass of the window, from whence she slithered to the ground, careless now of what injury she might do herself. There was no sign of the two lead horses, which she had hoped might return, and she set off down the rutted, dusty track on foot, fear and guilt lending her wings.

After a while, all sensation of time left her. Numb with shock, she stumbled on through the gathering darkness, only dimly aware of her surroundings and of the direction she must take, tripping blindly over exposed tree-roots but always picking herself up and staggering on.

When Timothy Dawson and two of his convict workers came riding toward her, Lucy would have passed them by, but Timothy, recognizing her, dismounted swiftly and caught her in his arms.

"Lucy—Lucy Tempest! For God's sake, child, what has happened, what is wrong? Two of the carriage horses came into the yard with their traces broken an hour ago. Has there been an accident?" He shook her gently. "Lucy, it's Tim Dawson. You were with my wife, were you not? Tell me where she is, for pity's sake!"

But Lucy could only sob incoherently and point, with a trembling hand, in the direction from which she had come. Finally, realizing that she was too shocked to tell him more, Timothy lifted her onto his saddlebow and rode on. They found the carriage a short while later, and one appalled glance into its interior confirmed all his worst fears.

Compassionately, he sent Lucy to the farmhouse with one of his men.

Two days later, Jethro Crowan arrived with Luke Cahill to escort her to Yarramundie, and Lucy, conscience-stricken and still deeply shocked, accompanied them without a word of protest.

The newly dug graves of Henrietta and the coachman reproached her as she rode past them on Luke's saddlebow, but she had wept without ceasing during the past two days and had no more tears to shed. The funeral service, conducted by the Reverend Cartwright, had been an ordeal, and she shivered involuntarily as she recalled the words he had spoken as Henrietta's coffin had been lowered into its last resting place.

"She was a noble and well-intentioned lady, who will be sorely missed, not only by her sorrowing husband and children, but by the whole community. . . ."

A stifled moan escaped Lucy's tightly pursed lips, and Luke's arms closed pityingly about her. He had matured into a big, handsome man in the intervening years, and leaning back against his muscular chest, she took comfort from his strength and gentleness.

By comparison, Archie MacNaughton and Philip Connor were, she told herself bitterly, arrogant and irresponsible boys, whose friendship had brought her nothing but misery. . . .

CHAPTER XII

On the morning of September 8, the convict transport *Canada* lay off Port Jackson Heads awaiting a change of wind to bring her into the harbor. Just before noon, Andrew Hawley went out to her in the pilot cutter, accompanied by the harbor master, Robert Watson, and other port officials.

It was the ship's second voyage under government contract to the colony. She was a roomy two-decker of 403 tons burden whose master, Captain John Ward, had a better reputation than most for dealing humanely with his unwilling passengers and, according to Watson, landing them in good health. This voyage was, it seemed, to be no exception. The master reported with satisfaction that he had made a fairly fast passage of 169 days, calling at Rio de Janeiro and the Cape.

"One hundred and twenty-two female felons loaded, sir," he told Andrew. "And I shall be putting ashore one hundred and twenty-one, all decently clad, well fed, and free of disease. The only deaths we had were of a poor, aged woman who should have never been considered fit for transportation, and the wife of a noncommissioned officer of His Majesty's Seventy-third Regiment. She, God rest her soul, departed this life only two days ago."

Andrew nodded his understanding. "What was the cause of the deaths, Captain? Old age, presumably, in the first . . . but what of the other?"

He had asked the question purely as a formality, in order to report on the matter to the Governor, but to his surprise, the gray-haired master became guardedly evasive.

"You had best speak to my surgeon, sir," he advised. "I'll pass the word for him, if you wish. The husband—that is, the widower—is on board. Sergeant Major Campbell, commanding the draft for the Seventy-third. They were men who were left behind in Portsmouth when His Excellency's convoy sailed last year."

"Was there not an officer in command of the draft?" Andrew inquired.

Captain Ward shook his head. "I understand the officers came out in the *Anne*." He gave precise details and then added soberly, "Mrs. Campbell's death leaves two small children motherless. But Campbell told me he has an older stepdaughter already in the colony, so doubtless she will care for them once they go ashore. Now, sir—" He gestured hospitably in the direction of the after companionway. "If you and the harbor master would care to join me in my day cabin, we can dispose of the necessary formalities over a few glasses of madeira, and then you can have a word with the surgeon."

The surgeon, when Andrew was introduced to him an hour later, proved only a little less evasive on the subject of Mrs. Campbell's death. He, too, was an elderly man, with a nervously hesitant manner, and while seemingly more than willing to discuss the general health of the transport's women passengers and even to wax eloquent on the advantages of the antiscorbutics he had prescribed for them, he was reluctant to give any details of whatever malaise had cost Elspeth Campbell her life.

"I was exceedingly sorry to lose her," he admitted, eyeing Andrew anxiously as he spoke. "She was a fine woman, and to die when in sight of her destination . . . well, that was ironic, was it not? She was one of the few who really *wanted* to come out here. Mainly, I suppose, on account of the daughter who is already here and of whom she was very fond. But that may be a blessing, of course—the captain will have told you that Mrs. Campbell has—had—two small girls on board?"

"Yes," Andrew confirmed. "He told me that. But . . ." He was still puzzled. "Was the poor woman ill for long before she died?"

"No. She was pregnant—six months pregnant—but perfectly healthy. Her demise was . . . it was sudden, Captain Hawley. Mrs. Campbell was brought to bed prematurely and of a stillborn child."

Normally Andrew would have left the matter at that. There were always deaths on board convict transports, he knew. Deaths from infectious diseases, malnutrition, ill-treatment, and even, on occasion, from judicial hanging, when convicts attempted mutiny . . . and women died in childbirth. The *Canada*'s surgeon had done well, and his care must have been exemplary for so few lives to have been lost on the nearly six-month passage; but something about the older man's manner made Andrew persist. The thin, stoop-shouldered surgeon was clearly ill at ease, Andrew sensed, and now, having said all he was seemingly prepared to say on the subject of Mrs. Campbell's death, he appeared anxious to turn to another topic—any other topic, so long as it did not concern the sergeant major's wife.

Finally he spoke of the war, of England's new hero, Lord Wellington, and of the terrible losses in the previous year during the retreat to Corunna.

"But His Lordship showed them what British troops are made of at Talavera," the old man asserted with pride. "And General Beckwith's force took Martinique, as I expect you will have heard, capturing two of Bonaparte's Eagles, and—"

Andrew broke in with quiet insistence. "Doctor, I think I should have a word with your sar'nt major, if you've no objection, before I return to the shore."

"I . . . er, why yes, if you wish. I'll send for him. I . . . er, did Captain Ward tell you? He had asked me to say nothing. There's no proof, and Campbell's a fine soldier, well respected by his men."

"Captain Ward told me nothing, sir," Andrew said. "But I fancy it might be as well if you were to do so. Of what is there no proof?"

The surgeon eyed him in dismay. "Why, that . . . er,

that is to say, the poor woman, Mrs. Campbell, had certain injuries which were not, in my view, caused by a fall. She claimed that she had fallen. But . . ." He shrugged unhappily and went on, with obvious reluctance, to describe the injuries.

Blackened eyes, a broken nose, and severe bruising of the lower part of her body seemed unlikely in the extreme to have been the result of a fall, Andrew thought, as he listened, and he asked crisply, when the old surgeon came to the end of his recital, "But you and Captain Ward decided that there was no proof that her husband had assaulted her?"

"She denied it, sir. Even when she became aware that she was dying. And Campbell was with her at the end. He was deeply moved, and he never left her side. I am quite sure, in my own mind, Captain Hawley, that his grief was heartfelt and . . . and genuine. As I told you, he is a fine soldier. A strict disciplinarian, well aware of his duty and a credit to his regiment. I hope, sir—" His gaze was still unhappy, Andrew saw, as the surgeon added, "I hope that no words of mine will cause trouble for Sergeant Major Campbell, for truly there *is* no proof that he beat her on this occasion."

"Was he in the habit of beating her?" Andrew demanded.

"Men do beat their wives, sir," the *Canada*'s surgeon reminded him. "Amongst the—er, the lower classes, it is almost a sign of virility, is it not?" He moved to the curtained doorway leading to his sick bay and dispatched his steward to summon Sergeant Major Campbell. "If you prefer to talk to Campbell in private, sir, you are at liberty to use this cabin."

"Thank you, Doctor," Andrew acknowledged. "I shall not require it for very long."

Sergeant Major Campbell answered the summons promptly. He came in, saluted smartly, and remained at attention, a tall, stiff figure, whose heavily jowled face was shuttered and devoid of expression. Even when bidden to stand at ease, he did not relax, and his eyes, dark and deep-set, were wary and watchful, although he replied readily to questions concerning the voyage and the draft he had brought out with him from Portsmouth. His manner was overly obsequious, his speech punctuated with too many deferences to Andrew's rank, and his accent thick and uneducated, smacking more of Glasgow than of the Highlands, from whence most of the men of the 73rd hailed.

But he was undoubtedly, as the ship's surgeon had claimed, a fine soldier—efficient, impeccably turned out, and well versed in his duties. When, at pains to make no premature judgment of him, Andrew expressed sympathy on his recent bereavement, the gaunt face clouded over, and the brisk, soldierly veneer seemed suddenly to crack.

"I've a gey sore hairt, sir, for 'tis a loss I'd never expected tae have tae face. And tae come when we were no' but a few days frae here . . . indeed, sir, that maks it awful hard tae bear. And I've two puir wee bairns, who are missing their mother sorely, as maybe the surgeon will hae told ye."

"Yes, he did," Andrew confirmed. "He also mentioned you have an elder daughter, who came out in the *Dromedary*."

Sergeant Major Campbell inclined his head. "Aye, a stepdaughter, sir. A scatterbrained wee girl who somehow contrived tae get hersel' overlooked when the *Dromedary* sailed. The families' quarters were overcrowded, and it was decided tae land a number o' us at Portsmouth, when His Excellency Colonel Macquarie came aboard. Jessie wasna wi' her mother, you see, sir, for all I'd left instructions for her, and the ship weighed before I could send a boat back tae bring her ashore." He shrugged, his tone rueful. "So the lassie came out by hersel'. But the women will have cared for her, I don't doubt, and she'll be wi' one o' the families now."

Despite the rueful tone, there was an underlying hint of anger in the big man's voice, and Andrew eyed him searchingly. There might, as the *Canada*'s surgeon had insisted, be no proof that Campbell had beaten his pregnant wife, but if he had in fact done so, it augured ill for the young stepdaughter who had "contrived to get herself overlooked" when the Governor's ship sailed, instead of going ashore in accordance with his instructions.

"Well, you will be able to reclaim her, will you not, Sar'nt Major?" Andrew suggested, with a touch of asperity. "What is her name—Jessie Campbell?"

"No, sir," Campbell answered woodenly. "Her mother wouldna permit her to take my name. She goes by her ain feyther's name—Maclaine. She'll be known as Jessie Maclaine here, likely."

"Jessica *India* Maclaine?" Andrew exclaimed, startled.

"Aye, that was the daft name Murdoch gave her. It couldna be called a Christian name, could it, sir, when the Indian people are all heathen savages? Murdo Maclaine was aye a damned, senseless fool!" Campbell's dark eyes suddenly narrowed, and the scorn in his voice changed to uncertainty. Forgetting the respect he had hitherto shown, he fixed Andrew with a coldly accusing gaze and demanded harshly, "For God's sake, how is it that the girl is known tae you? Ye're no' a Seventy-third officer, are ye?"

"No, Sergeant Major Campbell, I am not," Andrew conceded. "But I am about to transfer to the veteran company of the Seventy-third. At present I am serving on His Excellency's staff at the Government House and acting as port naval officer. That is how I come to know your stepdaughter. She is employed as a maid—"

"A maid, is it? Is yon no' another name for the whores who keep house for the officers here?" Campbell burst out. Andrew had spoken with crisp formality, intending to keep the big man in his place, and the angry interruption took him by surprise, as much by its vehemence as by the implication it drew. "The damned wee beezum! But I might have known, for I've heard plenty about the way females behave in this colony. Aye, and the way the officers take advantage o' the ones that canna support themselves. Jessie hasna a trade nor any skills—I might have guessed what she'd be driven tae left on her ain. Though she was brought up strictly in a good Christian household. I saw tae that, I gie ye my word, sir."

The "sir" was belated, and Andrew drew himself up. "That will do, Sar'nt Major!" he snapped. "You have been misinformed as to the moral state of this colony now that order has been restored. Your stepdaughter's behavior has, to the best of my knowledge, been exemplary. And she has been exceedingly well cared for . . . by the Governor's lady herself, with whom she is in service as a personal maid. Mrs. Macquarie engaged her during the passage out, I believe, and seems to have a high regard for her, so you need have no anxieties on that score. And you will, I think, have to employ a maid or a housekeeper to care for your two young children—initially, at all events. Their Excellencies are on tour, and Jessica is with them."

The sergeant major regarded him sullenly, but Andrew's rank and the sharpness of his reproof had their effect. He came to attention, mindful of discipline. "Aye, sir, I understand. But Mrs. Macquarie canna keep the lassie when I'm in such sair need of her. I've two motherless bairns on ma hands, sir, and—"

"You will have to speak to your commanding officer of that matter," Andrew told him. "Very well, Sar'nt Major, you may go."

Campbell hesitated, as if wanting to say more, but then, thinking better of it, he saluted and turned on his heel. Still uncertain what to make of him, Andrew left the surgeon's cabin and went to conclude his official business with the *Canada*'s master. A little over an hour later, when he was preparing to rejoin the pilot cutter for what promised to be a long pull, under oars, up the six-mile length of the harbor, he saw the sergeant major come on deck with his two children.

Both little girls were neatly dressed, and although subdued, they evidently were on affectionate terms with their father. Campbell, for his part, seemed totally absorbed in them. Hoisting the younger child onto his shoulders, he took the elder by the hand and paced the after deck with them, pointing out objects on shore and going to considerable pains to keep them amused and entertained.

Perhaps, Andrew thought, he had been wrong about the man and might even have done him an injustice. He had a temper, but . . . he appeared to have won the good opinion of both the ship's master and her surgeon, and both officers had had over five months to observe and judge him. Whereas he himself had only a brief interview to go on. He shrugged and, having taken leave of Captain Ward, followed Robert Watson into the cutter.

Little Jessica India Maclaine was, he told himself, in no danger from her stepfather.

The viceregal tour had begun auspiciously with a drive along the newly completed turnpike road to Parramatta. It was a fine road, built of stone, with a gravel surface and a ditch on either side, and the Governor's carriage, surrounded by its mounted escort and with Joseph Big on the box, had bowled smoothly along it, to draw up outside Government House, Parramatta, at seven o'clock in the evening.

There had been cheers all the way; little groups of settlers had come running from their farms, and in the small township of Parramatta itself, every resident, convict and free, had turned out by lantern light to line the street and bid an enthusiastic welcome to the travelers. Riding in the carriage with her mistress, Jessica had thrilled to the prevailing excitement, proud and happy to be even an insignificant part of the triumphant scene.

In the eight months since his assumption of the governorship, Colonel Macquarie had transformed Sydney. The old rows, as they had been called, had given place to streets fifty feet wide, cleared of roots and of the larger livestock that had previously been permitted to roam at will . . . and they had been renamed. His Majesty and the royal dukes had given their names to George, York, Gloucester, Kent, Clarence, and Cumberland streets; the colony's former Governors were remembered in Phillip, Hunter, King, and Bligh streets; the Colonial Secretary in Castlereagh Street; and Macquarie Place and Elizabeth Street completed the sequence.

Bridges had been widened, markets enlarged and rebuilt; a new hospital, a post office, a justice court, and numerous other public and private buildings were in the course of construction; and on what had been common land, on the south side of the town, a fine new park and a racecourse were taking shape, to be known as Hyde Park.

Parramatta was, by contrast, small and somewhat dilapidated, although the approach to it, from the summit of a low hill, had taken Jessica's breath away, with the spring-flowering wattle turning the surrounding, parklike countryside into a vista of golden yellow blossom, brilliant even in the fading light.

The township itself consisted of a single, mile-long main street, with Government House at one end and the river, with its wharf and wooden storage sheds, at the other. Government House, despite its pretentious title, was small and had but a single story, built on straggling lines, yet—unlike Sydney's viceregal residence—it was neither damp nor in need of constant repair to prevent its collapse.

After a meal prepared by convict cooks, the Governor had received the local magistrates and civil and military officers, but he had gone early to bed, and soon after dawn the following morning, he and Mrs. Macquarie had set off on horseback, followed by their retinue, to cross George's River and break their fast at the home of a wealthy settler named Moore.

Jessica, left behind in Parramatta, had occupied part of the morning exploring the township of white-painted, weatherboard houses and visiting the church—which was larger and infinitely finer than Sydney's St. Philip's. In the afternoon, she had traveled to the next projected overnight stop with the Government House servants, in ox-drawn carts laden with tents, which had been set up by early evening, ready for the arrival of the Governor and his party.

After that, however, to Jessica's delight, Mrs. Macquarie had insisted that she must travel with the viceregal retinue. She had ridden in India as a child and, although out of practice, had acquitted herself well enough on horseback when her mistress chose to travel thus; and, for the rest, she had traveled somewhat less comfortably in the carriage. Yet, for all the inevitable stiffness, the saddle sores, and the jolting, for her the journey was one of endless enchantment.

Through green pastureland and newly seeded arable, winding among the thickly timbered hills and along a track alive with kangaroos, emus, and other strange animals, the cavalcade made its unhurried way. Flocks of gaily hued parakeets rose skyward in alarm as Sergeant Whalan's escort of dragoons clattered past. In the eight months she had spent in Sydney, Jessica had never seen any of the native inhabitants at close range; but now each day she saw them, peering out from their hiding places beneath the trees, frightened yet insatiably curious.

Everywhere the flowering shrubs added their golden beauty to the scene, and Captain Antill named them for her, so that soon she was familiar not only with the ever-present wattle but also with the heavenly blue of jacaranda, the heavily scented frangipani blossoms, and the sarsaparilla bushes, from which, Dr. Redfern told her, the first settlers had brewed their "Botany Bay tea."

They rode southward to the Cow Pastures and made camp there, witnessing the alarming spectacle of two wild bulls fighting for supremacy, and hearing, as the darkness fell, the bellowing of the great herd that had bred and increased almost a hundredfold from the domestic cattle Governor Phillip had imported, twenty years before.

They saw the fine flocks of purebred Merino sheep on the Macarthur estate at Camden and, sheltering temporarily in a bark hut at Benkennie, came upon Mrs. Macarthur herself, supervising some half dozen of her assigned convict laborers in the construction of a fence designed to keep the wild cattle out.

Jessica was impressed by Elizabeth Macarthur's friendliness and by her cheerful, open manner, and as the party sat round the campfire that evening, she watched the forging of a bond of friendship between her mistress and the wife of the man who, seemingly, was feared and hated by most of the colony's inhabitants. But Mrs. Macquarie, as always, judged the merits of all new acquaintances for herself, and later, as she disrobed in her tent, she told Jessica very firmly, "Elizabeth Macarthur is a woman after my own heart. She has great courage, and her knowledge of cattle and sheep rearing, as well as of horticulture, surpasses that of anyone else I have met in this colony. Whatever her husband may or may not have done to provoke the rebellion against Commodore Bligh, I will hear no criticism of that most admirable woman."

They moved on next day, waved on their way by Elizabeth Macarthur from her new boundary fence, and made camp beside a ford across a river, which Dr. Redfern identified as the Nepean.

From James Meehan, the black-browed Irish emancipist surveyor whom the Governor had included in his party, Jessica learned of the confusion the first explorers of the area had met with when they had endeavored to follow the course of the river through the trackless wilderness of the bush country.

"The early maps, made in Governor Phillip's day, showed parts of the Hawkesbury River attributed to the Nepean, so they did," the Irishman explained. With a stick, he drew a widely curving line in the damp sand at his feet to illustrate the point he was making, and then, an odd little smile curving his lips, he gestured to the distant mountains. "One day, please God, I truly believe that we shall be after finding a way to cross those mountains. 'Tis my prayer that I may be there when we find it, for there will be more and even greater rivers to be surveyed and tracked to their source. And then you will see a vast expansion of this colony, Miss Maclaine, just as Governor Philip prophesied when he first landed here."

Jessica listened with awe, but she only half believed him. To her, as the vicerega party moved on from one well-stocked farmstead to another, it seemed that the colony was already interminable, the grazing sheep and the lowing cattle so numerous as to be beyond her power to assess. From the campsite known by its native name of Kirboonwallie, they rode some ten or twelve miles to Menangle, where Mr. Robert Campbell's grant was situated, and the gum forest gave place to what was almost a small village. A fine, stone-built family residence was surrounded by laborers' cottages, stables, barns, and cattle sheds, and in the lush paddocks, sheep were grazing as far as the eye could see.

A series of rainstorms delayed further progress for two days, but then the sun and the cloudless blue skies reappeared, and the oxcarts were sent lumbering ahead to make camp within sight of the mighty Hawkesbury River. Here, at a place called St. Andrews, on Bunburry Creek, the Governor halted in order to inspect the farm of the recently deceased Andrew Thompson, who had willed it to him.

It was a beautiful place, set in the most picturesque surroundings, with acres of growing crops, every variety of livestock, and a splendid residence, all in perfect order. There was even a floating bridge across the river, built by the late owner, and Mrs. Macquarie waxed enthusiastic about the unexpected legacy and expressed the wistful hope that his duties might permit the Governor to spend some time there in the not too distant future.

"The late Mr. Thompson is an example of what can be achieved by the emancipist settlers, if they are prepared to work hard and put the past behind them," she told Jessica. "Governor King made him chief constable for the Hawkesbury district, and Colonel Macquarie had recently appointed him to the magistracy, after Dr. Arndell's health compelled him to retire from office. I believe he was only a lad of sixteen when he was sentenced to deportation . . . and he was not forty when he died. Like that young man Mrs. Ovens said you were so taken with at our farewell ball for Commodore Bligh," she added, smiling at Jessica's embarrassed blushes. "Justin Broome—that was his name, was it not?"

"Yes, ma'am," Jessica stammered, wishing that the kindly Mrs. Ovens had kept a still tongue in her head. "But I only—"

Mrs. Macquarie waved her to silence. She went on, following her train of thought to its conclusion, "Like Justin Broome, who was born here to emancipist parents, Mr. Andrew Thompson risked his life to save others. But he, poor soul, was not spared to continue the good work he was doing in this district. He contracted an affliction of the lungs, I understand, as a result of the noble efforts he made to rescue people who were cut off in the floods earlier this year. Nevertheless, despite his premature death he was, I feel sure, proof that His Excellency's policy is the right one, in regard to those who came out here as convicts and earned their freedom by diligence and good conduct. And there are others, Jessica—many others. We shall meet them, as we travel farther afield."

And indeed they did; some small landholders on thirty-acre grants, living in primitive wattle-and-daub cabins which, when the mighty Hawkesbury River was in flood, were frequently washed away and then just as frequently rebuilt. Each smallholding had its domestic animals—hens, a few hogs, occasionally a house cow—and each had its fields, painstakingly cleared from the bush and growing wheat and maize, fruit and vegetables.

There were many large farms, like that of the late Andrew Thompson, but for the most part, the Hawkesbury settlements were worked by men and women who had come out in chains and, as Mrs. Macquarie had said, earned their freedom—and their thirty-acre grants—by diligence and good conduct. Not all were successful, but when a man failed, lost heart, or proved incapable, his land was sold or reclaimed and allocated to someone else.

Jessica, unversed in map reading, lost track of where the Governor was leading them, but as she grew accustomed to riding fifteen or twenty miles on horseback, her interest in the wilder parts of the country came almost to match that of her mistress. Elizabeth Macquarie was seemingly tireless. Dismounting from her horse, she climbed tree-clad hills on foot, the better to view her surroundings, and often she and Jessica were well ahead of the gentlemen of the party as they all tackled a steep ascent.

A brief return to Parramatta, for two days' rest and an opportunity for the Governor to compose a dispatch to the Colonial Office, and the tour was resumed. This time, with the deputy government surveyor, Mr. George Evans, and Mr. Gregory Blaxland added to the party, the carriage was left behind and only the horsemen and the slow-moving oxcarts set off to explore new land recently discovered by Evans, and a river he had called the Western, which he believed was a tributary of the Nepean.

Heading westward, beyond Prospect Hill, halts were made and hospitality offered at some of the larger land-holdings. Lieutenant Nicholas Bayly's property on South Creek, and the farms of Dr. D'Arcy Wentworth and Mrs. King, widow of the late Governor, were inspected and admired, and supper taken at Emu Ford, where Mr. Blaxland had a small farm. After that, to Jessica's joy, they headed into the wilds, bivouacking on the west bank of the Nepean beneath the shadow of the Blue Mountains.

At dawn next day, a boat was launched and they rowed up the wide river, beneath lofty, tree-girt banks and in brilliant sunshine. At ten o'clock they went ashore to break their fast, half a mile from where the newly discovered tributary flowed into the Nepean. The chosen picnic site was on the right bank, on a flat rock, which formed a natural terrace at the foot of a perpendicular cliff fully four hundred feet high.

Jessica was entranced by the beauty of the scene and by the birds flying among the trees that covered the rugged cliff-face right up to its summit. An aboriginal, hired as a guide, gave the native name of the new river as the Warragamba, and the Governor, delighted by the sound of this name, directed Surveyor Evans to mark it thus on the maps he was preparing.

They rowed an additional three or four miles upriver, but then found their progress halted by a spectacular waterfall and were compelled to turn back, reaching the tented camp as darkness was falling.

After that, the party went northward, Mrs. Macquarie finally wearying a little, but the Governor riding tirelessly for up to thirty miles a day, making detours so as to visit isolated farms and settlements and selecting sites for the new towns and hamlets he planned to establish. Finally, they were back at the Hawkesbury and crossing in the floating bridge from Andrew Thompson's farm to the Green Hills.

"It will be a relief to rest for a few days," Elizabeth Macquarie confided, as they made their way through a little crowd of cheering settlers to the picturesque Government Cottage prepared for their reception. "And," she added ruefully, "although I have seldom enjoyed myself so much, it will also be a relief not to be eaten alive by leeches and flying insects."

She sought her bed as soon as they reached the cottage, built on the slope of a low hill overlooking the river and the sun-bleached wooden houses of the township, and as Jessica helped her to disrobe, she said, in a strained whisper, "Jessica child, say nothing to a soul, but I think I am again pregnant. God grant that this time I may carry the baby to its term!"

Jessica echoed her prayer, feeling tears come welling into her eyes as she did so.

"Will you wish to go back to Sydney, ma'am," she asked anxiously, "if it is so?"

"Yes, if it is so," Mrs. Macquarie agreed. "But it may not be, and in any event, I shall rest here quietly until I am sure. His Excellency will have duties to perform, people to meet, and places to see. He will not mind if we delay here for a little while."

The delay lasted for a week, during which Mrs. Macquarie kept to her bed and the Governor occupied himself by riding out to visit settlements in the neighborhood, planning still more new townships and detailing the additions he wished made to those already in existence. He gave names to each and decided to change the name of the Green Hills to Windsor—a decision that met with only guarded approval from the inhabitants.

But they feted him, called public meetings, and read loyal addresses, and when Mrs. Macquarie was rested sufficiently to rejoin her husband, a dinner was given in their honor, at which loyal toasts were proposed and drunk to the new settlements, although as yet most were only names on the maps the two government surveyors were preparing.

The day before the viceregal party was due to leave for Sydney, a wedding took place in the tiny, weatherboard church, and the Governor was invited to stand in the place of the girl's father—now deceased—and give the bride away. He did so gladly, and attending on her mistress, Jessica witnessed the marriage of Lucy Tempest to Luke Cahill, a handsome young emancipist who, it seemed, was employed on his bride's sister's property at Yarramundie.

It was a joyous occasion, attended by all the landowners from miles around, and the service was conducted by the Reverend Robert Cartwright with impressive eloquence. Jessica recognized many of the wedding guests from seeing them at Government House, although she could put names to only a few. Abigail O'Shea, the bride's sister, she remembered well; Mr. Dawson, from nearby Upwey—still in mourning for his wife—Dr. Arndell and his family, and Mr. and Mrs. Jasper Spence were among those she knew; but the majority were strangers to her, and she was glad enough to forgo the wedding breakfast when Mrs. Macquarie, pleading fatigue, left after the church service.

"It occurred to me, Jessica," the Governor's wife observed when they were alone in the seclusion of her bedroom in the Government Cottage, "that Mrs. O'Shea was not ill-pleased by the match her sister has made, for all the young man is what His Excellency sometimes satirically terms an 'untouchable.' And I am sure that *he* will be pleased, for both young ladies are gently bred, the daughters of a naval officer, and Mr. Cahill came out here as a convict. It will be the first marriage between our two social extremes, I am almost certain, and perhaps others may be encouraged to follow their example."

Jessica contented herself with a dutiful "Yes, ma'am," not fully understanding the logic of her mistress's reasoning. An untouchable was, she knew, an Indian term for low-caste Hindu menials, and the Governor, of course—having spent many years in India, on military service—would be conversant with all that the term implied. Luke Cahill had not seemed to her to bear any resemblance to a humble Indian outcaste; indeed, he had appeared well-dressed and gentlemanly, but . . . She sighed and reached for her mistress's hairbrush.

Even in the servants' quarters at Government House, the gulf between convict and free was apparent—greater and more insurmountable than that which existed between the regiment's rank and file and its officers. She had accepted both without question until now. Now, as she gently plied the brush, she suddenly found herself thinking of Justin Broome, who was a "currency kid," or so he had derisively styled himself. As the son of New South Wales emancipist parents, would Justin be considered acceptable by London society, she wondered . . . and would the Lords of the Admiralty grant him a commission in the Royal Navy?

Mrs. Macquarie's voice broke into her thoughts. She said approvingly, "Your touch is so soothing, Jessica, you have almost sent me to sleep. Stop now, child, and help me into bed."

Obediently, Jessica put away the hairbrush and went to turn down the coverings on the big four-poster bed. Her mistress lay back on the heaped pillows, smiling at her sleepily.

"I think I must be pregnant," she asserted, "because I feel so tired—which isn't like me, is it? But I have not yet told His Excellency . . . I dare not risk disappointing him again. He wants a son so much, and I would gladly give him his heart's desire." She went on speaking, as she often did, more to herself than to the listening Jessica. "I am His Excellency's second wife—I expect you knew that, did you not? His first wife was called Jane, and when our little daughter was born—the baby who died, just before we came out here—he wanted her to be christened Jane. Jane had never given him a child, you see, and . . . oh, that is why *I* want to give him a son." Her voice changed, taking on a brisk, resolute tone. "I must stop riding on horseback, Jessica, and climbing mountains and having late nights. You must help me, you must remind me, should I forget. Will you do that?"

"Yes, ma'am, of course I will," Jessica assured her eagerly. "I'll do everything I can."

"You are a good child," Mrs. Marquarie told her. "Indeed, Jessica India, you have become the treasure I hoped you would! And truth to tell, I should find it very hard now to do without you." She took a hand from beneath the coverlet and clasped Jessica's. "Are you happy, working for me?"

"Oh, yes!" The answer came unhesitatingly. She was,

Jessica thought, happier than she had been since her
childhood, bound to the kindly, charming woman on the
big rumpled bed by ties that would be hard to break. Only
to her mother had she previously given her unstinted devotion, but that devotion had been strained almost beyond endurance until, like her brother, Murdo, she had made an
end to it by running away.

She bit back a sigh and bent to straighten the ruffled
coverlet. There had been no word of Murdo, no letter from
her mother, but no doubt her stepfather would have seen to
that. . . . Mrs. Macquarie again grasped her hand.

"I need you, child," she said softly. "More than ever
now, if God grants my prayer and this pregnancy is to run
to its full term. You will not leave me, will you, Jessica?
Promise you will not?"

"I will never leave you, ma'am," Jessica promised, her
throat tight. "Never—as long as you have need of me!"

But, three days later, on the return of the viceregal party
to Sydney, she found her stepfather waiting for her, and
the promise she had made so willingly had, after all, to be
broken . . . and at her mistress's insistence.

"Sergeant Major Campbell's need is greater than mine,
Jessica," Mrs. Marquarie said regretfully. "He has suffered a most tragic loss, and there are your two poor little
sisters to think of. I must not keep you, when it is your
duty to go to him and try to take your mother's place."

"But ma'am, I was giving you my word. In truth, I
would sooner be staying with you."

"Your duty is to your family, Jessica. It will break my
heart to lose you, but I release you from your promise."

It was, Jessica knew, useless to protest. That afternoon,
with a heavy heart, she left Government House to walk the
short distance to the barracks and her stepfather's quarters
in what was now called Clarence Street. Fergus Mackinnon, who appeared pleased by her change of dwelling, escorted her, carrying her dress box and small bundle of possessions.

"It will be turning out for the best, Miss Maclaine," he
told her. "You will see. Now that you are no longer in His

Excellency's household, I can be asking your father's permission to keep company with you, perhaps, and—"

In a rare burst of temper, Jessica rounded on him. "He will not give it, Piper Mackinnon! And he is my *stepfather,* not my father. All he is wanting me for is to skivvy and cook for him, whatever tale he has spun for Their Excellencies."

"There are the bairns," Fergus pointed out reproachfully. "Your sisters—that is, your half-sisters—who will be sorely wanting your love and care."

He was right, Jessica knew. Their mother's death—the news of which had left her numb with grief—must have come as an appalling shock to Janet and little Flora.

Her fears and her bitter anger faded when Fergus left her at the door of the neat, brick-built quarter and the two little girls, prompted by the woman who had been caring for them, came running to meet her, crying her name. She fell to her knees, arms outheld, to hug them and kiss their small, well-scrubbed faces. At first they were shy of her, and Flora hung back, whimpering and seeming not to recognize her, but Jessica persisted, and soon laughter was mingled with their tears, as old jests and quips from the past were remembered and shared again. Finally, with each holding a hand, they led her into the house, chattering like magpies.

"Jessie's back, Feyther!" Janet exclaimed excitedly. "Our ain sister Jessie, do you see?"

"Aye, I see that." Her stepfather, Jessica saw, stood in front of the fireplace, tall and imposing, his gaunt face grimly set, as if he were experiencing difficulty in controlling his emotions. He dismissed the woman—evidently a soldier's wife, pressed into service—with a brusque word of thanks and, when she had gone, turned dark, angry eyes on Jessica.

"This is a house of mourning," he reproved her coldly. "Such laughter is unseemly; even if you are no' mindful that your mother is lately deid, the weans are . . . and so am I. I'll thank ye tae remember it."

The reproof was unjust, but Jessica, anxious to avoid dissent, bowed her head submissively and said nothing.

Throughout the rest of the day, she cooked and cleaned, tended the two little girls, and endeavored to keep out of her stepfather's way, conscious always of his brooding gaze, which followed her wherever she went. The children's touching pleasure in her company heightened her determination to give him no cause for complaint, but nevertheless it was with a sense of relief that, after the evening meal, she heard him say that he was going out.

The children were in bed when he returned, and Jessica, sorting out a pile of their soiled clothing and neglected mending, which the soldier's wife had allowed to accumulate, was taken by surprise. Realizing that it was too late to make the escape she had planned to the comparative safety of the children's room, she remained where she was, praying that he would ignore her and go straight to his bed without entering the kitchen.

In the old days, she recalled, Duncan Campbell had always been violent when he had been drinking, but her mother had known how to counter the violence—or had suffered it, rather than permit him to vent his drunken rage on Murdo or herself. But her mother was dead, she thought, panic-stricken. Her mother, God rest her brave soul, could no longer come to her aid . . . and her stepfather had clearly been drinking.

He had stumbled as he opened the street door, and hearing an ugly stream of obscenities as he picked himself up, Jessica looked about her wildly for some weapon with which to defend herself. His pipe-clayed belt, with scabbard and bayonet, lay on the chair on which, in readiness for the following morning's parade, he had draped his scarlet tunic, and with trembling hands, she drew out the gleaming length of honed steel and thrust it under the piled garments on the table. She was endeavoring to extinguish the lamp by which she had been working when, with an oath, her stepfather came staggering into the kitchen.

"Dinna think ye can hide from me, ye damned wee huzzy!" he shouted at her wrathfully. "Leave the light be— I ken fine ye're there. And we've an account tae settle, have we no'? Did you not run awa' when the troopship was at Portsmouth and I'd tell't ye tae come ashore wi' yer mither and the bairns?"

Jessica shrank from him, all the remembered fear she had known since her childhood threatening to overwhelm her. "Yes," she admitted, in a tense whisper. "Yes, I did."

"Yes, *Feyther*!" he roared. "Divil tak' ye, lassie, have ye not yet learned how tae address me?"

Her stomach churning and her mouth dry, Jessica could only stare back at him in terrified silence. Her failure to give him the answer he had demanded added fuel to the fire of his anger.

"Runnin' off as ye did, damn your eyes, 'twas enough tae break yer mither's hairt," he accused. "She was never the same, after you left us. She had nae spunk, nae will tae live, and 'tis you I'm holding tae blame for that, Jessie! You and yon pulin' wee brother o' yours. 'Tis on your account my two puir bairns are left wi'out their mither."

Jessica started to speak and then bit back the words. Of what use was it to tell him that her mother had urged her to run away, had helped her to hide from him, on board the *Dromedary*? Or that Murdo had also fled, with their mother's connivance, because he had made life unbearable for them both? Of what use was it to try to tell him anything when, as he always had, he held the whip hand and would bully her into submission?

"Ye cunning wee beezum, getting yoursel' yon fine job wi' Her Excellency," Duncan Campbell sneered. "Hobnobbin' wi' the officers, awa' on tour wi' the Governor and, they tell me, riding in a carriage, as if ye were a lady born! Weel, lassie, a' that's over, for I've put a stop tae it. . . ." The rasping, bitter voice ranted on, and Jessica tried in vain to shut her ears to it.

Only the thought of the two little girls in the bedroom beyond kept her from taking refuge in flight. Their father was fond of them both, she knew, and he had always treated them affectionately, but . . . She stifled a sob. For their sake and for the sake of her poor dead mother she must endeavor to placate him, until the effects of his drinking wore off.

"Leave me be, Father," she pleaded. "I am sorry I ran away, and I am sorry if I—if I did hurt my mother. I loved her, I truly loved her, and I never intended to hurt her. I—"

"Aye, but ye did, Jessica! *You* broke her hairt, I'm tellin' ye, and her death's at your door, no' mine." He towered over her, swaying a little, his bloodshot dark eyes bright with menace. "I'll need tae punish ye for that and for running awa'. 'Tis ma duty and what she would ha' wished."

He reached for the belt at his waist and started to unbuckle it, his fingers clumsy in their haste, and for a paralyzed moment, Jessica did not move. Always before, throughout her childhood, he had subdued her thus; she had been too weak to defend herself against his brutal assaults, too frightened of what he would do to her mother or Murdo, if she attempted to defy him. But . . . her mother was dead, and Murdo was not here, she told herself, fighting down panic.

He had the belt looped round his hand when, at last, all fear left her and, thrusting beneath the pile of clothing on the table, her fingers closed about the hilt of the bayonet she had hidden there.

"No!" Jessica's voice was high-pitched with strain, but she held the gleaming bayonet steadily in front of her, grasping it with both hands. "I will kill you if you lay a hand on me! Put away the belt."

Duncan Campbell stared at her, his jaw dropping in ludicrous surprise. Then he recovered himself and lurched toward her, swearing, the belt raised high above his head.

"Why, ye damned wee bitch! Ye've asked for it and, by God, you shall have it!"

The bayonet tip came to rest against his throat, above the loosened collar of his tunic. Jessica did not speak, but the resolute courage with which she faced him gave even Duncan Campbell pause. He let his hand fall, and the belt fell with it, as the sharp tip of the bayonet nicked the skin of his neck and a small trickle of blood ran down the front of his shirt.

"D'ye mean it?" he demanded, in a shocked voice.

"Damme, ye've drawn blood! Do ye really mean ye'd kill me, Jessie?"

"Aye," Jessica confirmed. "I mean it. You'll not beat me again—you'll never beat me again, as long as I live! And I *will* kill you if you try!"

She had not expected him to capitulate so easily, but to her relief, he did, taking refuge in bluster. And suddenly he was robbed of all menace; feeling only scorn and disgust, she listened to his excuses, his insistence that he had acted for her own good, and then watched him stagger sullenly away to his own room.

For the next three days, she hugged her small victory to her, satisfied that her stepfather ignored her, while giving all his attention to his own two daughters, who basked happily in the warm glow of his approval. He remained sober and spent more time than usual in the barracks, but as a precaution, Jessica retained his bayonet, hiding it beneath her bedclothes when she slept.

On the fourth day, toward evening, he brought a pleasant-faced, buxom woman back with him. She was evidently well-known to Janet and Flora, who greeted her arrival with cries of delight, but Jessica had no inkling of the purpose of her visit until her stepfather turned to her and said brusquely, "Pack your bags, Jessie, and awa' back tae Government House—I'll no' need ye any mair. This is Agnes Hope, who is a guid, God-fearing woman and a widow. We're tae be wed, as soon as I can pay the license, so you'll not have tae concern yoursel' wi' my bairns or me any longer." Agnes Hope touched his arm, and reddening, he added in a more placatory tone, "Ye may visit wi' the bairns when ye wish. But they'll be fine wi' Mrs. Hope— she came out wi' us in the *Canada*."

Jessica summoned a startled smile and then, thankful that the ordeal was over, went to pack her bags. When this was done and she returned to the lamplit kitchen to take leave of her little half-sisters, she found Flora seated on Mrs. Hope's lap and Janet crouched contentedly at her feet. The sound of their laughter stilled the prickling of her conscience. Agnes Hope, she realized, studying the round, apple-cheeked face, must have come out as a convict on board the *Canada,* since soldiers' widows were seldom, if ever, permitted to accompany regimental drafts overseas. But she seemed a good and kindly woman, for all that, and both children were evidently fond of her. Probably she would care for them better and more capably than she herself had been able to . . . which was what her mother would have wanted above all else.

Her initial doubts finally dispelled, Jessica closed the door of the quarter behind her and set out, once again, on the familiar road to Government House, certain, this time, of the welcome that would be awaiting her. And, as she walked slowly through the evening dusk, it was borne on her that she had left her childhood behind and with it the fears that had, for so long, tormented her.

Duncan Campbell had been revealed to her at last for the cowardly bully he was. She had stood up to him and defied him, and he had turned tail and run. "Oh, Mam!" she whispered to the darkening sky, "I wish you had been here to see him run!"

CHAPTER XIII

"If it please you, sir," the elderly Admiralty clerk said, lowering his balding head in a respectful bow, "Admiral Moorsom is free to see you now. Be so good as to follow me, sir."

Captain Pasco rose at once and, his cocked hat tucked correctly beneath his arm, moved toward the door of the anteroom. Reaching it, he paused to give the waiting Justin a smile of encouragement.

"The great and revered Lord Nelson once told me that he was kept cooling his heels in this room for three hours, whilst Their Lordships debated the wisdom of granting him a lieutenant's commission. Let us hope that your wait is not as long, Mr. Broome."

And that it would be equally successful, John Pasco thought to himself, as he followed his guide along a wide, picture-hung corridor to the Second Sea Lord's room.

Rear Admiral Sir Robert Moorsom greeted him affably and waved him to a chair. The rear admiral was a distinguished officer, now in his fifties, who had been in command of the seventy-four-gun *Revenge* at Trafalgar, and like Pasco himself, he had been severely wounded in the battle. Another bond between them was the *Hindostan*, which Sir Robert had commanded twenty years earlier, on first attaining post rank, and he asked now, with nostalgia, about the old ship.

"Razeed her since you paid her off, have they not, and renamed her, too?" he suggested. "A sad day, John, when an old war-horse loses her guns and comes to the end of her fighting life."

"A sad day indeed, sir," Pasco agreed.

The admiral shrugged his slim, epauletted shoulders. "You brought back the rebel Corps from Botany Bay, I believe . . . and Commodore William Bligh with 'em? Not an easy passage for you, I imagine."

"It was less—er—less difficult than I'd anticipated, sir." He smiled. "The commodore was on board my ship, and most of the rebel regiment was on board the *Dromedary*. We lost their commanding officer, Lieutenant Colonel Paterson, off the Horn. Natural causes, sir; he was a sick man when he left Sydney, and if the truth were told, it was a miracle he lived as long as he did. And, something else"— his smile widened—"just after we weathered the Horn, my wife, Rebecca, gave birth to a son. A strapping eight pound boy, sir!"

"Did she, by Jove!" Moorsom's smile echoed his warmly. "My felicitations to you both. That's splendid news. But now, refresh my memory, if you please . . . you made a fairly fast passage, I think?"

"Not unduly, sir," Pasco amended. "A hundred and sixty-six days to Spithead. If it had been just my *Hindostan,* we would have been here long before. As it was, the old *Dromedary* is a slow sailer, and we were held up in Rio for three weeks for repairs to the *Porpoise*. We made Spithead on October twenty-fifth of last year."

"How did Commodore Bligh take the delay?"

"Well enough, sir, in the circumstances."

Prompted by questions from the admiral, John Pasco went into details. He was anxious concerning his future, eager to learn whether his request for a new command was to be acceded to and his overdue promotion assured; but knowing Moorsom, he was careful to betray neither his anxiety nor his eagerness. It was evident from the older man's manner and from the questions he was asking that he had something on his mind; he was not, it seemed, entirely satisfied that the passage from Sydney had been as comparatively uneventful as he himself had implied.

"You know, of course," Admiral Moorsom said suddenly, "that the court-martial of the New South Wales Corps's commandant, Lieutenant Colonel Johnston, is to take place very soon?"

"I heard so, yes, sir."

"Bligh's charging him with high treason, John. A damned serious charge. But . . . you've been out there, you've been in the colony. What's your view? Is the charge justified?"

Pasco hesitated, conscious of the admiral's deep-set blue eyes fixed searchingly on his face.

"In my view, sir," he answered at last, "the charge is entirely justified. But . . ." Again he hesitated, searching for the right words. "It should also be brought against a certain gentleman—formerly a captain in the regiment but now a civilian—who was the real instigator of the rebellion against Commodore Bligh."

"You mean Mr. John Macarthur, I take it?"

This time Pasco replied without hesitation, realizing that the Second Sea Lord was well informed as to the complexities of the impending trial.

"I do, sir, yes." Again, under Moorsom's brisk prompting, he went into detail, giving chapter and verse of what, in Sydney, was now called the Rum Rebellion. He had talked to both factions in the dispute, to the loyal supporters of the deposed Governor and to those who had connived at his arrest, and he had listened to the accusations made against John Macarthur—some by his erstwhile adherents. "I've never met the man, sir," he admitted. "But I heard a great deal about him when I was in Sydney—little was to his credit, sir. And Commodore Bligh was not the first Governor with whom he crossed swords. The late Governor King, I was told, referred to him as 'the secret assassin of my honor and reputation.' Damning enough, as I'm sure you will agree."

"He's raising plenty of influential support here," Admiral Moorsom observed distastefully. "Lord Camden, of course, and His Grace of Northumberland; even, it's said, Admiral Hunter, and a host of others." He ran through a list, ticking the names off on his fingers. "But the worst he's done is spread a positive spate of malicious rumors concerning Bligh . . . aided and abetted by a fellow named Foveaux, who came home, I understand, in *your* convoy from Rio, John."

"Lieutenant Colonel Joseph Foveaux," John Pasco supplied, with equal distaste, "who was not involved in the rebellion but acted as Governor when he arrived back from leave, after Bligh had been deposed and held in arrest. An unprincipled fellow, in my opinion, but . . . he ingratiated himself with Governor Macquarie before he left Sydney." He shrugged. "He arrived in Rio on board the *Speke,* sir, having come from New Zealand. The *Speke* joined us, and Foveaux instantly had himself transferred to another packet . . . he was determined to get to England before Commodore Bligh."

Moorsom grunted. "He and Macarthur gave evidence at Lieutenant Kent's court-martial, as I expect you know. Kent's acquittal did not aid William Bligh's cause."

"The Commodore will be vindicated when Colonel Johnston is tried, sir," Pasco asserted confidently.

"I hope to heaven he is," the admiral returned, with feeling. "Well, you've told me what I wanted to know, John, and I'm glad to hear you speak so well of Bligh. As a seaman and navigator, he probably has no peer, but from what I've heard about him, he has a fiendish temper. But he's due for his flag, and I, for one, would like to see him given it, although the Lords Commissioners won't hear of promoting him until after Johnston's trial. Sir Joseph Banks is giving him impassioned support, and that alone would suffice for me, I must confess—Banks is a gentleman of great integrity and a very good judge of character."

"Yes, indeed, sir," Pasco agreed. He waited, avoiding the admiral's eye, and Moorsom said, with an indulgent smile, "As to yourself, John . . . the First Lord's closeted with the Prime Minister and likely to be for the rest of the morning. Spencer Perceval is horrified by the naval estimates, which isn't surprising, but Yorke's a damned fine First Lord. He'll talk him out of it. However, I digress. . . . The board met a week ago, and I'm at liberty to tell you that you'll be made post from the eleventh of April. None too soon, eh, thanks to Admiral Nelson?"

Greatly relieved, Pasco stammered his gratitude, and Admiral Moorsom's smile widened. "John Quilliam robbed you of five years' seniority, did he not? And the board gave him command of the *Crescent,* whilst all I can offer you is the *Tartarus.* She's a sixth-rate of twenty guns, at present undergoing a refit at Devonport. But you *will* be made post, John. The First Lord recommended it personally, and Admiral Duckworth interceded for you. You met him again at Portsmouth, I believe, when you paid off the old *Hindostan?"*

"Yes, sir, I did. He was kind enough to put myself and my family up at Admiralty House." Pasco looked up to meet Moorsom's smiling gaze, remembering the young midshipman he had left—to cool his heels, as Nelson had done, in the anteroom. Was this, he wondered, the moment to put Justin Broome's case? The boy deserved it; he had done exceptionally well on the passage home. He had impressed even Bligh with his skill as a cartographer, had replaced the *Dromedary*'s sick master and navigated her across the Pacific to the Horn and, since his arrival in England, had sat for and passed his lieutenant's examination, earning the praise of the board of captains who had examined him. He was a first-rate seaman and an excellent officer, but . . . Pasco frowned, seeking for words.

"Sir, may I prevail upon you to consider the merits of a young man I brought back with me as a volunteer, at the request of His Excellency Governor Macquarie? His name is Broome, sir, and—"

Admiral Moorsom cut him short, his smile fading. "Broome . . . is that not the young man of whom Colonel Macquarie wrote officially to the Lords Commissioners? You delivered the letter yourself, the last time you were here and . . . damme, I have it on my desk! The Secretary, Mr. Croker, drew my attention to it. Damned efficient fellow, Croker, *and* he's an M.P. . . . the honorable Member for Felixstowe or some such place." He rummaged among the papers on his desk. "Yes, here it is. Just give me time to glance through it, like a good fellow . . . it's a trifle wordy."

Pasco waited obediently, deeming it best to volunteer no information until he was asked to do so. For all his easy, friendly manner, Admiral Sir Robert Moorsom was a taut hand where official matters were involved, and he did not like to be rushed.

The questions came, a few moments later, and he replied to them as fully as he could, at pains to sound impartial, while not detracting from the merits of his young protégé.

Moorsom listened impassively. "I take it," he suggested, when Pasco ceased talking, "that you have promised the boy your patronage?"

"Yes, sir, I have—and very gladly. Commodore Bligh also offered his interest, and—"

"At the present time," the admiral said dryly, "I fear that may do Broome more harm than good. However, that is not what the board have against him. We . . . that is, my brother Lords Commissioners and, in particular, Lord Mulgrave, are reluctant to set a precedent. This young man is the son of felons deported to the penal colony of New South Wales for crimes committed here, and . . . damme, John, for that reason we *cannot* grant him a commission in His Majesty's Navy! However good you say he is, such an appointment simply cannot be countenanced because of his background."

"His father served as a master's mate in the navy, sir, and as master in Captain Flinders's *Investigator*. He was given command of a colonial sloop by Admiral Hunter," John Pasco began, "and—"

Admiral Moorsom waved him to silence. "He can enter the masters' branch, if he wishes. We'll appoint him as assistant or second master—there would be no objection to that. We are in need of good men, the Lord knows. You can take him with you to the *Tartarus* if you've a mind to, and he shall have his warrant at once."

Pasco sighed. Justin Broome was a proud young man, he knew, and he had set his heart on making a career in the Royal Navy . . . but as a commissioned officer. He rose, taking the admiral's final words as his dismissal.

"Thank you very much indeed, sir. I'll put it to Mr. Broome. He's here, sir, waiting for me in the anteroom. I cannot be certain, of course, but I expect him to refuse."

"He'll be a fool if he does," Moorsom said, his heavy brows lifting in surprise. "But . . . you know the lad, I don't." He held out his hand. "I give you good day, Captain Pasco. My felicitations to your dear wife."

Returning to the anteroom, John Pasco found Justin still patiently waiting. There were others there now, and he drew the boy aside. As kindly as he could, he explained what had passed between Admiral Moorsom and himself and saw the bright light of hope flicker and die in his young midshipman's eyes. But he accepted the verdict with dignity.

"Thank you, sir, for putting my case and . . . for all you've done for me. I am grateful, believe me, sir, and happier than I can tell you to learn of your step in rank."

"I've been given the *Tartarus,* Justin," Pasco reminded him, "and I'll take you with me most gladly if you are willing to come."

As he had expected, Justin Broome shook his head. "It is good of you, sir. But I shall go back to . . . to the land of my birth. It's where I belong, after all. I'll work my passage back to Sydney. Maybe I'll delay long enough to sit the examination for a civilian master's ticket and try for a mate's berth in a transport."

John Pasco was loath to let him go thus.

"I've taken a small house in Portsmouth, for Rebecca and myself and the baby—we could not impose on the port admiral any longer. You would be welcome to stay with us until you're ready to return to Sydney."

"Thank you very much, sir. But . . ." The youngster's face lit up, as if from some inner radiance, and his voice softened, losing its studied calm. "That swine of a French Governor has released Captain Flinders at last—Captain Matthew Flinders, sir—after holding him captive at Ile de

France for over six years. And he's here in London, with his wife. He has rooms in Nassau Street, Soho, where he is engaged in writing an account of his explorations in the *Investigator*. He has invited me to stay with him, sir, to read the manuscript and help him to reproduce the charts he lost."

Matthew Flinders, Pasco thought—poor devil, Their Lordships had given him scant reward for all he had done, scant compensation for all he had suffered at the hands of Bonaparte's Captain General, the unspeakable Decaen. His post rank had only just been granted, and he had not been given a command.

"The book he's writing, sir," Justin volunteered eagerly, "is to be entitled 'A Voyage to Australia.' Captain Flinders deems that a better title than 'Terra Australis.' I think it is, too, sir, don't you? It has a—a ring to it."

"It has indeed, lad," John Pasco agreed. "You will have to suggest it to His Excellency Governor Macquarie when you return to Sydney." He put an arm round Justin's shoulders, and they walked out into Whitehall together.

John Pasco was conscious of a pang when they parted in the rain-wet street outside the Admiralty building, and he watched his tall young midshipman go striding off in the direction of Soho.

It was the navy's loss, he told himself, and he had done all he could.

Justin waved the last water lighter away from the *Admiral Gambier*'s starboard side and, crossing her deck, shaded his eyes in the hope of seeing the quarter boat, with the transport's two missing passengers, put off from the shore. But there was no sign of the boat; the mate had been gone now for something like four hours, he realized, yet for some reason he had failed to make contact with the missing men.

It was April 11, 1811; the ship, with her cargo of two hundred male convicts, stores, provisions, and the master's trade goods, was ready to sail, and he, for one, was eager to get under way. He had spent almost six months in England—unhappy, trying months, during which he had not only endured the humiliation of being refused a commission by Their Lordships of the Admiralty, despite the recommendations of both Commodore Bligh and Captain Pasco, but also witnessed the deterioration of the man who had been his boyhood hero . . . poor Matthew Flinders.

Justin's throat tightened. Flinders was a dying man; his health, his courage, and the ambitions he had once cherished undermined and finally destroyed by the long years of captivity, from which his own countrymen and the Admiralty had, it seemed, made scant effort to free him. He was bitter and disillusioned; angry because François Peron—one of Commodore Baudin's scientists—had, under the title of *Voyage de Découvertes aux Terres Australes,* published a book in which *his* discoveries were falsely claimed by the French, without credit to him anywhere.

Flinders's own book would, of course, be published and would refute Peron's exaggerated claims of self-importance, but . . . the work would inevitably take time and, Justin feared, might well drain the *Investigator*'s erstwhile commander of the little strength he had left, long before it was ready to be sent to the printers.

Matthew Flinders had his loving, devoted wife—his beloved Annette, of whom he had spoken so often on the voyage of circumnavigation—and he continued to enjoy the support and patronage of Sir Joseph Banks. But, largely because of the Admiralty's parsimony and his belated promotion, his circumstances were straightened, and the modest rent of the lodgings in Nassau Street—four rooms above a jeweler's shop—took almost all he had, leaving little for extravagance.

Justin had stayed for a much shorter time than he had anticipated in Nassau Street, for his own means were insufficient to pay for his keep. He had worked on the charts for the book, sitting up until the early hours and working by candlelight in order to provide as many maps and drawings as he could in the shortest possible time. Then, taking Captain Pasco's advice, he had set about gaining his master's ticket from the Maritime Brethren of Trinity House, shipping as deckhand in a collier, so as to earn enough money

to pay for the cost of the examination . . . and to save the
price of lodgings ashore.

He had done what he had set out to do—the coveted
parchment certificate of competence was his, and it had
enabled him to apply for and obtain his present berth, that
of second mate of the *Admiral Gambier,* bound for Sydney
under the command of Edward Sindrey, her master.

He knew the ship, from her previous stay in Port Jackson; but Sindrey, a black-browed, taciturn little man, was a
stranger to him, appointed for the present voyage in place
of Captain Harrison. He was . . . Justin turned, hearing
heavy footsteps behind him, to confront the man of whom
he had been thinking.

"You sighted our quarter boat yet, mister?" the captain
demanded.

Justin shook his head. "No, sir."

"Plague take it!" Sindrey glanced up at the scudding
clouds above his head. "A fine wind to take us down-
Channel, and we're like to lose it, on account of two
damned passengers, who can't make the rendezvous on
time!" He swore irritably and then spun round on his heel,
clearly intending to return to his cabin, where he had been
entertaining the pilot. "Call me as soon as you see 'em,
mister, and prepare to weigh the minute they step on
board."

"Aye, aye, sir," Justin acknowledged. From force of
habit, he drew himself up, only to receive an ill-tempered
grunt for his pains. "This ain't a King's ship, Mr. Broome,
and I don't stand on ceremony. Just you do your job and
obey my orders and we'll get along well enough."

"As you wish, Captain," Justin answered.

"That's as I wish," the stout little master informed him
tartly. He added, almost as an afterthought, "When the two
gentlemen do come aboard, send 'em below to report to
me."

He did not wait for Justin's acknowledgment but
stumped off, still swearing to himself, to vanish down the
after hatchway, with an explosively audible "Damn their
eyes, the sodding redcoats!"

Presuming Sindrey was referring to the expected passengers, Justin found his interest quickening. Redcoats, the *Gambier*'s master had said, but . . . the draft for the 73rd Regiment was already on board, consisting of an ensign and twenty other ranks. If the belated pair were army men, they must be officers, since two of the best passenger cabins on board had been reserved for them. . . . He frowned thoughtfully. Captain Sindrey had not mentioned their names and, indeed, had been curiously secretive concerning them, as if . . . Justin's frown deepened. He had gone ashore in Portsmouth, to call on the ship's chandlers on Sindrey's behalf, and an odd-looking fellow had accosted him, as he was returning to his boat—a man who had asked questions as to the *Gambier*'s destination and what passengers she was carrying.

He had thought nothing of it at the time, and in any event, since Captain Sindrey had not seen fit to reveal their names, he had been unable to satisfy his questioner's demands or assuage his curiosity. But the fellow had mumbled something about Mr. Macarthur and had appeared to know more than most of the folk he had met in England about the colony in general and the New South Wales Corps in particular. He had spoken of Colonel Johnston's impending trial and had expressed strong views on it, displaying an unmistakable bias against Commodore Bligh, until— Justin grinned to himself—until he had sent him about his business, and in no uncertain fashion.

The trial, by military court-martial, was to take place early next month, according to the newspapers. At Chelsea Royal Hospital, if he remembered rightly, but the announcement had merited only a brief paragraph, on one of the back pages. Neither this nor, indeed, the colony itself seemed greatly to interest the majority of people, who—no doubt understandably—seemed to think and talk of little save the war with France.

Justin glanced shoreward again and then let his gaze stray to where three ships of war lay at their moorings, each with lighters tied up alongside, provisioning them for sea. One was a towering two-decker, a seventy-four, flying a rear admiral's flag; the other two were frigates, the nearer of the two, H.M.S. *Amphion,* loading powder and shot from an ordnance tender. Waiting their turn to come alongside were three boatloads of scarlet-jacketed marines—reinforcements or, more probably, replacements for men killed or wounded in action.

The frigates had been in action in the Adriatic recently, he knew, for he had seen them make port, their sails pock-marked with holes from enemy cannon fire and the *Amphion* under a jury-rigged foremast, her hull badly shattered. But they had brought in prizes and were evidently preparing to go into battle again and in haste, for he had watched their crews working through the night, stepping a new foremast head and repairing damaged deck planking.

For a moment or two, standing there on his own ship's quarterdeck, Justin was conscious of regret. Had he swallowed his pride and accepted Their Lordships' grudging offer, he might have been on board one of the three King's ships, sailing off to fight his country's battles, as his father had done sixteen years before. But . . . He expelled his breath in a long-drawn sigh. England was not his country, he reminded himself; he belonged to the vast unexplored land Matthew Flinders called Australia. The land that had given him birth and to which both his parents had been exiled, without thought or pity and without even a chance to appeal for clemency.

He owed England nothing, for God's sake! And he did not appreciate what he had seen of it; least of all did he like the dirty, overcrowded city of London, where life was easy and luxurious for the rich and a veritable nightmare for the poor and helpless. He—

"Boat's comin', Mr. Broome," a passing seaman warned. He pointed and Justin clicked open his glass. It was the quarter boat, he saw, with the unmistakable red head of the mate, Zeke Lander, clearly visible when he focused the glass on it. There were two men in the sternsheets with him, both in dark, civilian garb. At that distance, even with a glass, neither was recognizable, and Justin turned to the seaman.

"Aye, it's our boat," he confirmed. "With two passengers. Cut aft and tell the captain, will you, lad? Say I'm preparing to weigh as soon as I've got the quarter boat inboard."

The boat was within hailing distance when he looked again, and this time he had no difficulty in identifying the two soberly clad passengers. One was Lieutenent William Lawson, of the Corps, with whom—despite the difference in their ages—he had formed a friendship during the latter part of the voyage from Sydney in the *Dromedary*. The other was also a Corps officer, Archibald Bell, recently promoted from ensign to lieutenant, and . . . Justin smothered an exclamation of surprise, as the boat came nearer and he saw that there was a third passenger, crouched uncomfortably in the bows. Lieutenant Nicholas Bayly, also in civilian dress, had been at one time one of John Macarthur's closest friends and supporters and had stood bail for him at the infamous trial, which had led to the Rum Corps's rebellion and the arrest of Governor Bligh. Later, during the rebel administration, they had fallen out, but . . . Justin stared down at the three upturned faces, frowning, as the implications of their unexpected presence slowly sank in.

He had heard the impending trial discussed often enough during the long voyage and was well aware that all three officers were to be called as witnesses in Colonel Johnston's defense. Bayly and Bell were, perhaps, of small importance to the accused colonel's case, but Lieutenant Lawson, because he had been a member of the court that had tried John Macarthur in Sydney, four years earlier, was—damn it, he was a vital witness! Yet now, on the eve of the court-martial hearing, he was about to take passage back to New South Wales . . . and secretly, in civilian dress, having almost certainly paid the *Admiral Gambier*'s avaricious little master well in excess of the normal fare, in order to ensure that his own and his brother officers' departure might be made without attracting official attention.

That explained why the boat had been kept waiting for so long, and . . . yes, it probably explained the probing questions of the odd-looking fellow who had accosted him in the ship chandler's, a week or so ago. But Captain Sindrey had talked of two passengers, and . . . there were three, all of them supporters of the rebel administration and bitterly critical of the Governor they had actively helped to depose.

Justin snapped an order to the men he had detailed to winch up the passengers' baggage and made his way to the entrypost, just as the bowman hooked his boathook on to the ship's starboard chains.

William Lawson, round-faced and dapper, was the first to come on board. He accepted Justin's steadying hand and then, as recognition dawned, stared at him in some dismay.

"Good God, our young Mr. Broome! What in the world are you doing here, boy? I had supposed you to be destined for a career in His Majesty's Navy, with Bligh and Pasco as your patrons!"

"And I, sir," Justin answered, with a hint of defiance, "had supposed *you* to be awaiting a summons to Chelsea Hospital."

"Ah, yes." The other two officers joined him, and Lawson said, "See whom we have here, gentlemen."

"It is a small world," Nicholas Bayly observed. But he was smiling, Justin saw, the smile friendly and even faintly amused, as he held out his hand in greeting. "So you've tired of Old England, have you, Justin? Or were Their Lordships slow to appreciate your worth?"

"I have no place here," Justin answered. "And Their Lordships offered me none that I wanted to fill."

"And you've a family awaiting your return to New South Wales," Bayly suggested. "Haven't we all? Wives, tender young children, fair lands, and positions of influence . . . I cannot wait to go back! Besides, I approve of the new Governor, with certain reservations. Tell me, when do we sail? We're to join a convoy as far as Rio, are we not?"

"The convoy has already sailed," Justin told him. He glanced below, to see that the last of the baggage was being winched up. Zeke Lander waved. "We'll weigh as soon as your gear and the boat are in-board, and we should overhaul the convoy by tomorrow morning, if this wind holds."

He turned to Lieutenant Lawson. "Captain Sindrey will be obliged if you would wait on him, sir. Be good enough to follow me."

He led the way, the three officers close on his heels, and at the door of the master's day cabin, William Lawson put out a hand to grasp his arm, drawing him to a halt.

"We want no part in the trial, Justin," he said softly. "I least of all, for I cannot justify or defend what was done any more, God help me, than I can condemn it . . . and I'll not lie on oath, as certain others seem prepared to. Not even to save George Johnston's neck! In any event, he has plenty of supporters, and they include Admiral Hunter, as well as a formidable array of legal advisors; and our late judge advocate, Mr. Atkins"—his voice took on a cynical note—"has signified his willingness to speak out against Bligh, and Crossley's not here to contradict him, which may well tip the scales our colonel's way. He'll not need our testimony."

"If you say so, Mr. Lawson," Justin returned stiffly. He had liked the older man very much, he reflected regretfully, and had admired his talents and ability. Lawson was a qualified surveyor and a first-rate farmer; he owned a large property in the Concord area and, during the long nights at sea, had talked of his cattle breeding and of a desire to find a way over the Blue Mountains to the great pastures that he was convinced lay on their other side. But he had supported the rebellion, served in the rebel administration and now, it seemed, was seeking to escape the consequences, with scant regard for the loyalty that Colonel Johnston, as his commanding officer, was surely entitled to expect from him.

Justin's stiffness did not pass unnoticed. Lawson said, as if reading his thoughts, "Damme, boy, I'm not running away! None of us is, for God's sake; and you should know by now that we hold no brief for Captain Bligh. But there's a rumor that, when the trial ends—and whatever its outcome—no officer of the regiment will be permitted to return to the colony. And as Nick Bayly mentioned just now, we all have wives and families, as well as property, in New South Wales. I've got six children, who are dependent on me, and every penny I own is tied up in my land. I daren't risk staying for the trial, if there's any danger of my not being allowed to go back."

It was a reasonable argument, Justin had to concede. He nodded his understanding and leaned forward to knock on the door of the master's cabin.

"Captain, sir, the gentlemen are here," he announced.

"Send 'em in then, mister," Captain Sindrey bade him curtly. "Get our hook up and tell Mr. Lander to set tops'ls and courses as soon as we're clear of the anchorage. I'm wanting to catch up with that convoy before we have any plaguey frog privateers on our trail."

He had the grace to rise, but his greeting of the three Corps officers when they entered was, if anything, more abruptly worded than his orders had been, and his reaction to the presence of the three of them—instead of the expected two—struck Justin as decidedly surly. But, for all that, Justin's heart was light and his spirits buoyant as he went back on deck to convey the master's orders to Zeke Lander.

What, he asked himself, did anything matter, save the fact that the ship was about to get under way? He was going home, back to the land of his birth, to the people and the places he knew and loved. Going back perhaps, God willing, to help finish the work of exploration that poor Matthew Flinders and his friend Surgeon Bass had begun . . . His lips curved into a smile.

He would hold Simeon Lord to his promise. He would build a new trading sloop in Lord's yard and, with the pay for this voyage from the *Admiral Gambier*'s owners, would be able to equip her properly, instead of penny-pinching, as he had been compelled to do in the past.

True, he would not be returning to Sydney as he had hoped—in naval uniform, with a lieutenant's commission and a fine new sword at his side. Abigail O'Shea would probably still look at him askance, as she had the last time he had waited on her, but . . . Justin closed his eyes, seeking to conjure up a vision of her face. The vision came faintly, almost reluctantly—the blue eyes, the proudly held head, with its crown of golden hair—and then it abruptly faded, to be replaced by that of another girl, seen only once, yet—to his own surprise—vividly remembered.

He saw the small, piquant face of the girl with whom he had danced at the Governor's ball and to whom he had talked so earnestly when the dancing was over. Jessica, Jessica India Maclaine, who had told him that she was maid to the Governor's lady and not the officer's daughter he had supposed her to be . . . His smile widened, as he recalled the look in her eyes when she confessed to him her menial status. Then, brought back to the present by a shout from the mate, he crossed the deck to the big, red-headed man's side and repeated Captain Sindrey's instructions.

"In a hurry, is he?" Lander grinned. "Well, come to that, so am I—those infernal passengers kept me waiting for long enough." He paused to shout a string of orders, and then added, eyeing Justin curiously, "You know 'em, don't you?"

"Yes," Justin admitted. "They're Rum Corps officers, all three of them. Lieutenant Lawson, Bayly, and Bell."

"And like you, I suppose, they reckon they're going home," the mate suggested. "Well, no accounting for taste, is there? All right, Second, up anchor . . . and don't look so damned pleased with yourself or I'll have you keel-hauled!"

Justin echoed his grin. "Put your backs into it, my lads!" he bade the sweating men grouped about the capstan, and led them in the familiar chanty chorus as they strained on the bars:

> Yeo ho! Heave ho!
> Round the capstan go . . .
> Tramp and tramp it still!
> The anchor must be weighed . . .

Slowly the great anchor came up, and the topmen scampered aloft, ready to unfurl and sheet home as soon as the order was given. The anchor was catted; with topsails and jibs set, the *Admiral Gambier* moved majestically toward the open sea. Hands waved in farewell from the frigate's deck, and then, from the orlop, came a concerted, moaning cry. The convicts, Justin thought—poor devils; although they could see nothing, the movement of the ship and the pounding of feet on deck told them that the long voyage had begun and they had seen the last of England.

"Some of our passengers," Zeke Lander observed cynically, "ain't as keen as you and your friends to get to Botany Bay, are they, Justin?"

Justin shook his head. After a while, the cries faded into silence and were not repeated. Had his mother wept when she left these shores over twenty years ago, he wondered—had she, too, cried out in bitter, helpless protest, as the nameless, manacled prisoners below in the dark confines of the orlop had cried out? Perhaps she had, all those years ago, and yet his mother had found happiness, love, and a purpose in the new life to which Governor Phillip's ship had brought her. She had no regrets. Perhaps these convicts, too, would come to love their new land.

The wind freshened, blowing hard and easterly. Night fell, but no orders came to shorten sail. When Justin relieved Zeke Lander for the forenoon watch, they had passed through the Needles and their convoy was in sight, topsails just visible through the morning mist.

CHAPTER XIV

At ten o'clock on the morning of May 7, 1811, the trial by court-martial of Lieutenant Colonel George Johnston, commanding the 102nd Regiment of Foot, was opened in the Great Hall of Chelsea Hospital, London.

After the members of the court had been sworn in and Colonel Johnston had been escorted to his place, the judge advocate general, the Right Honorable Charles Manners Sutton, read out the charges against him.

Addressing the accused by name, he declared in a resonant voice, "You are charged that on January the twenty-sixth, in the year eighteen hundred and eight, you did begin, exact, cause, and join in a mutiny, at the head of the New South Wales Corps, of which you were acting commandant, arresting and imprisoning William Bligh, commodore in the Royal Navy, then His Majesty's Captain General and Governor in and over the territory of New South Wales. How do you plead?"

Colonel Johnston, a round-faced, somewhat portly figure in his gold-laced scarlet uniform, answered, after a barely perceptible hesitation, "Not guilty, sir."

Seated in the row of straight-backed chairs reserved for the members of the press, young Damien Hayes, representing the *Provincial Courier* in Sussex, had found himself in awe-inspiring company, flanked on either side by veterans of the London press corps. This was his first reporting assignment; his news editor had awarded it to him with the condescending air of one bestowing a favor, but he had omitted to brief the young man on any of the personalities involved, and Damien had been puzzled when, on entering the courtroom, he had found that—apart from his fellow newspaper reporters—it was virtually deserted.

It was far from crowded now, and as he listened uncomprehendingly to the objections being raised by several members of the court to the apparent lapse of three years before a warrant for the trial had been issued, his initial bewilderment increased and he was emboldened to whisper a question to his right-hand neighbor.

The gentleman, a gray-haired, bewhiskered personage, whose credentials had proclaimed him the representative of the London *Chronicle,* eyed him with ill-concealed disdain. He took a gold snuff box from a pocket in his handsome brocade waistcoat, tapped a few strong-smelling powder grains onto the back of his hand, and sniffed loudly, his rheumy gray eyes subjecting Damien to a careful scrutiny. But then, evidently taking pity on the young reporter's manifest inexperience, the great man relented and answered quite kindly, "The general public has little interest in an event that took place so long ago in a remote penal colony. That is why so few have troubled to attend." He waved a hand at the half-empty courtroom. "It is our task—yours and mine, my young friend—to publish our account of the proceedings in such a manner as to awaken the public interest. Far too much space has been taken up, of late, in our columns with reports of battles fought by our army in Portugal and Spain—of setbacks and enforced retreats and of victories won at a fearsome cost in killed and wounded. Our readers think of little else. This case may, at least, serve to distract them."

Damien nodded agreement. His own newspaper had been filled with such reports, made the more vivid and heartbreaking by firsthand descriptions, written by officers serving under Lord Wellington's command.

The most recent battle, fought on the heights of Barossa on March 5, had seen the defeat of one of the Emperor Napoleon's generals, Marshal Victor, by a greatly outnumbered British force, brilliantly led by General Thomas Graham. But the Spanish general, La Peña, had failed to give his support, and barely a week later, his compatriot, Don José Imaz, Governor of Badajoz, had surrendered the city to Marshal Soult, rendering the British sacrifice of over a thousand men killed or wounded a vain and bitter one.

Damien shuddered as he recalled a description of one town laid waste by the retreating French. The words of the dispatch were still imprinted on his mind: *We found young women lying in their houses brutally violated, the streets strewn with putrid corpses of murdered peasants . . . and a few starved male inhabitants, looking like so many skeletons, permitted to leave their graves that they might seek vengeance . . .*

"You see, my dear boy . . ." His distinguished colleague was smiling down at him, and Damien flushed guiltily, returning to the present. "You, too, think of little save the war. But if you are to succeed in your profession and become a reliable purveyor of news to your readers, you must concentrate on whatever is your current assignment, to the exclusion of all else. Let me test your knowledge of what is happening here at this moment. Do you know, for instance, who is the president of this court?"

Shamefacedly, Damien shook his head. "I know his name, sir. It is Keppel, General Keppel."

"Lieutenant General Sir William Keppel, late of His Majesty's Sixtieth Rifles," his companion supplied. He lowered his voice as the judge advocate again stood to address the court. "His father and two of his uncles commanded at the capture of Havana forty years ago. One of the uncles was the Earl of Albemarle; the other was the illustrious Viscount Augustus Keppel, former First Lord of the Admiralty. The Keppel family fortune was built on the Havana prize money, you know. Lord Albemarle's share was rumored to be a hundred and twenty thousand pounds." He shrugged, his expression frankly envious. "Sir William himself has had a distinguished career, and although his father never married his mother, he was recognized as the heir and nominated to a knighthood of the Bath."

"Indeed, sir?" Damien was astonished, seeing the bemedaled and brilliantly uniformed president with new eyes. The general was a handsome man, alert and ramrod stiff.

"Seated to his right," the *Chronicle*'s representative went on, "is Lieutenant General Baird—Sir David Baird—one of the heroes of the Indian wars and the campaign in Egypt. He lost his right arm at Corunna, when serving under the late Sir John Moore. On his right is Lieutenant General Milner, but . . ." The older man paused and gestured toward an officer in naval uniform who had just entered the courtroom, and whose presence had evidently caused the judge advocate temporarily to resume his seat. "Do you know who *that* is?"

"No, sir," young Damien was forced to admit. He studied the new arrival with interest, taking in the stocky figure and, when the man turned his head, the striking blue eyes and smoothly rounded features, and pale, almost sallow complexion. "Unless—could he be Captain Bligh? Bligh of the *Bounty*, sir?"

"He could and he is, my boy. The late and—if the charges we have just heard read by the judge advocate general are correct and can be proven—the illegally deposed Governor of New South Wales. What, pray, do you know of Captain Bligh and the circumstances that have brought him here?"

Damien Hayes lowered his embarrassed gaze, again red with shame. "N-nothing, I fear, sir. Except that he drove the crew of his ship the *Bounty* to mutiny in the South Seas. One of his officers, whose name was Christian, I believe, led the mutiny, and neither he nor the *Bounty* have been heard of since. But some of the mutineers were captured, and . . . were they not hanged, sir? Despite evidence that Captain Bligh used them with great harshness and brutality? I seem to recall that—"

"You have much to learn," his companion put in severely. "And when the court recesses for luncheon, I shall endeavor to dispel some, at least, of your ignorance. Suffice it now to say only that Captain William Bligh served with distinction under the great Lord Nelson and that he is probably the most renowned navigator and explorer living today. But now, if you please, pay attention. The judge advocate is about to address the court, and I wish to take note of what he says."

Abashed, young Damien groped in his pockets for his own notebook, but because of the ignorance of which his colleague had accused him, he was unable to follow the points that Mr. Manners Sutton was making with such eloquence. But over luncheon, to which the *Chronicle*'s representative treated him in a nearby alehouse, he learned much of the personalities involved in the case. His new friend, whose name was Reginald Deighton, was a mine of information, and by the third day of the trial, Damien was able to identify those who were called to give evidence, and to assess the value—and even the truth—of their depositions, his assessment based on the information Mr. Deighton had supplied as to their backgrounds and motives.

The pages of his notebook rapidly filled; he became absorbed in the drama of what he was hearing, fascinated by the questions the judge advocate put to each witness, by their replies, and by the manner in which, when not satisfied that these were accurate, the lawyer swiftly and skillfully demolished them.

By the end of the first week, he had begun to hold and to voice opinions of his own, and Reginald Deighton, with thinly disguised delight in his pupil's aptitude, subtly encouraged him.

"What is your view of Colonel Johnston, Damien?" he inquired, as they sat together in his favorite Fleet Street tavern.

"That he is lying," Damien answered, without hesitation. "Not all the time; but when he claimed that the populace of Sydney was in an uproar against Commodore Bligh's tyranny and injustice, I am sure he was not speaking the truth, Mr. Deighton. Governor Bligh was in no danger— there was no necessity for him to call out the troops in order, as he said, to place Commodore Bligh in protective arrest. Dr. Harris was the only one who supported that claim, and General Baird tied him in knots! And the master mariner, Captain Walker—who was an impartial wit-

ness—swore on oath that *he* saw no sign of any disturbance, until after the Governor's arrest. Hours after, he said.
Then there was the matter of what they called the requisition, sir."

"The document, purporting to have been signed by over
a hundred of Sydney's respectable citizens—as well as by
all the officers of the Corps—in which Johnston was 'im-
plored,' I think the word was, to place Governor Bligh in
arrest? Is that what you mean?" Deighton suggested.

Damien nodded vigorously. "Yes, sir. Mr. Blaxland
swore that he could recall no general discussion—yet his
name was one of the first on the requisition! He admitted
that the decision to march on Government House was
taken by Colonel Johnston, after talking for only a few
minutes with Mr. Macarthur . . . and that it was Mr.
Macarthur who wrote out the note and was the first to sign
it."

"Damien, my boy, I am proud of you!" the older man
exclaimed, beaming. "Given time, you will, no doubt, become a first-rate law court reporter, for you are learning
fast. But now tell me . . . what is your considered opinion
of Mr. John Macarthur? And what part do you suppose *he*
played in the rebellion?"

Damien gave these questions careful thought. His first
impression of John Macarthur had been a favorable one; he
was good-looking, highly articulate, and had been courteous
in manner when he had made his initial address to the
court. But the judge advocate had halted his oratory, showing him again and again to be at fault in his recollection of
facts that had been proven by other witnesses; and under
the lash of the lawyer's tongue, Macarthur had undergone
an almost visible transformation. Gone were the courtly
manners and the exaggerated compliments; his hatred of
Governor Bligh had become nakedly apparent, and with
pouting underlip, like a small, sullen boy, he had indulged
in scurrilous accusations that palpably had no foundation
in truth. At times he had even made accusations against
Colonel Johnston and other defense witnesses, and, Damien
recalled, the unhappy Johnston had gone deathly pale as he
listened.

"I believe, sir," he said at last, "that Mr. Macarthur was the instigator of the rebellion. It seems to me that he had been plotting just such an outcome, in secret, long before it took place. Whilst he was on trial, he was working to that end, and he deliberately placed the officers who were trying him in jeopardy, to ensure their support." Damien hesitated, looking anxiously at his mentor. "My opinion is, sir, after listening to the evidence that has so far been called, that . . . well, sir, that Colonel Johnston is not the man who should be on trial for his life."

"You think it should be Macarthur?"

"I . . . yes, I do think so."

"Of course," Deighton reminded him, "we have been deprived of the evidence of Lieutenant Lawson—who was a member of the court that tried Macarthur—and of two other officers who, I am led to believe, took ship back to Botany Bay some weeks ago. But I'm inclined to agree with you, young man. Poor Johnston has been cast for the role of scapegoat because he was in command of the troops and is still a serving officer."

"Does that mean that Mr. Macarthur will escape scot-free?" Damien asked indignantly. "Because he sold his commission?"

"He cannot legally be tried here by court-martial, Damien. But"—Reginald Deighton flashed him a wintry smile—"from inquiries I have made, it would appear that Lord Castlereagh has sent specific instructions to the present Governor of New South Wales, Colonel Macquarie, that should Macarthur return to the colony, he is to have charges of high treason preferred against him in the Colonial Court. He will not dare to return."

"And Colonel Johnston, sir?" Damien questioned.

His colleague's smile vanished. "He will have to take the consequences, my boy."

"Do you mean . . . the death sentence, sir?"

"It is probable, if the court finds him guilty of mutiny. It is within their power to impose a lesser sentence, but I do not think they will. General Baird is a stickler for loyalty to the Crown—General Paget, too, and both are only lately returned from the bloody battles of the Spanish peninsula.

They will have little sympathy to spare for the officer who has commanded a regiment of rum traders." Deighton shrugged. He then asked quietly, "Have you changed your opinion of Commodore Bligh?"

Again Damien hesitated, considering the question. With a murmured apology, he consulted his notebook, its pages now almost filled.

"Sir, we have not yet heard the commodore's evidence; but yes, I have changed my opinion of him," he admitted. "Captain Walker stated, if I may read from my notes, sir . . . 'I always heard the settlers say that Governor Bligh was the only Governor that ever studied the interests of the colony.' And Mr. Robert Campbell, who struck me as a gentleman of great integrity, swore that 'The Governor was always impartial in his administration of justice, and the colonists in general and the settlers in particular approved of his government. But the officers of the Corps were dissatisfied, because the Governor would not permit them to receive such large quantities of spirits as they had done formerly and hence could not make large profits by its distribution.' "

"Quite so," Reginald Deighton approved. "Go on, my boy."

"Well, sir, there is so much evidence that seems to me to prove that Commodore Bligh was the very reverse of a tyrant." Damien leafed through the pages of his notebook. "The settler, Mr. George Suttor; the Reverend Henry Fulton; the secretary, Mr. Griffin; Mr. John Palmer, the chief commissary; and Mr. Gore, sir—especially Mr. Gore, whom the rebel administration sent to Coal River as a felon. He was provost marshal, and . . ." He looked up into Deighton's searching eyes. "These are good men, and what they said had the—the ring of truth. All were agreed in their approbation of Commodore Bligh's governorship; none held him to be other than just and honest. He had his instructions from the Colonial Office, sir, to put an end to the rum trafficking of the Corps officers, and this, it seems to me, is what he endeavored to do. And it was because of this that they deposed him . . . egged on by Mr.

Macarthur, whose profitable commercial interests the Governor threatened."

"What of their counterallegations against Bligh?" Deighton said.

"I think that most were trumped up, sir. Some were quite absurd, and those put forward by Mr. Richard Atkins just plain spiteful. Lieutenant Minchin and the sergeant major, Whittle, had to withdraw theirs, under cross-examination, did they not? And—" Damien searched through his notes. "The two noncommissioned officers who arrested Commodore Bligh and accused him of cowardice—Sutherland and Marlborough—contradicted each other *and* Lieutenant Minchin, although admittedly Marlborough's evidence was in the form of an affidavit."

"Bligh's naval record absolves him of any such accusation, my dear boy," the *Chronicle*'s representative asserted. "I wonder that they saw fit to make it. Whatever else he is, William Bligh is no coward. Well . . ." He lumbered heavily to his feet. "Let us call it a day, shall we? Bligh's opening speech was restrained, as I'm sure you'll agree. But tomorrow, when he will make reply to Johnston's charges and insinuations, I fancy we shall have our answer beyond all shadow of doubt."

His forecast proved to be correct. Next day, when the court again assembled, Commodore Bligh was called to the witness stand, and the brief simplicity of his address seemed to Damien, as he scribbled furiously in his notebook, to carry complete conviction.

The deposed Governor spoke first of Colonel Johnston's dispatch to Lord Castlereagh, dated April 11, 1808.

"In this, gentlemen, I was accused of having acted upon a predetermined plan to subvert the laws of the colony, to terrify and influence the courts of justice, and to bereave those persons who had the misfortune to be obnoxious to me of their fortunes, their liberty, and their lives. You have seen the dispatch—it forms the basis for the defense Colonel Johnston has made of his conduct. The charges, although unsubstantiated, were made also by the two officers who acted in my place and usurped my office during my imprisonment, which they continued—Colonel Foveaux and the late Colonel Paterson."

He paused, looking about him, and then went on, in the same level tones. "It has been stated, on oath in this court, by Mr. Macarthur, that—and I quote—*'so much dread was created in the public mind'* lest the six officers who were officiating at his trial should be sent to jail, that *'nothing could have prevented an insurrection'* but the arrest of myself, the lawful Governor. No proof has been shown to you, sirs, that there was any danger of an insurrection; and indeed none existed."

Damien's pencil broke, and in a hurried search for another, he lost the next few sentences. Reginald Deighton smiled and passed him his own.

"Write on, boy," he whispered. "I'll take my notes from yours."

Damien turned to a fresh page and heard Commodore Bligh say tellingly, "Gentlemen, it has been claimed that I was guilty of offenses which rendered me unfit to govern the colony to which I was appointed. Permit me, if you please, to sum up for you my alleged offenses: The barter of spirits, a source of emolument to other Governors, I prohibited. The confined distribution, an advantage to myself in common with all the officers, I extended to all free settlers. The former practice of irregular committal to prison I abolished. The limits of arbitrary punishment I contracted. I consulted the general good of the colony, instead of allowing myself to be guided by the selfish policy of a few individuals, and I determined that all ranks alike should be respectful and obedient to the law."

Bligh again paused, his gaze directed at the row of distinguished officers composing the court. Then, in ringing tones, he went on, "These, gentlemen, were the offenses which rendered me unfit to govern! In other words, it was no longer convenient to my accusers, or suited to their purposes, that I should continue to govern. Accordingly a scheme was devised to remove me, which—after all that has been heard in evidence—the court will perhaps think took longer to digest than the short time Colonel Johnston retired into the next room with Mr. Macarthur and emerged, with a requisition demanding my arrest and deposition. A requisition, may I venture to remind you, which had over a hundred signatures appended to it when it was produced in evidence. Yet virtually all were obtained long after Colonel Johnston led his regiment to Government House to effect my arrest!"

There were some questions posed by members of the court and the judge advocate, but Colonel Johnston, sitting slumped in his chair, asked none. Commodore Bligh bowed and retired to his own seat, and Sir William Keppel, after consulting his pocket watch, announced the luncheon recess.

"It is all over, Damien," Reginald Deighton asserted when they were seated together at their accustomed table, "and the result a foregone conclusion. Did you see the expression on the learned Mr. Frederick Pollock's face when his client resumed his seat? Commodore Bligh is vindicated—he'll get his promotion to flag rank. That was a masterly reply to Johnston's attempt to vilify him, by the Lord Harry it was! Made with dignity, too, and offering proof positive that there *was* a plot to depose him, conceived and carried out by Macarthur long before his own trial. Damme, they had the bonfires ready to light and the effigies made, and that rogue of a sergeant major—what's his name?—Whittle, doling out liquor and cadging signatures to the requisition." The waiter came, and Reginald Deighton grinned at Damien across the table. "Let us celebrate our first collaboration, shall we? A bottle of your best claret, my man, if you please; and for myself, one of your famed steak and kidney pies."

Damien stammered his thanks. "When, sir," he asked, "will the court announce its findings?"

Deighton shrugged. "Tomorrow, most probably—by afternoon, I expect. We shall have to compose ourselves to await their deliberations, which may be prolonged. The hearing has lasted for thirteen days, and a total of—let me see—" He opened his own notebook. "—Forty-two witnesses gave testimony. Have you all their names?"

"I think I have, sir, yes."

"Good." The waiter brought their claret, and when it had been tasted and poured, the veteran reporter raised his glass. "Your health, young Damien . . . and to your future success in our honorable profession!" He drank the toast, and his smile was kind as he set down his glass. "I have read the draft of your article on the trial, and it is good. Indeed it is very good. Have you thought of your future, boy? Do you intend to return to the provinces?"

"I've been giving the matter some thought, sir," Damien answered. He had enjoyed his brief sojourn in London, but—for no reason that he could have explained—he had no wish to stay in the bustling city. An idea had, however, occurred to him a few days before—a not altogether practical idea, but one he had been unable to put from his mind. The prospect of returning to his native Sussex and the dull office of the newspaper that had given him employment had ceased to appeal to him, but . . . He sighed.

Mr. Deighton would probably laugh him to scorn if he revealed what was on his mind, and yet something impelled him to do so. He reddened and managed uncertainly, "I have heard so much of New South Wales during the past two weeks, sir, that I—well, I'm tempted to go out there and see it for myself. I've no ties to keep me here. My parents are dead, and I was an only son. And it seems to me that the colony has much to offer to any young man who is prepared to work—and I am prepared to work, Mr. Deighton."

"In your profession?" Deighton queried sharply.

"Yes, if it's possible. Some of the witnesses spoke of a Sydney newspaper called the *Gazette*, but if there were no opening for me there, I'd turn my hand to anything. I—" Damien's color deepened. "You will suppose me foolish, I don't doubt, sir, but it is a new country, becoming more settled and prosperous under a good Governor, and I—well, sir, my aim would be to start my own newspaper eventually."

To Damien's surprised relief, Reginald Deighton beamed on him approvingly. "You are a young man after my own heart, Damien," he said. "Damme, it's what I would do, if

I were your age!" He leaned across the table and clasped the boy's hand warmly. "I had thought of offering you an introduction to my managing editor, in the hope that he might be able to find room for you on the *Chronicle*'s staff, but—this is better! It offers opportunity and adventure, a golden chance to fulfill your ambitions. Have you the means to pay your passage?"

"I'm not sure what it would cost, sir," Damien admitted. "I have some money my parents left me, about a hundred pounds. There are a few small debts to pay, and I should need to keep some money by me until I could find employment. But—"

"That should suffice," Deighton assured him. "But, if it does not, you may count on me to make up the difference and a few pounds, to tide you over when you reach Sydney. No, no . . ." He cut short Damien's stammered thanks. "I am a comparatively wealthy man; I shall not miss such a sum. And you can repay me—you can send me news of the colony, articles about the countryside, the native people, the flora and fauna. I will use them for my column in the *Chronicle*, and I'll see that you are paid for any I use. Ah!" The waiter came with their meal, and he broke off. "Let us eat, my boy. We can talk more of the prospects awaiting you in New South Wales when we have eaten, can we not?"

The following morning, after a brief announcement that Sir David Baird was absent owing to extreme pain from his recent wound, the court retired to consider its verdict. This was given, unanimously, as guilty—a verdict that occasioned little surprise when it was delivered in the sparsely attended courtroom.

The sentence, however, had the reporters agog and reaching for their notebooks.

"The court," the president announced gravely, "having duly and maturely weighed and considered the evidence adduced on the prosecution, as well as what has been offered in defense, are of the opinion that Lieutenant Colonel Johnston is guilty of the act of mutiny, as described in the charge, and do therefore sentence him to be cashiered."

To this, the judge advocate added crisply, "Whilst it is not considered necessary for the public service to institute proceedings against the military officers involved, this is mainly because the Hundred and second Regiment has been removed from the colony. But it would be mischievous if any of the officers connected with the regiment during the commotion in the colony are now residing in, or likely in a public capacity again to return to that settlement, or any of its dependencies."

"The Prince Regent is not likely to be pleased by that sentence," Reginald Deighton muttered, putting away his notebook. "Nor is his brother, the commander in chief, but . . . George Johnston has powerful friends, and I suppose justice has been done after a fashion. The puppet should not be punished for the crime committed by the puppet-master!" He gestured to the retreating back of John Macarthur, as he left the courtroom alone, save for one of his young sons.

By contrast, Damien saw, Commodore Bligh was receiving enthusiastic congratulations from those who had given evidence for the prosecution, and from a dignified-looking, white-haired gentleman who, Deighton told him, was the renowned Sir Joseph Banks, naturalist, explorer, and Bligh's most influential supporter.

"I will endeavor to procure you an interview with the great man, if you are really determined to go out to New South Wales," the older man promised. "But, as you can see, Sir Joseph is old and frail—this is the only time he has attended the court." He eyed his young colleague searchingly. "Are you still determined on this course?"

"More so than ever, sir," Damien answered, without hesitation.

Reginald Deighton took his arm. "Then we have much to do, boy! First we must write up our report on the trial and its outcome, and then, together, we will make inquiries concerning your passage. Does it matter to you how soon you sail?"

"No, sir," Damien assured him. He drew himself up, shoulders squared and head held high. "Not at all, sir— indeed, the sooner the better!"

Three weeks later, he boarded the transport *Friends* at Portsmouth, his fare reduced to thirty pounds in consideration of his acting as clerk to the master, Captain Ralph, and with letters of recommendation from Sir Joseph Banks and Mr. Reginald Deighton in his pocket.

CHAPTER XV

Justin set down his hammer and with the end of his kerchief wiped the sweat from his face and chest. His new sloop was taking shape; the bare, curving ribs that had for so long stood in seeming mockery in the stocks were now decently covered and ready for caulking. Simeon Lord had supplied good teak for the deck planking, and he himself had purchased a disused hulk, together with spars and cordage, which he would put to use as soon as he could engage the necessary labor to assist with the task.

But . . . He sighed in frustration. Skilled labor was impossible to come by in Sydney these days. Sammy Mason was fully employed in Robert Campbell's yard and could give him only occasional spare-time help, and Governor Macquarie had monopolized the services of virtually every carpenter in the colony—convict or free—for the large-scale building program in which he was engaged. Everywhere in the town, new public offices and private residences were springing up; new wharves and warehouses mushroomed on both sides of the cove, gardens were fenced in, and fine, wide streets had replaced the rutted cart tracks that had once sufficed to carry Sydney's traffic.

A start had been made on the building of a hospital; a new military barracks and an extensive jail were nearing completion; the bridge over the Tank Stream had been re-

placed by a wide stone structure; and there was talk of a
two-story courthouse, with a residence for Judge Advocate
Ellis Bent attached to it and space provided for the offices
of a bank. There were schools, both fee-paying and
government-financed, and a wharf and warehouse at Cockle Creek, where produce from the Hawkesbury farms was
now landed and stored. Straying livestock had vanished
from the streets, the government domain around Government House was being turned into a picturesque garden,
and the innumerable rum shops in the Rocks area had
been reduced to a handful.

For all his grumbling at the lack of available labor, Justin could not but approve of the changes. Sydney was growing, its buildings had dignity and beauty, and there was
order in the town instead of the earlier drunken lawless-
ness. Most of the convict workers had been freed of their
chains; the new arrivals wore distinctive yellow garments,
and men undergoing special punishment were clad in
black, but for the rest, there was nothing about their ap-
parel to distinguish them from the settlers and emancipists
with whom they mingled.

And they worked well, for Governor Macquarie was
known to frown on the overseers' excessive use of the lash,
and he gave pardons to all deemed worthy of reward. The
two old men Justin was currently employing, although feeble and incapable of strenuous effort, were at least punc-
tual and willing to work, he had to admit; and because they
were hoping for remission, neither had ever attempted to
steal from him. But . . . He picked up his hammer again,
wishing that Cookie Barnes were not still at sea. For all the
hours of toil he himself put in and the midnight oil he
burned, his *Flinders II* was still a very long way from completion, and it was now nearly ten months since he had laid
down her keel.

He worked away, holding the nails in his mouth and
moving the big whale-oil lantern as he progressed, letting
his thoughts drift back to all that had happened since he
had left England nearly a year and a half ago.

The passage out had been uneventful. The *Gambier* was
a well-run ship and a fast sailer, and Captain Sindrey, de-

spite his taciturn manner and occasional bursts of ill temper, was an efficient and experienced master . . . and
there had been no trouble, either with crew or convicts.

He had made two good friends on the voyage, Justin
reflected—the mate, Zeke Lander, and, rather to his surprise, William Lawson. During the long, comparatively idle
hours when the ship had been running before the steady
westerly winds and not a sail or a sheet had to be touched
for days, he had talked long and enthusiastically with the
Rum Corps lieutenant . . . and always of one subject. The
possibility of finding a way over the barrier of the Blue
Mountains had become an obsession with the older man,
and before long, it had become equally so for himself.
What had been only a vague idea on the voyage to England
had hardened into a definite plan on the return trip, after
the *Gambier* left Rio, and the friendship between them became established on a firm foundation.

Bayly and Bell had held aloof; their intentions, Justin
had sensed, remained what they had always been—locked
in the desire to enrich themselves. But Lawson was different, and although he never openly said so, he wanted to
repay what his adopted country had given him in wealth,
prestige, and prospects.

"I have sons, Justin," he had explained, more than once.
"Lads like yourself, born in the colony, whose future lies
there. And imagine what that future could be, were we
able to cross those mountains and find the vast, rich land
that every instinct I possess tells me must lie beyond! I
shall petition the Governor as soon as we reach Sydney and
request his support for the launching of a well-prepared
exploratory expedition. Colonel Macquarie is a farsighted
man, with the prosperity and expansion of the colony his
consuming aim. I feel sure that he will encourage the venture."

Justin paused in his hammering, once again to wipe the
sweat from his eyes and face. William Lawson had been as
good as his word. He had approached the Governor and
laid his carefully prepared plans before him; but instead of
the expected encouragement, he had been peremptorily
ordered to wait. Governor Macquarie had other matters on

his mind; he was busy touring the colony, establishing new settlements and townships, building roads.

"He wants to consolidate what we now have," Lawson had reported. "He is planning a tour of Van Diemen's Land and a visit to Coal River in the *Lady Nelson* and wants us to wait until he returns. But I have his promise that he *will* give consideration to my request at the earliest opportunity. So . . . be patient, Justin, my dear boy. Build that sloop of yours whilst you're waiting. I've taken a commission in the veteran company and have been given temporary leave of absence to attend to my farms. I intend also to use the time to right a wrong and delight Samuel Marsden's overmoral heart . . . I am going to legitimize my sons and my nine-year union with their mother. My faithful Sarah and I will be married at St. John's Church, Parramatta, and you will be welcome to attend the ceremony, if you feel so inclined."

He had done so, Justin recalled, on his way to visit his mother at one of the Governor's newly established settlements, on the Nepean River near the foothills of the Blue Mountains. The fact that his mother had, at long last, sold her beloved Long Wrekin to Timothy Dawson was, he thought, one of the most startling of the changes he had found on his return from England, and at first, when Simeon Lord had told him of it, the news of his mother's decision had greatly shocked him.

But any doubts as to the wisdom of the exchange had faded when he arrived at the new farm. It was sheep country, well watered but removed from the danger of floods, which the Hawkesbury had always threatened, and his young brother, William—grown almost out of recognition now—was in his element. His mother, too, had seemed happy; her health, even to his anxious eyes, had improved greatly, for all she was overthin, with telltale white streaks in her bright auburn hair.

The farmhouse was built of solid timber and more than twice the size of the house at Long Wrekin, with extensive outbuildings and stockyards, a fine barn and shearing shed, and accommodation for two married convict laborers. Andrew had taken up the Governor's offer of a commission in the veteran company and was in command of the settlement garrison, a post that allowed him adequate time to work on the land.

"We have done the wisest thing in coming here to Ulva, Justin," his mother had assured him. "It is best for Andrew, of course, since he has not had to relinquish his commission, which he has always been loath to do. William, as you can see for yourself, could ask for no more, for all our sheep are in his charge. Rachel continues at school but spends her holidays here, and Tom and Nancy Jardine are in trusted charge of Long Wrekin."

"And you?" Justin had asked.

"I am content," his mother had answered quickly—too quickly, perhaps, Justin reminded himself. "I would not have fancied living in Sydney Town, as dear Frances Spence urged me to . . . I like it here very much, for it is beautiful country. And I still have some of my horses, my brood mares, you know . . . and a colt sired by my poor Sirius. The only progeny he left, Justin, but Young Sirius is the image of his sire."

She had talked much of her horses, although in spite of her brave words and the eagerness with which she spoke, Justin had been left with the contradictory impression that her heart was no longer in the breeding of horses. Certainly she did not ride very often, seeming to spend most of her time in the house, cooking and sewing—pursuits that were alien to the hardworking mother he remembered from his childhood, who had toiled from dawn to dusk on the land.

But he had allowed her the reticence she evidently wanted, and she, in turn, had not sought to question him too closely as to the reason for his return to the colony. Beyond expressing regret that he had failed to obtain a commission in the Royal Navy, his mother had confined her queries to more general topics, anxious to learn what he had thought of England, of London in particular, and of the ports he had called at when serving in the Newcastle-based collier.

She had told him of Henrietta Dawson's death and of Lucy Tempest's marriage to the young emancipist laborer, Luke Cahill; but beyond a passing reference to the fact that

Abigail O'Shea had left the management of the Yarramundie property to her sister and Luke, and had herself gone back to Sydney, his mother had scarcely mentioned the girl. She had not asked him if he had seen or called on her, Justin recalled, and—since he had put off paying a call on either the Spences or Abigail until he felt able to risk a rebuff from Abigail—the conversation had veered to other topics.

Andrew's questions had been less tactful. He and Justin had traveled back to Sydney together—Andrew having been summoned to sit on a court-martial—but his stepfather's interest had lain more in the reasons for the Admiralty's refusal to commission him than in more personal matters. In any case, his probing had been easy enough to counter, and for most of the time they had spent in each other's company, they had talked of the war and of recent naval actions, and Andrew, who was well informed on the subject, had given him chapter and verse of the Governor's new projects, loud in his praise for the majority of these.

"Colonel Macquarie is the best Governor we have had, Justin," he had reiterated. "He is a man of vision and of great integrity, and because he has the wholehearted support of Colonel O'Connell and the officers of the Seventy-third, he's been able to bring in most of the reforms Commodore Bligh sought and failed to bring in. And needless to tell you, I applaud his attitude toward the emancipists, although this is increasingly criticized by what used to be termed the Botany Bay faction—which includes most of John Macarthur's old associates . . . save, of course, those of them who *are* emancipists!"

They had laughed together over this, he and Andrew, but, Justin thought, he had been astounded later to learn that Simeon Lord had been among those appointed to the magistrates' bench. Respectability was, it appeared, measured at times by worldly success and wealth, to both of which Lord could now lay claim . . . although, Andrew had added cynically, the Reverend Samuel Marsden had opposed his appointment strenuously.

"They serve together, under protest, on the Parramatta Turnpike Board, which is a bitter pill for poor Marsden to swallow, but . . . he has swallowed it, temporarily, at all events. Young William Charles Wentworth is acting provost marshal pending Gore's return, his father has the contract for the building of the new hospital, Dr. Redfern is high in the viceregal esteem, and James Meehan accompanies the official tours and plans the new settlements. What more can the Governor do?"

What more indeed, Justin thought. He climbed up to the skeleton deck of his vessel, drawing in great gulps of the night air. The wind had veered to the east and it was cooler, he realized thankfully, and . . . The devil take it, he would smoke a pipe and allow himself half an hour's respite. No man worked well when he was stiff and tired, his muscles aching.

His pipe filled and drawing, he squatted down cross-legged in the bow of his half-built sloop, staring out across the anchorage. The moon rose, bathing the whole cove in silvery light. Apart from two sandalwood traders owned by Robert Campbell, and an American whaler, the harbor was deserted. The *Lady Nelson,* with the Governor's party on board, had not yet returned from Van Diemen's Land, although she was expected within the next week or two, and . . . Justin sighed.

It had been his intention to further his acquaintance with Jessica Maclaine, but she was in constant attendance on the Governor's wife, who accompanied her husband on his travels about the colony and who had, of course, gone with him to Hobart on their current tour. They had met, it was true, on half a dozen occasions—once at Parramatta's first fair, twice at race meetings in Sydney, and several times in town—but always in public, when it had been impossible to do more than exchange a distant greeting.

Indeed, Justin reflected glumly, he was not even certain that Jessica had remembered him or, come to that, that the Governor had, either. His doffed hat and his bow had been acknowledged, but he had not conversed with any of the viceregal entourage; and when he had made his formal call at Government House to report his return, it had been the Lieutenant Governor, Colonel O'Connell, who had received him.

Together with a score of others who . . . He sat up, startled. A ship was entering the cove, heralded by the creaking of her pumps and the echo of a spate of orders bawled through a speaking trumpet. The vessel herself was a ghostly, barely discernible shape in the moonlight, but even so, he was able to see that she was listing to larboard and appeared to be taking in as much water as her straining pumps could cope with.

For a moment, he took her for the *Lady Nelson,* but then, as the moon rose higher, he saw that she was much larger—a ship-rigged brig, painted in Nelson checker and flying the Union ensign of the Royal Navy. A sloop of war, pierced for—eyes narrowed, Justin counted—pierced for sixteen guns, with carronades mounted on her upper deck.

She fired no salute, and having, it seemed, entered and traversed the harbor without the assistance of port officials or pilot, she came to anchor in the cove without ceremony, like the wraith she had appeared to be when he had first glimpsed her.

Within minutes a boat was lowered—a gig, with four men at the oars—but instead of making for the government wharf, the boat headed for where Justin was standing, and he stared at it in astonishment as it approached. There was an officer in the sternsheets, enveloped in a thick boat cloak, and as soon as the gig grounded, he flung off his cloak, jumped ashore, and came striding across the yard. Halting a few yards from the stocks, he peered critically at the half-built vessel and then called out a greeting.

"I saw your light. You're a shipwright, I take it?" Without waiting for Justin's reply, the new arrival gestured to his ladder. "Come down here, like a good fellow, so that I can talk to you. I'm in urgent need of your services."

Justin tapped out his pipe and obediently descended. "Sir," he acknowledged. "You are?"

"William Case, commanding His Majesty's ship *Semarang,*" the stranger supplied. He was tall and deeply tanned, wearing the single epaulet of a naval commander, and as nearly as Justin could judge in the dim light, he was in his early thirties.

"Justin Broome, sir," he volunteered. "How can I serve you?"

"In any way your skill allows," the sloop's commander returned. "And at once. My carpenter is down with the scurvy, and his mates are damned ignorant dolts! As you can probably see, we're listing badly, and the last sounding showed twelve feet of water in the well. I've had the pumps going night and day and men bailing with buckets, but the infernal water's gaining on us, and she'll sink at her moorings, unless you can help us. Come out with me now and see for yourself, Mr. . . . ah, Broome."

He grasped Justin's arm, propelling him toward the waiting gig and giving impatient details of the damage he estimated to the *Semarang*'s hull . . . the result, it appeared, of striking a shelf of coral when under full sail, three days previously.

"Damned Admiralty charts are no use on this coast—worse, they're infernally misleading," he complained. "Wouldn't have come near your plaguey settlement, only I've a consignment of bullion to deliver—ten thousand Spanish silver dollars, which your Governor's been crying out for. He's going to start a bank, I understand." He waved Justin into the gig, brushing aside his objections. "Tools, you say? Damme, we've all the tools you're likely to need . . . what we're lacking is a man with the skill to use 'em. But you're a shipwright, are you not?"

"I've served my time, sir, yes," Justin began. "But—"

Captain Case rapped an order to his men to put off. "That's a pretty useful looking craft you have on the stocks," he observed. "Building her yourself, I take it?" Receiving Justin's nod of assent, he turned to subject him to a faintly puzzled scrutiny. "You're young. What are you, eh? A convict? Time expired, pardoned, or whatever they call it in this place?"

"I was born here," Justin answered. He offered no other explanation, and Case evidently expected none. He waved a hand to his ship.

"I think we'll find," he said, "that the copper's badly damaged. Up to you to say, of course, but I imagine it will be necessary to careen her. Can that be done here?"

"It can, yes. But there is a shortage of labor, and—"

"Skilled labor, you mean?"

"Any labor, sir. His Excellency the Governor has extensive building and road-making work in hand, and . . ." This time Justin attempted to explain, but William Case cut him short.

"The requirements of one of His Majesty's ships of war must take precedence," he asserted, with lordly arrogance. "And I'll soon make that clear to—what's his name?— Governor Macquarie. Soldier, is he not? Colonel of some Scottish regiment, spent most of his time in India? Well, labor's plentiful enough there, and it ought to be here, I should have thought, with all the convicts we're shipping out from England. I'll have a word with Colonel Macquarie."

"He is on a tour of inspection in Van Diemen's Land at present," Justin told him, nettled by his tone. They came alongside the *Semarang*, and without conscious thought, as he stepped on board, he saluted the quarterdeck, then heard Captain Case give vent to a surprised exclamation.

"You've served at sea with His Majesty's Navy, have you?" he demanded, observing the doffed cap. "And ran, eh?" he added, again not waiting for Justin's reply to his question. "Well, we can soon rectify that, my lad. Keep my ship afloat and, damme, you can fill the warrant carpenter's berth, and no questions asked!"

"Permit me to inspect the damage, if you please, sir," Justin requested, with difficulty containing his growing irritation. "I may not be able to keep your ship afloat."

A preliminary inspection confirmed the seriousness of the damage. A jagged hole had been torn in the sloop's hull beneath the waterline, forward and on the larboard side. In spite of the thrummed topsail her crew had managed to haul under the hull and secure over the damaged area, tons of water had poured in and continued to do so. Her list, too, was increasing, although all the larboard main deck guns had been shifted to starboard in a vain attempt to hold the ship on an even keel.

Aided by the two carpenter's mates and a volunteer working party of seamen, Justin began the task of repair, at times almost up to his neck in water. He had thought at first that the sloop might have to be beached, but gradually he found that they were making headway against the water, and with the pumps going and both watches forming a bucket chain to bail, the level slowly decreased.

By noon of the following day the leak had been sealed off. The weary seamen thankfully dismantled the pumps and stowed away their bailers, an extra tot of rum was issued, and one watch was piped to dinner. Justin, soaked to the skin and even more exhausted than his working parties, went to report to the *Semarang*'s commander, whom he found on the quarterdeck, engaged in a heated altercation with Robert Watson, the harbor master.

He waited, shocked into silence when he heard Captain Case order Watson off his ship; but when the affronted port official had departed, the captain's manner changed.

"My dear fellow, you have performed a miracle!" he exclaimed. "Come to my cabin and let me offer you some refreshment." Seeing Justin's gaze go to the harbor master's boat, he added nonchalantly, "That officious little swine was not only insolent—damme, he was drunk! I sent him about his business, and I shall report his misconduct to the proper authorities. To the Governor, if necessary, only . . . devil take it, didn't you tell me the Governor's not here?"

"He is on tour in Van Diemen's Land," Justin confirmed. He continued to stare after the departing boat, concerned on Robert Watson's account. "Sir," he began, "Mr. Watson is a good man. He—"

William Case cut him short. "Possibly when he is sober, his manners may leave less to be desired, Mr. Broome," he conceded haughtily. "And I don't doubt that, when he returns to his senses, he'll ask my pardon. But enough of the miserable fellow . . ." He gestured to the after hatchway. "I've some capital Cape brandy below, and you look as if you're in need of it, after all your exertions. That and some dry clothing. I'll tell my steward to fit you out."

Later, dressed in borrowed shirt and breeches and with a lavish tot of brandy in front of him, Justin made a careful report on the repairs he had been able to make.

"Your ship won't sink at her moorings now, sir," he ended. "But if you will take my advice, you will arrange for her to be beached and careened as soon as it is possible." Again he went into details, stressing the extent and nature of the damage. "Meanwhile I suggest you put your guns ashore and relieve her of as much deadweight as you can. She'll need caulking and—"

"Yes, yes, I understand all that," Captain Case put in impatiently. He tossed off his brandy and refilled the glass, eyeing Justin thoughtfully over its rim. "*You* are a good man and you know your work. I want you to undertake the repairs to my ship, Mr. Broome. You'll be well paid, of course—I will see to it that you are given an Admiralty draft to cover your wages and those of the laborers you employ. You—"

"Forgive me, sir—" Justin's interruption was diffident. "But I am a private individual, and I have the use of Mr. Simeon Lord's yard, by personal arrangement between us, for the purpose of building my own trading vessel. I fear, sir, that you must seek the requisite authority for repairs to your ship. As I mentioned to you last night, there is a shortage of skilled labor here, and although there are facilities for careening vessels, there is a dearth of trained caulkers and riggers. And for a ship of this size . . . well, I doubt whether the necessary repairs could be undertaken at once."

Captain Case gave vent to an angry oath. "The—devil take it!—the requisite authority you spoke of, Mr. Broome—to whom were you referring?"

At pains not to betray the satisfaction he felt, Justin said quietly, "The acting port naval officer, sir—Mr. Robert Watson. The miserable fellow you ordered off your quarterdeck just now. He is also the harbor master. And now, sir—" He got to his feet, setting down his barely touched glass. "If I may trouble you for use of your boat, I should like to get back to the shipyard."

William Case rose with him, eyes blazing but his lips tightly compressed. "Very well, Mr. Broome. I'm in your debt and I acknowledge it. But—*are* you a deserter from His Majesty's Navy?"

Justin faced him unsmilingly, "No, sir, I am not."

"But you have served in a King's ship?"

"Yes, sir, I have."

"A plague on you, Broome!" Captain Case exclaimed, losing his temper. "Which ship, man? And under whose command?"

"The *Hindostan,* sir, under the command of Captain Pasco. I was rated midshipman and master's mate. My request for a commission was turned down by Their Lordships, and I was discharged from His Majesty's service." Justin drew himself up and reached for his cap. "Have I your permission to go ashore, sir?"

Case threw back his head and laughed, with genuine amusement. "Damme, you're an insolent young devil, but I admire your spunk! And your professional accomplishments—master's mate, eh, and Their Lordships wouldn't commission you?" He put an arm round Justin's shoulders and led him to the foot of the hatchway, from whence he bellowed an order to the officer of the watch to call away his gig. Turning again to Justin, he held out a conciliatory hand. "If you feel inclined to return to His Majesty's service, I'll take you right gladly as a volunteer. My patron is Vice Admiral Samuel Hood—Sir Samuel Hood, now commander in chief in the East Indies. He would ensure that Their Lordships changed their minds on your account, Mr. Broome, if I requested it. I was his first lieutenant in the *Centaur* for three years and am on exceptionally good terms with him."

"Thank you, sir," Justin acknowledged. He shook the proffered hand cautiously, still not quite certain of his feelings for the tall, arrogant young captain. "Perhaps I may be permitted to think over your kind suggestion."

"Oh, by all means, my dear fellow," Case assented readily. He shrugged and added, "If the repairs to my ship take as long as you seem to think they will, then I can allow you plenty of time to consider my offer. In any event, I must await the Governor's return. When do you suppose he's likely to return?"

"I cannot tell you, sir," Justin answered. "Within a week or two, I believe . . . certainly before Christmas, because plans are being made for a reception at Government House. His Excellency will be back for that."

"I see. Well, they say it is an ill wind turns none to good, do they not? I shall let my ship's company have a run ashore, for God knows they've earned it! I work 'em hard when they are at sea, every man jack of 'em, but I'm not one to keep them from their pleasure when we make port. They are lusty fellows." The captain's smile was indulgent. "I take it that Sydney Town can provide them with what they need in the way of taverns and women?"

Justin nodded. "In plenty, sir." For all Governor Macquarie's new laws and restrictions, Sydney was still a corrupt and lawless place, he thought grimly. After dark, in the Rocks area, it was the den of iniquity the Rum Corps had made of it, over the years, in their quest for profit from their liquor trading . . . and old habits died hard. The Governor's compulsory church services and the Reverend Samuel Marsden's fiery denunciations from the pulpit had not, as yet, induced the women in the bawdy houses to reform . . . and shore-going seamen, with money in their pockets, were easy prey.

"I'd keep a weather eye on your men, sir," he advised, "until they have the measure of this town. It can be a dangerous place."

"Be damned to that!" Captain Case retorted. "It's not my way. My lads are tough fighting men, and I don't mollycoddle 'em. Well . . ." A hail from the deck above announced that the gig was alongside, and he gestured to Justin to precede him. "I'll give you good day, Mr. Broome. And my thanks, once again, for your most able assistance."

"Good day, Captain Case," Justin responded.

Grasping the bundle that contained his wet clothing, he descended to the gig, to find himself waved to a seat in the bows by a haughty young midshipman. The boy, he realized, took him for a convict and was treating him accordingly. But he made no objection. The navy, he assured himself, was not for him, and Captain Case could forget his offer. Twenty minutes later, whistling cheerfully, he was back at work on his own ship.

CHAPTER XVI

Governor Macquarie sat at his desk in Sydney's Government House, regarding with unconcealed dismay the mountainous pile of official papers, Colonial Office dispatches, and private correspondence that his secretary had set before him.

True, a tersely worded communication from the Horse Guards had informed him of his promotion to the rank of brigadier general, and that was pleasing, but . . . Macquarie sighed.

For the past two months, he and his wife, with a small staff, had been carrying out the functions nearest to his heart, those that he himself firmly believed should constitute the prime duty of any colonial governor. In the process they had braved the storm-wracked waters of the Tasman Sea in the eighty-ton *Lady Nelson* and, after the most perilous voyage he had ever experienced, had finally entered the sanctuary of the Derwent River and landed in Hobart Town.

Hobart Town was a straggling, ill-planned collection of flimsy wooden buildings, erected haphazardly, wherever and whenever a need had appeared to exist. It had taken him and his staff days of painstaking work to devise a new plan for the town, dividing it into a principal square and seven streets, with a much larger hospital and a strongly constructed barracks for the garrison.

All the new streets had been named, and Damien Hayes, the youthful journalist he had decided, almost on impulse, to take with him, had made a sketch of the orderly town he envisaged and sent this, together with an article explaining its future prospects, for publication in the London *Chronicle*. This, when it was read in London, might well attract new settlers and the capital investment that was badly needed if Hobart were to prosper.

He would, of course, have to report unfavorably on the trading activities of certain of Hobart's officials—the chaplain, the Reverend Henry Knopwood, among them—and on the profligate spending by the acting Lieutenant Governor, Lieutenant Lord, on his predecessor's funeral, but . . . Macquarie's frown deepened. He had advised—nay, had besought the Colonial Office to appoint Colonel Foveaux as the late Colonel Collins's successor, but his pleas had been disregarded. The home government had sent instead one of Admiral Phillip's First Fleeters—and a Royal Marine major named Thomas Davey, a heavy drinker whose manners were uncouth and who was said to have been up to his ears in debt when he had left England. A plague take the home government and his lordship of Liverpool! Did the politicians imagine that they could direct the affairs of a colony that none of them had ever seen—and from a distance of twelve thousand miles—without taking into account the views and the carefully considered advice of the man on the spot? They had appointed him as Governor, they had saddled him with immense responsibilities, and yet, in their arrogance, they had refused to listen to him!

Davey would, without doubt, ruin all the plans he had made for Van Diemen's Land, Macquarie told himself glumly. Damn it, had he not suffered and submitted his companions—including his dear wife and her maid—to unbelievable hardship, in order to cross from Hobart to Launceston overland, so that he might judge of its future prospects at first hand, and then report on them to the Colonial Office? They had risked life and limb, had ridden for miles and tramped part of the way on foot, so that Meehan might select the best site for a road.

Weary and saddlesore when at last they came in sight of
the hamlet that was Launceston, he had written of it . . .
Macquarie picked up his draft, memory stimulated as he
savored the words he had jotted down that evening in his
tent.

> The grand view and noble and picturesque land-
> scape that presented themselves on our first coming in
> sight of Launceston and the three rivers, the fertile
> plains and the lofty mountains by which it is bounded,
> were highly gratifying and truly sublime—equal in
> point of beauty to anything I have ever seen in any
> country. . . .

Foveaux could have been relied upon to carry out the
removal of the northern capital to York Cove, which he
had proposed, but Davey . . . Lachlan Macquarie's mouth
tightened. If the Colonial Secretary mistrusted Foveaux,
there was his own brother, Charles—now Colonel Charles
Macquarie, commanding the Second Battalion of the
73rd—whose name he had put forward as a possible alternative. But Liverpool had sent only the drunken, uncouth
Davey, who could be relied on to do nothing, save abuse
the hospitality extended to him and insult those emancipists
who had been invited to dine at Government House.

In a surge of bitter exasperation, the Governor let his
report fall and started to pace the room in long, impatient
strides. It was a damnable pity, he reflected, that after the
most successful, as well as the most distant, tour he had
undertaken, he had had to return to Sydney, with its war-
ring factions and the constant attempts by the Colonial Office to undermine his authority.

Apart from Davey, the commander of His Majesty's
sloop of war *Semarang* was also proving a thorn in his side.
Case's ill-disciplined seamen, permitted unlimited shore
leave while their ship was careened and undergoing repair,
were running wild, fighting with the civilian population
and the watch, and setting an appalling example to the hitherto well-behaved soldiers of the 73rd. He would have to
take stern measures to curb them, but . . . Captain Case

was not one to take his strictures lying down. Already there were two notices of complaint lying somewhere on his desk, Macquarie recalled irritably, in which Case asserted that charges brought against his men were—how had the infernal fellow worded it?—"Ungenerous, groundless, and false . . ." And this, when the charges were against two of his officers, caught red-handed by the constables when causing willful damage to property! That episode had been described by their indulgent commander as "a mere frolic," for which, he insisted, all charges should be withdrawn.

The Governor shook his head in angry disbelief. His restless pacing took him to the widow, and hearing the sound of approaching carriage wheels, he paused there and peered out.

The carriage contained two ladies and a small, dark-haired boy, and as he saw his wife come from the veranda at the front of the house to welcome them, his earlier irritation swiftly faded. Mrs. Jasper Spence and the lovely young widow, Abigail O'Shea, had called, bringing with them the latter's little deaf and dumb son, who was a particular favorite of Elizabeth's.

Indeed, he thought, as he watched the little boy run to her and be eagerly enfolded in her arms, his wife could not have been fonder of small Dickon if he had been her own. It was an infernal pity that he was not, Lachlan Macquarie thought sadly. Elizabeth longed for a child—for a son—as he did himself; but, poor, brave soul that she was, it was not to be. She had suffered so many miscarriages since coming out here, so many disappointments, that in light of both her age and his, it had begun to seem unlikely that their dream could now be fulfilled.

Maurice O'Connell had been more fortunate. Commodore Bligh's daughter Mary had given birth to a son a year after their marriage, and he and Elizabeth had stood as godparents to the child at the christening. He had been conscious then of his wife's longing, Lachlan Macquarie recalled with a pang, and conscious of envy, too. But . . . such matters were in the Lord's hands, and it was not for mere mortals to question His wisdom or the manner in which their prayers were answered.

Yet, as he continued to watch little Dickon O'Shea respond to Elizabeth's affectionate coaxing, he found himself offering up a silent prayer. He loved her, heaven knew, and perhaps after all it was not too late for that love to bear fruit.

"May I take Dickon to look at the flowers, Abigail?" he heard his wife call out.

Receiving the expected assent, the two walked across the well-tended lawn to the flower beds that George Caley, the botanist from Kew, had established among the vines and shrubs Admiral Phillip had planted over twenty years before.

The little boy was making the high-pitched sounds that, in his case, passed for laughter, and Elizabeth was chattering happily away, careful to keep her face turned toward him, so that he might read her lips and understand what she was telling him.

After a while, recalled to her duty as hostess, she joined her two guests on the veranda, and Dickon was left in the care of Jessica Maclaine, who came running from the house, smiling and bouncing a ball in front of her to capture the attention of her charge.

The girl was undoubtedly a treasure, Macquarie thought, watching her in turn. She was good with children, and Elizabeth trusted and depended on her and had been thankful to get her back after losing her to her stepfather—a widower, who had come out two years ago, in charge of a regimental draft. But the man had remarried, and Jessica seemed to want nothing better than to serve her mistress with single-minded devotion, oblivious—or, at any rate, indifferent—to the various young men who from time to time had sought her attentions.

His piper, the stolid 73rd man, Mackinnon, whose intellect did not match his splendid physique, had been one; the boorish young reprobate, Ensign MacAlpine—whom he had been compelled to send home in disgrace—had been another; and . . . The Governor smiled indulgently, as he turned away from the window.

During their recent tour of Van Diemen's Land, the London *Chronicle*'s talented new correspondent, Damien Hayes, had paid marked attention to little Jessica India, and for all her innate shyness, the girl had appeared to enjoy his company. Hayes would make an eminently suitable match for her when the time came, as he and Elizabeth were agreed—and a step up, socially, to which she could scarcely remain indifferent in this socially conscious place.

With a resigned sigh, Governor Macquarie returned to his desk and picked up his report again. For the next hour, he concentrated on setting out, in unequivocal terms, the impression he had gained of the Coal River settlement and his suggestions for further development of its resources. He had gone there direct from Launceston; and although still under the spell of the scenic beauty revealed during his twenty-mile ascent of the magnificent Hunter River, he was well aware that, so far as the Colonial Office was concerned, whatever suggestions be made must be practical. Practical and, of course, commercial; the home government was anxious to ensure that the colony should become self-supporting, and in his latest communication, Lord Liverpool had made this abundantly clear.

Wearily, Governor Macquarie reread the dispatch:

> I repeat to you the positive commands of His Royal Highness that, while you remain in charge of the Colony of New South Wales, you use the most unremitting exertions to reduce the expense at least within its former limits. . . .

Impatiently, he turned the page, skipping over the comparisons the Treasury had made, yet still faintly shocked to see that his own expenses for his first year in office amounted to 72,600 pounds, while Bligh's had been half that amount, and even that of the rebel administration had not exceeded 50,000 pounds.

The next page continued in the same vein, Lord Liverpool taking him to task for not having obtained the permission of His Majesty's government before entering into agreements pertaining to building programs. The free settlers, the Colonial Secretary maintained, were supposed to bear the cost of erecting quays, wharfs, and bridges; if they could not, then that alone was evidence enough that such projects were not needed—the colony not having grown sufficiently prosperous to require them. The circularity of his lordship's logic brought a weary sigh to the Governor's lips.

On the subject of the proposed and, heaven knew, sorely needed new hospital for Sydney, Lord Liverpool had waxed even more indignant, quoting the Privy Council as well as the Treasury to emphasize his doubts as to the wisdom of financing the building costs by means of a license to import rum:

> It would have been advisable that no engagement of this nature were entered into, until you had an opportunity to learn the sentiments of His Majesty's Government upon its propriety. . . .

Conscious of a deep-seated feeling of resentment, Macquarie picked up the draft of his report on Coal River and tore it to shreds. The damned report would have to be rewritten; he had simply been wasting his time. If the Prince Regent and his ministers questioned the need for a new hospital in Sydney, if they begrudged the expenditure for roads and wharfs in the colony's administrative capital, they were unlikely to permit him to expand the harbor at Port Stephens or build a road to encourage settlement in the fertile Hunter Valley. And as for his plans for Hobart and Georgetown . . . He looked down regretfully at the torn scraps of paper scattered on his desk and reached again for his quill.

Somehow he must endeavor to make Lord Liverpool understand that the expenses he had incurred would, in due course, be repaid, since they would secure the colony forever from the danger of famine, which, from the day of Admiral Phillip's landing, had always existed. Only by

opening up new lands for growing crops and raising cattle
and sheep could the danger be averted. But to do so there
must be roads and . . . He smothered an exclamation.
The devil take it!—they must somehow find a way to cross
the mountain barrier that hemmed the colony in! Once that
was found, a road could be built, and the fertile plains
Phillip had visualized would banish the specter of famine
for the rest of time.

Let the profligate, unreliable Davey do his worst in
Van Diemen's Land—since, in any event, he would, and
there was scant chance of stopping him. And let Newcastle
and its coal mines remain a place of punishment for the
escapers and the malcontents. He would, in future, concentrate on Sydney and the settlements he had contrived—
despite the home government's parsimony—to establish
and expand.

During the festivities that had marked his return from
the tour and his fifty-second birthday in January 1813, the
Governor recalled, Gregory Blaxland had put forward a
plan for an attempt to cross over the Blue Mountains, and
earlier, Lieutenant Lawson had made a similar proposal.
But neither had received much sympathy, with so many
other matters of more importance on his mind. No, not of
more importance . . . simply of greater urgency.

But *this* was urgent now, in the light of Lord Liverpool's
harshly critical dispatch. Admittedly, Blaxland and his
elder brother had been supporters of John Macarthur and,
like William Lawson, had connived at Commodore Bligh's
arrest; but they were respectable men of good breeding,
large landowners, and successful farmers. Colonel Foveaux
had spoken well of them, as he had of Lawson, and . . .
had not Gregory Blaxland made two previous attempts to
find a way over the mountains?

True, he had failed, just as Governor Phillip had failed,
and General Tench and the unhappy Colonel Paterson in
the early days. Successive governors had sent out expeditions—Surgeon Bass and Henry Hacking in Hunter's day,
Lieutenant Barrallier, and even the botanist, George Caley,
in King's, with perhaps a score of others, whose efforts were

unrecorded and forgotten, or who had vanished forever into the mountain mists.

But all had shared the conviction that beyond the precipitous rocky peaks and the deep gorges of the unconquered mountain barrier lay well-watered pastureland and a fertile plain, stretching as far as the eye could see.

Caley—although he had returned to England with Commodore Bligh—had been wholly convinced that he had penetrated farther than any who had gone before him. And he had left a carefully documented report, Macquarie recalled, for the use of any who might come after him.

Coming swiftly to a decision, the Governor rang for his secretary.

"Be so good as to look for George Caley's papers in the files," he requested. "Those pertaining to his explorations . . . I wish to study them. And, John . . ."

John Campbell, quiet and self-effacing, waited expectantly. He had observed the torn scraps of paper on the desk but, wise in the ways of the man he served, did not remark on them. "Your Excellency?"

"Send a note to Mr. Gregory Blaxland and say that I should deem it a favor if he would wait on me, as soon as he finds it convenient."

"Very good, sir," Campbell acknowledged. "And your report for the Colonial Office . . . is that ready for me to transcribe?"

Lachlan Macquarie shook his head. "No, it is not. But I intend to write it now, and I shall have it ready for you by this evening. That's all, John, thank you."

Alone once more, he again drew pen and paper toward him and wrote quickly and without hesitation:

> Conscious of my own integrity and rectitude and of the honorable purity of my motives, I shall now proceed to give your lordship such full and clear explanations of the grounds upon which this unusual expenditure has been sanctioned by me that your lordship will, I feel confident, agree that it was imposed by imperious necessity. . . .

With the meticulous attention to detail that came from having served as a military staff officer, he described the conditions he had found on his arrival in the colony. The Hawkesbury floods, the failure of the wheat crop, and the reckless depletion of stores and provisions by the rebel administration were among the problems he cited, but the list was long, and the situation was complicated by the arrival of the eight hundred men of the 73rd Regiment and their five hundred wives and children, who had also to be fed, clothed, and housed.

Dusk fell; a servant came with a lighted lamp, and Lachlan Macquarie wrote on, oblivious to the passage of time as he described the state of dilapidation and decay in which he had found the public buildings, the hospital, and the storage warehouses and wharfs, and even his own official residence. Of Government House he wrote bitterly:

> When I took up my residence here, I found the building so ill-constructed and in such a decayed and rotten state that it was unsafe to live in, and in point of size, altogether inadequate for the accommodation of even a private gentleman's family, much less that of a Governor in Chief. . . .

His pen spluttering with the force he was exerting on it, he concluded his dispatch with what, he knew, was a truthful claim:

> I believe I may without vanity assert that I have already done more for the general amelioration of this Colony, the improvement of the manners, morals, industry, and religion of its inhabitants than my three predecessors, during the several years they governed it.

A knock at the door just as he was finishing heralded the arrival of his wife. She came to him, affectionate and anxious, and resting her hands on his bowed shoulders, she laid her soft cheek against his.

"Lachlan dear," she chided him gently, "you work too hard. Stop now, I beg you, and let us dine. Henry Antill is just returned from meeting the *Minstrel* transport, off the Heads. He says that Colonel Johnston is on board."

The Governor stared at her in astonishment. "*George* Johnston—the rebel they cashiered?"

Elizabeth confirmed this gravely. "The ship is loaded with his trade goods and livestock, Henry told me. Lachlan, I thought that he had been found guilty of treason at his trial. Is he . . . is he permitted to return here?"

Wearily, Lachlan Macquarie got to his feet. Lord Liverpool, he could only suppose, had countenanced George Johnston's return. It would be as a civilian, of course; the court-martial had stripped him of his military rank. But he had been a good soldier once; they had campaigned together in America, he remembered, and Johnston had acquitted himself well enough to earn a mention in Lord Cornwallis's dispatches.

And besides . . . He shrugged and started to move to the door, grasping Elizabeth's arm with stiff fingers. The onetime commandant of the Rum Corps had a common-law wife and family in New South Wales, and so far as the court-martial was concerned, it was widely accepted that he had been the unfortunate scapegoat—"Jack Boddice's tool," as the satirical song had implied.

"I have nothing officially against George Johnston, my dear," he said at last. "And no instructions to bring charges against him, either. John Macarthur *would* be liable to arrest were he to come back to the colony, but Johnston is not. He has stood his trial and forfeited his commission. I shall seek to exact no more from him, if he has come here to live peacefully with his family."

"I see," Elizabeth said. Reaching the door, she halted and turned to face him, and to his surprise, Macquarie saw that there were tears in her eyes. "I wonder," she added, with deep feeling, "whether people of this colony know what a just and honorable man their Governor really is? Or what a kind heart he possesses?" Rising on tiptoe, she kissed his cheek. "I am so proud of you, Lachlan," she whispered, with more emotion than she usually permitted herself to display. "And I do so dearly wish that I could give you a son. Even if he were like poor little Dickon O'Shea . . . because he is quite a darling, you know, in spite of his handicap."

The Governor held her close, suddenly bereft of words, his square, bony face brick-red. But the anger he had felt after reading Lord Liverpool's admonitions drained swiftly away. "There, there, my dear," he managed awkwardly. "It doesn't matter . . . I have you, have I not?"

CHAPTER XVII

Jessica left her stepfather's quarters in Clarence Street to find that darkness had already fallen. It had not been her intention to prolong her visit, but Duncan Campbell had been absent on guard duty at the barracks when she arrived, and both the children and her new stepmother had persuaded her to stay for the evening meal.

Agnes Campbell was a kindly, pleasant woman and an expert cook . . . and, Jessica reminded herself ruefully, it had not taken very much persuading to get her to stay for dinner. But outside in the street it was very dark, moon and stars obscured by scudding clouds that brought with them the threat of rain. She hurried, her footsteps echoing on the boarded sidewalk and her head down as she turned into the blustery wind and felt the first heavy drops of moisture on her cheeks.

Her way took her down a narrow alley, leading to steps cut in the rock—it was a shortcut into George Street, which passed the rear of the commissariat store and Simeon Lord's shipyard and was the route she usually followed in daylight. In daylight there were always people about; but now, she realized, as she reached the head of the steps, the convict working parties had gone from the stores, the yard appeared to be deserted behind its high brick wall, and those who resided in the area had closed their doors against the expected rainstorm.

Normally none of this would have caused her concern; she was accustomed to running errands for her mistress and Mrs. Ovens, and she knew this part of the town so well that she could have found her way through it blindfolded, but . . . Jessica caught her breath as the sound of ribald laughter reached her and voices rose in bawdy, drunken song.

Fool that she was, she had forgotten that the King's ship *Semarang* had returned to anchor in the cove and that her seamen—who had acquired an evil reputation among Sydney's inhabitants—would follow this route back to their ship, after their evening's carousing in the taverns of the Rocks.

And they were coming down the alleyway behind her, a mob of perhaps a dozen, judging by the noise they were making, catcalling and jeering and clearly out for trouble. Jessica looked about her, seeking a place to hide until they had gone past. There was a house set back in the rock, but no light shone from its windows, and receiving no response to her frantic knocking, she quickened her pace, frightened now but hoping to gain the street below before they could catch up with her.

There were women with them, she realized—harridans with strident voices—but their presence was a measure of relief to her, since it meant that whatever mischief the seamen were bent on, they would not be seeking female companionship. So long as she kept out of sight, she told herself, the chances were that they would pass her by. George Street was patrolled; it could not be long before the watch became aware of the disturbance and made their appearance, to hustle the unruly mob into the boat that would be awaiting them at the wharf.

She was almost at the foot of the steps when disaster struck. The steps were uneven and weed-grown, and in her haste, Jessica missed her footing and stumbled, giving vent to an involuntary cry of pain as her right ankle twisted beneath her.

She was up in an instant, but one of the seamen, staggering unsteadily ahead of the rest, heard her cry and yelled out to his companions as he came in pursuit.

"Come on, me lucky lads! Here's another wench to give us a run for our money!"

It was the signal for a disorganized chase, the men swearing and tumbling over one another as the women who were with them tried vainly to hold them back. Impeded by her twisted and rapidly swelling ankle, Jessica reached George Street only twenty yards ahead of her pursuers, and they would undoubtedly have caught up with her had not the gate into Simeon Lord's shipyard suddenly opened. A man emerged, to stand for a moment framed in the aperture, and then, swiftly taking in her plight, he called out something she could not hear and came running to meet her.

"Quick, this way!" His arm was round her, supporting her, and he led her toward the gate, moving with sure-footed ease over the rain-wet cobbles of the street. A gust of wind blew the gate further open, and Jessica's rescuer thrust her inside, relinquishing his hold of her in order to turn and push the gate shut behind them. It closed with a loud creak of unoiled hinges and a resounding crash, and she heard him curse as one of the seamen came pounding after them, shouting to warn the others.

"The wench went into the yard! Come on, boys—that's where she's gone, plague take her!"

Her unknown rescuer slid a wooden bar into place at the back of the door and, bending swiftly, picked Jessica up in his arms.

"It'll take them all their time to break in here," he told her. "And they may give up and seek some other distraction. But in the meantime, we might as well take cover. My ship's on the stocks over there and should give us all the cover we'll need."

His voice was vaguely familiar, Jessica realized, but it was not until he gently set her down on the far side of the wooden structure that contained the skeletal outline of his ship that memory stirred and she recognized him.

"Are you not Mr. Broome?" she asked. "Mr. Justin Broome?"

"That I am," he confirmed. "I was hoping that you might remember me, Jessica India Maclaine." As he spoke he was unlocking the door of a small lean-to shed, and with a waved hand he invited her to enter. "My toolshed, Miss Maclaine. It will keep the rain off us and, God willing, your pursuers out. They are stubborn swine, though— they're not giving up."

A chorus of shouted threats and obscenities and persistent battering on the yard gate testified to the truth of his words, and Jessica's heart sank. "They are sailors from the *Semarang*, I think," she said uncertainly. "But I did nothing to provoke them, Mr. Broome. I was on my way back to Government House, through the cut from my stepfather's quarters in Clarence Street. Perhaps it was foolish to come that way after dark, but I was late, and . . . I just did not stop to think."

"They need no provocation," Justin assured her, a hint of anger in his voice. "They are out to hold the town to ransom, and their officers aid and abet them. I've had some dealings with their commander, Captain Case, and King's officer or no, he is determined to stir up as much trouble as he can . . . until he gets what he wants. He—"

"But what does he want?" Jessica put in, puzzled. "Their Excellencies have entertained the captain at Government House, and the officers, too. Some of them are dining there this evening, and they have been most civilly treated."

"He wants provisions we cannot spare and skilled labor we do not possess, to speed up his repairs," Justin answered flatly. "He wants to denude us of canvas and cordage and to press any prime seamen he can lay his hands on into his ship's company—" He broke off abruptly as, with a crash of splintering wood, the gate to the yard came down.

Triumphant shouts and cheers applauded its fall, and within moments a mob of yelling men came hurtling into the yard.

"The devil take them!" Justin exclaimed. "They're in! And it's not just the *Semarang*'s people. . . ." He was by the door, looking out apprehensively. "They've collected a crowd of riffraff from the Rocks by the looks of it. Miss Maclaine, you must stay out of sight." His tone was crisp, brooking no dissent. "Here, under my workbench . . . slip down and I'll cover you up. And for pity's sake, don't stir from there, whatever they do. The swine have got lanterns and cudgels, and they mean business. I've got to stop them from raiding our stores."

He was piling planks in front of her hiding place, deaf to Jessica's protests, and peering out from behind them, she saw him pick up what looked like a crowbar that had been leaning against the wall. He intended to use it as a weapon, she could only suppose, and sick with terror, she cried out to him to leave her and make a run for it.

"Could you not go for the watch before they see you? They were chasing me, but if they don't find me, surely they will go away?"

"The watch won't tackle a mob this size," Justin retorted grimly. "Bide quietly where you are, Miss Maclaine. I'll see if I can get rid of them."

And then he was gone, closing the door of the lean-to behind him and leaving Jessica trembling in the darkness. But her fear, she realized, as she heard the key turn in the lock, her fear was for him, rather than for herself. . . .

The rain had ceased, Justin observed when he emerged from the shed, and he cursed it—a heavy rainstorm might have deterred the drunken troublemakers before they could do any serious damage. But as it was . . . Partly concealed by the timbered shell of his half-built vessel, he took stock of the invaders.

There were now at least forty or fifty of them, with perhaps twenty of the *Semarang*'s seamen at their head, and they had armed themselves—as Sydney's riotous mobs invariably did—with palings torn from the fenced gardens they had passed on their way. A few women, denizens of the brothels and the so-called cock-and-hen clubs of the Rocks, lingered uneasily on the edge of the crowd, silent for the most part and ready to take flight at the first indication that they might be courting trouble, should the watch arrive. Some of the men, harmless drunks, appeared also to be wavering, and they, too, Justin decided, would probably make off if they were not provoked. Like moths drawn to a candle flame, they had simply been attracted by the noise the seamen had created and had followed them, in the expectation of witnessing yet another pitched battle with authority—a spectacle to which, several times since the *Semarang*'s arrival, her people had treated them.

The seamen constituted the only real danger. They were obviously as drunk as any of the others, but they were fit fighting men, whose commander, for reasons of his own, had deliberately released them in order to cause havoc in the town, and . . . Justin drew in his breath sharply. They had virtually no fear of retribution, since Captain Case could be counted on to protect them from any action the civil—or, come to that, the military—authorities might take, however outrageous their behavior.

Now, although they were still swearing and shouting to one another about the wench who had vanished, they were laughing and engaging in horseplay, pretending to do battle with their improvised cudgels. Recognizing their leader as a man he knew by name, Justin reluctantly decided to appeal to them to return to their ship.

He stepped from his concealment and, cupping his hands about his mouth, made his bid for their attention. "Bo'sun's Mate—Tom Dodge! This is Mr. Lord's shipyard . . . you should know better than to look for wenches here. Get back on board—your boat's been waiting for you this hour past. You don't want to have your liberty stopped, do you, by overstaying your shore time?"

Dodge heard him and grinned. He came striding up to Justin's side, his gait a trifle unsteady, but his manner not ill-humored.

"Well, look who's here, lads!" he exclaimed. "The shipwright, by God—the fella that won't lend us a hand with our caulkin'! An' playin' the officer now to the manner born! Good evenin' to you, *Mister* Broome, sir! Touch yer forelocks to Mister Broome, lads—it seems he's in command o' this yard."

They gathered round him, jostling and nudging each other, knuckling their foreheads in mock respect.

"We don't mean no harm," one of them asserted sol-

emnly. "But we lost a wench, an' we seen 'er come in 'ere.
We'll go when we find 'er."

"You won't find her," Justin declared. "So take yourselves off before there's trouble. I don't want to call the
watch, but you've broken in here and—"

A chorus of derisive laughter cut him short.

"Let the swine come. We'll break their skulls for 'em if
they do!"

"The bloody watch won't tangle wi' us, after what we
done to 'em last time they tried!"

The boasts were probably true, Justin thought ruefully.
But the civilian hangers-on were starting to melt away, he
saw, as if sensing that the anticipated fracas was unlikely
now to materialize. He gestured in the direction of the departing knot of women and again addressed Tom Dodge.

"The wenches you had are leaving you, Bo'sun's Mate.
Hadn't you better go after them?"

The big petty officer shook his head. "Nah, we had all
we want of 'em. We wasn't taking 'em back on board
anyways—cap'n's orders. No women on the mess deck.
Gotta keep 'is Majesty's ship *Semarang* clear o' convict
scum." He hiccoughed loudly and flashed Justin a sly
grin. "That's a tidy craft you're building here, Mister. I
never got a proper look at her till now."

"She's a long way from being completed," Justin pointed
out.

"Aye, so I see. But I reckon you'll have all the spars an'
canvas an' copper you need for her stashed away, ready.
An' that's teak you're using, ain't it? Good stuff, real good.
Now if we had some o' that for our ship, Cap'n Case'd be
over the moon." Dodge's callused hands caressed the
planking, his grin undeniably malicious, and Justin tensed,
conscious of danger.

"I need what I have. And I paid for it, Bo'sun's Mate."

The big man ignored his protest. "It's what you got
stashed away I'm interested in, Mr. Broome. Wouldn't
mind having a peek into that shed o' yours 'fore we call it a
night—eh, lads?" He jerked his head in the direction of the
lean-to as the men gathered round him. "Let's get it open,
shall we?"

They stared back at him owlishly, most of them still too drunk to follow what he was saying.

"Is the plaguey wench in there, Tom?" one of the younger men asked. "Soon get 'er out if she is."

Justin did not wait to hear Dodge's reply. Grasping his crowbar in both hands, he positioned himself in front of the shed door. The men surged uncertainly after him, but he held his ground.

"Better go back to your ship, Dodge," he warned. "And take your lads with you. No one gets into my workshop, understand? I'll report you to Captain Case if you try." He hoped fervently that Jessica Maclaine could not hear the loud altercation that followed, but fearing that she might and thus be tempted to reveal herself, he moved forward, the crowbar raised above his head. "Out of here, the lot of you!"

They retreated before the fury in his voice and eyes, and Justin might have won the brief battle of wills had not a shout from the retreating crowd at the gate distracted his attention.

"The watch! The watch is coming!"

"Take him, lads!" Tom Dodge thundered. "Before them swine get here!"

They were on him and Justin swung at them with his crowbar. One man went down, clutching a shattered arm; a second cried out in agony as a glancing blow caught him on the side of his head. Robbed of the crowbar, Justin felled Dodge with his fists, but his assailants were too many for him, and he went down under a concerted rush of bodies. With boots and cudgels they beat and pounded him into insensibility, and the last sound he heard before he lost consciousness was the sickening crash of splintered timber.

Blind instinct told him it was his half-built vessel that had become the object of their vengeance. . . .

Hours later, he came to his stunned senses to find himself in manacles and leg-irons, lying prostrate on the bare brick floor of what, he realized with dismay, must either be the jail or the watch house. Sunlight filtered wanly through a barred window high above his head, but when he attempted to rise in order to get his bearings, the effort proved beyond him and he lapsed back into unconsciousness, too weak even to call out.

It was evening when a constable brought him food, water, and a candle, and assisted him to move his bruised and aching body to the trestle bed beneath the window. He removed the wrist fetters, but made no reply to Justin's bewildered questions.

"There's a visitor for you," he evaded. "Mr. Robert Watson—him that's harbor master. Maybe he'll be able to tell you what happened, 'cause I don't know. I wasn't there." He gestured to the jug of water he had brought. "Best clean up afore he sees you. You're in a right mess, lad, an' no mistake! But happen it'll teach you a lesson. The surgeon don't reckon you're hurt too bad."

Justin did his best to follow the jailer's advice, but Robert Watson, ushered in five minutes later, exclaimed in shocked astonishment at the sight of him.

"God in heaven, Justin, those ruffians worked you over properly! And now they're claiming that *you* assaulted them . . . but to my way of thinking, the boot's on the other foot. Sit down on the bed, boy, and I'll sponge your face for you."

The story emerged as the older man deftly plied soap and water. Warned of trouble at the yard by one of those who had earlier taken part in it, he had dispatched the fellow to summon the watch, while he himself called out his boat's crew and rowed across from the government wharf.

"It was all over when I got there," Watson said apologetically. "I shouldn't have delayed, but—well, I've had some pretty rough dealings with those blackguards from the *Semarang* lately. Their captain's accused me of everything from drunkenness to dishonesty, and I wanted my own lads with me as witnesses, see? I shouldn't have left it to those yellow-livered constables of the watch, though, and believe me, Justin, I wouldn't have, if I'd known it was you that was involved. I'm sorry, lad, truly I am, because it's turned out to be a real bad business."

Justin brushed the apology aside. "But what happened, Bob? I don't recall anything much, after they came at me. Except . . ." He drew a quick, uneven breath as memory partially returned. "Oh, dear heaven—that poor lass! Jessica Maclaine . . . they were chasing after her, and I hid her in my workshop. Did you find her? Is she safe?"

"Aye, safe and back at Government House," the harbor master assured him. "I took her there myself in my cutter. But she was worried sick on your account, which is one reason I'm here. I promised her I'd find out how you were faring and let her know. She was afraid they'd killed you."

"Well, they didn't," Justin retorted bitterly. "Though that wasn't for want of trying! But why in God's name am I here, Bob? Am I in arrest?"

Watson inclined his head gravely. "The constables had you in irons and on your way to the watch house when I reached the yard. And it was a shambles! You put three of the *Semarang*'s seamen in the hospital, and it's touch and go whether one of 'em dies. They claim you smashed his head in with an iron bar, lad . . . and there's a score of them ready to swear to it."

"You mean they're making charges against me?" Justin's head was throbbing, and he stared incredulously at the stout harbor master, the two rows of silver buttons on his jacket seeming first to recede and then to spin in crazy circles as Justin tried to focus his gaze. "But they broke in—they smashed the gate into the yard and attacked me! And the swine were drunk."

"That wasn't the story they told the watch, Justin."

"And the plaguey watch believed them?"

"The watch ain't heroes, lad," Bob Watson reminded him dryly. He laid a hand on Justin's shoulder. "They're a bad lot, those *Semarang*s, and most of us know it, for they've done nothing but brawl and stir up trouble since they got here. Still, with twenty of 'em, still spoiling for a fight and all telling the same tale, you can't hardly blame the constables, can you? It looked bad. And they hadn't found the girl . . . *I* found her, after they hauled you off."

"She can testify to the truth," Justin said. "And I am sure she will . . . she's a fine lass, she won't be afraid." His hopes rose at the thought but were as swiftly shattered when Bob Watson said reluctantly, "They have an officer backing them up, Justin . . . one of their lieutenants, named Horton. He says that—"

"But there was no officer with them!" Justin interrupted. "Only a petty officer, a bo'sun's mate. Dodge, Tom Dodge. It was he who started the fight . . . damme, Bob, it's all coming back to me now! Dodge wanted to raid my stores and—" He broke off, licking at lips that had suddenly gone dry as he recalled the last sound he had heard before his senses had deserted him. "Did they do any damage to my *Flinders*?"

Watson shrugged resignedly. "Some," he admitted. "But you don't want to trouble your head about that now. You—"

"How much?" Justin insisted, tight-lipped. "How much damage, Bob? I have to know."

The stout harbor master got to his feet. He said, avoiding Justin's gaze, "They stove in her bows, Justin, and knocked down your stocks. But they claim the mob did that, and there weren't any witnesses. The mob from the Rocks didn't stop to be questioned." He hesitated, and then added emphatically, "You'll have to prepare to defend yourself against their charges, lad, because you'll be up before the bench in a day or so, if Captain Case has his way. He reckons to sail for the Cape for the supplies he can't get here, and the Governor won't want to hinder him. He wants to see the damned *Semarang* quit this anchorage as much as I do . . . or maybe even more. So there'll be no delay."

"No delay?" Justin echoed. For a moment, futile anger threatened to overwhelm him, but he managed somehow to control it. "Will you be seeing Miss Maclaine?" he asked thickly.

"Aye, that I will," Watson assented. "Do you want me to ask her if she'll speak up for you in court?"

"Yes, I'd be obliged if you would." Justin rose with some difficulty from the bed and held out his hand. "Thank you for coming and for telling me what's afoot. I'm grateful, Bob, believe me. And I'm going to fight those damnable charges all the way!"

But when the door of his cell clanged shut behind the stocky, blue-uniformed harbor master, and the full enormity of his situation began slowly to sink in, Justin came perilously close to despair. With his ship damaged and the work of months wasted, and with the *Semarang*'s people seemingly ready to perjure themselves in order to saddle him with the blame for their misconduct, his future prospects were, at best, uncertain.

It was a far cry from the proud day when he had donned the King's uniform, he thought wretchedly. Even in Hobart, when Tobias Cockrell had set out to ruin him, he had been able to fight back, because the mate had played into his hands. But now—now, with the crew of a King's ship ranged against him, what chance had he? Surely he had an unhappy propensity for landing himself repeatedly in difficult scrapes, and he began to wonder if perhaps he truly merited the term "currency kid" and all that it implied.

He stumbled back to the bed and buried his aching head in his hands. . . .

"Justin Angus Broome, by a majority verdict, the findings of this court are that you are guilty of all save one of the charges preferred against you. On the fifth charge— namely, that you unlawfully obtained possession of certain naval stores, required for the repair and maintenance of His Majesty's ship *Semarang*—you are found not guilty and accordingly acquitted."

Judge Advocate Ellis Bent made the announcement with fitting gravity, his gaze straying for a moment in mute reproach to the officer who had dissented from the verdict of his fellow magistrates.

Lieutenant Lawson, he thought, had admitted to being well acquainted with the accused and, indeed, had made a telling speech on the young man's behalf, stressing his previous good record and not inconsiderable achievements. And this had resulted in the imposition of a comparatively lenient sentence, with which he personally could only concur.

For the rest, however, the trial had followed the course he had intended it should. He bent forward to pick up the paper with his notes, affecting an inability to find it in order to give himself time to reflect on what had happened . . . and, with satisfaction, on the annoyance it would cause the Governor, when the verdict was made known to him.

During the voyage out from England, he had been on excellent terms with Colonel Macquarie and his wife, Bent reminded himself. The Macquaries were a dull couple, a trifle too puritan in outlook to be entirely to his taste, but, he had supposed, sufficiently well bred and versed in the niceties of class distinction to occupy their viceregal position with dignity. Above all, he had expected Macquarie, as a King's officer, to maintain those barriers which, in a penal colony, must very strictly be adhered to . . . the social barriers, between officialdom and the lower orders.

All convicted felons, whether emancipated or still under sentence, constituted the lower orders, in his own view, but Governor and Mrs. Macquarie had sadly disillusioned him when they had insisted on sweeping away the barriers. He, a barrister of Lincoln's Inn—and, worse still, his lady wife—had been compelled to sit at table with disbarred attorneys, with mutineers from the *Nore,* with robbers and forgers and common thieves. When they attended divine service, they had had to listen to sermons delivered by Irish traitors and, for medical treatment, had had no choice but to seek the advice of convict emancipists, married to women of similar origin.

"Mr. Judge Advocate!" The voice was the Reverend Samuel Marsden's, harshly impatient as ever; and although he did not respond as Marsden clearly wanted, by reading out the sentence, he smiled politely and continued to make a show of searching for the required papers.

Marsden shared his views, of course; the outspoken Yorkshireman had repeatedly made them known to Colonel—no, he was a brigadier general now—to General Macquarie. And more openly than he had felt able to express them himself, but . . . he was dependent on the Governor's goodwill for the furtherance of his career, and Samuel Marsden was not. Besides, there was still the question of his brother Jeffrey's appointment to the colonial judicature. . . . Ellis Bent sighed.

The prisoner, he noticed, was waiting as impatiently as Marsden, but that he did not mind. Young Broome was a protégé of the Governor's; but upstart that he was, he had squandered his chances by brawling with the *Semarang*'s seamen, and even the biased Macquarie could scarcely condone his behavior . . . or offer him any second chance to—what had the rogue aspired to, with Macquarie's encouragement?—to make a career as a commissioned officer in the Royal Navy, no less! But since he was the son of a convicted felon and the stepson of one of Bligh's aides, Broome had been an unsuitable choice, in any event . . . and Their Lordships of the Admiralty had made that abundantly clear, when he had been presented to them.

Perhaps, after today's conviction had been recorded, the Governor's attitude to the so-called currency kids might undergo a significant change . . . he might begin, at last, to see them for what they were. Certainly Mrs. Macquarie would be upset and even angered by the revelations concerning her personal maid that this trial had brought to light. It had been a fortunate chance that had led him to question her stepfather—a sergeant major in the Governor's own regiment—for *his* evidence, his suggestion that the girl was deceitful and wanton, had most effectively destroyed her credibility as a witness. And she had been the only witness young Broome had called. . . .

"Mr. Bent . . ." This time it was Lieutenant Lawson and not the Reverend Marsden who intruded on his thoughts, and Ellis Bent met his gaze with a stony stare.

"Sir?" he questioned haughtily.

"Are we to be kept sitting here all day, sir," Lawson demanded, "whilst you rummage endlessly amongst your briefs? We are busy men, with other duties to perform outside this court, even if you have not."

"I am seeking the necessary authority to enable the prisoner to be transferred to your custody, Mr. Lawson," Ellis Bent informed him. He gestured to his clerk, and although the document to which he had referred was in his own hand, he directed the man to look for it. Observing, however, that Samuel Marsden was showing further signs of impatience, he forestalled an outburst by once again addressing himself to the prisoner in the dock.

"In view of your previous record, Broome, the court has decided to show you clemency by imposing a light sentence on you. You will serve for the next six months at hard labor; and at his request, you will be assigned to the service of Lieutenant Lawson, of the veteran company of His Majesty's Seventy-third Regiment. On production of the requisite authority, you will be released into Mr. Lawson's custody." He jerked his bewigged head at the two constables on duty over the dock. "Take him down!"

Just for an unguarded instant, the judge advocate was taken aback by the naked pain he glimpsed in Justin Broome's eyes, but then the constables hustled him away and his clerk ventured nervously, "Begging your pardon, Mr. Bent, sir, but I am unable to find the form of assignment."

Bent nodded in dismissal and went through the pantomime of himself searching for the missing document, finally producing it with a flourish. He entered the court's findings and the sentence imposed, initialed it, and passed it to the bench for the magistrates to append their signatures.

The girl, Jessica Maclaine, had slipped out, he observed, and he wondered what sort of reception Mrs. Macquarie would accord her. A reprimand, certainly, for having—if Sergeant Major Campbell's evidence were true—permitted the *Semarang*'s seamen to pick her up in the street, like a common prostitute, and then to have run away from them, thereby causing the brawl.

"A sly wee beezum," Campbell had called her, using a Scottish term that apparently was intended to imply that the girl was of doubtful morals. Indeed, he had stated positively that, when out of his care and freed from the restrictions of the Governor's household, she was not to be trusted . . . and the magistrates had duly discounted her evidence.

There was, of course, the possibility that Campbell had *not* been telling the truth. He was clearly a martinet, with strong religious prejudices, and he had not attempted to hide a vindictive disapproval of his stepdaughter, but . . . Ellis Bent dismissed his lingering doubts. It did not matter. The evidence of the seamen had been overwhelming and borne out by one of their officers, Lieutenant Horton. As a result, a subtle blow had been dealt to the Governor's cause, and his own part in dealing it would not be apparent.

He started to gather up his papers as the magistrates filed out, and he was on the point of following them when he found Damien Hayes at his elbow. Hayes was a journalist, the judge advocate recalled, and another of Governor Macquarie's protégés, who had accompanied him on the recent tour of Van Diemen's Land. If not, perhaps, of particularly good breeding, at least he was not an emancipist.

"Well, Mr. Hayes?" he inquired, civilly enough. "What can I do for you? You were, I presume, present during this trial—are there any legal points on which I can enlighten you?"

The angry vehemence of Hayes's reply shattered Bent's complacency. "I'm no lawyer, sir, but I believe that I have witnessed a travesty of justice during this trial," the journalist flung at him. "I have seen an innocent man condemned. And—God knows for what *legal* reason, Mr. Judge Advocate, since clearly you would have obtained your conviction without it—I have been compelled to listen in silence to the . . . Oh, the devil! To the destruction of a fine young woman's good name! I refer, of course, sir, to Miss Jessica Maclaine, with whom I have the honor to be acquainted. She—"

Ellis Bent interrupted him furiously. "Since on your own admission you are no lawyer, sir, and since I am a member of the English bar, I will thank you to keep your opinion to yourself!"

"And that, sir, is what I will *not* do," Damien Hayes

countered. He had his rage under control now and spoke with measured calm. "I have the power of the press behind me. I intend to prepare a report for the London *Chronicle* on what I have witnessed in this courtroom today. It will not make pleasant reading for the benchers of the English bar, I can assure you, Mr. Bent."

Cramming on his hat, he was gone before the judge advocate could find words with which to answer him.

Jessica, to Damien's relief, had not gone far from the court building. He found her standing disconsolately by the water's edge, looking out over the anchorage with her back to the Government House gateway.

She did not turn at his approach and, even when he called her by name, gave no acknowledgment of his presence. Sensing that this was because she was reluctant to let him see that she was weeping, he laid a hand on her shoulder and said gently, "Please listen to me, Jessica."

Still she did not turn to face him. "He shamed me," she managed, in a voice choked with sobs. "And he was lying, Damien, just as the sailors were lying. There was not—not a word of truth in what he said."

"I know that," Damien assured her. He drew her back toward him, aching to hold her in his arms and offer her comfort. "Surely you did not imagine that I believed him?"

"No," she conceded. "But the magistrates did. And now poor Justin Broome is having to suffer, when all he did was simply to—to try to help me."

"He will not fare badly with Lieutenant Lawson, Jessica. They are friends—Broome will not be treated as a convict, I feel sure."

"But the stigma will remain," Jessica said sadly. "He will never be given a commission in the Royal Navy now, will he? And I . . . Oh, Damien, I shall not be able to hold my head up here, ever again! And Mrs. Macquarie . . . how can I be facing her, after this? Perhaps she will not believe that Duncan Campbell was lying."

"Mrs. Macquarie knows you too well to have any doubts," Damien asserted with conviction. "As do I."

Under his gentle urging, she came nearer, letting her small, dark head rest against his shoulder. Holding her thus, feeling her slim body close to his own, and looking down into her tear-wet, unhappy face, he was conscious of a feeling of great tenderness and of an almost overwhelming desire to protect her. From her bullying, sanctimonious stepfather, from the judge advocate's insinuations, and . . . Damien caught his breath. Perhaps even from Mrs. Macquarie, should she, after all, give credence to Sergeant Major Campbell's cruel lies.

He had little knowledge of women, he reflected ruefully. His only intimate contact had been with a London prostitute—an experience that had disgusted him and, in any case, taught him nothing that he needed to know now, in approaching the gentle Jessica Maclaine. . . .

During the time they had spent touring Van Diemen's Land, he had come to enjoy her lively but well-mannered company, to share her pleasure in the beauty of their surroundings, and to talk to her without having to keep a guard on his tongue. Yet it had not occurred to him to attempt to make love to her or to put their friendship on a more intimate footing; he had been content simply to ride with her over the lovely, untamed countryside and marvel at the pleasure she found in chance glimpses of strange plants and animals.

But now . . . Damien felt the sweat break out on his brow and in the palms of his hands, as a sobering thought flashed into his mind. The government printer, Mr. George Howe, who produced the Sydney *Gazette,* had not been able as yet to find paid employment for him. And although the London *Chronicle* had agreed to keep him on a small retainer and to pay him for the articles he sent them, he had, he reminded himself regretfully, barely sufficient funds at present to maintain himself.

Certainly he did not earn enough to support a wife, although . . . Damien braced himself, still holding Jessica diffidently in his arms. Governor Macquarie had expressed approval of the tentative suggestions he had made concerning a newspaper for Hobart Town and had promised financial aid from the government of New South Wales, were he of a mind to start one. And he had been of that mind, lacking only the courage—or the incentive—to translate ideas into action. He had talked to Jessica of his ideas, and . . . His arms tightened about her.

"If I were to go to Hobart with Major Davey," he burst out. "If I were to start a newspaper there, would you come with me, Jessica?"

She was startled, unprepared for the question and clearly bewildered by it. He had been clumsy, Damien thought ruefully, acting on impulse, as all too frequently was his habit.

"I mean," he added hastily, "would you come with me as my wife? You would be free of clacking tongues there and of your stepfather. And I . . . I would deem it an honor if you would consent to wed me, Jessica."

"Wed you? I . . ." Jessica broke free of his encircling arms and backed away from him, her cheeks flushed and her gaze oddly reproachful. "Because of what was said of me in court? Out of—out of pity, Damien? Is it out of pity that you are asking me to wed you?"

"No!" Damien exclaimed, hurt. "Of course it is not!"

"But you are not in love with me!" she persisted. "You have spoken no word of love to me before."

"That would come. There is no one else, Jessica—no other woman I would wish to wed, I give you my word. I am seeking to protect and care for you . . . that is not pity, surely?"

But seemingly his protestations failed to carry conviction, and Damien cursed his own lack of finesse when Jessica answered with bitter pride, "It is not love, Damien. You are wanting me to run away to Hobart—to hide, just as if my stepfather had spoken the truth! He did *not*, and I will not run away on his account. He shall not drive me away from Sydney with his malice. I can find other work, if my mistress—if Mrs. Macquarie does not wish to continue my employment. I will stay until my name is cleared."

"Even if I go to Hobart?" Damien asked wretchedly.

She faced him, the tears gone and her head held high. "I *must* . . . not only for my sake, also for Justin Broome's. Had it not been for my stepfather, my evidence might well have cleared him. I owe it to Justin to stay, I . . ." Sensing Damien's discomfiture, she softened her words. "It was good of you to offer to wed me, and I am grateful. But I . . . I could not think of accepting under the present circumstances."

"But you will think of it, in the future?" Damien urged.

Jessica hesitated, and then, to his relief, she bowed her head in acquiescence. "I will think of it and of you, wherever you are. I am truly grateful for your offer. It has given me courage."

She was smiling when she took her leave of him, and Damien stood where he was, watching her out of sight. Courage, he told himself, was a quality which he, too, would need if he went to Hobart. But he might need even more if he were to write the article with which he had threatened Sydney's judge advocate . . . a very great deal more.

And in his mind, he found himself composing the article as he walked slowly back to his lodgings.

CHAPTER XVIII

"We leave on Tuesday, from South Creek, and cross the river at Emu Ford," Justin said. He saw his mother exchange an anxious glance with Andrew and added reassuringly, "There's little risk, Mam, with seven of us, including Mr. Blaxland, who has been on two exploratory expeditions already. And old Byrne—the one they call Lucky Byrne—has hunted kangaroos in the foothills for years. He's volunteered to act as guide."

"Are you taking horses?" Andrew inquired.

Justin nodded. "Yes, four, to carry our provisions as far as possible. That may not be very far, if we strike a gorge with no way round. But Mr. Blaxland's idea is to follow the main ridge between the Warragamba and Grose rivers and keep on high ground, as George Caley did. He described it as being similar to walking over the tops of houses in a town. Look . . ." He took a sketch map from his breast pocket and spread it out on the table. "This is only a rough copy—Mr. Lawson has the final draft. I compiled it from Caley's and Barrallier's reports and from a sketch Dr. Bass gave me, years ago."

He went into careful detail, indicating on the map the routes other expeditions had taken and the estimated distance they had traveled.

Andrew listened with keen interest, occasionally offering a suggestion or asking a question, but his mother, Justin sensed, was holding deliberately aloof from their discussion. His conviction and sentence had come as a severe blow to her, he was unhappily aware, and their present relationship, although still warm, was under something of a cloud. She had wanted him to appeal against the court's findings—if necessary to the Governor himself—and his refusal to do so had hurt and disappointed her. But . . . He stifled a sigh, as he folded the yellowing map Surgeon Bass had given him when, as a boy of seven or eight, he had first tried his 'prentice hand at shipbuilding.

George Bass, he recalled, had made a most determined attempt to find a way across the great dividing range of the Blue Mountains, equipped with ropes, scaling irons, and climbing hooks of his own design. Accompanied by Henry Hacking and the ship's boy, Billy Martin, he had penetrated some twenty miles into the unknown but had returned, disconsolate, claiming to have found only an endless succession of peaks and ridges, with ravines and gullies between them. And his verdict had been that the mountain barrier was impassable overland—a verdict with which Francis Barrallier had reluctantly concurred, after the failure of his second attempt to find a crossing, in November 1802.

But the taciturn botanist, George Caley, had refused to admit defeat and, two years later, had reached a formidable gorge—which Colonel Paterson had earlier sighted, naming it Grose Valley—only to be driven back because his companions were exhausted and his provisions were running out. The Yorkshireman's meticulously detailed notes were, however, the basis on which Gregory Blaxland had made his plans, and Justin, who had studied the notes carefully during the past month or more, was now convinced that their own expedition—profiting from Caley's mistakes—would have a fair chance of succeeding where his had failed.

"You have His Excellency's approval for this attempt, I take it?" Andrew said.

"His consent," Justin amended, with a faintly rueful smile. "But not his wholehearted approval, I fear."

"Who obtained the Governor's consent, Justin?" his

mother asked, a slight edge to her voice. "Not you, I suppose?"

Justin shook his head, anxious to evade the subject of his present convict status. "Mr. Blaxland saw him, and Will Wentworth, who has decided to join us. He—"

"Do you mean Dr. D'Arcy Wentworth's son? The young man who is acting as provost marshal?"

"Yes," Justin confirmed. "His elder brother is to be commissioned in the army, but—"

His mother interrupted quickly, "Through the Governor's favor?"

"Yes," Justin was compelled to admit. "But you must understand, Mam, Dr. Wentworth is now chief surgeon, and his position is such that—"

His mother was not to be deflected. Again she cut him short, "And he came out here as a convict, just as your father and I did. Oh, Justin, please . . . why will you not appeal to Governor Macquarie against your conviction? You said that the evidence against you was perjured, that those drunken rogues of seamen lied about everything, and that their officer was not even present! Surely you have a right to appeal?"

Justin expelled his breath in a long-drawn sigh. "Because it would mean subjecting Jessica Maclaine to a fresh ordeal, Mam. She came forward willingly to speak in my defense, and her swine of a stepfather, out of pure malice, did all in his power to blacken her name. It made no difference to Mrs. Macquarie, of course, and she took Jessica back into her employ, but . . . damme, I cannot and will not ask her to go through it all again!"

"Not even to restore *your* good name, lad?" Andrew demanded.

"No!" Justin exclaimed vehemently. "What have I suffered, compared with that poor, innocent girl? I've lived at Prospect with Mr. and Mrs. Lawson. I've been treated as one of their own sons and afforded the chance, which I welcome, to take part in this expedition. I've had my say as to the route we shall follow, and the only time I've had fetters on me was when I was arrested." His gaze sought his mother's, and he added gently, "I was refused a commission in the navy long before the brawl with the *Semar-ang*'s people, so I've lost nothing, have I?"

"You have lost the ship you were building," Jenny pointed out.

Again Justin shook his head. "I can still build her, after I've served my time."

"The *Semarang* is back in Sydney Cove," Andrew volunteered, with a wry smile. "I saw her last week, when I was in Sydney for a court-martial. She lost her foremast off Cape Pillar in a storm and limped in with all her pumps going."

"Did she, by heaven!" Justin's mouth tightened. Like most of Sydney's inhabitants, he had not expected to set eyes on the arrogant Captain Case and his ship again, but if she had returned, then perhaps . . . He glanced again at his mother and then bit back the words he had been about to voice. It was best to say nothing, he decided. Case was a slippery customer.

Andrew, intercepting his glance, covered his involuntary pause with ready tact. "You heard, I suppose," he said, his smile fading, "that when he sailed—supposedly for the Cape—Robert Watson's cutter failed to dip her ensign and Case fired a shot across her bows? An insult to a King's ship, he claimed. When Watson brought-to, Lieutenant Horton boarded her and pressed six of her crew into His Majesty's service . . . convicts, all of them!"

Justin stared at him incredulously. "No," he answered. "I have not heard about that, Andrew."

But it had, perhaps, been fortunate that he had been with the Lawsons at Prospect, instead of working on his skeleton vessel in Simeon Lord's yard, he thought, recalling what Captain Case had said to him, on the occasion of their first meeting. If the *Semarang*'s commander had made up deficiencies in his ship's company by pressing the harbor master's convict boatmen, he might well have been tempted to send Lieutenant Horton to the shipyard, in order to fill the warrant carpenter's berth . . . the brawl and its unhappy consequences conveniently forgotten. And Justin had only his conviction to thank for his absence from Lord's yard at the time. . . . As Case himself had remarked, it was an ill wind that turned none to good, Justin reflected, a trifle cynically.

His thoughts were still of the *Semarang* and her captain when, having taken leave of his mother and Andrew, he rode with William to the border of the Ulva holding.

His impression of Captain Case had not been entirely unfavorable, he reminded himself. True, the man was arrogant, but he had served with some distinction under the redoubtable Admiral Hood, and surely was not one to countenance perjury on the part of any of his men . . . if he indeed was aware that they had committed perjury at the trial. It was possible that he was not aware of it but had simply accepted Petty Officer Dodge's account as the truth—and Lieutenant Horton's, too—and had inquired no further.

If the *Semarang* were still in port when he was freed, a personal call on Case might serve to set the record straight, Justin decided. Certainly it could do no harm, since the harm was already done, particularly where little Jessica Maclaine was concerned. Yes, once his freedom was restored—and that would not be long now . . . his sentence would end within a week or so of the expedition's return—he would go straight to Captain Case, then to Jessica.

He parted cheerfully from his brother William and, with the boy's good wishes still ringing in his ears, put his borrowed horse to a canter and headed for the Nepean River and Gregory Blaxland's farm.

On the morning of Tuesday, May 11, 1813, the party left South Creek, their four packhorses laden with provisions, spare ammunition for their muskets, and a few tools with which to construct the bark shelters they planned to use instead of tents. Old Lucky Byrne, the kangaroo hunter, had his half-breed dogs with him—five bony animals, more dingo than dog—and Gregory Blaxland had brought two of his convict farm workers, both sturdy, reliable men, who would cook and care for the horses.

Gregory was the younger of the two Blaxland brothers and had, Justin knew, come out as a free settler eight years before, from Newington, in the county of Kent. His elder brother, John, had followed a year later, with his wife and family. Gregory was a tough, determined man and, like William Lawson, was in his late thirties, the owner of a prosperous, well-worked farm property, on which he bred cattle and sheep. Two succeeding years of drought and a recent plague of caterpillars and winged insects had played havoc with his grazing land, and since he was anxious to increase his stock, the search for fresh pastures provided the motive for his decision to attempt the mountain crossing.

William Charles Wentworth's motives were not quite as practical, but his enthusiasm for the project exceeded even Lawson's. He was twenty, a gangling, somewhat awkward young man, with a cast in one eye and an unruly thatch of auburn hair which, like his dress, was always untidy. His education had been obtained at an English public school, and Justin found him intelligent and exceptionally well read, but with a sarcastic manner and an almost aggressive defensiveness, which became apparent whenever he felt himself slighted. The Governor's choice of so youthful an incumbent for the temporary office of provost marshal had not been a popular one with either the military officers or the traders and shipowners of Sydney, yet despite his lack of experience, the younger Wentworth had succeeded well in his difficult role.

With Justin, since they both were native born, he was usually quite at ease, and as they plodded steadily along toward their first objective, he talked excitedly of the prospect ahead of them.

"If we can find a way to reach the land beyond the Blue Mountains, this colony will become an asset instead of a liability to the British Crown. New settlers would come here in the hundreds, enough of them to found a nation. The nation of Australia, Justin, as your friend Captain Flinders would have it. I read his book, you know—or rather, the first part of it, in manuscript, after meeting him in the office of the cartographer, old Jacob Arrowsmith, entirely by cance."

"He is a sick man," Justin said, with infinite regret. "But I trust he will live to see his work published."

"He wanted it to be entitled 'A Voyage to Australia.'" Wentworth went on. "But for some reason, Sir Joseph Banks did not approve. He wanted the title altered to read 'Terra Australis,' with the inevitable implication that the land is still unknown. But do you know what Captain Flinders said? He insisted that such old names were outworn. This is a new world, a world for youth to conquer, he told me. 'Archipelago or continent,' he said, 'I call the whole land Australia.' I repeated all that to the Governor, and I think he was impressed."

"You mean that Governor Macquarie may decide to use it officially?" Justin asked eagerly. "That would delight poor Matt Flinders's heart, no doubt of it."

"Perhaps," Wentworth confided, smiling. "If our expedition should prove successful, we shall be in a position to convince him of its suitability." He added, gesturing toward the distant mountains, "And we shall succeed! *'Nil mortalibus ardui est'*—'no height is too arduous for mortal man'!"

By four o'clock, they had crossed the Nepean at the Emu Island ford, and after proceeding two miles in a southwesterly direction, through forest land and good pasture, it was agreed that they should make camp at the foot of the first ridge.

Justin slept dreamlessly and well, and by nine the following morning, they began to ascend the ridge. The land was covered with scrubby brushwood, very thick in places, and the horses found the going difficult and had to be coaxed and, at times, dragged unwillingly up the steep slope. Justin went ahead, with William Lawson, to make a check of their bearings. Keeping to the summit of the ridge, he reckoned that they had covered some three miles, their direction varying from southwest to west, the ridge being singularly hard to follow, with deep rocky gullies appearing without warning and necessitating constant changes of direction and detours.

With the aid of Caley's map, Lawson identified the high-land of Grose Head, bearing north by east and, as nearly as he could judge, six or seven miles distant. When the rest of the party caught up, the horses were so exhausted that Blaxland advised that they make camp where they were, at the head of a deep gully. Justin climbed down, with Byrne, in search of water, and on their return to the camp they came across a young kangaroo that had fallen victim to a predatory eagle only a few minutes before. Roasted over the campfire, it made excellent eating.

By the third day they had fallen into a routine, but unable to travel through the brush until the dew was off, they made slow progress, and the horses had become more of a liability than an asset.

"We should leave the damned animals and proceed on foot," William Wentworth said, making small attempt to hide his impatience. "I doubt we've covered a mile as the crow flies since we left camp." As if to lend emphasis to his words, one of the horses stumbled on the rocky surface of the track they were following and went crashing down, scattering its load.

"We'll rest them," Gregory Blaxland agreed, his tone curt. "If you are in such an infernal hurry, William, go on and scout out our route for tomorrow. Byrne can take the dogs and try to shoot some game."

"Very well," Wentworth agreed. "Coming with me, Justin?"

Justin nodded, not trusting himself to speak; but as the two of them set off, the sheer enormity of the task before them struck him with the force of a physical blow. All around them were the jagged peaks, stretching for mile after mile in seemingly endless succession, their tree-clad slopes separated, one from the other, by precipitous rocky gorges and gullies hundreds of feet deep. And in the direction they were all agreed that they must follow, the brush grew so thickly that, in order for the horses to negotiate the ascent, a way would have to be hacked out before they could even begin.

"Let's see if we can find an alternative route," Wentworth suggested, after inspecting the tangled mass of brush with a despairing eye. "We'll separate—you go nor'west, and I'll go south by west."

But after two hours' searching, both returned to the agreed rendezvous to report the same unhappy result—there was no alternative route, and the brush would have to be cleared before they could move on.

"I came across a track that was marked, I should suppose by a European, by cutting nicks in the bark of the trees," Wentworth said. "But the track ended, as they all seem to, in a narrow gully—too steep to be possible for us, even on foot, without the horses."

"I think Mr. Dawes marked that track," Justin answered. "He left a cairn of stones about four or five miles further on, but the brush has evidently grown over the route he took." He looked at William Wentworth's red and sweat-soaked face and added wryly, "I fear that these infernal heights may prove too arduous for us poor mortals, Willie."

"We shall not fail for want of trying," Wentworth vowed obstinately. "By heaven we shall not!"

Their flagging spirits were once again raised when old Lucky Byrne reappeared with two small kangaroos that his hunting dogs had pulled down, and after a satisfying meal, Gregory Blaxland called on them to volunteer to tackle the brushwood next day.

"We must keep to the main ridge," he went on, with conviction. "It is the only one that is even likely to lead us to our objective, and if that entails cutting a track for the horses, then so be it. And . . . I think it would be wise if we set a watch throughout the night. Byrne says he came across some native huts, with signs of recent occupation. We don't want to take any risk of being attacked—these are not the most friendly of their kind."

Leaving the convict servants to guard the horses and their provisions, the explorers worked to the point of exhaustion for the next two days, slashing a path through the thick, unyielding brush with knives and axes. Five miles of track took them to a high point, only to find that another low ridge lay beyond the one they had cleared with so much labor, this new obstacle also overgrown and impassable for the pack animals unless it, too, was cleared.

They worked on, their hands blistered and swollen and the sweat pouring from their weary bodies, worried now by the absence of water and a lack of suitable fodder for the horses. But they had made progress, however little, and Blaxland declared that Sunday—the sixth day of their journey—should be set aside, to enable them to rest and recoup their strength. When night fell, however, fear of a native attack deprived them of sleep. Byrne's dogs ran off, and the nightlong howling of a large pack of wild dingoes reduced the two convict servants to such a state of apprehension that it was all Blaxland could do to persuade them to continue. He and Lawson, armed with muskets, were compelled to remain with the badly frightened men to ensure that they, like the dogs, did not run off.

Such grass as they could find was loaded onto the horses, in addition to the burdens they were already carrying, and with infinite effort, the parched animals were half-dragged, half-led up the newly cleared track.

Justin, with William Wentworth, went ahead and selected a campsite in the late afternoon between two seemingly bottomless gullies, with Grose Head bearing northeast by north and Mount Banks northwest by west. A streamlet ran through one of the gullies, and with no water to be found on the summit, Justin made a perilous descent of some six hundred feet in order to bring up a scanty supply.

He was utterly spent and badly bruised and cut by the sharp rocks when, just before dusk, he clambered slowly back to the ridge, the glory of the sunset and the shadowed beauty of the mountains seeming to mock him as, at last, he flung himself down by the campfire and let his heavy lids drop.

It was hopeless, he thought, and they were risking life and limb to little avail, for even if by some miracle they were able to cross the barrier of trackless mountains, how could any settlers follow them—still less with sheep and cattle, when horses could barely do so?

After an unappetizing meal of salt meat and biscuit, washed down with only a mouthful of their precious supply of water, he confided his doubts to William Lawson.

"We do not know for certain that there *is* pasture and

grazing land on the other side of the range. My mother"—
Justin smiled thinly—"is convinced that there is, and has
been since she landed in Governor Phillip's wake. At this
moment, Mr. Lawson, I just wish that I could believe she
was right!"

Lawson looked round at the hunched forms of their
companions, huddled about the dying fire with the abandon of men tried almost beyond endurance, and shrugged
despondently.

"It's hard for any of us to believe it from where we are
now," he conceded. "But we *must* believe it, Justin . . .
or turn back, admitting defeat as all the others who tried to
find a way across finally did. But you're not one to give in
easily, are you?—any more than I am."

Justin shook his head. "I'm not for turning back, sir. My
fears are for what we may find when we've made the
crossing. A swamp, perhaps; a barren desert; or, as Barrallier believed, an inland sea."

"We can only hope," Lawson said, "and pray to the God
of our fathers. But we will not turn back . . . we'll go on,
until we know for certain what lies beyond those mountains."

William Wentworth roused himself to murmur sleepily,
"For Australia, Justin—remember? For the Australia Flinders dreamed of . . . 'nil mortalibus ardui est'!"

They went on, grimly, wearily, but with ever-growing determination, with little variation to the pattern of their
days. Now the path had to be cut, as before, through thick
eucalyptus scrub; now a great pile of fallen rock barred
their passage and had to be laboriously cleared, rock by
rock, so that the horses might stagger on. Again and again,
deep chasms were encountered, forcing them to make a
detour, but they held to their westward direction, sometimes by taking a path along a ridge barely twenty yards
wide, rimmed by perpendicular cliffs, and occasionally by
following a creek bed or a kangaroo track through a forest
of close-growing trees.

They found the cairn William Dawes had left to mark the
furthest point he had reached; and after ascending the sec-

ond ridge in the barrier that faced them, blazing a trail as they went, they found themselves looking down on the settlements they had left behind them ten days before.

Justin took their bearings, and William Lawson recorded each with meticulous care. Prospect Hill bore east by south, the Seven Hills east-northeast, Windsor northeast by east, with Grose Head still to the northeast. Elated because they were on course, they camped that night at the head of a stream of good water; and in the swampy area nearby, the horses found a plentiful supply of coarse grass. But caution was needed on the flatter land through which the stream ran, and Byrne's dogs—three of which had returned—gave warning of an aborigine party that apparently had been tracking them. A few musket shots swiftly put the would-be marauders to flight, but once again a nightly watch had to be kept, lest they should decide to return.

On Saturday the twenty-second, after enduring a heavy rainstorm, they gained the summit of the third and highest ridge to the south of Mount Banks, calculating the distance covered from Emu Ford to be eighteen miles in a straight line. The top of the ridge was flat, covered with short, coarse grass and free of trees and scrub, with a stream of clear, fresh water. They made camp, tired but their spirits running high, for it seemed the end was at last in sight. But when, next morning, they resumed their journey, it was only to find that their progress was barred by an impassable barrier of rock, which appeared to rise perpendicularly from the side of the mountain, like a vast wall of stone.

Justin and William Wentworth made an abortive attempt to scale it, first descending some four hundred feet from the ridge to the foot of the rock face, but were compelled to return, defeated, unable to find even a toehold on its forbidding surface.

"We must head north," Gregory Blaxland decided, "and endeavor to find a way round. But," he added, seeking to revive their flagging hopes, "the worst is over—the way is there to be found."

They struggled on, having once more to hack their way through thorny brushwood and seldom covering more than three miles a day. More aborigines were sighted, and game became more plentiful, water easier to find. But the horses were now in sorry condition, and their loads had to be carried by the party themselves, each man strapping a bundle on his back and stumbling on as best he could over the rocky, treacherously slippery ground.

Tempers inevitably became frayed; Blaxland lapsed into taciturnity, Wentworth ceased to quote his airy Latin tags, and even the quiet, controlled Lawson resorted to angry outbursts when the incessant grumbling of the two convict servants became too much to tolerate. Justin, however, for no reason that he could have explained, found himself growing in confidence and beginning at last to believe in Governor Phillip's promise concerning the colony's future. Dirty, unshaven, and unbearably weary, he flung himself on the hard ground to sleep after a day of back-breaking toil, and as he drifted into unconsciousness, he heard his mother's voice as clearly as if she were beside him:

> "Here are the fertile plains . . . here are interminable pastures, the future home of flocks and herds innumerable . . ."

On Monday, May 31—the twentieth day after fording the Nepean River—the dream became reality. They had covered six miles through well-watered forest land, bringing the horses down from the summit of a steep ridge by dint of cutting a zigzag track for them with hoes. That night they made camp near a hill shaped like a sugarloaf, with two smaller, similarly shaped hills on either side. From the summit of the highest, they had looked out over a wide area of fine pastureland, which Gregory Blaxland, in a voice choked with emotion, declared would suffice the colony for the next thirty years.

Kneeling by their campfire, chilled by the sudden cold of their new surroundings, they gave thanks in prayer. According to William Lawson's calculations and Justin's carefully recorded compass bearings, they had traveled fifty miles through the mountains and eight miles through the forest beyond.

The decision to return without exploring the new pastures they had discovered was made of necessity. Their supplies were running out, the horses were barely able to walk, and the men themselves were worn out, their clothing in rags, their strength and endurance tried to the limit. But the journey back was easy by comparison, for the trail had been blazed, and the natives, to their relief, made no attempt to molest them.

On Sunday, June 6, with the last of their provisions exhausted, they were back at Gregory Blaxland's farm at South Creek, sick from weariness but triumphant. They had crossed the Blue Mountains to the unknown land beyond and had found that it was just as Governor Phillip had predicted, and not the desert or vast inland sea that William Lawson now confessed he had feared might meet their eyes at the end of their arduous journey.

Lawson wrote his report when he and Justin went back to Prospect, and Justin read it, his throat tight.

> Here is a great extent of fine land—forest, and the best-watered pastureland of any I have seen in this colony. This country will, I have no doubt, be a great acquisition to the whole colony, and there will be no difficulty in making a good road to it, if its contours are taken into account.
>
> In case of invasion, it will be a safe retreat for the inhabitants and their families and stock, for this part of the country is so formed by nature that a few men would be able to defend the passes against a large body.
>
> I also have every reason to believe that the same ridge of mountains we traveled on will lead into the interior of the country and that a communication can easily be found from this to the head of the Coal River, where, to my knowledge, is a large extent of fine grazing country. . . .

After taking ten days to recoup their strength and compile reports on the crossing, the party once more joined forces and rode to Sydney, in order to report in person to the Governor.

It was when they came in sight of the cove that Justin interrupted an argument that had developed between Gregory Blaxland and William Wentworth as to whether they had, in fact, traversed the entire mountain range.

Below them, the King's ship *Semarang* and three trading schooners lay at anchor, and Justin's shout of mingled astonishment and pleasure, while it halted the somewhat acrimonious exchange between his two companions, caused them to turn on him in almost simultaneous annoyance.

"What the devil has that plaguey ship to do with me?" Blaxland demanded. "I had supposed she had long since sailed for the Cape."

"She suffered storm damage and had to put back," Wentworth explained. "All the same—what has caused you so much excitement, Justin? You are surely not anxious to renew your acquaintance with her people, are you?"

"It's *my* sloop I'm interested in," Justin returned. He pointed, scarcely able to believe the evidence of his own eyes. "In God's name, Willie—*look at her!*"

The vessel he had left on the stocks in Simeon Lord's yard, barely half-completed and with part of her bow stove in, was now in the water, tied up to the end of the wharf, and finished in every particular as far as he could make out. Both lower masts had been stepped, and the standing rigging was in place. About a score of men, in the garb of seamen and wearing sennit hats, were moving purposefully about the wharf, on which they had a pair of sheerlegs in efficient operation.

As Justin watched incredulously, the fore-topmast was hauled up and lowered into place, and a second party, on the sloop's deck, set to work to fid and rig it. A tall officer was directing them, bawling impatient orders, and even at his present distance, Justin recognized him and shook his head in stunned bewilderment.

"Forgive me, sir," he said to William Lawson, "if I don't accompany you. But I have to find out what is going on—

that's Captain Case, you see, on board my sloop. It looks as if . . . dear heaven, Mr. Lawson, it looks as if his people have built my vessel for me!"

Lawson shrugged. "A fitting payment, if that's the case, Justin. Off you go, my dear boy, and make your peace with His Majesty's Navy. I shall, of course, see to it that the Governor is made aware of the part you have played in our recent exploration. The least reward you may surely expect is a pardon." He leaned across to take Justin's rein. "You can leave the horse with me."

Captain Case greeted him with typical lack of contrition.

"Ah, so you are back, Mr. Broome. I had hoped to have this finished"—he waved vaguely about him, as his men toiled, sweating in the hot sun—"and your sloop ready to put to sea. But you've upset my calculations by returning a trifle prematurely. I trust, however, that your—ah—your venture into the unknown met with success?"

Justin eyed him warily. "It did sir, yes. But you . . . may I ask why you have set your ship's company to work on my vessel?"

Case flashed him a faintly malicious smile. "It keeps them off the streets, does it not? And prevents their molesting innocent young damsels and hardworking young shipwrights." His smile faded and he laid a slim brown hand on Justin's arm. "Mr. Broome, my third lieutenant, in the mistaken belief that we had seen the last of Sydney Town, confessed to me what some of these villains of mine had done to you. He also admitted that he had perjured himself at your trial, in order to save them from retribution. Well, I have done all in my power to set the record straight." He counted on the fingers of his hand. "Firstly, Lieutenant Horton has repeated his confession to the judge advocate, and your conviction and sentence have been quashed. Secondly, Bo'sun's Mate Dodge received two dozen lashes and has been disrated. Thirdly—and I trust to your satisfaction—half the men under my command have, perforce, learned the skills required of shipwrights and carpenters, and having worked initially on repairs to the *Semarang*, they have completed the work you had begun on this fine small vessel."

Bereft of words, Justin continued to stare at him in disbelief. William Case's immaculately tailored arm went round his shoulders.

"Justice has been done, Mr. Broome, and I hope most sincerely that you will not think too ill of me. We shall sail—this time in the confident expectation that we shall *not* return here—at the end of this week, provided the wind is favorable. I have helped myself to some of your teak for my own ship, but have left you, in exchange, a suit of canvas for yours. May I take it that—ah—we part as friends? Unless, that is to say, you care to reconsider my offer of a berth as master's mate, which is still open?"

Justin found his tongue at last.

"Thank you, sir," he managed. "But I—"

"You could sell your sloop," the *Semarang*'s commander put in. "And I would promise you a commission, when we pay off. What do you say, Mr. Broome, eh? Yes or no?"

"It must be no, sir," Justin answered; and to his own surprise, he was conscious of regret. "You see . . ." Searching for a reason, he recalled suddenly the green vista of the pastureland he had seen from the summit of the last rocky hill he and his party had conquered, and he added with newfound pride, "My future is here, sir. I saw it stretching before me less than two weeks ago."

Captain Case held out his hand. "Very well, Mr. Broome. I can only bid you farewell and good fortune. And I hope that you are right!"

He had another reason for staying here, Justin thought, as he shook the extended hand. Justice had not yet been done to little Jessica Maclaine.

CHAPTER XIX

The report in the Sydney *Gazette* was brief, and Justin read it in some bewilderment.

> The party led by Lieutenant William Lawson of the Veteran Company and Mr. G. Blaxland, whose departure on an excursion of discovery we announced on the 18th ultimo, returned without the slightest injury from fatigue or accident on the 13th instant.
>
> Both gentlemen, and Mr. W. C. Wentworth who, we understand, accompanied them, called on His Excellency the Governor earlier this week. They report having found a prodigious extent of fine level country lying in the direction they pursued on the north side of the Western River, which time may render of importance and utility to the Colony and entitle the gentlemen employed in the discovery to the thanks of the inhabitants.
>
> No further particulars of the expedition have, however, as yet reached us.

"The Governor did not doubt my statement," Gregory Blaxland explained, with barely concealed resentment. "But he appeared dissatisfied, giving me reason to suppose—damme, not to put too fine a point on it—that he had neither expected nor wanted us to succeed! Furthermore, he insisted that we should not speak freely or openly of our discovery, lest convict escapers be tempted to follow our route and—supposedly driving stolen livestock before them—seize possession of the new land!" He crashed his big fist angrily down on the table onto which Justin had laid the copy of the *Gazette*. "Small wonder Will Lawson's taken himself off to Prospect in disgust."

"Has he, sir?" Wentworth questioned. "But—"

Blaxland ignored him. "That wretchedly inadequate report—from which Justin's and Byrne's names were omitted—was censored by Secretary Campbell, I don't doubt, on the Governor's instructions. In fact, Campbell probably wrote it, not George Howe. That other young newspaperman—what's his name? Hayes, is it not, Damien Hayes? The fellow who appears to represent the London *Chronicle*, at all events—well, he was sniffing round the *Gazette* office, obviously scenting a story, and I was sorely tempted to present him with ours. However, in view of the Governor's attitude, I refrained . . . and damme, now I hear that Hayes has taken passage to Hobart on board the *Semarang*! And she sailed this morning!"

"His Excellency did promise that he would arrange for an official expedition to survey our route," William Wentworth offered, in a placatory tone. He met Justin's puzzled gaze and shrugged. "He suggested that George Evans, from the surveyor's office, should be sent, to examine the possibility of constructing a road. Because unless a road *can* be built to enable settlers and their livestock to cross the mountains, our discovery will be of little value to the colony as a whole. And we did *not* traverse the whole of those mountains, Mr. Blaxland."

"So you keep on reminding me, William," Blaxland retorted, refusing to be placated.

"Well, we can scarcely expect rewards for what we did not succeed in doing, can we, sir?"

"Who is talking about rewards, devil take you, boy?"

"I had supposed," the younger man murmured, his smile malicious, "that you might be. Apart from our friend Justin here—who has returned to find his skeletal vessel built for him—it cannot in truth be said that the risks we took to life and limb have gained us even acclaim!" He gestured to the crumpled pages of the *Gazette*. "That is not my notion of a eulogy, with all due respect to Secretary Campbell." Striking an attitude, he quoted solemnly, " 'And nearer seen the beauteous landscape grew, opening like Canaan on rapt Israel's view!' At least old Lucky Byrne was rewarded—His generous Excellency gave the old fellow ten pounds for his trouble, in holey silver dollars."

Still irritated, Blaxland brushed his sarcastic comments aside. "Will Lawson is a trained surveyor and engineer, and *he* says that a road could be built. Not a carriage road, perhaps, but one suitable for the passage of cattle and sheep. I don't understand why Macquarie insists on secrecy and delay."

"For the reason he gave, sir," young Wentworth asserted. "To offer no temptation to escapers, bushrangers— call the rogues what you will. Speaking, and quite seriously, as acting provost marshal and head of the colony's constabulary, I must applaud His Excellency's caution . . . even if I am thereby robbed of acclaim. We need the convicts to labor for us, to build houses and roads—not to make off with the settlers' livestock in search of the promised land. And I'm looking for no tangible reward, any more than Justin is—eh, Justin, my friend? Now that you are a free man again, I imagine you'll be back off to sea, will you not?"

Justin nodded somewhat absentmindedly. For some inexplicable reason he had found himself thinking of little Jessica India Maclaine, and it was only with some effort that he brought himself back to the present. "Yes . . . yes, indeed. I'll take the first charter I can get . . . to Coal River or Hobart or the Hawkesbury." He smiled. "Captain Case presented me with a compass and a fine chronometer before we sailed. I can be ready to put to sea in a week."

"Splendid!" William Wentworth exclaimed. "Then I fancy I know from whom you could expect a charter. Mrs. O'Shea, the charming Abigail, is anxious to visit her property on the Hawkesbury. She has some stock to transport, and she is worried about her sister, she told me. She has had no word of late, and . . ." He talked on, but Justin scarcely heard him.

The recollection was almost painful, yet he could not but think back . . . Abigail, dear Abigail! Even after all this time, if there were the slightest chance on earth of his being of service to her, he would grasp it with both hands! He would need a crew, but Cookie Barnes was back in port and willing to sign on with him again, and there should be little difficulty in finding another man. Or, come to that, a good boy might suffice, provided old Cookie was fit.

"I'll call on Mrs. O'Shea," he said, breaking into William Wentworth's lengthy explanation. "Thank you, Willie, for the suggestion." Abigail's younger sister, Lucy, he recalled, had married the emancipist, Luke Cahill, a decent, hard-working lad, whom the Boskennas had first employed at Yarramundie. Lucy Tempest had caused something of a sensation by her wild behavior before Justin had sailed for England, and he had not greatly liked her, but . . . He rose, unable to disguise his eagerness, and took his leave.

" 'Nil mortalibus ardui est'!" William Wentworth called after him, in friendly mockery. "Good hunting, Justin!"

There was another call he must make though, Justin reminded himself; and he must make it before he pledged himself to a charter. Until two days ago, his sentence had exiled him from Sydney. But now he was a free man again, and he had debts to make good. . . .

At Government House, however, the housekeeper, Mrs. Ovens, told him that Jessica Maclaine was off duty.

"She will likely be at Sergeant Major Campbell's quarter in Clarence Street, visiting her sisters," the woman added helpfully. "But you will not find the sergeant major there, Mr. Broome. Jessica does not visit when he is at home."

Which, Justin thought wryly, was not surprising. He found the quarter without difficulty, its front door standing invitingly open, and was about to enter when a man's voice, shouting wrathful accusations, brought him abruptly to a halt.

"Ye damned wee slut! I'll no' have ye here, leadin' ma lassies astray wi' your talk! Was it no' enough that ye broke your puir mither's hairt an' drove her tae her death? But

here ye are, sneakin' in when ye think ma back's turned!
Weel, ye're no' welcome, Jessie—so awa' wi' ye; out o' my
sight, d'ye hear me?"

A woman's voice broke into the tirad. "Jessie has done
no harm, Duncan. And the little girls enjoy her visits, as I
do myself. Besides, did you not give her permission to
come? Did you not say—"

"Whist, woman!" the man's voice thundered. It was
slurred, Justin realized; evidently Sergeant Major Campbell
had been drinking. Jessica had been silent until now, offering him no provocation; and expecting her to leave the
house, Justin stepped back, anxious that the girl should not
suspect he had been eavesdropping. He would duck down,
out of sight, he decided, and catch up with her farther
down the street. That would spare her humiliation and—
Jessica's agonized cry stopped him in his tracks.

"Maun I tak' ma belt tae ye, then?" Campbell demanded
thickly. Justin heard the swish of the descending leather,
heard the blow, and a savage anger caught at his throat.
He threw caution to the wind and flung himself into the
room. He was so filled with pent-up rage that, for a moment, he could not speak or attempt to explain the reason
for his presence.

"What the devil!" Campbell, in breeches and a crumpled
tunic, stood with jaw dropping, his thick leather belt still
held aloft as if, even now, it were his intention to continue
to use it on his defenseless stepdaughter. Justin grabbed his
upraised arm and, with the advantage of surprise, wrested
the belt from him and flung it away, simultaneously pushing Campbell backward so that the big man tripped over a
stool and fell heavily to the floor.

The occupants of the room stared at Justin in varying
degrees of bewilderment. Jessica, he saw, had a livid weal
across her cheek, the sight of which added fuel to the
flame of his anger. He muttered something, and the other
woman—Campbell's wife, he could only suppose—cried
out in alarm; and then, as if aware that nothing she might say
would deter him, she gave a smothered gasp and, moving
swiftly to where two small girls were crouching by the fireplace, gathered them both into her arms.

"Now, Mr. Campbell," he said menacingly, "let's see how you'll fare, matched against someone nearer your own size!"

"What . . ." the big man swore, staring up at Justin stupidly. "Who in God's name are ye, tae come bustin' in here, intae ma house and . . ." Recognition dawned slowly, and he rose unsteadily to one knee and emitted a loud roar of derision. "I ken ye now, ye damned young blackguard! Ye're the mealymouthed wee toad Jessie's daft enow tae fancy, and 'twas you that dragged her intae court! Well, tae hell wi' ye! I'll not tak' lip frae any plaguey convict!" He rose to his feet and rounded on his wife. "Awa' an' call the constables, and tak' the bairns wi' ye. . . . Make haste, now! Tell them an escaped convict has broken in here!"

The woman obeyed him, and Justin heard Jessica cry out in sudden fear. "Justin, he means it . . . and he'll lie! Go, oh please—go! He'll only make trouble for you if you do not."

"I'm not going," Justin grated, "until I've taught this drunken swine a lesson he'll remember. He shall not raise his hand to you again, I swear. Well, Campbell," he challenged, with biting scorn, "are you all talk and bluster and filthy lies? Or have you the guts to stand up and fight?"

For answer, Campbell stripped off his uniform jacket and gestured sullenly to the back door. "Outside," he invited, "an' I'll show ye, damn your eyes! 'Tis you will be taught the lesson, no' me."

They faced each other in the small, fenced-in garden, Campbell with his arms raised in the style of a trained pugilist, his shaven, bullet-head lowered and his dark eyes ablaze. He had the advantage in height and weight, Justin thought soberly, and probably in technique and experience, too, but . . . the years of heavy drinking had taken their toll of his big body, and for all his weaving and swaying, he was slow, his movements cumbersome and his muscles slack.

Whereas he himself . . . Justin's tension relaxed, as he deftly sidestepped his opponent's first, bull-like rush. Then, as the big man ground to a halt and turned himself clumsily around, Justin's two fists smashed in turn into the man's gaping lips. The soldier swore and, a trickle of blood coursing down his chin, his booted foot came out, catching Justin in the groin.

The blow was unexpected, and Campbell followed it up with a pounding attack, using both feet and fists, as Justin, off balance and in pain, momentarily lowered his guard. But the big man was breathing hard, the perspiration running off him, his rasping threats barely audible, and Justin, recovering quickly, landed two rapid punches to Campbell's soft belly. He heard his opponent gasp for breath, but Campbell, as if belatedly recalling the skills he must once have learned in the prize ring, warded off Justin's next blow with powerful arms crossing and weaving defensively in front of his chest.

His strategy might have succeeded had he not attempted, once again, to kick his way out. This time Justin was ready for him, and as the booted foot left the ground, he grabbed Campbell's ankle and pushed upward, sending him crashing heavily down onto his back. The man rolled over, groaning, and Justin stood back.

"I've had . . . enough," the big man gasped, crawling away on his elbows and struggling for breath.

Disgust succeeded anger, and Justin had just begun to turn away when Jessica screamed, and simultaneously he realized his mistake.

But Campbell was already on his feet, lurching toward him with a rusty garden spade held menacingly aloft and murder blazing in his eyes. The improvised weapon descended, missing him by inches as he leaped aside. Now, the full force of Justin's anger unleashed, he went bull-headed for his opponent, wrenched the spade from him, and threw it out of his reach.

"Now," he vowed furiously, "you shall have that lesson, and by God it shall be one you'll remember for the rest of your days! And, you misbegotten swine, if you ever lay a hand on Jessica again, I'll come from the ends of the earth to repeat it!"

Duncan Campbell was sobbing and begging him for mercy long before Justin's fury had spent itself. He pounded

the man's face into a bleeding pulp, smashed his fists re-
morselessly into the flabby muscles of his swelling paunch
and, fingers biting into the fleshy throat, shook him as a
terrier might a rat.

Only when Jessica made her voice heard, pleading with
him to have done, did his anger subside. Suddenly sickened, Justin let his bruised hands fall to his sides, and it
was then that Jessica managed to draw his attention to the
soldiers.

"The guard," she told him, in a choked voice. "Agnes
called the guard from the barracks, not the constables. Justin, they are here!"

A tall sergeant came toward him, and Justin faced him,
warily eyeing the two armed soldiers at his back. To attempt to make his escape was, he knew, futile. They would
arrest him, once again he would be arraigned before Sydney's magistrates, and there seemed little doubt that he
would be convicted of brawling. With his previous record—
although the earlier conviction had been quashed—he
could hardly expect to be acquitted. His anger started to
rise anew, when, to his astonishment, the sergeant winked
at him and clucked in the direction of Campbell's inert
form. "We were seeing Sergeant Major Campbell commit a
breach of the peace, sir, and witnessed the unprovoked attack he made on your person with"—gravely, he gestured
to the fallen spade—"an offensive weapon. I shall have the
sergeant major taken to the guardroom, and it will be my
intention to report him for being drunk and disorderly."

Unable to believe the evidence of his own eyes and ears,
Justin stared at him speechlessly. The sergeant's stern expression relaxed suddenly in a smile.

"If, sir," he suggested quietly, "you were to leave now,
in order to escort wee Jessica Maclaine back to Government House, my men and I . . . why, we shall be blind,
you understand. We shall say that we were unable to identify the person Sergeant Major Campbell attacked. As to
his injuries . . . well, now"—the lilting Highland voice
held a note of unexpected cynicism—"who is to say that he
did not sustain them when resisting arrest? Campbell is a
violent man when he is drinking, and 'twas his wife—

Agnes Campbell, sir—who was reporting him to the orderly officer. She was saying that he was drunk and that she was in fear of what he might do. My orders were to take him into custody."

Justin felt Jessica's small, trembling hand close about his. The livid weal across her cheek was fading, and seeing this, Justin felt the tension slowly drain out of him.

"This is Sergeant Macrae, Justin," she whispered. "He has known my—my stepfather for many years . . . and my mother also. He will do only what is right. For your own sake, you should not involve yourself further."

Good sense told him that she was right; he had his new sloop and his livelihood to consider, and . . . Justin's heart lifted. There was also, God willing, the prospect of Abigail O'Shea's charter to the Hawkesbury, and the *Flinders II* must be given her sea trials before he could undertake any charter.

He looked at Sergeant Macrae, anxiously searching the lined, leathery face. "What will befall him, if I take your advice, Sergeant?"

"Colonel O'Connell will order him to be reduced to the ranks, that is for certain. But it will be no bad thing." Macrae strode over to where Campbell lay, barely conscious and breathing stertorously. Frowning, he stared down at the man's battered features for a long moment and then gestured to the men of his escort to pick him up. As they carried him away, the sergeant added thoughtfully, "I am thinking that Duncan Campbell has had this coming to him for a long while. If it had not been you, it might well have been myself or others in the regiment, for we were not liking the manner of man he had become." Then, becoming brisk, he returned to Justin's side. "You had best be away now, Mr. Broome—you and Jessie both. I am wanting to forget that I have seen you here, you understand, and I must speak with Mrs. Campbell, so as to be sure that she also understands."

Justin thanked him and offered Jessica his arm. She took it, after a barely perceptible hesitation, and together they walked out into Clarence Street. For a while she was silent, and Justin made no attempt to break into her thoughts, sensing that, for the second time in their brief acquaintance, her stepfather's treatment of her had left her humiliated and ill at ease.

They crossed into Bridge Street and were in sight of the Government House gate when, at last, Jessica nerved herself to thank him for his intervention. "It was . . . good of you, and I am grateful. But you must think that I . . . oh, that I bring you nothing but trouble. First it was those sailors, and now . . . now this. I feel so ashamed."

"You have no cause to be ashamed, Jessica," Justin protested. "You least of all!"

Walking beside her, her arm linked in his, he was conscious of an odd stirring of the senses, coupled with tenderness and an instinctive desire to console and protect her. She was so small and vulnerable and yet so courageous, to have borne for so long what her brute of a stepfather had made her suffer. "Jessica," he began, "you—"

But she was not listening. "It was my fault that you were convicted," she insisted. "The evidence *he* gave at your trial"—she could not bring herself to utter Campbell's name, and her tone was bitter—"led to your being found guilty. Because they did not believe me, that was why."

Justin shook his head. "Only because the *Semarang*'s people perjured themselves. That was not your blame. In any event, they finally admitted that they had lied, and my conviction was quashed. That was why I called on you this afternoon . . . to tell you that I'm a free man again and that Captain Case made generous amends. The sloop I was building is completed, ready to take her sea trials and enable me to go to work. I've not suffered, believe me."

"You had to serve two months of your sentence, did you not?" Jessica halted by the low seawall and turned, her dark eyes searching his face anxiously.

Justin smiled down at her. "That was no hardship. I was able to accompany Mr. Lawson and the others on their expedition into the Blue Mountains. If I'd been at sea, I should never have been given the opportunity. And it was the adventure of a lifetime!"

"You were with them—with Mr. Blaxland and Mr. Wentworth? I read the report in the *Gazette*, and I heard the Governor speaking of it to Mrs. Macquarie. Oh, Justin, that was a fine brave thing to do!" The dark eyes were shining now. "You climbed those mountains—you found the way across! I did not know . . . your name was not printed in the *Gazette*."

"I was classed with the convict servants." Justin shrugged, dismissing it with feigned indifference, lest she again seek to blame herself for his omission. "It's of no consequence. The Governor wishes there to be no talk of our expedition until the possibility of building a road across the mountains has been explored. So . . . you had best forget it."

"Yes, but—"

"His Excellency has his reasons," Justin put in. "I . . . Jessica, I called on you this afternoon simply because I wanted to thank you for attending my trial. That was why I came to your stepfather's house—I'd no idea he would be at home. I'd no intention of playing the eavesdropper or of picking a quarrel with him, but when he struck you . . . Oh, the devil! I've no regrets on that score, believe me— save perhaps on your account. I may have made things worse for you."

"No, you did not do that." Color flooded Jessica's cheeks, and she turned away, staring out across the cove with tear-misted eyes. In a small, unhappy voice, she said, "You know that he—my stepfather—lied about me, just as the sailors did. I . . . I'm not a wanton, Justin. And I loved my mother. Whatever he said, I did not break her heart, I—"

"I know that well, Jessica India," Justin asserted. He reached out to take her hand and turn her face to him, only to wince with pain as his raw knuckles brushed against the top of the seawall, and she exclaimed in swift concern, "You are hurt!"

"It's nothing," he evaded. "Just skinned knuckles. Come—I'll see you to the gate."

She went with him, but upon reaching the gate, with its patrolling sentry, she gestured toward the house. "At least come to the kitchen and let me bathe those bruises. The housekeeper will have bandages and a salve, and—"

"No!" Justin cut her short, his tone harsher than he had intended. "For heaven's sake, it would set every tongue in His Excellency's household clacking! I want none of that, I . . . I'd best leave you here, Jessica. I've my boat to attend to and a charter to seek. I'm told that Mrs. O'Shea—Abigail O'Shea—wants to take passage to the Hawkesbury. You know her, perhaps?"

"Oh, yes, I know her . . . I sometimes take care of her little boy, when she calls on Mrs. Macquarie. Dickon—poor mite, he is deaf and dumb. But he's a lovely child, and his mother is very beautiful." Jessica hesitated, avoiding his gaze. "Will you be gone for long?"

"For a week or so, if I'm given the charter," Justin answered lightly. "Wish me luck, Jessica!"

"I wish you luck, Justin," Jessica echoed, in a small, flat voice. She took her leave of him briefly, her face still averted, and, gathering up her skirts, ran up the driveway to Government House.

Justin waited, but she did not pause or look back, and he turned away, glancing instinctively at the sun to ascertain the time he had left before dark. Three hours, perhaps; enough to allow for a run down the harbor, to get the feel of his new sloop under headsails and test her steering.

Then, after cleaning himself up, he would call on Abigail O'Shea with the offer of his services. If she was worried about her sister Lucy and young Cahill, clearly she would want to sail without delay for Yarramundie, and he must be ready to fit in with her wishes.

Whistling cheerfully, Justin set off for Simeon Lord's yard. He was at once gratified and—since it deprived him of the opportunity to call on Abigail—disappointed to find Timothy Dawson awaiting him there, with the firm offer of the charter, made on her behalf.

"I'll come with you, lad," the wealthy settler added. "If we find that all is well at Yarramundie, then you can set me ashore at my place on your return passage. There's stock to deliver and . . ." He went into careful detail. "When can you be ready to load?"

Justin considered the question, sensing a controlled urgency in the older man's voice.

"Give me twenty-four hours, Mr. Dawson," he said, "and I'll be at your service."

"You have a crew?"

"Not yet, sir. But I'll find the men I want this evening— one of them, anyway. I shall need two."

Dawson nodded his satisfaction. "Good! Then I shall leave it to you, Justin. But no delays. Abigail is anxious, you understand?"

"I understand," Justin assured him. Tim Dawson had changed since his wife's tragic death, he thought, watching the tall, now slightly paunchy figure crossing the wharf. It was not so much that he had aged as that he seemed more distant and aloof, and certainly less approachable than he had been a few years before. There had even been a time, Justin recalled sadly, when Dawson had been "Uncle Tim" to him, and until his own father had come back to the colony to claim him, he had—since boyhood—regarded Dawson in that light. It had been Henrietta Dawson who had raised a barrier between them—between all of them, and his mother in particular, whom she had openly and bitterly despised as a onetime convict and a social inferior.

And yet . . . Justin sighed. The marriage had been the basis for Tim Dawson's wealth, for his success, and for the position he occupied in the community. Without his father-in-law's money and influence, he would not now be the owner of three well-stocked farms or possess a share in a fine Indiaman, trading between Sydney and Calcutta. And he might still, but for that marriage, have been "Uncle Tim" instead of the formal "Mr. Dawson"—although that, it seemed, was the way he preferred things to be.

Justin shrugged. It was not that he minded. For God's sweet sake, he told himself, he should be accustomed to such treatment by this time, for had he not known it all his life? Disgruntled, he glanced again at the sky. Old Cookie Barnes would probably be in one of the Rocks taverns, and if the *Flinders II* were to be ready for sea in twenty-four hours, as he had promised Tim Dawson, he might as well go in search of the little man before he imbibed too freely. His ship would handle better with Cookie crewing her, and they could take her out at first light in order to get the feel

of her, and then run round to the public wharf in Cockle
Bay in readiness to load the stock.

And soon after that, Abigail would come on board.
. . . Justin was smiling as he strode briskly across Simeon
Lord's congested yard and headed toward the Rocks.

On board his own ship, he would be the equal of any
man, convict or free, he reflected proudly. Be damned to
Their Lordships of the Admiralty, and a pox on the lieutenant's commission they had refused to give him! And to
hell with Tim Dawson, if he was tempted to play the elitist!
Currency kid he might be, but today he had bested Jessica's bullying swine of a stepfather in a fight that had been
anything but fair, and tomorrow the beautiful young
woman whom, for so long, he had worshipped from afar
would come a little nearer. Near enough, perhaps, to be
aware of him as a man. *Nil mortalibus ardui est,* Will
Wentworth had called after him, half in mockery, half in
challenge. No height is too arduous for mortal man to at-
tain, Wentworth had said was the meaning of the Latin tag.
And in that spirit, they had crossed the great dividing
range of the Blue Mountains and glimpsed the fertile
plains beyond the unmapped gorges and the towering,
rock-crowned peaks.

Justin's head came up and his smile widened as the shipyard gate clanged shut behind him.

It was, of course, to be hoped that all was well at Yarramundie and that Abigail's anxiety on her sister's account
would be allayed when they reached the farm, but . . .
He pursed his lips into a cheerful whistle and quickened
his stride. It was an ill wind . . .

CHAPTER XX

Without troubling to do more than kick off her shoes and unbutton the neck of her dress, Lucy Cahill flung herself onto the untidy, sagging double bed that had once graced her father's manor house in England and, burying her face in the pillows, willed herself to sleep.

But sleep would not come. God, she told herself bitterly, God was punishing her for the terrible wrong she had done to Henrietta Dawson. And He would continue to punish her, to exact retribution for the deception she had practiced. . . . She caught her breath on a sob, reminded of a text that the Reverend Caleb Boskenna had taken, years ago, for one of his sermons: *There is no peace, saith the Lord, unto the wicked.* . . .

And she had found no peace here, Lucy thought, but only loneliness and isolation, boredom and a marriage that had long since begun to turn sour. It was not that Luke was a poor lover . . . indeed, part of the trouble was that he possessed a strong animal attraction for her, which he exerted to the full, but without sensitivity or finesse in his lovemaking; and invariably, once his passion had faded, he left her angry and unbearably humiliated. He had no aptitude for conversation, no manners, and an innate coarseness that, for most of the time they spent together, actively disgusted her.

Looking back nostalgically to the life she had known in
Sydney served only to add to her wretchedness. Then there
had been parties, military parades, receptions, and dinners,
with a bevy of handsome, witty young officers eagerly
seeking her favors and vying with one another for her company. She had been able to talk and laugh with them, to
bask in their admiration, to interest herself in topics other
than those mundane concerns that now engaged all Luke's
attention. He spoke of little save his doings on the farm—
so many acres ploughed and planted, so many ewes in
lamb, so many of the miserable creatures suffering from
liver fluke or foot rot, and the prices they might expect for
beef and mutton carcasses.

Luke had immersed himself in the farm work, and he
and Jethro were like brothers, giving more time and certainly more consideration to each other than either seemed
able to spare for her—even in the evenings, when their
work was done.

Lucy sat up, mopping ineffectually at her eyes with a
corner of the rumpled sheet. Bowed beneath the burden of
her guilt after Henrietta's death, she had seen the isolation
of Yarramundie as sanctuary and marriage to Luke as a
means by which her enforced exile there might be made
endurable . . . and perhaps even happy. That it had not
was scarcely her fault.

Abigail had not approved of the marriage, of course; but
then her elder sister had approved of little that she had
done or contemplated doing for a long time, and at least
she had not withheld her consent. But . . . Lucy's small,
petulant mouth tightened obstinately. She had not given
Abigail the satisfaction of being able to say "I told you so,"
and had avoided making any admission of error concerning
her marriage by the simple expedient of not writing to her
or to anyone else in Sydney. Such restraint was foreign to
her nature, Lucy had to concede, and the time was now
fast approaching when she would be compelled—for the
sake of her own sanity—to end her brief defiance and tell
Abigail that she had suffered enough and could remain
here no longer.

Luke, she supposed indifferently, would stay at Yarramundie. It would not take much to persuade him, and she, with new freedom conferred on her by her married status, could return to the life and the social circles she had missed so sorely, with only the pangs of her conscience and the fear of continued divine retribution to trouble her. That both would continue to plague her she had, alas, no doubt; her upbringing, at the Boskennas' hands, had left her with a morbid fear of sin and the consequences of evildoing, but at least in Sydney she could count on finding distraction and, perhaps, forgetfulness. Tim Dawson clearly harbored no suspicions where she was concerned. He had accepted his wife's death as the accident it had appeared to be and, when he had visited Yarramundie earlier in the year, had offered neither reproach nor accusation.

Lucy lay back again, closing her eyes. The hum of voices in the kitchen below had ceased, which meant that Jethro had gone at last; and when Luke had finished totting up the endless accounts he kept, he would come clambering up the narrow wooden ladder to their attic bedroom expecting, as he always did, to take his will of her. Because it was late, there would be no attempt at tender preliminaries, no effort to rouse her—just an animal coupling that would leave him satisfied and herself sick with desire, the sleep into which he would sink still eluding her. Luke wanted a child; he talked often of the family he hoped for, but she . . . Oh, God in heaven! If there was anything she wanted when she had married, it was tenderness and affection from her husband, some understanding of her feelings. She . . .

He was at the top of the ladder, already peeling off his shirt and undoing the buttons of his soiled breeches, careless of the unsubtle revelation of his intentions their gaping front disclosed. He had not shaved for two days, and his thick, dark hair was disheveled and unkempt, the fingernails on the hand he put out to draw back the sheet black with the dirt of the day's toil.

Lucy sat up, edging away from him as she caught the whiff of spirits on his breath. He and Jethro had been drinking, her mind registered, and hearing him hiccough, she shuddered, her distaste for his drunken state extinguishing all desire.

"Go away!" she bade him contemptuously. "Sleep in the hayloft or the byre, where you belong!"

"I'm your husband," Luke reminded her reproachfully. "And I belong in your bed, my pretty." He noticed then that she had not undressed and, making a jest of it, let his breeches fall and, naked, knelt over her, chuckling as he lifted her skirt and used it to pinion her arms against the rumpled pillows at her back. "Am I to take you by force? Is that what you want?"

"You stink of the dungheap!" Lucy accused.

"That's where I work, in amongst the dung, with hogs and sheep. I'm a farmer, damme, working your land. I wasn't bred to it, and I never wanted to do anything of the kind. But what choice did I have?" He continued to reproach her, adopting an aggrieved, whining tone, and Lucy lost patience with him.

"I'm leaving you, Luke," she flung back imperiously. "You can stay here with your hogs and your sheep and their filthy dung! I want no more to do with you, do you hear? I am going to Sydney. I shall write to Abigail. She has a house there, and I'll lodge with her until I can find a place of my own."

"You married me," he pointed out indignantly. "You're my wife—I've a right to come with you."

"You've no right," Lucy retorted coldly. "You are on ticket-of-leave. You are a convict, Luke, had you forgotten that? You still have five years of your sentence to serve."

It was her final argument, one she had never used before, out of consideration for his feelings; but she used it now without compunction and saw the arrogance drain out of him, as the ruddy color vanished from his cheeks. His hold on her had never been anything but physical, she thought, and he had been too careless, too selfish to retain it. In Sydney, she would find plenty of others ready and eager to take his place—men who were officers and gentlemen, whose wooing she could enjoy.

He started to bluster, but, with icy dignity, Lucy freed

her arms and sat up, pulling down her skirt and gesturing him to get off the bed.

"You could have applied for a pardon for me," he said, with bitterness. She ignored the accusation and watched, without pity, as he slid awkwardly to the floor in obedience to her gesture and hurriedly donned the breeches he had discarded so confidently a few minutes before.

Standing there, slim-hipped and broad of chest, face and body deeply tanned, he still possessed some remnant of the attraction he had once had for her, but . . . Lucy caught the sweaty stench of him and drew back, drawing the sheet about her in swift distaste. He used to wash and shave before coming to her bed, she reminded herself, and her resolution hardened.

"I love you, Lucy," he said, changing his tone, his dark eyes pleading with her. "If I've done aught to offend you, then you've only to tell me and I'll mend my ways. True, I took a drink with Jethro just now, but I work hard—we both do, Jethro and me. And we work for *you*, Lucy."

"You are a convicted felon—a common forger, who stole from his employer," Lucy told him, with conscious cruelty. "You were sent here to work, to expiate your crime, Luke. Never forget that."

His crime, she thought, made her own wrongdoing pale into insignificance. Henrietta would probably have died without her intervention; she had done no more, if the truth were known, than hasten the inevitable end. And no one *did* know the truth, not even Timothy Dawson. She was safe, and heaven help her, had she not paid the price! God could not go on punishing her, and if she went to Sydney, if she freed herself of this place and of Luke, forgetfulness would come and she would sleep again. It was the answer to all her problems, and the only surprising thing was that she had not arrived at it before. . . .

"Lucy, you're my wife," Luke whispered brokenly. "You're my wife, and I love you! We love each other, Lucy, you know that's so. If you must leave Yarramundie, let me come with you."

He was on his knees beside the bed, distraught and trem-

bling and, Lucy realized, defeated. She pursed her lips to
give him his answer and to complete her victory over him,
but the words were never said.

From the yard below came a hubbub of voices; a man
shouted something she could not catch, and from some distance away from the house, a single musket shot rang out,
followed by a high-pitched scream.

"Raiders!" Luke gritted, instantly alert. "Plaguey escapers!" He was on his feet, swiftly extinguishing the bedside
lamp. "Lie here, Lucy, and keep quiet, whatever they do.
I'll go and tackle them."

He was in command, himself again, no longer the shivering supplicant who had knelt to plead with the woman he
had married, but a man of courage and resourcefulness,
preparing to defend his own.

"Give them what they want," Lucy begged. "They're
armed—that was a shot I heard. Supplies . . . a boat, perhaps. We—oh, Luke, we don't want anyone killed; we
must avoid bloodshed!"

"I said I'd tackle them," Luke snapped. He jerked the
sheet over Lucy's head. "And I'll be armed, too, don't you
worry. Now for pity's sake, cover yourself up and don't
move. They'll get nothing from us, unless it's over my dead
body, I promise you that!"

"Take care," Lucy managed, in a muffled voice. "Take
care!" She had been insufferably cruel to him, she thought,
cruel and wickedly unfair. "I . . . Luke, I *do* love you!"

But he was gone, clattering down the ladder into the
darkness below. Cowering beneath the bedclothes, Lucy
could not be sure whether or not he had heard her parting
words.

There was a second shot, a few minutes later, sounding
much louder than the first, echoing and reechoing through
the house as if . . . Lucy drew in her breath sharply. As
if it had been fired inside, in the room below. Luke, she
thought, Luke must have opened fire on the intruders from
the door or through the window, and . . . She strained
her ears, listening, and then, sickened, heard the sound of
voices and the thud of a falling body.

A voice yelled, "Got the bastard!" The voice, she knew,

was not Luke's, nor were the heavy booted feet now mounting the ladder.

And there were two pairs of feet, not one, her straining ears told her, and more voices in the room below.

Lucy lay where she was, not moving, her heart pounding like a living thing in her breast and the sheet drawn so tightly across her face that it almost suffocated her.

"Oh God," she prayed silently. "Dear God, have mercy on me . . . help me! Please God, don't let them find me!"

There was, of course, no answer to her panic-stricken prayer, but, unbidden, another of the Reverend Caleb Boskenna's favorite texts echoed through her head, dredged up from her childhood memories as clearly and emphatically as he had thundered it from his pulpit: *God is not mocked! His anger is not turned away . . . His hand is stretched out still!*

His vengeful hand, stretched out to inflict further punishment on her . . . Lucy bit frantically into her lower lip but could not still the pent-up cry of despair rising in her throat, as the first of the intruders stepped off the top of the ladder and into her room.

He heard her and emitted a grunt of satisfaction. "Reckon there's a woman in here, Silas . . . we're in luck, boyo!"

Rough hands dragged the concealing sheet aside; hot, spirit-laden breath fanned Lucy's tear-wet cheek, and a man's voice exclaimed hoarsely, "By God, there is! Light the lamp, Silas, an' let's see what we've got here."

There was a brief delay, and then, as the oil lamp flared again into life, Lucy saw a dark, bearded face looking down at her. She tried to shrink away, but the hands held her as if in a vise, a pair of glittering dark eyes boring into hers and adding to her terror. The second man, younger but also heavily bearded, stumbled drunkenly up to the side of the bed, the lamp held aloft. By its flickering light, Lucy saw that both men's wrists bore the scars of convict fetters and that the younger of the two was clad in the broad-arrowed, shapeless garments which had recently begun to be issued to newly arrived felons.

He met her frightened gaze with a leer.

"God almighty!" he breathed excitedly. "She's young, an' she's a beauty! I've not set eyes on her like since them swine o' redbreasts clapped me in Newgate. Let me have her first, Ben, will you? It'll kill me to have to wait!"

"Then consign your plaguey soul to hell," the man addressed as Ben retorted aggressively, his fingers already tearing at the buttons of Lucy's dress. "We agreed to share an' share alike, didn't we—food, liquor, women, anythin' we took? I found this wench first. You c'n have her when I've done. Hey!" he said as Lucy started to struggle. "Hold her, Silas! Set down that bloody lamp an' hold her, d'you hear!"

Lucy screamed, fighting frantically to free herself. It was Luke's name she cried out in her terror, and the big, bearded convict smashed the back of his hand brutally across her mouth.

"No use callin' for no Luke or for anybody else, come to that," he told her. "There's only us here now, my fine lady. The others are dead, or they ran. So just you do like we want, an' you'll come to no great harm. We'll be leavin' at first light."

The scream died in Lucy's paralyzed throat. The second man had her by the shoulders, forcing her down, and conscious that her strength was ebbing, she ceased to struggle.

"Oh please," she managed to gasp despairingly. "Please, I beg you . . . let me go!"

Her plea was ignored. Breathing hard, the black-browed Ben ripped the remnants of her clothing from her and heaved himself onto the bed beside her.

She did not move, and he growled at her impatiently, "A plague on you—come on! You know what's what—bin married, ain't you? Then do as I bid you, woman, an' stop tryin' to play the innocent!"

She had been married, Lucy thought, her heart close to breaking. She had been married to Luke, and these wicked, merciless men had killed him . . . and Jethro, too, she supposed, if they had found him. And the servants had run; there was no one to help her. She made a futile at-

tempt to free herself, and Ben cursed and cuffed her painfully into quiescence.

His heavy, sweat-drenched body covered hers and he
took her savagely, without compassion, deaf to her sobs.
When he had done, he rolled off her, grunting, and before
Lucy could collect her scattered wits, the man he had
called Silas took his place. She cried out and struggled
anew, and he struck her again and again, until, at last,
blessed unconsciousness silenced her bitter weeping.

When she came to—she knew not how much later—it
was like waking from pleasant sleep into a horrible nightmare.

"The woman's still there," she dazedly heard a voice say,
"and the night's still young, boys. Take your time, God
roast you! There's food an' liquor aplenty to fill your bel-
lies an' slake your thirst. Let none o' you scallywags say we
didn't fall on our feet, comin' here, 'cause we did, right
enough. But just don't forget we're on the run, with every
man's hand against us. At first light we gotta be on the
move again, with all the provisions we can carry."

"And the woman?" one of the men asked. "Can we take
her along with us, Ben?"

"A sack o' potatoes'll be more use than she'll be, where
we're goin'," Ben snarled, and Lucy quailed before the
menace in his voice, the last vestige of hope fading. He
meant to kill her, she sensed, for these were desperate men,
escapers—as one of them let slip—from the notorious Coal
River settlement, to which only the most recalcitrant and
hardened malefactors were now sent. And they already had
murder on their conscience; they had killed poor Luke and
would not hesitate to serve her in the same fashion, once
her usefulness to them was over.

Lucy drew a long, shuddering breath. Why not end it
now, she asked herself, if only to avoid further torment,
further humiliation? If she made a bid to escape them, they
would have to kill her, they . . . But she was too late.
Laughing, their good humor restored by Ben's words, they
pushed a gangling boy of about sixteen up the ladder and

onto the bed, and she turned her head away, sickened, as a chorus of ribald voices offered advice, supposedly intended to combat his inexperience. Nothing loath, the youth endeavored to act upon the foul suggestions they made, hurting her badly in the process.

It was the final, unendurable humiliation, and Lucy screamed her agony aloud. Relief came unexpectedly when a voice shouted up from below.

"There's a bloody sailboat comin' upriver, Ben. Looks like it's makin' for this place."

All the men were instantly alert. "Shut her mouth," Ben ordered harshly, and the youth's thin hand was clamped over Lucy's bruised lips. "What kind o' sailboat is it?" the raiders' leader yelled down.

"Two-master. Seagoing, I reckon," came the reply. "Handy lookin' craft, Ben. An' I only counted four men on deck."

The implication was not lost on the other men. They started to clamor for action.

"Four o' them an' ten o' us—it'd be a walkover!"

"A seagoing boat . . . our luck's in, an' no mistake! We could sail to Timor in her, or to South America!"

"Christ, Ben—what are you waitin' for? Let's go!" It was the man called Silas, and he was already heading for the ladder.

"We've got to plan *how* we'll take her," Ben growled. He pushed past Silas. "I'll look her over, an' all o' you better come with me, so's we can be ready if the crew land."

"What about the woman?" the boy asked.

Ben was already halfway down the ladder. He called back callously, "Cut her throat, Seamus—or tie the bitch up. We're finished with her, an' we'll burn the house down afore we leave."

Left alone with her, the boy Seamus caught his breath on an outraged sob, and Lucy, despite her terror, realized suddenly that he was as frightened and almost as shocked as she. He took his hand from her mouth and stood looking down at her in trembling uncertainty.

"You won't . . . oh God, you won't kill me, will you?"

she whispered. "Please, Seamus—do you want my death on your conscience, as well as everything else?"

He shook his head, his eyes full of tears. "Holy Mother of God, mistress, I do not! 'Twill be hard enough to live with what I done to you. I'd never . . ." He gulped. "Not in my whole life bin with a woman, but I . . . ach, you've seen the way they are. And Ben Croaker's a fiend out of hell."

"Then why are you with them?" With the last remnants of her flagging strength, Lucy sat up, pulling the stained sheet about her and fumbling for her torn clothes.

The Irish boy shuddered. "I'd no choice, mistress. I was in their work party when they killed the guard and ran. I had to go with them. But—" He looked down at her, hope lighting his red-rimmed, frightened eyes. "Could we not run together, you and me? Could we not hide from them, or maybe get to that boat before they do? There'll be armed men on board, will there not?"

"I don't know," Lucy said bitterly. "But we could hide." She was too shocked to reason, too dazed even to wonder which boat might have come upriver, or who might be on board. But the instinct for self-preservation was strong; she arranged her torn garments about her the best she could and held out a shaking hand. He took it in both of his.

"Are ye able to walk?" he asked apprehensively. " 'Twill be all up wid us if they see us. We'll maybe have to take to our heels."

"I can walk," Lucy assured him. She started toward the ladder, unsteadily at first and leaning on him heavily, her bruised and aching body threatening to betray her. Then courage returned, and with it the realization that whoever the unknown men were in the two-masted sailing vessel, they might—unless they were warned—walk straight into a murderous ambush. At the head of the ladder she paused, forcing herself to think, to devise some way of giving them warning. The foul-mouthed Ben—Ben Croaker—had said that they would burn the house down before they left, but . . . She drew a long, agonized breath. If it were seen to be burning now, that should be warning enough. If . . .

"Hurry, mistress," Seamus urged.

"Wait," Lucy bade him. She relinquished her grasp of his arm and, turning, stumbled back into the room. Picking up the lamp, she spilled some of its contents onto the rumpled bedclothes and then flung it down, still burning, onto the bed.

The flames took swift hold. The mattress was ablaze before she and the young Irish boy had reached the foot of the ladder. By the time they emerged warily into the backyard, the top of the house was on fire, lit like a beacon against the dark night sky.

Surely warning enough to the crew of the sailboat, Lucy told herself, and then had to bite back a cry of horror as Seamus stumbled over the limp and lifeless body of a man and she saw that it was Luke. He was lying as his killers had left him, a few yards from the open back door.

They found Jethro a little later, by his sheep pen, surrounded by bleating ewes and their lambs. He had been badly beaten and was barely conscious, but to Lucy's sick relief, he was alive.

Justin glimpsed the flames rising from the farmhouse roof as he and Tim Dawson nosed the *Flinders*'s oared boat into the concealment of a clump of mangroves at the river's edge.

"You were right," he observed grimly. "It *is* a raid! But please God we'll be in time."

"Don't count on that, Justin," Dawson responded, tight-lipped. "These swine of escapers call themselves bushrangers now, and they move around the isolated settlements in gangs of a dozen or more. We've even had them prowling round Upwey. They're armed, no doubt, and we'll need to go carefully if we're to do anything at all to aid the Cahills. By the sound of the voices we heard when we dropped anchor, this is a big gang . . . at least a dozen, I'd say."

Recalling the shouts and the raised and drunken voices wafted to them across the darkened water of the river, Justin did not doubt that his companion was right. It had been at Dawson's suggestion that he had anchored the *Flinders* in midstream, instead of tying up to the Yarramundie wharf, as he normally did when he had stock to put ashore. Tim Dawson had been convinced that all was not well, and although he had made light of his fears to Abigail, he had insisted firmly that she must remain on board the sloop until they had made sure that it was safe for her to land.

She would be on deck now, Justin thought, and the sight of those leaping flames would keep her in an agony of suspense, for the blaze, although distant, would be all too clearly visible from the *Flinders*. He wished, for a moment, that he might have been there to offer her consolation; she still held him at arm's length and seemed unaware of his devotion, but . . . He grimaced to himself. This was no time for such regrets, and Abigail was in no danger; Cookie and the new deckhand, Eli Williams, were both armed, and they had their orders. Any attempt by the raiders to board the *Flinders* would be met by musket fire long before they could swim or maneuver a boat alongside.

"Are you ready?" Tim Dawson asked. He squinted impatiently up at the lightening sky. "It'll be dawn in an hour."

Justin secured the boat's painter to a mangrove root and, grasping his musket in one hand, balanced himself on the bow thwart and jumped nimbly onto the firm earth of the bank. Tim Dawson followed him, but, less adroit, he landed among the mangroves with a resounding splash and swore ruefully as he waded ashore.

Justin, alarmed by the noise his companion had made, eyed him reproachfully but said nothing. They had landed downstream of the Yarramundie wharf, with plenty of cover between the river and the farm buildings, and assuming that the raiders would have left the house before setting fire to it, he had counted on making a swift and silent approach, in case any of them were still about.

"I'm a clumsy idiot," Dawson said apologetically, wringing the water from his trouser legs. "But the swine will probably have made off by now, with all the food and drink they can carry. Usually the last thing they do is put a torch to the buildings, in the hope of covering their tracks."

"They may have seen us coming upriver," Justin argued, conscious of uneasiness. "And if they did—"

"If they did," the settler asserted, "then they'll have even more reason to make themselves scarce. We'll head for the house, Justin—and pray that Lucy and her husband aren't still inside."

He took the lead, and Justin followed close on his heels. Tim Dawson was one of the magistrates for the Hawkesbury settlements and, in that capacity, obviously had more experience of the depredations of the so-called bushrangers than he had himself, but . . . Justin felt his gorge rising.

"You think they're dead, don't you?" he suggested, in a tense undertone. "You think we'll be too late to save them?"

"I'm afraid of that," Dawson admitted. He paused at the edge of a clearing in the trees, from whence most of the farm buildings could be seen, and his gesture in the direction of the fiercely blazing farmhouse was despairing. "It's almost burnt to the ground—look! And these men aren't like the ordinary run of escapers—they're killers, who rob and murder and live as outlaws in the bush for months, sometimes for years. We hang them out of hand when we catch them, and hunt them with guns, like wild animals . . . which is what they become. And," he added grimly, as he started across the clearing, "they show no mercy to the poor souls they rob."

"Not even to the women?" Justin questioned, thinking of Lucy, his stomach churning.

"Still less to the women, God help them!"

His meaning was plain, without the need to put it into words, and Justin's fingers tightened about the stock of his musket. "It will break Abigail's heart if Lucy has suffered such a fate at their hands," he said hoarsely. "She—"

Tim Dawson cut him short. He burst out with unexpected anger, "You need not concern yourself with Abigail O'Shea's feelings, Justin. Leave me to care for her, understand? And if we *do* find that the worst has befallen her unfortunate young sister, the—the details must be kept from her. On no account must she be told the truth, by anyone."

His voice was choked with emotion, and Justin glanced at him in surprise, puzzled by his vehemence. But before he could make any reply, a ragged figure broke cover from the dark bulk of the farm outbuildings ahead of them, and Dawson, without hesitation, raised his musket to his shoulder, took quick aim, and fired. The range was long, his aim a trifle too hurried, and the ball struck the ground harmlessly some yards short of its objective.

The figure halted, both arms raised in token of surrender, and a scared young voice besought them not to shoot.

"Come here with your hands up!" Dawson ordered. "Keep him covered, Justin, while I reload."

The sound of his shot would have alerted any of the raiders who might still be in the vicinity, Justin thought ruefully, but . . . He watched, his own musket at the ready, as the ragged figure approached, to reveal itself as a thin, fair-haired youth, whose frightened gaze darted this way and that, as if anticipating a second attempt to kill him.

When none was made, he halted thankfully in front of Tim Dawson. "I'm Seamus O'Hare, sorr," he stated in a strong Irish accent. "An' the lady—Mistress Cahill—sent me to find you. I was after helping her to escape, sorr, and—"

"She's alive!" Dawson exclaimed.

"Praise be to God she is, sorr. Like I tell't you, 'twas I helped her to hide, and—"

"Where is she?" Dawson snapped.

The boy pointed in the direction from which he had come. "Hidin' in the feed store, wid one o' the farm people—Jethro, she called him, who's hurt bad. But she sent me to warn you, sorr. They . . . that is the others, Ben Croaker and the others, are plannin' to seize that sailing vessel o' yours. I seen 'em as I come from the feed store."

"How were they planning to seize my vessel?" Justin demanded.

The boy spread his hands helplessly. "I don't know, sorr, I swear to God I don't. But Mistress Cahill said there's an oared boat, tied up below the wharf. And they was makin' for the wharf, the last I seen o' them."

Jethro's old, rotting launch, Justin remembered. It was usually kept below the wharf, covered with some remnants of canvas. Or it had been, in the Boskennas' time; but probably the Cahills had replaced it with a more serviceable craft in the intervening years. And if they had . . . He turned urgently to Tim Dawson.

"We'd better go after them, Mr. Dawson. If they find the boat . . ." He did not complete the sentence, knowing that Dawson would understand, and less sanguine now as to the ability of Cookie and Eli to defend themselves and their vessel against a determined assault by overwhelming numbers. And with Abigail on board . . . He grasped Seamus roughly by the shoulders. "How many of them are there, O'Hare?"

"Nine, sorr, not countin' meself."

"You were with them?" Dawson accused, a sharp edge to his voice. "You young rogue, I thought, when you failed to run, that you were one of the Cahills' laborers!"

The boy launched into a wordy explanation, but Justin cut him short. "It's of no consequence now, lad. Go back to Mrs. Cahill and tell her that you have seen and warned us. Tell her to keep hidden, and we'll come for her just as soon as we're able. All right?"

"Sure, sorr," Seamus answered. "But . . ." He shuffled his feet, eyeing Justin uncertainly. "I'd come wid you, if you want me to. I—they're armed, sorr. They've two muskets, so they have."

And any more they might have stolen from the Cahills, Justin thought. He thrust the boy from him, aware of what it must have cost him to defy his erstwhile companions in order to come to Lucy Cahill's aid. "You've done bravely, Seamus lad. Off with you now, and take care of Mrs. Cahill and the shepherd. Don't any of you show yourselves till we get back."

"I'll do as you say, sorr," Seamus promised, and with a quick smile of gratitude, obediently took to his heels.

Tim Dawson said, a trifle sourly, "I'm not too sure that he's to be trusted. But since you appear to be taking command, Justin, what do you propose that we should do?"

Justin shrugged. "Let us try to find out what *they're* doing, Mr. Dawson, and then decide what we can do. The boy said they were making for the wharf, so I suggest we go back to the river."

Using what cover there was, they made their way to the riverbank without encountering any of the raiders. The *Flinders*, to Justin's relief, lay where he had left her, in midstream, moving gently to the pull of the current. They had extinguished all lights before leaving her, and as far as he could make out in the darkness, no attempt had as yet been made to board her. And Cookie, he was sure, would be keeping a vigilant lookout from the deck.

He was reminded, as he studied the darkened, silent vessel with narrowed eyes, of the occasion when he and David Fortescue had boarded the *Dolphin* where she had lain at anchor off Gull Island in Hobart's North Bay, after Tobias Cockrell had made off with her. The young ensign of marines, Enoch Finch, had made a wry jest concerning their approach . . . "muffled oars and over her stern." . . . Justin stiffened, every sense alert as he caught the sound of a faint splash, followed a moment later by a second.

Muffled oars or swimmers, cautiously entering the water, perhaps . . . Justin strained his ears in a vain attempt to identify the sounds. Beneath the high, tree-grown riverbank, the water was in deep shadow; fifty yards away, to his right, the wharf was in darkness, seemingly deserted—although that, too, was partially obscured by a clump of trees. Only the black shape of the *Flinders* was visible, silhouetted against the faintly reflected light of the crescent moon, emerging briefly from a mass of lowering cloud. But the light was her protection; a boat—even one approaching from the bank's shadow and allowed to drift downstream—would be seen once it emerged into the moonlit water in midstream.

And then suddenly he saw what had caused the splashes, and his whole body went rigid. It was neither boat nor swimmer, but a waterlogged tree that came within his line of vision . . . a gnarled gum, pulled up by the roots, with spindly branches and a crown of silvery leaves, floating slowly down on the current and heading toward the *Flinders*'s stern. A dark form lay stretched at full length along the half-submerged trunk, and pointing skyward was what, at first sight, appeared to be an unusually straight branch, but which could just as easily have been the barrel of a musket. And there was a second, protruding from among the twisted roots. . . . Justin drew in his breath sharply and thrust an elbow into Tim Dawson's side.

"That tree," he whispered. "There are two men on it, and I imagine the others are in a boat, lying under the bank, waiting to join them." He did not wait for Dawson's acknowledgment but took careful aim, and the silence was shattered by the crack of his musket. The ball struck the tree trunk, seemingly without harming either of the men clinging to it, but when Dawson followed his example and opened fire, Cookie, on the deck of the *Flinders,* loosed off a third shot, and he, too, was aiming at the same target.

Pandemonium broke loose. As Justin had expected, the rest of the raiding party abandoned the concealment the bank had provided. An oared boat was violently propelled into midstream, the men in it exchanging shots with the *Flinders*'s crew and then with Dawson and himself. He continued to concentrate his fire on the waterlogged tree, loading and reloading as fast as he could, but the musket barrel was hot to his touch before he had the satisfaction of seeing the tree's two passengers slide off it into the water. One managed to swim to his companions in the boat; the other vanished, and the tree bumped harmlessly against the *Flinders*'s side and floated on, robbed of its earlier menace.

The oared boat did not succeed in getting within thirty yards of its objective; caught between the fire of the *Flinders*'s crew and Dawson's and his own from the elevation of the riverbank, the raiders sought safety in flight. Tugging frantically at their oars, yelling and cursing at one another, they found refuge at last in the dark beneath the bank's overhang, and Justin heard them splashing ashore a few minutes later. When he and Dawson reached the spot where they had landed, they found only the abandoned boat, with a big, black-bearded man coughing his life away, spread-eagled across the bow, and the dead body of another, caught and held by the mangrove roots.

The bearded man used his last breath to curse them, then died with a blasphemy on his blood-flecked lips; but any regret Justin had felt at the killing vanished when, at last, they returned to the farm and Lucy Cahill sobbed out her story.

Sick with pity, he picked her up in his arms and carried her past the still-smoldering shell of what had once been her home. Cookie brought the *Flinders* alongside the wharf, and Justin relinquished his pathetic burden to Abigail and went back to help Tim Dawson and Seamus with the heavier burden of the unconscious Jethro. Finally they wrapped Luke Cahill's body in a sheet of canvas and loaded it in the forward hold.

"We'll put them all ashore at Windsor," Tim Dawson decided, his anger restrained but evident in the steely chill of his eyes. "Dr. Arndell will do what he can for that poor girl, and Jethro's strong—he'll get over it. I doubt if Lucy ever will, but . . ." He drew a long, pent-up breath. "We'll give Luke a Christian burial—Henry Fulton will see to that. And then . . ." He laid a hand on Justin's shoulder. "I intend to call for volunteers to aid me in bringing those foul swine to justice. I take it you'll come with me?"

Justin hesitated, but only for a moment. He thought of the look on Abigail's lovely face when she had caught her first glimpse of her sister, and he said quietly, "Yes, Mr. Dawson, I'll come. And we'll find them, however long it takes, I promise you."

In fact it took close on three weeks before the last of Ben Croaker's bushranging gang was run to earth in the foothills north of the river. Despite having initiated it, Tim Dawson did not join the search party, pleading a severe attack of gout, and it was Justin who led the two constables and the half dozen volunteers on their arduous mission.

He returned to the settlement at Windsor weary, saddlesore, and unshaven—but with his prisoners intact—to find a series of shocks awaiting him. His *Flinders* lay at anchor off the landing wharf, and he saw, with sick dismay, that her deck and upper works were twisted and blackened, her standing rigging hanging in ruins, and the paintwork, of which he had been so proud, flaking and blistered.

Cookie, toiling manfully to repair at least some of the damage, told him bitterly that Eli Williams had set fire to her in a fit of drunken madness.

"Went berserk, 'e did," the little man explained. "An' 'e was such a quiet feller, it was the las' thing I expected. Gawd knows what got into 'im! I come back an' seen 'er burnin' and tried me best to save 'er, with folks on shore helpin'. But you can see for yerself, Mr. Justin, the state she's in. I reckon we can just about get 'er to Sydney under sail if we take it very easy."

It would be possible, Justin decided, after making an exhaustive inspection—her masts were only superficially damaged, and Cookie had commandeered sufficient cordage to repair the essential rigging.

"What have they done with Williams?" he asked glumly.

"Put 'im in jail," Cookie returned, "in the same cell with that young Irish lad that saved Mrs. Cahill."

Justin nodded abstractedly. "And Mrs. Cahill? How is she?"

"Gorn back to Sydney. Mr. an' Mrs. Dawson took 'er. They—"

"Mrs. Dawson?" Justin interrupted, suddenly tense.

"Oh, aye," Cookie said innocently. "Mrs. O'Shea that was . . . Miss Abigail. The Reverend Fulton wed them 'bout a week after you left 'ere. Took the folks 'ere by surprise, I fancy, but they made a real fine do o' it, out o' sympathy p'raps. An' they've put Yarramundie up fer sale, lock, stock, an' barrel. Took Jethro Crowan, the shepherd, with 'em, in Mr. Burdock's *Fanny*. They . . ."

But Justin was not listening. He turned away, feeling the blood drain from his cheeks. Abigail, he thought with bitterness—his lovely, adored Abigail was now Tim Dawson's wife. His *second* wife, stepmother to his children, who were almost as old as she was.

Justin's throat felt tight. His sense of loss exceeded even his grief for his ship, but . . . The devil take it! He must not let Cookie suspect what his feelings for Abigail had been. She had never given him any encouragement, and he had had no real justification for the hopes he had cherished. Yet all the same . . .

He reached out blindly and snatched up the adze with which Cookie had been working. Then, forcing his stiff lips into what he hoped might pass for a smile, he strode aft and, using the adze as if it were a weapon, started to hack away at the blackened deck timbers that the fire had left in its wake.

CHAPTER XXI

"It's not *right* for Papa to marry again at his age," Julia Dawson declared resentfully. She appealed to Frances Spence, her blue eyes bright with indignation. "Is it, Aunt Frances? He's eighteen years older than Abigail!"

"Nineteen," her sister, Dorothea, corrected. "Abigail's birthday is in December. She's only twenty-two."

"Well, your grandfather was twenty years older than I was when I married him," Frances pointed out. "And ours has been a very happy union." During which, she reflected, the only concession she had asked for had been that she should be aunt and not grandmother to the Dawson children. She glanced at Jenny and saw that she was smiling, unmoved by Julia's indignation.

"Mama would not have approved," Julia persisted obstinately. "You know she would not."

Her mother would have been hard put to it to approve of any second marriage, Frances thought. Poor Henrietta had been intensely possessive, jealous of Tim's friendship with Jenny Hawley and still more so of the indulgence he had always shown to Abigail and Lucy. And Henrietta's attitude to her own marriage had been the only source of discord between Jasper and herself since he had wed her. . . . Frances sighed.

Seeking to change the subject, she turned again to Jenny.

"You saw Justin, I suppose? Has he decided what he intends to do?"

Jenny inclined her head. She had aged very noticeably, Frances thought, the glorious crown of vivid auburn hair now liberally flecked with gray. And she was thin—much, much too thin—which made her look older than her forty odd years. Not that, being the courageous woman she was, she ever admitted to being ill—or even tired, although she had taken the opportunity of one of her rare visits to Sydney to consult Dr. Redfern. She had not revealed the doctor's diagnosis; her talk had been of Justin and the terrible event that had taken place at Yarramundie, and now, in response to Frances's question, she again talked proudly of her elder son.

"Mr. Evans has been commissioned by the Governor, as you know, to advise on the practicability of building a road over the mountains. He is preparing an expedition, and he has invited Justin to join it, partly to act as guide and partly to help him with the survey."

"And will he do so?" Frances asked.

"He told me this afternoon that he would." Jenny's face clouded. "His *Flinders II* is an ill-fated vessel, I fear. The fire caused extensive damage, and when he sailed her here from the Hawkesbury, they ran into a storm and lost one of her masts. Replacing that may take weeks or even months, Justin says."

"Abigail," Julia put in sulkily, "should have married Justin, not my father, *I* think."

Aware of Jenny's feelings on the subject, Frances dealt out a sharp reprimand. "You are a foolish little girl, Julia! And you do not know what you are talking about."

"I do, Aunt Frances," Julia protested. "Rachel told me, ages ago—did you not, Rachel?"

The twelve-year-old Rachel Broome reddened unhappily but did not deny having betrayed her brother's confidence, and Julia added triumphantly, "You see—she did, and it's true! Justin has always fancied Abigail, even when she was engaged to be married to Lieutenant Fortescue."

"I think," Frances said firmly, "that it is time you children went to bed." She rose, brushing aside their objections. "You should know better than to join in your elders' conversation, Julia. And you certainly should *not* offer your opinion when it hasn't been invited. Say good night now, and off you go, all of you. Kate Lamerton will give you your milk. But see you are quiet—I don't want you to wake Dickon."

"Dickon wouldn't wake if we danced a jig round his nursery," Julia retorted defiantly. "He's deaf, Aunt Frances . . . deaf *and* dumb!"

Frances reproved her sharply. Henrietta's daughter was beginning to resemble her mother all too closely, she thought ruefully, and no doubt she herself was more than a little to blame. She was too lenient with all of them, and Julia took advantage of her softness. But both girls adored little Dickon, and Julia was not usually spiteful; it was, perhaps, a measure of the distress her father's unexpected marriage had caused her that she should behave so badly, and in Jenny's presence, too.

When the three girls had left the room, Frances said apologetically, "Julia should not have spoken like that, Jenny—I'm so sorry. She's not been herself since the news of Tim's marriage reached us. It has upset all of them, even Alexander."

"What she said was true though, Frances," Jenny answered. "Justin always has 'fancied' Abigail, as she put it, since he was—oh, goodness, about sixteen. And I think he feels her loss almost as much as he felt the loss of his first ship. But in fairness, I truly don't believe that Abigail was aware of his devotion. She is not by nature unkind or insensitive, is she?"

Frances shook her head. "No, certainly not. I like Abigail very much, and I think, given time, that she will make Tim a fine wife . . . and the children will get over it and accept her after a while. They were fond enough of her in the past, as I was myself. Concerning Lucy, I have to confess to having had reservations, but, poor young soul, I would not have wished the terrible fate she suffered on my worst enemy!"

"How is she now?" Jenny asked.

"Much the same, I understand—still badly shocked. I've seen her only once since her return here, and I was quite horrified by the change in her." Frances shivered involuntarily. "She is with Abigail and Tim, at Abigail's house . . . that is why the children and little Dickon are here with me. We thought it best, in the circumstances. Lucy won't speak to anyone. Mr. Marsden tried, and the Ellis Bents, but she refused to see them . . . not that I blame her for that! I do not honestly know which has become more insufferable of late, the chaplain or the judge advocate. Both are now bitterly opposed to the Governor, and they are quite determined to undo all the progress he has made to integrate emancipists of good repute into our society."

"It will be a great pity if they succeed," Jenny observed.

"Oh, I do not imagine they will," Frances asserted confidently. "Governor Macquarie is not easily turned from his purpose, once he has made up his mind, and his emancipist policies have wide support . . . including mine, as you might expect. And oddly enough, he has Mr. George Johnston's."

"You mean Colonel Johnston?"

"I do indeed. He caused a great furor among the elitist set by marrying Esther Abrahams soon after his return to the colony . . . and Mr. Marsden could scarcely criticize him for that, after his publicly expressed views on the evils of concubinage! Besides, Esther is a very fine woman, and they have a large family, as I expect you know."

Frances talked on, retailing items of news and gossip; but for all her efforts to distract her friend, Jenny displayed no more than a polite interest. Clearly, Frances thought, Jenny had other things on her mind . . . Justin's forthcoming expedition into the Blue Mountains with Surveyor Evans, perhaps, or . . . She studied the older woman's pale, thin face with some anxiety, seeking a clue to her feelings but finding none.

"It is rumored," Frances announced, smiling, "that Mrs. Macquarie is again with child and that this time there is a real hope that she may carry it to its term, which I believe will be March. Poor dear lady, she has suffered so many disappointments since she came out here, I do hope the rumor is true!"

Jenny's face lit up. "Please God it may be!" she exclaimed, with warm sincerity. "And that it may be a son."

It was the first real sign of animation she had shown, and Frances, pleased, endeavored to follow up her advantage.

"Dr. Redfern has been treating both the Governor and his lady and thereby striking another blow for the emancipists' cause," she said. "He is in high favor and is frequently invited to accompany them when they go on tour. And he has done wonders for little Dickon. That was why I suggested you should consult him, Jenny. He's a good physician, the best there is in the colony. Everyone says so."

The animation had faded from Jenny's face. She said reluctantly, "I have always relied on Dr. Arndell, as a friend as well as a doctor. He's aged a lot, of course, and he does not really practice now, though he makes an exception for his old friends. And he assured me that there was nothing wrong with me, apart from overwork and . . . well, old age, I suppose." She smiled thinly, avoiding Frances's gaze. "I don't overwork now; there's no need. Willie manages the sheep, Andrew helps in his spare time, and, best of all, Tom and Nancy Jardine decided to leave Long Wrekin and join up with us again. All I do is breed a few horses, which does not overtax my strength."

She broke off, still studiously keeping her eyes averted, and Frances put in quickly, "What are you saying, Jenny dear? That Dr. Arndell was wrong—that you *are* ill?"

"Dr. Redfern seemed to think so," Jenny admitted, the admission dragged from her. "He . . . Frances, if I tell you what he—what he said, will you promise that it will go no further? I don't want Andrew to know, or Justin—least of all Justin—and certainly not Rachel or Willie. It would worry them, and . . . Dr. Redfern has seen me only this once. He could be wrong, not Tom Arndell, who has known me almost all my life."

Dr. Arndell's own health was failing, Frances knew. Her husband—himself a magistrate—had told her that the aging surgeon now heard few of the cases that came before the Windsor bench. She stiffened, sensing Jenny's distress, and assured her gravely that her confidence would be respected.

"Jenny, you are my best and oldest friend, and I owe you—oh, so much that I can never repay. Let me help, if I can, at least by listening. What did Dr. Redfern say?"

Jenny looked at her then. Flatly she said, "He told me that I have a—a lesion, he called it, on my left lung, which was probably caused when I fell from poor Sirius and fractured my ribs. That was over four years ago, and I did have quite a lot of pain for a while afterward. But the ribs healed. I—I find it hard to believe that they could have done any serious damage."

Frances was less sanguine but was careful not to reveal the fact. Jenny, she recalled, had been in considerable pain when she had come to Sydney to bid Justin farewell, not long after her accident. She had not danced at the Government House ball, and had looked ill then, although she had taken part in most of the festivities that had marked Governor Bligh's departure and his daughter's wedding to Colonel O'Connell, and had complained of nothing more than feeling tired. And, of course, when the fleet had sailed, she had gone back to the endless toil of Long Wrekin, which could hardly have aided her recovery.

"Did Dr. Redfern advise any treatment?" Frances nerved herself to ask and, anticipating the answer, added gently, "Apart from rest, I mean?"

"No." Jenny's voice was still flat, quite devoid of emotion, but her lower lip was trembling. "He said there was no cure for my condition because I'd—I'd left it too late. The broken ribs have set now, and two of them are pressing on the lung. That's why I feel so tired most of the time."

She fell silent, forcing a mirthless little smile as she met Frances's concerned and searching gaze and then blurted out with bitter scorn, "He advised me to become a lady of leisure for the rest of my life! Imagine that, Frances—I simply wouldn't know how."

"You could try," Frances urged. "You could live here in Sydney."

"And leave Ulva?" Jenny's headshake was emphatic. "Oh, no! Andrew loves it, and so do I. William is utterly content, and Rachel will be leaving school soon—all she wants is to join us at Ulva. I . . ." She put out a hand to grasp Frances's, and her expression softened. "Dearest Frances, I told you before, did I not, that it's the only life I know? The farm, the stock, the land—it's these that have meaning for me, that have given my life a—a purpose. And for what is left of it, I don't want it to change."

Instinct told Frances that she had not yet heard all; Jenny was still holding something back, and guessing what it must be, she asked apprehensively, "Jenny, what else did Dr. Redfern tell you?"

Jenny's fingers tightened about hers. Sitting very erect in her chair, she answered in a quiet, controlled voice, "He gave me a year to live—a year or perhaps two, at the most. I made him tell me—he did not want to, but I had to know."

Jenny's admission was so much worse than she had anticipated that Frances, for a moment, could only stare at her in wordless pity. No wonder, poor dear, that she had appeared indifferent to Julia's ill-mannered criticism of her father's marriage a little while ago! Forgetting her own unstinted praise of Dr. Redfern's medical competence, she stammered miserably, "He could be wrong, Jenny. You said yourself that Dr. Arndell assured you there was nothing seriously the matter with you and that he's known you for so much longer than Dr. Redfern has. Besides—" The sound of men's voices in the entrance hall cut her short. Jasper and Andrew had returned from calling on the Governor, Frances realized; they would be expecting dinner, and . . . Jenny's hand closed convulsively about hers.

"You promised, Frances—don't forget, you promised! Please, as you value our friendship, not a word to Andrew about what I've just told you. He must not know, at least not yet."

"I'll not say anything, Jenny dear," Frances responded. Rising, she bestowed a sympathetic kiss on her friend's flushed cheek and then, forcing herself to behave as she normally did, crossed to the sideboard to pour drinks as her husband ushered Andrew into the room.

Dinner proved to be less of a strain than she had feared. Neither she nor Jenny contributed much to the conversation, but the two men, greatly concerned by what they had learned from the Governor, made up for the omission.

"Lord Bathurst is proving even more parsimonious than his predecessor at the Colonial Office," Jasper said indignantly. "At least Lord Castlereagh was prepared to *listen* to His Excellency's proposals before rejecting them! But Bathurst appears to have set himself out to withhold funds for building and road-making on principle. The poor Governor has pleaded for the services of a professionally trained architect, and he's to get one—a convicted felon named Greenway, who has been recommended by Admiral Phillip—as soon as the home government can arrange his passage. But the esteemed Colonial Secretary has laid down that local building projects must be paid for out of funds raised for the purpose here, with a view, he insists, to reducing the vast expense to which this colony has already put the mother country!"

"Furthermore," Andrew added derisively, "whilst Government House is to remain a mean, decaying, and shabby place, with His Excellency occupying worse accommodation than any private gentleman in the entire settlement, permission has been given to rebuild his stables—the reason for this somewhat odd decision being that Secretary Campbell had the brilliant notion of informing the Colonial Office that the stables could be constructed in such a way as to double as a fort, in case of a French attack!"

Even Jenny laughed at this, but Jasper went on gravely, "Our learned friend, the judge advocate, Mr. Ellis Bent, has annoyed the Governor mightily. His dwelling house, for which he received five hundred and fifty pounds sterling and two hundred gallons of spirits to defray expenses, is now complete . . . you've probably seen it. It is that extraordinary edifice on the corner of Elizabeth Street, with a gabled roof and two front doors. Well, Mr. Bent's contract called for the building to contain suitable accommodation and offices for the civil and criminal courts, but for these essentials, he has allocated only one small room on the ground floor! General Macquarie is furious about it, and to add to his understandable annoyance, he has just been informed by Lord Bathurst that Bent's younger brother, Jeffrey—a barrister of seven years' standing of Lincoln's Inn—is to be appointed chief justice to the colony, at a salary of eight hundred pounds a year! And Ellis is now demanding that a new courthouse be built in time for his brother's arrival!"

"A new courthouse?" Frances questioned, puzzled. "I thought it was to be included in the hospital building."

"And so it was," her husband agreed. "But Ellis Bent is out to scotch that idea. He has submitted plans for a building one hundred and forty feet in length, with a Doric portico at the main entrance copied from the Temple of Theseus at Athens. The design is by a settler named Daniel Dering Matthew, who, I strongly suspect, was in his cups when he conceived it."

This time there was no laughter. Watching Jasper as he carved the leg of lamb that constituted their main course, Frances found herself wondering how her husband had contrived to keep his sense of humor over the years. Perhaps, she thought, passing Jenny her plate, it was because he spent a considerable portion of each year in Calcutta, and as a wealthy shipowner and merchant, he was seldom affected, either commercially or personally, by the rapacious activities of people of Ellis Bent's character.

But he liked Governor Macquarie, she knew, and was an admirer of his lady. Despite the cynicism of his earlier remarks, Jasper deeply resented slights directed against the Macquaries—in particular those that emanated from the British Colonial Office, whose parsimony in relation to the colony always infuriated him.

Like Jenny's husband, he had given Governor Bligh his loyal support, allying himself with Robert Campbell and

John Palmer against the rebels, and he had been made to
suffer for it by John Macarthur. Yet . . . Frances felt a
warm flood of mingled pride and affection for him sweep
over her. More than anybody else—John Macarthur's erstwhile friends not excepted—Jasper had gone out of his way
to help Macarthur's wife, arranging the dispatch of letters
for her, importing livestock from India or the Cape whenever she required it, and visiting her, when he supposed
her to be lonely, at Parramatta and Camden.

If Abigail was half as fortunate in her marriage to Tim
as she herself had been in hers, Frances thought, then there
was much to be said for a difference in age, whatever Julia
might suppose. The girl would get over it, just as Justin
would.

"The Seventy-third's days here are numbered," Andrew
was saying. "The Governor told me today that they are
ordered to India and are to be replaced by the Forty-sixth
of Foot early in the New Year. I thought the old gentleman
would be reluctant to see his own regiment go, but he's not.
He says that they are being corrupted here and are losing
sight of their military duty by too close an intimacy with
the lower classes of our inhabitants. Which is true—far too
many of them head for the taverns of the Rocks the moment they come off duty."

"Will the O'Connells leave?" Frances questioned. "And
Captain Antill? They will be a sad loss, if they go."

She saw her husband and Andrew exchange glances, and
then Jasper said, with a wintry smile, "His Excellency does
not consider that Colonel O'Connell is a stern enough disciplinarian and—to be perfectly blunt, my dear—he fears
that Mary O'Connell exerts too much influence over him.
She's Bligh's daughter, and that's one thing she does not
forget. But—" He shrugged and helped himself to one of
the dishes the maid was offering. "I don't doubt they will
be back, do you, Andrew? And probably Henry Antill, too.
They both have considerable property here, and this colony
will afford them better prospects than His Majesty's
Seventy-third is ever likely to."

"Then are we to have a new Lieutenant Governor?"
Frances pursued.

"Yes," Andrew said. "That office will go to the Forty-sixth's commanding officer, Colonel George Molle. And the Governor seems pleased—Molle apparently served with him in India and Egypt and is an old friend. The Forty-sixth, he says, is a good regiment, with a distinguished record in the American War under General Wayne." Frances saw him cast an anxious look at his wife. Jenny's plate was scarcely touched, but intercepting her husband's glance, she started to ply her knife and fork with well-simulated eagerness.

In the brief silence that followed, she asked quietly, "Andrew, did His Excellency mention Mr. Evans's proposed expedition, the one Justin is to join?"

Andrew hesitated and then inclined his head. "Yes, indeed. He has authorized it—but rather, I think, from necessity than from conviction. The present drought and those damned bush fires that have done so much damage have forced his hand, but—" He appealed to Jasper Spence. "I had the impression, I must confess, that he does not believe, in his heart, that Blaxland and Lawson, when they assured him that a road could be built, really went into all the practical difficulties that its construction would entail."

"Least of all," Jasper said dryly, "did they consider what it would cost. Or whether Lord Bathurst would provide the funds to build it!"

"Then," Jenny suggested unhappily, "Justin may be wasting his time if he accompanies Mr. Evans?"

"No exploration is a waste of time, my love," Andrew countered, with deep conviction. "As His Excellency himself expressed it—if Evans can find a new tract of country where nature is more bountiful than within the present circumscribed limits of the colony, and if *he* is able to say that a road can be built, then funds will be found somehow. By local subscription, if his shortsighted lordship refuses to provide them. We *must* expand, if we are ever to prosper. Or, come to that, if we are ever to cease being a burden to the mother country, as Bathurst clearly intends that we should."

He reached over to Jenny, holding out a big hand to her small one. "Take heart, Jenny love—perhaps we really are on the verge of realizing that dream of yours, at long, long last."

Jenny distractedly smiled up at him. "The fertile plains," she answered softly.

"Let us drink to it," Jasper proposed. He topped up their glasses and raised his own. "To your dream, Jenny—and to Governor Phillip's—it was his, too, as well as yours, was it not?"

"Yes," Jenny confirmed. "Yes it was. But even I must admit that there were times when my faith was shaken, when I doubted and lost hope. But now"—her eyes were bright, Frances saw, and her head was held high—"now I drink to hope renewed—to the new land and to the road that, please God, will lead us there!"

"Amen to that," Frances whispered and, crossing herself, prayed silently that, this once, Dr. Redfern might be wrong.

By Friday, November 19, 1813, the expedition was at Emu Island, all its supplies packed up and across the Nepean River.

George Evans, his maps and instruments in a haversack, and a musket slung from his shoulder, looked at the members of his party and smiled.

"We are amply supplied with every comfort and necessity, and there will be sufficient to permit us to make a cache, at a suitable point, for our return journey. Rest whilst you may, all of you, and be ready, if you please, to make the ascent of the first ridge at sunrise tomorrow morning."

The colony's assistant surveyor of lands, George Evans, was a small man, with a round, pink-complexioned face and thinning, reddish-brown hair. He was, as nearly as Justin could tell, about thirty-five, toughened by the nature of his work and professionally highly competent—if perhaps a shade too conscientious. Although officially appointed to lead the expedition, he was diffident, inclined to defer to the kangaroo hunter, Lucky Byrne, on the grounds of Byrne's greater experience, and given to phrase his orders as polite requests.

Byrne, disrespectful and foulmouthed as ever, took full advantage of Evans's seeming uncertainty. Under Lawson and Blaxland, he had been permitted few liberties, Justin recalled, and had played his part well. Now, however, he was drinking surreptitiously from a flask he kept in the capacious pocket of his shabby leather jerkin, and the dogs—which were his responsibility—were already out of hand, snarling and barking at the other members of the party.

Besides Evans, Byrne, and himself, there were four others: a fresh-faced young settler named Richard Lewis, and three convict servants, Tygh, Cooghan, and Grover, chosen, Justin had decided after meeting them, for their physique rather than their intelligence. But all were pleasant enough, and Tygh, the oldest of the convicts, who was acting as cook, served up an appetizing stew of kangaroo meat, which they ate before retiring.

The following morning they awoke to find a thick fog swirling about their camp, and the ridge they had planned to climb hidden behind a thick curtain of moisture. Evans would have postponed their departure, but the horses were loaded, the men eager to make a start, and Byrne was confident that, fog or no fog, he could lead them to their destination—the campsite Blaxland's party had established at the top of the ridge.

They had scarcely set off when a heavy rainstorm soaked them to the skin. Cursing and grumbling, Byrne led them on and, predictably, led them astray, his boasting revealed for what it was. When at last, weary and disspirited, they stumbled on the remains of the old campfire, they had been climbing for over five hours.

Justin took Evans aside and said tersely, "I know the route we followed as well as Byrne does, and I'll stay sober. Let old Lucky hunt for us—it's what he does best—and let me act as guide."

"Certainly, Mr. Broome," the surveyor agreed without hesitation. "Yours is an excellent suggestion."

By the evening of Wednesday, November 24, they had crossed the first range, and keeping to the track that the Blaxland party had cleared with so much labor, by the fifth day they had reached the terminal point of the first expedition. Here, busy with his maps and measurements, George Evans was in high spirits. Names began to appear on his map—Mount Blaxland, for the mountains at whose foot they made camp, and Lawson's and Wentworth's sugarloaves, for the two odd-shaped pinnacles on either side of the rivulet from which they refreshed themselves.

The grass all around them was fresh and green, clear of trees and well watered, as Justin remembered it. Lucky Byrne took his dogs and went hunting, returning soon after nightfall with a young kangaroo and a brace of duck, so that, despite the almost continuous rain, they feasted royally, cooking the game in the shelter of a rocky outcrop.

The weather improved in the morning, and although it was still misty, they made good progress and, four days later, had passed over the main dividing range and found themselves looking out over a forty or fifty mile expanse of the finest pastureland any of them had ever seen. The spirits of the whole party rose, and Evans was in ecstasies as he added more names to his map. They descended to the plain, undeterred by the return of the rain, and followed the course of a fine river, abounding with fish, to its junction with a second, bright with wattle that grew in clusters along its banks. The horses were failing and had frequently to be relieved of their loads, but Evans pressed on, deaf to the grumbles of the convict servants and to Byrne's more loudly voiced complaints and warnings of disaster.

Justin caught his feverish enthusiasm and began also to contribute names to the map, for this indeed was the fulfillment of all their hopes and dreams—the promised land, which could make the colony prosperous. William Lawson's optimistic report was vindicated, and the Governor's doubts as to its validity could be set at rest.

Carefully, protecting the paper from the teeming rain, Evans wrote in his small, neat hand, grinning with delight as he did so. Fish River was an obvious choice; Bathurst, Macquarie, and O'Connell designated the lush plains; the second river, which they crossed by fashioning a bridge of cut logs, became the Campbell, and the third, with which it finally merged, the Macquarie. A modest tributary was given Evans's own name, Justin and young Lewis gave theirs to waterfalls along its course, and even the reluctant Byrne was similarly honored.

Justin himself made careful notes on the nature of the terrain—half for his mother's benefit, and half to while away the long evening hours he spent, cold and wet, in his tent. In the late afternoon of December 5, which Evans had declared a rest day for men and horses, Justin wrote:

The nights are very cold, the mornings misty, and we have met with almost continuous rainstorms since leaving Emu Plains. Despite the discomfort caused by having to travel in wet clothing, what we have so far seen of the country beyond the Western Range has filled us with hopes for the future.

It is fine grazing land, well watered and extending as far as the eye can see, which I judge to be forty or fifty miles from the spot where we are now encamped. The soil is loam and fit for every variety of cultivation; the country from the first river abounds with red and black granite, and its whole aspect appears as if it had undergone some great convulsion of nature, with hills heaped upon hills, and deep gullies in between, some with streams running through them, and all clothed with trees to their very summits.

There is plenty of wild game. Emus, kangaroos, opossums, wild duck, black swans, and geese, and a great variety of other birds, including cockatoos, plovers, orioles, magpies, and crows. Byrne's dogs are very successful in hunting kangaroos, but for some reason they will not attempt to chase the emus.

We have suffered no molestation by the native tribes, who seem timorous in the extreme and ready to run at the sight of us. The few with whom we have made contact have had to be persuaded to accept our gifts; they speak a different language from those around Sydney and Parramatta. Because of the ex-

treme cold in these mountains, they have learned to
fashion themselves cloaks of opossum skin, sewn together by the sinews of the kangaroo and emu.

They hunt with wild dogs, as their Sydney brethren
do. Of a party that approached us yesterday, one, an
old woman, was blind, two children leading her and
seeming to show her much kindness.

Tomorrow we move on, to follow the course of another river and, it is hoped, to explore the surrounding
flat country, with a view to future settlement.

Four days later, on December 9, they camped on the
bank of the river Evans had marked on his map as the
Macquarie, and considering it a perfect site for settlement,
the surveyor thoughtfully penciled in the name Bathurst.

"A cart road to this point can be built," he told Justin.
"And I shall assure His Excellency that it is a feasible prop-
osition and likely to be most richly rewarding, for the land
is better by far than any in the colony."

For another week, the conscientious surveyor delayed
their return, however, intent on exploring the country beyond, identifying varieties of trees and shrubs, measuring
gradients and marking in distances. According to his reck-
oning, they had traveled a hundred and fifty miles into
hitherto unknown country and ninety-eight miles farther
than the Blaxland party had reached when halting at the
sugarloaf peaks.

"We will start back tomorrow," he finally declared. "We
have done enough to satisfy His Excellency. I'd have liked
another week to follow the westward course of the river,
but . . . the horses are worn out, and Tygh's complaining
that we have only four days' supply of flour left. Better
not to tempt providence, eh? And tonight we must dine
well. I will try my hand at rod and line if you would like to
take Byrne and shoot us a kangaroo or a few duck, Justin."

Byrne had vanished, however, as he all too frequently
did, and leaving Evans and Lewis placidly fishing, Justin
set off on his own. Without the dogs, he would have small
chance of bagging a kangaroo, he knew, but just before
dusk the wild duck usually came down on the swampy

ground at the confluence of the two rivers, and he headed in that direction, his musket loaded and primed.

Luck was with him. He had three good-size ducks to show for his pains two hours later, and was about to start back for camp when he heard Byrne's dogs giving tongue some distance beyond the swamp. To his surprise, the kangaroo hunter appeared, saw him, and then, ignoring his hail, took to his heels, yelling out something Justin could not catch. It had sounded like a warning, but Byrne was so often drunk that Justin did not take it seriously, until he saw that the man had abandoned a kangaroo carcass he had been carrying. Puzzled, and reluctant to leave a good meal to the wild dogs, Justin started to circle the swamp in order to retrieve the carcass.

The light was going with the suddenness that it always did, and it was not until he was within fifty or sixty feet of his objective that he saw the aborigine. The dark figure was alone; it was bent low and seemed unaware of his approach. Supposing that the native was also after Byrne's abandoned prize, Justin shouted to him to leave it.

Instantly the lithe body was galvanized into action, and a spear point was leveled at Justin's chest. They faced each other, neither one advancing or retreating, Justin having instinctively raised his musket to meet the spear's challenge. The native was a boy of perhaps ten or twelve, and he was holding his weapon awkwardly in his left hand. Even in the dim light, the reason was plain enough: His right arm was broken—and badly, too, the bone protruding from the brown skin of his forearm, the hand uselessly dangling and visibly swollen. Justin lowered his musket and approached warily.

He knew that the few native phrases he had learned while living on the Hawkesbury would do him no good now, but he attempted, nevertheless, to make his intentions clear. He stopped, laid down his musket and, forcing a smile, held out his empty hands.

"*Kamarooka!*" he pleaded. "*Jumbunna!*"

The spear did not waver; his invitation to wait and talk went unheeded, but the young native's fear was as plain as his mistrust, and Justin found himself wondering whether

Byrne had been responsible for his injury. The shattered arm might well have been caused by a blow from a musket butt, and if it had . . . He sought vainly for some means of reassurance, and finally gestured to the kangaroo. "*Koonook* . . . take it!"

The boy's eyes widened. Then, without warning, he began to sway, the spear slipped from his grasp, and Justin rushed up and caught him as he fell. He weighed almost nothing, and his whole body felt as if it were on fire . . . The poor little devil had a raging fever, which at least cleared Lucky Byrne of any complicity. The broken arm apparently had been suffered days before.

As carefully as he could, Justin lowered him to the ground. He had a flask with him, and he poured its contents recklessly onto the jagged wound, hoping to cleanse it. The boy did not move. Realizing that he was unconscious and that, if he were to be helped at all, it had better be now, Justin tore a strip from his shirt to serve as a bandage. The spear, broken in two, would have to be used as a splint, he decided.

Working in the dim afterglow of the setting sun, he did what was possible to set, splint, and bandage the arm. The boy came to and whimpered softly, but made no attempt to escape; and when Justin rose to his feet, the boy rose with him, to stand staring at him with puzzled eyes. His tribe would find him, no doubt, or he would find them in due course, and the kangaroo could be left as a peace offering. Or the ducks might be easier for him to carry . . . Justin reached his haversack and laid the three feathered bodies at the aborigine's feet.

"*Koonook!*" he said again, smiling. Then, shouldering his musket, he took the kangaroo by its hind legs and hefted it onto his back. The boy said nothing and made no effort to detain him.

He was within sight of the camp and its glowing fire when he heard a footfall behind him and, turning, saw that the boy was there, carrying the ducks. Justin swore good-naturedly.

"They're yours, lad. *Koonook!* Off you go and take 'em with you. Eat 'em!"

Evidently this time he had made himself understood. The aborigine dropped two of the birds at Justin's feet, flashed him a smile, and was gone.

Next morning, however, when they broke camp, he was there, and he trailed them throughout the day. George Evans said dryly, "It seems you have made a friend, Justin, and he's not going to leave you."

"Well, if he's still around when we get back to the Nepean," Justin declared, "I'll take him to my mother's. He can stay at Ulva until his arm mends."

The boy—whose name they finally learned was Winyara—continued to pad after them until, after crossing the Nepean at Emu Ford, Justin parted company with the others. Then, without a word, the boy disappeared, and after a cursory search, Justin thought no more about him and set off for Ulva.

He was aching with weariness but happily conscious of what they had achieved.

To his mother, he said, "We found the interminable pastures, Mam—they are there for the taking, and I truly believe they will support our flocks and herds for at least a hundred years. And the road will be built—George Evans has gone to Sydney to tell the Governor that it can be done."

His mother hugged him, and he heard her whisper, "Oh, thank God!"

CHAPTER XXII

On the evening of Saturday, March 28, 1814, Governor Macquarie prepared to receive forty invited guests by himself.

Elizabeth had gone into labor at three o'clock that afternoon, and her husband waited in an agony of suspense for news that might well break his heart once again . . . or fill it with such joy as he had never previously known.

Dr. Redfern, beaming with confidence, had sought to reassure him. "Mrs. Macquarie has gone to her full term, sir, and the movements of the infant are as strong and lively as I've ever seen. She will give birth to a healthy child, I'm in no doubt of that. And Mrs. Reynolds—who is a most experienced midwife—shares my opinion. Try to be patient, sir, for it will take time."

Patient, the Governor thought miserably—how could he be patient, when all his hopes depended on the outcome of the next few hours? He had celebrated his fifty-third birthday two months earlier, and Elizabeth was herself already thirty-six. If this child should be stillborn—or, most calamitous of all, should die, as their daughter Jane had died, at a few months old—there was unlikely to be another pregnancy. He could not, in all conscience, submit his poor Elizabeth to further torment, for had she not already suffered disappointment enough in her valiant endeavor to give him the child for which he longed, and which she had set her heart on giving him?

Macquarie bit back a sigh. He had already changed into his formal dinner clothes, although the guests would not arrive for at least another hour, and he strode impatiently across to his desk, seeking to distract his thoughts during the time of waiting. As always, the desk was piled high with papers—Colonial Office dispatches, petitions, requests for land grants, for building permits, for pardons . . . the demands on him were endless. And there were alarming reports of the increased activities of bushrangers in the Hawkesbury area and in Van Diemen's Land—particularly in the latter, where Major Davey's rule was proving, as he had feared, exceedingly lax.

A band of convict escapers had seized the brig *Unity* at Hobart Town; another gang of the wretches had pirated the *Speedwell* when she lay at anchor in the Hunter River at Newcastle and had made off with her, eluding all attempts at recapture. True, thanks to the prompt action of young Justin Broome and the Windsor constables, the rogues who had raided Abigail O'Shea's property at Yarramundie had been brought to justice and . . . He clicked his tongue. Abigail was Mrs. Timothy Dawson now; he must remember and cease calling her O'Shea. Despondently, he returned to the report.

The natives, too, were becoming troublesome. They were hungry; the still prevailing drought had caused a shortage of fish and wild game, and raids on settlers' stock and crops were occurring with increasing frequency. Worst of all, perhaps, was the aboriginals' habit of setting fire to growing crops, in order to deter pursuit; and this year's harvest was, heaven knew, liable to be the poorest for many years. He would be hard put to it to feed the colony, the Governor thought grimly, if the drought continued and he could not prevail upon the civil police to exert themselves, in order to protect property in the outlying settlements from predators.

A punitive raid on the Hawkesbury tribes by the military

might be a possibility, once Colonel Molle's regiment had settled in and had been brought to full strength. At present this was out of the question; only Molle himself had as yet arrived, with a small advance party, and the transports were standing by to receive the departing 73rd. Indeed, the reason for this evening's ill-timed dinner party was to bid Godspeed to Maurice O'Connell and his wife and to welcome George Molle and his second-in-command, but— The sound of footsteps on the main staircase brought the Governor instantly to his feet.

He waited, sick with apprehension, but the sound receded; and guessing from the lightness of the footsteps that his wife's maid, Jessica Maclaine, had been sent on some errand to the kitchen, he forced himself to relax. Redfern had said that it would take time and had counseled patience; he must, he knew, attempt to take the doctor's advice.

Still seeking distraction, Governor Macquarie found his restless fingers closing about a bundle of handwritten sheets, which he identified as the land surveyor George Evans's lengthy report on his recent Blue Mountains expedition. Evans had returned at the end of January with an enthusiastic account of the excellence of the land that he and his party had found beyond the mountain barrier. The maps he had drawn were attached to the report, and Macquarie leafed through them, reading the notes at random.

> The river now forms large ponds; at the space of about a mile, I came on a fine plain of rich land, the handsomest country I ever saw; it surpasseth Port Dalrymple . . . I have named it after the Lieutenant Governor 'O'Connell Plains.' . . .
>
> At three o'clock, we halted at the commencement of a plain still more extensive and very pleasing. I could not see the termination of it to the north; the soil is exceedingly rich and produces the finest grass, intermixed with a variety of herbs. The hills have the look of a park and grounds laid out; indeed, I am at a loss to find words to describe its beauty and fair promise. I named this part the 'Macquarie Plains.' . . .

Yesterday's trace led us much north of west. The extent of the plain following the river is eleven miles and about two wide on each side, the whole excellent land and the best grass I have seen in any part of New South Wales . . . Graziers could keep stock here to great advantage. The feed is exceptionally good, particularly for sheep. . . .

There was more in the same vein, and the Governor found himself smiling as he read on. He had, of course, read it before, but not, perhaps, with such attention; he had tended to concentrate more on Evans's plans for the proposed road and its probable cost. Yet now . . . Suddenly conscious of excitement, Macquarie turned the pages, his attention caught and held by Evans's lyrical descriptions of the newly discovered land.

The road to Windsor was all but completed, and so, also, was the turnpike to Liverpool. The chain gangs, recently instituted by the Reverend Samuel Marsden—who now sentenced all the felons brought before him to work on the roads—had made rapid progress. They could be employed to build a turnpike as far as Emu Ford, and then . . . The Governor hunted among his papers, seeking a note he had received from William Cox of Clarendon.

Cox had been lieutenant and paymaster of the Rum Corps but had retired prior to the rebellion, in order to farm his extensive land grant in the Mulgoa area, south of the Nepean. He had had considerable experience as a builder and had recently finished the construction of the Glebe House at Castlereagh, which had met with widespread approbation.

They had discussed the possibility of a road over the mountains, the Governor recalled, and he had been compelled to admit that he had no one in mind to whom so hazardous and laborious an undertaking could be entrusted. Cox had said nothing at the time—there had been others present, and he was a man who was inclined to keep his own counsel—but a few days later, he had written, offering his services, and . . . Devil take this accumulation of papers! Where was his note?

He found it at last and, spreading the single thin sheet of paper on the desk in front of him, perused it carefully.

William Cox's terms were modest in the extreme. He asked for thirty convicts—men of his own choosing—to be allocated for the actual work of road building, specifying that they should be "convicts who volunteered their services, on the condition that they should be granted emancipation for their extra labor," once the road was built. His other requests were for a military guard to protect his laborers from attack by hostile natives, for oxcarts, blasting tools and powder, axes, saws, and hoes "to be specified in detail later," and for the services of another retired New South Wales Corps veteran, Lieutenant Hobby, to act as his assistant. His own fee he would leave to the Governor's discretion, but he would not, the onetime paymaster stated, with admirable modesty, "make any untoward or unreasonable demands on the Colonial Treasury."

Even Lord Bathurst could scarcely quibble at such an offer, Macquarie told himself; nonetheless, he rose and paced the floor for several minutes before returning to his desk. Evans had estimated that it would take three months to build the road; Cox, more cautiously, specified six to eight, and promised a track that "would admit of a provision cart passing over it."

Coming finally to a decision, Governor Macquarie reached for his pen and a sheet of paper. Swiftly he wrote:

> I now most readily avail myself of your very liberal and handsome offer regarding the construction of a cart road from Emu Ford to the newly discovered land known as Bathurst Plains. I do hereby invest you with full power and authority to carry this important design into complete effect, government furnishing you with the necessary means to enable you to do so.

He addressed it to William Cox, Esquire, and signed his name, leaving the letter propped up on the desk top for his secretary to seal and dispatch.

Time enough, he thought, to acquaint the miserable skinflints at the Colonial Office with his decision. Already they were questioning the wisdom of his contract with Dr. D'Arcy Wentworth for the building of the new hospital— Bathurst had passed on another acid comment from the Prime Minister as to the impropriety of linking the project with the spirit trade. At least William Cox had not asked for an import license. . . . He sighed deeply and returned to his restless pacing, halting occasionally by the door to listen.

But no sound came from the upper floor; no infant cries to warm his heart and put an end to his anxiety, not even the light tripping footsteps of Jessica Maclaine on the stairway to the hall. Glumly, Lachlan Macquarie resumed his seat in front of the paper-strewn desk and, from his private file, took the most recent letter he had received from his brother Charles. He reread the war news, which seemed hearteningly good, with Bonaparte "going as fast to the devil as his greatest enemy could wish," according to Sir David Baird, and smiled, a trifle cynically, over his brother's announcement of betrothal to "a highly accomplished young lady in Edinburgh, with a fortune of twelve thousand pounds."

Charles, it seemed, no longer minded that he had not been appointed to the lieutenant governorship of Van Diemen's Land and that the other candidate Lachlan had sponsored for the office—Joseph Foveaux—had been promoted. He— A knock on the door had the Governor leaping nervously to his feet.

"Yes?" he snapped, as Sergeant Whalan stood framed in the open doorway. "Yes?"

"His Honor Colonel O'Connell and Mrs. O'Connell are here, Your Excellency," Whalan answered woodenly. "I showed them into the anteroom, sir."

"Thank you, Sergeant. Ah . . . there's no word from Dr. Redfern, I take it?"

Whalan's round red face expressed the sympathy he could not voice. "No, sir. The doctor is still upstairs, sir, with Her Excellency."

The O'Connells, when he greeted them, were delighted

by his news. "I'm so pleased, sir, that we shall be here to celebrate the happy event," Maurice O'Connell volunteered. He put an affectionate arm about his wife's slim shoulders and added, smiling, "We know, do we not, Mary, my dearest, how much a child can add to marital happiness?"

"And how is my godson?" the Governor asked, bowing over Mary O'Connell's hand and making an effort to be sociable.

"He is in bouncing health, I'm delighted to say," Mary assured him. She had received the sad news of her mother's death in England only a few weeks before, Macquarie recalled, and she was in mourning, but looking as lovely as ever in her somber black gown. He raised her hand to his lips, the stiff but courtly gesture intended to smooth away any past differences that had arisen between them. She was a fine woman, he had to concede, and an exceptionally courageous one; Maurice O'Connell was a lucky man, and . . . damn it, so was Bligh, to have fathered a woman of Mary's caliber! Loyalty was a quality that he himself had always valued, and if the late Governor's daughter found it difficult to forgive those who had deposed him, small blame could be attached to her for that.

"Colonel and Mrs. Molle," Sergeant Whalan announced, from the door. "Major Cameron . . . Mr. and Mrs. Riley . . . Mrs. Redfern."

The guests were all arriving now, and he must play the host, the Governor knew, without reference to his poor Elizabeth, enduring the agonies of childbirth in the room above. He wrung George Molle's plump hand, greeting him with all the warmth of an old friend and comrade-in-arms, bowed to his wife and the Rileys, and kissed Mrs. Redfern on the cheek.

Whalan, playing the role of majordomo with military precision, announced Ellis Bent and his wife, Eliza, who swept in like royalty, contriving to thrust ahead of Henry Antill, who was escorting one of the newly arrived officers of the 46th. The Reverend Samuel Marsden was just behind them, and the Governor, suddenly irritated, stepped adroitly aside before the Bents could reach him and went to greet Timothy Dawson, whose name Whalan had not yet announced.

Abigail was with him, looking radiant in a green silk gown; she was a favorite of his wife's, Macquarie knew, and he himself enjoyed her company, together with that of her little son, who in spite of his handicap was a charming, lively little boy.

"Dawson!" he said. "My dear fellow . . . and Abigail. My warmest congratulations to you both!"

Behind him, he heard Eliza Bent emit an affronted exclamation, and satisfied with the success of his ploy, he turned without haste to receive her, his greeting coolly correct.

"Dr. Milcham . . ." Sergeant Whalan intoned from the door. "Mr. and Mrs. Campbell . . . Dr. Wentworth, Lieutenant Wentworth, Mr. William Wentworth."

Thirty-eight guests finally sat down in the dining room, and to the anxious Governor, the meal seemed endless. But by eleven-thirty all save the O'Connells—who were staying in Government House overnight—had taken their leave.

Still there was no word from upstairs, and left alone, Lachlan Macquarie resumed his restless pacing, oblivious to a fall of plaster from the dilapidated ceiling, which the white ants in the fabric of the building were steadily eating away.

In the great bedroom—the only room in Government House that had been rebuilt—Jessica scurried from bed to washbasin with cloths wrung out in cold water, in a vain attempt to bring some relief to her mistress's suffering.

Mrs. Macquarie had now been in labor for over fourteen hours, with Dr. Redfern and Midwife Reynolds in constant attendance. But there was, it had become evident, nothing they could do to hasten the birth, and very little to allay its agonies.

Mrs. Macquarie, infinitely courageous, uttered no complaint, and save for the occasional muffled cry when the pains were beyond even her endurance, she had suffered the long ordeal stoically. But she was exhausted now, Jessica realized, and no longer able to obey Dr. Redfern's pleas to her to bear down.

At midnight, in response to a message from below, the doctor left the room for a brief conference with the Governor, and Mrs. Reynolds seized the opportunity afforded by his absence to refresh herself from a bottle she had secreted in her midwife's bag. To give her credit, Jessica thought, the stout, perspiring woman had worked hard, but . . . She laid yet another cool cloth on her mistress's forehead and whispered gently, "Rest, ma'am, for a little while, to recoup your strength."

"It is taking a long time, is it not?" Mrs. Macquarie questioned anxiously.

"No longer than usual, Mrs. Reynolds says," Jessica answered, not quite truthfully, for the midwife's remark had been made several hours before. "Can I be fetching you something, ma'am? A cup of tea or gruel, or a little brandy?"

"A glass of water, perhaps," Mrs. Macquarie managed. "I am parched, Jessica."

But Mrs. Reynolds intervened when Jessica brought her the water. "No, ma'am, I'm sorry. Not without the doctor orders it." A spasm of pain convulsed her patient's hunched body, and she shooed Jessica away imperiously. "Bear down, Mrs. Macquarie! Your baby won't be born unless you help it by using the pains like you should. Pull on that strap I fixed for you . . . pull!"

The spasm passed, leaving the poor lady exhausted. Jessica wiped the beads of moisture from the thin, pale face and heard her say bitterly, "My baby will be born dead if this goes on for much longer. Is that not so, Mrs. Reynolds?"

"That is a possibility, ma'am," the midwife confirmed severely. "If you would just bear down when the pains come, 'twill be better for us all. *Now!*"

Mrs. Macquarie grasped the end of the strap fixed to the bedhead and strained with what was left of her strength, but to no avail. Despairingly she gasped, "I cannot—God help me, I cannot!"

"You must try, Mrs. Macquarie," Mrs. Reynolds reproached her, and Jessica caught the whiff of spirits as the woman bent over the bed. She made a quick examination beneath the sheet and clicked her tongue with ill-concealed impatience. "You are fully dilated—it needs but a little effort, ma'am."

Dr. Redfern returned. The midwife went to him, talking in a hissing whisper, and Jessica saw the doctor shake his head. He was a kindly man, gentle with all his patients and very skilled . . . little Dickon O'Shea, she recalled, adored him. He came to the bedside and said quietly, "I've had a word with His Excellency your husband, Mrs. Macquarie, and, I trust, have reassured him. I want you to drink this—" He held a glass to Mrs. Macquarie's lips, and Jessica lifted her head. "We'll call a halt for half an hour, and you shall rest. After that, I am quite sure, all will be well."

"But the baby might die," Mrs. Macquarie objected fearfully. "While I am . . . am resting."

"No fear of that, I promise you," Dr. Redfern answered, smiling. He gave Jessica the glass, and his hands moved purposefully beneath the covering sheet. "Lively as a cricket—do not worry, dear lady. No harm will come to the most eagerly awaited babe in this colony!"

Obediently, Mrs. Macquarie lay back and closed her eyes, only to open them an instant later. "Dr. Redfern!" she whispered hoarsely. "The young Macquarie is permitting me no time to rest . . . it is now!"

She clasped Jessica's hands and flexed her weary body with newfound urgency. Dr. Redfern called to the midwife, and to Jessica's unbounded joy, the struggle was over. The baby's cries filled the room, and the doctor, after a brief delay, held up the tiny, squirming body.

"It is a boy, Mrs. Macquarie!" he exulted. "A fine, healthy boy—the son and heir your husband wants so much!"

Half an hour later, the baby washed and lying gurgling in his cot, and Mrs. Macquarie in a fresh nightgown and with her hair neatly braided, Dr. Redfern ushered in the Governor. He fell to his knees beside the cot, his thin, austere face lit by a joyous smile, and Dr. Redfern motioned Jessica and Mrs. Reynolds to follow him from the room. To the O'Connells, waiting in their nightclothes at the door of the guest room, he said simply, "It is a boy!"

Mrs. O'Connell's relieved and happy "Thanks be to God!" found its echo in Jessica's heart.

"Duncan," Agnes Campbell said, careful to avoid any mention of their relationship, "wishes to see you before we sail, Jessie. I'd take it very kindly if you would come back with me to the house."

Jessica eyed her uncertainly across the scrubbed kitchen table. When Mrs. Ovens had summoned her to receive a caller, she had not expected it to be Agnes, to whom she had already bidden farewell. The Indiamen in the cove were busy loading the 73rd Regiment's baggage; tomorrow the men and their families would go on board—just as, Jessica remembered with a pang, they had boarded the *Dromedary* and the *Hindostan* to come out here, five years ago.

Then she had endeavored to conceal herself in a store cupboard in the barracks, in terror of her stepfather, but now . . . She started to shake her head.

"Please," Agnes begged. "Is it so much to ask? He has changed a great deal, you know. These last few months have not been happy for him. He has felt the loss of his rank very sorely, and John Gould—the soldier they hanged for murder—was a friend of his. To see one of their own dispatched like a common criminal has dealt a blow to the regiment's pride, Jessie. I tell you truly, Duncan Campbell is not the man he was."

"Is he not?" Jessica questioned, finding this hard to believe. The case of Private Gould had, she knew, shocked the Governor greatly, too. Gould, in a fit of drunken rage, had murdered a woman by the name of Margaret Finnie, with whom he had cohabited, and he had then endeavored to conceal her body, while denying all knowledge of her whereabouts.

"Duncan has given up the drink," Agnes asserted. "He has not touched a drop since they sentenced him to be reduced to the ranks." She laid a hand on Jessica's arm and added pleadingly, "We shall be gone in a few days, and I doubt if we shall see one another again. We go to India, as you know, and no doubt you will wish to stay here . . . and I'd not blame you, for you have a fine post with a truly fine lady in Her Excellency. But you are on poor Duncan's conscience, Jessica, and he wants to make his peace with you."

It would be ungenerous to refuse the proffered olive branch, Jessica thought, and she had nothing to lose. Besides, Agnes was a good woman and an exemplary stepmother to the two little girls.

"Very well," she said, "I'll come with you now, if Mrs. Ovens will give me leave."

The housekeeper gave her permission readily. "You've bin up most o' the night, my lass—you're entitled to a few hours off. In any event," she added, a shade tartly, "that Mrs. Reynolds seems to think that *she's* rulin' the roost abovestairs, an' I doubt if she'd even let you through the door o' the mistress's room this mornin'. It was all I could do to get inside meself, just for a glimpse o' young Master Lachlan Jarvisfield Macquarie!"

Jessica smiled, and Agnes, overhearing Mrs. Ovens's somewhat acid comment, asked eagerly about the new arrival. The topic occupied them as they walked to Clarence Street.

"That's quite a mouthful—Lachlan Jarvisfield Macquarie," Agnes remarked incredulously. "Is that really what Their Excellencies intend to call the poor wee mite?"

"Lachlan certainly," Jessica assured her. "After his papa. I'm not sure about Jarvisfield, but I think it is the name of His Excellency's estate in Scotland."

"Was it a difficult confinement, Jessie?"

"It was a long one," Jessica admitted. "And my poor lady was sorely tried."

"But the babe is strong and healthy?" Agnes pursued.

"He seems to be, thank heaven." Dr. Redfern had expressed some concern for the new baby's breathing, Jessica recalled, and had frowned a little as he listened to it with a small instrument he carried in his pocket. "Please God he is."

"And will you be looking after him?"

"I do not know. Helping to, perhaps."

They left the Government House grounds, and Agnes gestured to the two big transports lying at anchor in the cove. "I am not sure if I shall be glad or sorry to leave this place. Glad in some ways, I suppose, seeing that here I'm classed as an emancipated convict and never allowed to forget it, for all I'm respectably married."

"What were you convicted of?" Jessica asked curiously. Agnes had never talked of her past, even in moments of intimacy, when, as now, they were alone together. She had confessed to having been a widow, but that was all.

"You want to know?" The older woman's lips curved into an odd little smile that held a hint of defiance.

"Not if you are not wishing to tell me. I wondered, that was all."

"There is no harm in you knowing, Jessie. I was charged with arson. Myself and four other poor souls."

"*Arson?* But surely—" Jessica was taken aback. This quiet, domesticated woman was the last person in the world she would have supposed guilty of such a crime. Fire-raising was common enough here, in the colony, but only hostile natives and escapers indulged in it.

Agnes let a sigh escape her. "We set fire to a coal owner's mansion in Derbyshire. But it was no more than he deserved. There was a roof-fall in his pit—one they called the Long Drift Mine at Whitwell—and it was entirely his blame. He tried to save money by using rotten wood for pit props. The forward workings caved in and buried my husband and my two sons alive, with half a score of others. My boys were twins, just eight years old, poor young things."

"Oh, Agnes!" Jessica whispered and could only look at her helplessly, regretting her thoughtless question.

Agnes linked an arm in hers. "It is all a long time ago, Jessie, and I have put the memory behind me. At the time, though, I was very bitter. It took more than a week to dig all the bodies out, and I kept thinking that my husband, who was the pit deputy, had begged the owner repeatedly to close the forward workings until the props were replaced. But he would not." She repeated her sigh. "There is not much more to tell. After the funeral, the five of us—all widows—went up to the big house and burnt it to the ground. They arrested us, of course, and we pleaded guilty to the charges. The court showed us leniency, in view of what had happened. The other women were given short sentences, but I—I was the ringleader, so they sentenced me to seven years."

Jessica was silent, bereft of words. Agnes forced a smile. "Your father—your stepfather, I mean—saved me from having to serve my sentence in full. He married me, and I am grateful, not only for that but also for those two little girls. Janet and Flora have taken the place of my boys, Jessie. They have helped me to start my life anew. And as I told you, Duncan Campbell is a changed man." Her gaze went again to the anchored troopships, and her smile widened. "He is eager to return to India and forget the past, as I have done. You will see the change in him, truly you will."

And indeed, when her stepfather rose to greet her, the change in his manner was very evident, Jessica had to concede. His greeting was friendly, and Janet and Flora, with whom he had been playing, were urged to bid their sister welcome in almost effusive tones.

"You'll no' see her again for an awfu' lang time, ma weans. That is if I canna persuade her tae come wi' us tae Calcutta, as she's mair than welcome tae do. How aboot it, Jessie lass? Ye're still on the regimental strength—it wad no' tak' much arranging, if ye're of a mind tae bide wi' your ain folk."

The two little girls, thus prompted, added their shrill-voiced pleas to his, and Jessica, even as she refused, felt a twinge of conscience. But Duncan Campbell accepted her refusal with a good grace.

"Dinna reproach yoursel'—'twas what I expected ye'd say, and wha's tae tell ye ye're wrong? Ye've guid prospects here, nae doot o' that. An' maybe the fact that yon fine young piper, Mackinnon, has gi'en ye up and married the pipe major's bucktoothed daughter will hae something tae do wi' it?"

He was eyeing her with a hint of his old malice, and Jessica flushed, controlling the impulse to voice an indignant denial. She knew of Fergus Mackinnon's marriage; he had courted his bride since being relieved of his post as the Governor's personal piper and returning to the regimental band, and she had not set eyes on him for months.

Meeting Agnes's anxious gaze, she answered without heat, "Piper Mackinnon was never courting me."

"Was he no'? Weel, 'twas my impression that he was wanting tae." Duncan Campbell shrugged, dismissing the subject. He stood looking down at Jessica with narrowed eyes, tall and imposing, his turn-out impeccable. Only the faded patches on his sleeve, where the sergeant's chevrons had been, looked out of place. She had cost him those, Jessica thought. She and Justin Broome . . . She drew in her breath sharply, the old fear of him returning; but contrary to her expectation, he offered affably, "Ye'll tak' a bite o' lunch wi' us, will ye no', lassie?"

She hesitated, seeking for an excuse. "No, thank you, I . . . they'll be wanting me back, you see." It sounded unconvincing, even to her own ears, but Agnes came to her rescue.

"Her Excellency gave birth to a son last night, Duncan. Jessie will be needed." She signed to the two little girls to follow her and made for the kitchen. "I'll brew a pot of tea. You'll have time to drink a cup before you go, at least."

The door closed behind her, and Duncan Campbell smiled. " 'Tis no' all beer and skittles at Government House, then?" he suggested. "Ye've tae work at your grand job?"

"Yes," Jessica agreed. "But I enjoy it. Mrs. Macquarie is very good to me."

"And now she has a son?"

"Yes."

"Yes, *Feyther*," he reproved her. "De'il tak' ye, Jessie—I'm your feyther! And I'm wantin' us tae part on guid terms. Can ye no' find it in your heart tae meet me halfway? For your puir mother's sake, if no' for mine, dammit a'!"

Perhaps her mother would have wanted it, Jessica thought, her conscience again plaguing her. It was little enough to ask, and her stepfather had made the first move to end the breach between them. He had swallowed his pride by asking her to come here, so that they might bid each other farewell and, as he had put it, part on good terms.

She looked up. "Yes, Father," she managed huskily. "I *do* want to meet you halfway."

"Guid!" Campbell acknowledged. He rose, still smiling, and crossed to a small deed box that stood, with several other boxes and packages, piled up in readiness for departure. Opening it, he extracted what appeared to be a newspaper cutting, glanced through it, and then strode back to his seat.

"This is the main reason why I sent for ye, Jessie. " 'Twas gi'en me by a friend, and I . . . weel, I think ye should see it." He held out the cutting. "Read it, lassie."

Puzzled, Jessica took the crumpled scrap of newsprint from him. The report, which was dated nine months earlier—June 1813—was headlined "Death Sentences for Mail Coach Robbers." It continued:

> At Southampton Assize Court yesterday, the three men—believed to be members of the infamous Vickers gang—charged with holding up and robbing the London mail coach outside Winchester on the 10th ultimo, were found guilty.
>
> Mr. Justice Devereux pronounced sentence of death on Richard John Farmer, Septimus Todd, and Murdoch Henry Maclaine, and it is expected that all three will meet their fate at Winchester Prison on Tuesday of next week.

A description of the holdup followed, and Jessica attempted to read it, but the print blurred before her tear-filled eyes. Sick with shock, she let the cutting fall, as realization slowly sank in. Murdo—her brother, Murdo, a highwayman, a thief, brought to trial and condemned to death! It could not be true; Murdo was not a thief. He was . . . Biting back her tears, she picked up the cutting with a shaking hand and forced herself to read the name again. But it was there, in black and white, and it was *his* name—their father had called him Henry after Major Antill, and . . .

Duncan Campbell said softly, "Aye, it's him right enow, it's that damned young rogue Murdo. Your ain brother, Jessie!"

"But it *can't* be Murdo!" The cry came from Jessica's heart, and she stood up, trembling violently, her voice a thin whisper of sound. "There must be—be some mistake. He . . . Oh, no, it cannot be true!"

" 'Tis his name, is it no'? Newspapers dinna make mistakes, lassie."

Her stepfather was savoring his triumph, Jessica realized. It was for this that he had wanted her to come, not to effect a reconciliation, not to salve his conscience. The leopard did not change its spots, and Duncan Campbell had not changed. The newspaper cutting was nine months old—he must have kept it for at least three months, waiting his moment to give it to her, to taunt her with it, to . . . to . . . Hatred flared, just as it had in the past—the futile, childish hatred she had always felt for him.

She struck out at him blindly, but he caught her arm, drawing her toward him, his eyes bright with malice.

"He's deid, ye damned wee fool . . . your precious Murdo's deid! Hanged by the neck in Winchester Prison, can ye no' understand? Ye'll never set eyes on him again, and guid riddance, I say. 'Tis God's judgment on the pair o' ye!"

The thick, back-street Glasgow accent jarred on her ears, bringing back memories she had tried to forget. Dun-

can Campbell released her arm, and Jessica shrank from
him, numb with despair. For he was right, she thought
dully, although she had not at first taken it in. If the newspaper reporter had not made a mistake, if the Murdoch
Henry Maclaine he had named was indeed her brother,
then . . . Murdo was dead. She would never set eyes on
him again, because he . . .

As if he had read her thoughts, her stepfather said
harshly, "They dinna bury them in hallowed ground, Jessie—yon pulin' wee Murdo will be rotting in a felon's
grave, ye ken. Served the same way they served puir
Johnny Gould here, and—"

Jessica could bear no more. As Agnes came into the
room with a laden tray, she managed a choked good-bye
and, ignoring the woman's plea to her to wait, took refuge
in heartbroken flight.

Out in the street once more, she ran blindly, without
conscious thought or direction, her only desire to escape
from Duncan Campbell's bitter, taunting voice.

At the gate to Simeon Lord's shipyard, Justin turned at
the sound of her running feet. He recognized her and came
quickly to meet her, looking down with concern at her
white, tear-stained face. But he asked no questions—
simply put his arm round her and led her through the yard
to where his half-repaired *Flinders* was moored.

"We've just rigged a new mainmast," he explained apologetically. "But the cabin hasn't yet been touched, and it is
in rather a mess, I'm afraid. However, we can talk there in
private, if you've a mind to talk, Jessica. I take it that you
have been to your stepfather's house?"

"Yes," Jessica admitted miserably. "I—I went to bid
them farewell. The children and *him*. But . . ." She
choked on a sob, and could not go on.

Justin, still with his arm about her, led her to the cabin,
clearing a space in its smoke-blackened, cluttered interior
for her to sit down.

"Now," he invited gently, squatting down in front of her
and taking her hands in his. "Tell me about it, Jessica India. If I can help, if I can serve you in any way, rest assured that I will."

She told him, making a brave effort to speak calmly and quell her tears. The newspaper cutting was, she realized, still in her possession, although she had no recollection of having taken it with her from the house. She gave it to him and saw him frown as he read it.

"Campbell—your stepfather—showed you this without warning?" His tone was accusing.

Jessica nodded unhappily. "Yes. I had no idea. Agnes said that he wanted to make his peace with me before the regiment leaves, and I . . . I believed her. She insisted that he was a changed man. But he has not changed, Justin."

"There is still time," Justin suggested grimly, "to make him pay for it. The troops are not embarking until tomorrow, and believe me, I'd take pleasure in teaching him another lesson."

Jessica shook her head. "No, let him go. Please, Justin, it would only make trouble for you and for Agnes and the children, and I'd not want that. He's going and . . . he will be as . . . as dead to me as poor Murdo is now, when the ships sail."

Justin was angry enough to argue, but she succeeded, finally, in persuading him to let the matter pass. "I suppose he was only telling me the truth. I had to know, and . . . I will get over it, once he is gone." She managed a smile, for the first time since she had entered the cabin. "It was the shock—I let it upset me. But it has helped to talk to you."

To her surprise, he leaned forward and took her into his arms. His kiss was gentle and undemanding, intended more as consolation than as wooing, but a wave of tenderness swept over her, and for a moment she clung to him, liking the clean, fresh sea-scent of his body and the reverence with which he held her.

Justin, too, seemed oddly moved. He said, with studied restraint, "You are a sweet girl, Jessica India, and I've been blind, I think. But—" He jumped nimbly to his feet and held out his strong, brown hands to help her to rise. "I'll take you back to Government House. They say Mrs. Macquarie has had a son—is it true?"

"Yes," Jessica confirmed, "it is true." And her mistress would be wanting her, she thought guiltily, recalling the trauma of the birth. She had already been away too long.

Justin said, as they gained the deck, "I should like to take you to Ulva to meet my mother one day soon, Jessica. I'll be going there when they start building a road across the mountains, to help with the final survey and the chaining. Would they grant you leave to come?"

She had never asked for such a favor before, Jessica reminded herself, but Mrs. Macquarie had talked of engaging a nurse for the baby, so that . . .

"I think they would," she answered, with newfound confidence.

"Good," Justin acknowledged. Smiling, he offered her his arm. As they walked together across the yard, she glanced back at the troopships and could not suppress an involuntary shiver.

"They'll be gone by this time tomorrow," Justin observed, with swift understanding. His fingers tightened about her arm. "And you will be free, Jessica India!"

She remembered his words, next day, when she watched the two big Indiamen working out of the cove, the men of the 73rd crowding the decks and the pipes and drums playing their farewell to Sydney. Standing in the window of her mistress's bedroom at Government House, she watched them out of sight, saw the guard of honor on the government wharf dismissed, and the thin, stooping figure of the Governor leading his officers back to the house.

She breathed a silent prayer for the soul of her brother and turned away, conscious of relief.

"Jessica!" Mrs. Macquarie called softly. Mrs. Reynolds had brought the baby to her, and there was a look of radiant happiness on her tired face as she held the small, shawl-wrapped bundle in her arms. "Be so good as to tell His Excellency that his son is on view. He will want to see how well the dear wee soul takes his evening meal. The ships have gone, have they not? It is over?"

"Yes, ma'am. The troops are marching off, and I saw His Excellency on his way back. I'll tell him."

Jessica had reached the door when the Governor's wife said unexpectedly, "You should marry and have babies like this one. I am selfish to keep you here. Would you not like to be married, child?"

Jessica hesitated, taken by surprise at the question. "I—I'm not sure, ma'am. I—perhaps I would."

"Is there not some young gallant you fancy?" her mistress persisted.

Jessica's cheeks flamed. She thought of Justin's kiss, and the invitation he had extended, and stammered confusedly, "There is one, but he—I am not sure, ma'am."

"Do not leave it as late as I did, Jessica India," Mrs. Macquarie advised. She gave the baby her breast and added, a catch in her soft Highland voice, "This child is a miracle, you know."

CHAPTER XXIII

William Cox began the construction of a road over the Blue Mountains with winter at its height. By mid-July, he had his labor force assembled at Emu Ford—thirty carefully chosen convicts, some from his own farms, all sturdy, reliable men, accustomed to field work. For superintendent, he had enlisted the services of Thomas Hobby, his onetime brother officer in the New South Wales Corps, and old Lucky Byrne was to fill the dual roles of guide and game hunter. Together with a sergeant and eight men of the veteran company to guard against attacks by the native tribes, this constituted his entire force—few enough, Justin thought, when he joined them, bringing with him the maps made by William Lawson and Surveyor Evans.

The task facing them was daunting. The Governor had specified that the road was to be at least twelve feet wide, "cleaving through the forest to the fine tract of open country to the westward lately discovered," and ending at the site for settlement, which Evans had named Bathurst—a distance of just over one hundred miles. Cox's instructions called for him to "grub up the stumps in forest country and fill in the holes, so that a four-wheeled vehicle could negotiate the surface without difficulty or danger."

"Our highway," the barrel-chested Cox declared, after a day spent inspecting the terrain with Justin and his maps, "must climb over four thousand feet and pass through more than seventy miles of sandstone cliffs and gullies; and a great many of the trees that must be felled are hardwoods. True, the way is marked out for us—we know *where* we're to go. But my problem is *how*. Still, we must thank the Lord for small mercies, must we not?" He gestured to the lowering sky. "At least fog and rain will keep the aborigines off our trail. You heard, I suppose, that we had a running battle with them at Mulgoa a few weeks ago?"

"Yes," Justin confirmed, reminded momentarily of his encounter with the boy Winyara. "I heard. And there were attacks at Airds and Appin and an attempt to fire growing crops at my stepfather's property ten days before I got here. Mrs. Macarthur's shepherd was speared to death on the Cow Pastures, I was told. Do you really think that eight soldiers will suffice to guard your road builders, sir?"

"They will damned well have to, my young friend," Cox returned grimly, "since they're all I'm to be given. But they're all veterans, men I know well; and the sergeant, John Chisholm, is a first-rate fellow—he'll keep them up to the mark."

Certainly the morale of the party was high. Cox was a humane and generous employer, trusted and respected by his laborers. On his own large estate at Clarendon, he employed half a hundred men and had made himself independent, as far as this was possible, with his own shearing and weaving sheds, blacksmith and wheelwright shops, corn mills, cider presses, and, it was suspected, his own distillery. So free was he with the granting of leave passes to his men that other landowners complained of it and referred to his policy derisively as "Cox's liberty."

Justin had not known him well, until now, although he had met the family with William Lawson and had visited Clarendon on several occasions. But during the next few days, when they worked closely together on the initial planning of the road, he came to respect the onetime regimental paymaster for the resourceful, clearheaded individual he was. Going over the meager equipment with which the commissariat had supplied him, Cox had laughed hollowly and asserted, with cynical amusement, that even the British Colonial Office could scarcely complain of the expense entailed.

"One horse, six bullocks, and two carts," he had added, ticking each item off on his blunt-tipped fingers. "Ten felling axes, two crosscut saws, ten grub hoes and six common hoes, six pickaxes, four sledgehammers, two crowbars, and six tomahawks. And two sets of blasting tools and five-and-twenty pounds of powder, six spades, and six shovels . . . all listed in triplicate! It's fortunate that I'm able to supply my own blacksmith's anvil and bellows and spare ammunition for our muskets, is it not? The government issued forty rounds of ball cartridge—for Byrne *and* the soldiers! I don't blame the poor old viceroy, though—the home government's riding him on a very tight rein."

Next day, he had augmented the single workhorse by four of his own, and a fine team of oxen appeared, drawing behind them a prefabricated wooden hut in which, beaming, Cox established his sleeping quarters.

Regardless of the sleet and fog, he set his laborers to work, clearing timber, grubbing stumps, breaking rocks, and pounding the earthen surface into a level track, which slowly advanced along the plateau and then began to descend the steep western pass. The men worked hard, and Tom Hobby saw to it that they were amply fed and supplied with dry clothing and a generous ration of spirits when darkness put a halt to their labors.

Justin stayed with them longer than he had originally intended. The timber he needed to complete the repairs to his *Flinders* was in short supply in Sydney. Here, among the all-prevailing eucalyptus, were clumps of ironwood and cedar for the taking; and with Cox's promise to transport a small load to the river when the oxcarts went back for fresh provisions, he set about collecting what he required. In return, he assisted with rock blasting and pegged the route to be followed, sometimes with Hobby, sometimes with Cox himself.

Twice, when he was alone, the native boy, Winyara, found and followed him, his arm healed but still badly scarred and stiff. The boy did not speak, but he smiled and gave what assistance he could, loping silently off when any

of Cox's men or the soldiers appeared. Then, leaving a gift
of fish, he vanished and did not reappear.

By Sunday, September 4, the road was nearing the
eighteen-mile mark, reaching the cairn of stones left by
William Dawes. Here they were confronted by a steep gully
that had to be bridged if the road were to be made passable
for wheeled traffic. It proved a tedious and time-
consuming task, but Cox had chosen his men well, and despite the cold and inclement weather, it was completed in
less than two weeks. Of its eighty-foot length, thirty feet
was planked and the remainder filled up with stone and
rubble from the blasting.

Viewed from above, it appeared an impressive achievement, and Justin climbed to the top of the bluff, with
George Evans, who had come to inspect progress.

"The Governor will be overjoyed when I report this to
him," the surveyor said. "He's anxious for news. But the
worst is yet to come, is it not? The next sixteen miles will
be over a succession of steep hills, and I don't doubt that
you recall the immense difficulty we had in getting our
pack animals down from Mount York?"

"Indeed I do, Mr. Evans," Justin agreed feelingly. "But
Mr. Cox has planned to traverse that descent in a series of
zigzags, I understand."

"It will still be hazardous for wheeled vehicles," Evans
asserted. He was, Justin knew, more than a little put out
because Cox, rather than he himself, had been entrusted
with the building of the road. For all that, he was unstint-
ing in his praise of all he had so far seen, and his congratulations, when he finally took his leave, afforded the indefatigable William Cox great pleasure.

"He is a fine cartographer and well versed in every aspect of his profession," he observed to Justin, as they
watched the stout surveyor striding off across the new
bridge. "But George Evans is *not* an engineer. He sees haz-
ards where none exist and yet deems easy much that is
difficult—which is the difference between theory and
practice, Justin, my boy. But he is a good fellow, for all
that, and I respect him." He smiled a trifle grimly. "And

he is right about the descent from Mount York, for it will pose us some problems when we get there. I'm going to take a survey party to have another look at it tomorrow, if this infernal rain lets up on us. Perhaps you would like to come with me?"

Justin accepted eagerly, but a heavy thunderstorm and torrential rain during the night caused Cox to change his mind.

"We'll put it off for a week or so," he decided. "I'm going back to Clarendon to have some of our tools repaired. There will be space in the wagon to take that timber of yours, if you can have it ready for loading at the first depot by midday. I've only a couple of sick men to take down, in addition to the tools, and I take it you can arrange to send the timber to Sydney by boat, if we dump it on this side of the river?"

Only craft of shallow draft could navigate upriver to Emu Ford, but there were usually at least one or two available for hire, and Justin nodded.

"I'll take the opportunity of paying my family a visit," he said. "Thank you, sir. You'll have saved me a small fortune. Once that timber reaches the yard, I can have my sloop ready for sea again in a couple of weeks."

"And then you will desert us?" Cox suggested.

Justin smiled. "No, Mr. Cox—I shall be back before you come to Bathurst Plains. I want to see the end of the road before I quit."

William Cox clapped a friendly hand on his shoulder. "You will be warmly welcomed, lad, for you have contributed as much as anyone has, believe me. But . . ." He hesitated, eyeing Justin with a thoughtful frown, "I've sometimes wondered why. You're a seaman, and whilst exploring may be in your blood, I'd scarcely have supposed that road-building would be."

"No, sir, it's not." Reddening under the older man's scrutiny, Justin shuffled his feet awkwardly. "My mother came out with the First Fleet as a girl of barely seventeen, and she—well, she's always had a dream, sir, of a fine great pastureland beyond these mountains. And since we've found it at last, I want to see the road built, so that *she* can see it, too, and realize her dream. She's a pretty remarkable woman, my mother."

"I believe you, Justin," Cox said. "Well, off you go and get that timber loaded. It's five miles from the depot to Emu Ford, and I want to be there before dark."

Justin was already on his way, smiling to himself. He would bring Jessica Maclaine back with him, he thought, and introduce her to his mother and Andrew. The prospect was pleasing, and his heart lifted as he plodded up the steep incline of the Blue Mountain road.

Jenny sat in the old rocking chair that had been the first piece of furniture she had ever owned and, rocking gently, watched the sun go down behind the screening trees. It was not often that she sat in idleness—usually she had at least some mending or knitting to occupy her hands—but this evening she was tired. And she was also alone, without the need to keep up the pretense of healthy vigor she was at pains to maintain in front of her family.

Andrew had ridden out to visit the road builders' camp and replace two of the veteran company guards, injured by a rockfall during blasting operations. Rachel, home for the Christmas holidays, was attending the birthday party of a neighbor's child and was to stay there until Andrew returned to pick her up next day. And William . . . Jenny's lips curved into a smile.

William had gone to buy a ram from the new government stock farm below Emu Ford and would, almost certainly, take all day over the transaction. Where breeding stock was concerned, he was not easy to please and tended to drive a hard bargain, but the result of his hardheaded caution was to be seen in the Ulva sheep paddocks, and in the prices his wool commanded. Jenny's smile reflected her pride in fourteen-year-old William's achievement.

He had always been a most reluctant scholar, she thought indulgently. Unlike Justin, whose desire for knowledge was seemingly insatiable, William had skipped school whenever he could, wanting only to work on the land and with his sheep. And perhaps that was as well, in the present circumstances, since her own contribution to the daily work of the farm was now so much less—in terms of enthusiasm, if not of effort. The effort was there, it was true, but making it was, she knew, taking a heavy toll of her physical strength.

Jenny lay back, closing her eyes and letting her body relax. The pain in her chest was only a faintly nagging sensation now, her breathing quite easy and devoid of strain. But Dr. Redfern—the clever, competent young Dr. Redfern—had been proven right, and, alas, it took only a few hours on horseback or a walk down to the river to drive home the unpalatable truth.

Thank heaven, though, she had been able to hide that truth from all of them . . . even from Andrew. She had had to lie to them and lie, most of all, to Andrew, but . . .

Frisky, William's old collie dog, wakened suddenly to life beside her. Stiff-legged and growling, he crossed to the low wooden railing of the veranda, his graying muzzle aggressively lifted. Then, to Jenny's surprise, the growls ceased and the old dog ran with wagging tail and shrill yelps of delight to meet a mud-spattered figure in rough laborer's clothing advancing along the garden path toward the house. It was a moment or two before Jenny recognized Justin and jumped up eagerly to meet him. The sudden movement sent a spasm of pain coursing from one side of her chest to the other, but, accustomed to such attacks, she held her breath until it passed and then greeted him in what was almost her normal voice.

He hugged her, apparently noticing nothing amiss, and held her close, apologizing ruefully for his dirty and unshaven state.

"I'm just down from the road, Mam, and I've been loading and unloading timber for the *Flinders* in one of the worst rainstorms we've had. And the Lord knows we've had plenty!"

"Whilst *we* are complaining of drought," Jenny told him. She held him at arm's length, studying him with concern. "Poor Justin, you're soaked to the skin, and you look quite exhausted! I'll ask Nancy to put the big kettle on, and you can have a hot tub as soon as it boils. Andrew will have some clothes you can borrow, until those filthy things of yours can be washed and dried. Did you see him, by the way? He went up to the road this morning at first light."

He nodded. "Yes, very briefly. He was on his way up, and I was coming down . . . and the rain never ceased, so we only exchanged hellos. But I said I was coming here, and I gather that he expects to be back sometime tomorrow afternoon."

"And you will be staying for a while, I hope?"

Justin smiled apologetically. "Only for a couple of days—I have to take that timber to Simeon Lord's. But I'm glad to have you to myself, Mam. I—well, I've a favor to ask."

"A favor?" Jenny's brow furrowed. It was seldom that Justin ever asked for anything; he made his own way and gave much more than he could ever be persuaded to take, from either Andrew or herself. "Dear Justin, surely you know that you have only to tell me what it is?"

"Well . . ." He reddened a little. "There's a girl, one I like very much. She has had a bad time lately—it's quite a long story, and I'll tell you about it sometime. But I would like her to get to know you, because I'm sure it would be good for her. You've got so much courage, Mam, and you always seem able to meet setbacks and disasters without turning a hair."

"Do I?" Jenny stared at him incredulously. There was one impending disaster she had yet to find the courage to meet, she thought guiltily, but of that she could not, of course, speak to Justin. He was the last person in the world to whom she would ever be able to speak of it. A year, a year or perhaps two, Dr. Redfern had said, and she had already had ten months. . . . She forced her stiff lips into an encouraging smile. "I will be more than happy to meet this girl. Would you be able to bring her here, to Ulva, Justin, or do you want me to come to Sydney Town?"

"Oh, here—I'd like to bring her with me when I come back. Mr. Cox reckons he'll complete the road to Bathurst Plains soon after Christmas, and I want to be there when he does." Justin hesitated, looking anxiously down at her. "I was hoping that *you* would be there too, Mam, to see those pastures you've always talked about, because they are there—stretching as far as the eye can see. I remember how you used to talk about them to me when I was a child. Not that I had any idea what you meant. I just knew you believed in their existence."

"Yes," Jenny agreed. "I believed they existed and that they would be found one day." She laid her cheek against the rough stubble of Justin's, her throat suddenly tight. "But I never dreamed that *you* would be one of those who found them! Dearest Justin, you know how proud I feel, do you not? And how much I want to be with you when the road is finished."

He put her gently from him. "Mam, I'm filthy, and I haven't shaved for over a week."

Jenny laughed, her emotions under stern control again. She called out to Nancy Jardine in the kitchen, making a jest of it, "Nan, Justin is here and says he is filthy and hasn't shaved for a week—put the kettle on, will you?" Turning back to Justin, she asked, "About this girl of yours—what is her name?"

"Didn't I tell you? It is Jessica—Jessica India Maclaine. Her father was a soldier of the Seventy-third, killed in the battle of Seringapatam. She came out with Their Excellencies, as lady's maid to Mrs. Macquarie."

Then she was a far cry from Abigail, Jenny thought, with some relief. Perhaps, God willing, this girl would not haunt Justin endlessly, all for naught, as had his earlier love. . . . "Could you bring Jessica here for Christmas?" she asked.

"I think that might be possible. Er . . . she's not my girl, in that sense, Mam, but I . . ." Justin's unshaven face was aflame again. Then he grinned. "I've not sought permission to court her, you see. But I intend to, when I go back to Sydney. She's a very sweet girl, and I believe you will think so, too, when you meet her."

Had his been an impulsive decision, Jenny wondered uneasily—a reaction to Abigail's marriage? Searching her son's face for some clue to his feelings, she decided that it had not. Justin did not act impulsively; he took his time, gave careful thought to what he did—and he had had plenty of time, while he had been with Mr. Cox's road builders, to think and come to the right conclusion.

"I shall look forward to meeting her," she said. "Now, off you go and clean yourself up. Would you like a drink to take with you?"

He shook his head. "I'll get some tea from Nan, don't worry. And you said I could borrow from Andrew's wardrobe?"

"I'll see to that," Jenny promised.

"Thanks. And, Mam—"

"Yes?"

Justin came to take her hands in his. "Don't forget what I said about coming to the end of Mr. Cox's road, will you? You'll be able to ride all the way, and there are provision huts and good campsites at regular intervals. The weather should have improved by March, too."

"I won't forget, Justin." And she would not, Jenny thought, conscious of a chilling fear. She would not forget; but March was six months ahead, and she had already had ten months of the time Dr. Redfern had specified.

Justin left her, and she heard him talking and laughing with Nancy Jardine in the kitchen. She fetched the shirt and breeches from Andrew's closet, and, leaving them ready, returned to the rocking chair. Old Frisky settled down beside her, and she patted his head, staring out into the gathering darkness, dry-eyed and fighting down the fear.

She was glad that Justin had found a girl, glad that he had got over his infatuation for Abigail without, seemingly, being too badly hurt. God willing, she would see him married and . . . She prayed silently.

"Please, God, let me go with him to the end of that road. Let me keep enough strength to sit a horse until—" The pain came, like a knife thrust between her ribs, but she did not cry out, and after a while it passed. She drew a long breath and finished the prayer. "Please, Heavenly Father, let me see the interminable pastures before I must go. . . ."

*   *   *

"You must try to be kind and considerate to Aunt Lucy," Abigail warned, "like you are to Dickon, because—"

"Is she deaf and dumb, then?" Julia interrupted insolently.

"No, of course she's not. But she has been very ill. And we want to have a happy family Christmas, do we not, all of us together?"

"It won't be happy," Julia said with conviction. "Not like it used to be, when Mama was alive. Then it was lovely. We had candles and hot punch, and they roasted a whole bullock on a great big fire outside, so that the convict servants and the farm workers could join in."

"Well, I expect your papa will arrange for that this year," Abigail suggested, her tone placatory. But she was close to losing her temper, and Julia, sensing this, lapsed into a sullen and unresponsive silence. Alexander, taking his cue from her, sidled up to Dickon and pinched him surreptitiously, assuming an expression of angelic innocence when the little boy's face went scarlet and he emitted one of his odd grunts, which were the only sounds he ever made.

"I think Dickon's going to be sick," Alexander said scornfully. "Shall I call Kate to take him away?"

"No, you will not call Kate," Abigail retorted. She picked up her little son and soothed him gently. She felt exasperated by the Dawson children's unrelenting hostility. No matter what she did, she was unable to win their approval or even, come to that, she thought bitterly, their toleration.

Julia was the cause of it, of course. As the eldest of Timothy's children, Julia exerted a strong influence over the other two, and Dorothea, who had initially seemed ready to accept her, was now almost as difficult and demanding as her sister. And Tim did not understand her inability to control them.

"They're only children," he had said, more than once. "Exercise your authority, my dear."

Abigail sighed, holding Dickon to her and kissing the top of his dark, curly head. Dickon was an angel, loving and sweet, despite his terrible handicap, but the young Dawsons were making his life a misery. Even with Kate Lamerton's stout backing, Abigail was finding her stepchildren more and more difficult to control, and poor Lucy, still in a state of numb and uncommunicative shock, did not make the situation any easier.

It was all so frustrating. Abigail resisted the temptation to slap Dorothea, who had burst into tears for no apparent reason, and sternly ordered her to work on her sampler. The little girl obeyed with reluctance, and as Julia assisted her to sort out her embroidery threads, there was silence.

Abigail repeated her sigh. She was deeply in love with her new husband, and he, she had no doubt, with her. They had been ideally happy for the first few weeks of their marriage, and Tim had proved himself an eager, passionate lover. Lucy had not intruded on their happiness, and Frances had looked after all four children with her usual unselfish kindness. Tim and she had stayed in Sydney, enjoying the social life, attending the dinner parties and balls, the Government House receptions and the horse racing, the garden and picnic parties, the firework displays. The newly arrived regiment, the 46th, had outshone even Simeon Lord and John Blaxland with the lavishness of their hospitality, and Colonel and Mrs. Molle were, everyone was agreed, assets to the colony's society.

She had enjoyed herself, Abigail reflected, and Tim had indulged her to the full. He did not like parties, but without a word of complaint, he had escorted her to every one to which they were invited and had played the host, with unfailing goodwill, at those she had insisted they must give in return. But it could not last, and she had, of course, known that it could not. Tim was a landowner, with three large farms to manage, and the Spences were planning a voyage to Calcutta in the new year.

So they had closed the Sydney house and come back to Upwey with the children for Christmas. Once there, Tim had gone about his business from early morning until late at night, and . . . Abigail bit her lower lip fiercely, feeling it tremble. She had been left to her own devices, with three resentful and rebellious children for company.

She liked the house immensely. Since Henrietta's death, Tim had enlarged it, building on half a dozen more rooms, a cellar for the wine he was now experimenting with, new stables, and a mass of farm buildings whose purpose she had not yet ascertained . . . and a cottage for her faithful Jethro, which had been completed just before their return. They employed more than adequate labor, with a good cook and seven excellent house servants, who left her little to do—except, that was to say, to exercise her authority over the children. And Lucy—poor, unhappy Lucy—was to join them for Christmas, coming with Frances and Jasper Spence in their carriage from Parramatta. . . .

"Could we not go for a river picnic?" Julia's shrill voice broke into her thoughts, and Abigail stiffened, her first impulse to refuse.

"There are the Christmas decorations to prepare," she said weakly, "and your gifts to wrap and label."

"There's plenty of time," Julia argued, pouting. "And it's so dull, just sitting here in the house sewing. When Mama was alive, she used to take us on the river."

"Oh, yes!" Dorothea exclaimed, coming to her elder sister's support. "Please, Abigail, couldn't you take us? It's a lovely day."

Their refusal to address her as mother, as she had asked them to, was yet another source of irritation, but Abigail swallowed her resentment. Perhaps, she reflected, their strained relationship might be improved if she acceded to their request. It was not much to ask, and in the old days, when she had acted as their governess, river picnics had been one of her pleasures, as well as theirs.

"Very well," she agreed, "if you wish. It *is* a lovely day, too nice to spend indoors. We can go after lunch."

Delighted cries greeted her words and banished some of her resentment. She got to her feet. "I will go and see the cook. We can have luncheon early, and he can pack up a picnic basket for us. Alexander, go and see whether you can find Jethro and ask him to make an oared boat ready."

"We're not taking Jethro, are we?" Julia demanded disparagingly.

"Yes, of course we are," Abigail told her, her tone sharp. "The river has a strong current. We shall need him to row."

"But he's so uncouth," Julia objected. "And he smells of sheep always."

"He is a shepherd, Julia. He can hardly help that, can he?"

"He could wash. And we can't talk freely when he's there," Julia argued petulantly. "Besides," she added, "Alex can row, and so can I. We won't need Jethro."

Abigail gave in, despising herself nonetheless for having done so. She set Dickon down, freeing his clinging arms from about her neck. To her dismay, the little boy's face puckered and he looked up at her with tear-bright eyes, pleading with her mutely not to leave him. "You must stay, Dickon—I'm only going to the kitchen." Bending down, she spoke slowly and carefully, so that he could see and read her lips. "We shall be going for a picnic on the river, darling. You'll like that, will you not?"

Before Dickon could signify his understanding, Julia intervened. "Oh, surely we don't have to take *him,* do we? He's too small and stupid—he'll spoil everything!"

Abigail slapped her hard across the face, unable to restrain herself. Grasping Dickon's hand, she dragged him after her, closing the door on Julia's indignant wails.

The picnic party was not likely to be a success after this, she thought wretchedly, but for all that, the Dawson children had asked for it, and they should go, whether or not they now wanted to. And Dickon, however small and stupid they deemed him, should come too. . . .

Her resolve did not weaken, despite a sullen silence on Julia's part and rudeness from Dorothea and Alexander. Jethro had the boat ready, and with the two elder children at the oars, Dickon on her knee, and the picnic basket under the thwarts, they set off.

"We'll go upstream," Abigail decided, "whilst you are fresh, and then we can drift down on the current after we've had our picnic."

It was pleasant enough on the river, she had to concede—much cooler than on land, with a light breeze skimming over the sun-dappled water, and the trees growing on the high bank over their heads providing a welcome shade. The two older children, put on their mettle, rowed very competently, and gradually their sullenness was overcome by the beauty and interest of their surroundings.

There were birds in the trees—flocks of brightly colored parakeets which rose in alarm at the boat's approach; a pair of magpies; a white cockatoo; and wheeling high above them in a tight, wedge-shaped formation, half a dozen wild ducks, their bodies black against the sunlit sky. Alexander claimed to have heard the coach-whip bird; Julia, ever ready to outdo him, insisted that a platypus had passed close to her side of the boat; but their argument was good tempered, and Abigail gradually relaxed, letting the peace of the scene lull her into tranquil drowsiness.

"Let me look after Dickon," Dorothea offered. "The other two are rowing, and I've got nothing to do. I'll take care of him, I promise."

Dickon seemed quite ready to go to her, and Abigail relinquished him, amused to hear his gurgles of pleasure when Dorothea dipped a hand in the water and splashed his small face with drops of moisture. There were cushions piled up in the boat's stern, and Abigail leaned back luxuriously, letting her heavy lids fall. Perhaps, she told herself sleepily, if she were to have a child who would be closer kin to the young Dawsons than Dickon was, they might not resent her so much. And Tim wanted her to have his child, he . . .

"Oh, look out, Dodie!" Julia shrieked. "Look out—Dickon's slipping!"

Rudely awakened, Abigail sat up. Dickon, she saw to her alarm, had climbed up into the bow and was precariously balanced there, in imminent danger of falling into the river. To her credit, Dorothea acted quickly and bravely. She scrambled up beside him and, with all her strength, pulled the little teetering figure from his perch.

Dickon landed with a thud on the bottom boards, but the effort proved too much for his small savior. With a cry of terror, Dorothea, her arms flailing, fell backward into the water. She struggled frantically as the current caught her and started to bear her away, her struggles as ineffectual as her cries.

"She can't swim!" Julia exclaimed. "Oh, Abigail, Dodie can't swim!"

Abigail did not hesitate. She had a sudden, nightmare vision of a red-coated, half-drowned body glimpsed, years ago, from the deck of the *Fanny*, and then she was in the water, striking out with swift, strong strokes in Dorothea's direction. She had been a good swimmer all her life, and although impeded by her skirt, it was only a few moments before Abigail had the terrified girl in her arms. Dorothea clutched at her wildly, but, kicking off her skirt, Abigail freed herself and managed to turn the girl onto her back, grasping her arms firmly to prevent further struggles.

"Lie still, Dodie," she begged. "You're quite safe. I won't let you sink, truly I won't."

Julia and Alexander, handling the boat with considerable skill, maneuvered it alongside her. Between them, they hauled Dorothea from the water and then, on Abigail's instructions, held the boat steady to enable her to drag herself over the gunwale. Dripping and breathless, she took the still badly frightened Dorothea into her arms and, holding her tightly, bade Julia head back to the Upwey wharf.

"As fast as you can, Julia. The current will help. And be careful of Dickon, won't you?"

"Yes, all right, Abigail," Julia acknowledged in a subdued voice.

Tim was waiting when they reached the wharf. "In heavens name, my love!" he exclaimed, taking in their damp and bedraggled state with some concern. "What happened? Here, let me have that poor child."

He took Dorothea from her, and Abigail scrambled from the boat, shivering now with the chill of reaction.

"We had an accident—" she began, but it was Julia who answered her father's question.

"Dodie fell in and would have drowned, if it had not been for Abigail, Papa," she told him, in ringing tones.

"You should be proud of her; she—oh, Papa, she's a heroine, truly she is! She saved Dodie's life."

"Well, I'm damned!" Tim looked from one to the other of them in frowning bewilderment. Then his face cleared, and he set Dorothea down, holding out his arms to Abigail. He said softly, as she went into them, "I don't think, my dearest wife, that any of my offspring will question your authority ever again. But here . . ." He took off his jacket and wrapped it round her. Turning to Julia, he added crisply, "Up to the house with you, you and Dorothea. And run, understand? Alex, you look after Dickon."

The children obeyed him instantly, and Abigail's spirits lifted as she watched them depart. It was to be hoped he was right, but they were spirited young things and would probably defy her again. But at least, she thought, hugging the knowledge to her, she had won their respect, and that was something.

Tim tucked her arm under his, and they walked back to the house in the children's wake.

CHAPTER XXIV

The road over the Blue Mountains was completed—ahead of William Cox's estimate—on January 21, 1815. It covered a distance of just over 101 miles from its starting point at Emu Plains and reached as far as 141 miles from Sydney. A flagstaff, with the Union flag flying from it, marked the site of the future township of Bathurst, which the Governor was officially to name in a few weeks' time.

At present the site consisted of a handful of wooden huts and storage sheds, the former occupied by Cox and some of his men, with a guardhouse for the soldiers of the veteran company, under Sergeant Chisholm.

There was little enough to show for all their prodigious labor, Justin thought, and perhaps his mother would be disappointed, for until the Governor gave his formal permission and land grants were authorized, the flocks and herds of her dream could not be driven to the new pastures.

But the fertile land beyond their mountain barrier had not been found a day too soon, he knew. In the prolonged drought of the previous year, twelve hundred cattle, over twelve thousand sheep, and a thousand hogs had perished, and the wheat harvest had failed disastrously. Even at Ulva and other farms in the well-watered Nepean area, stock had died and crops withered in the ground for lack of rain, while, ironically, the mountain road and its builders had been hampered by the almost daily downpours and the frequent storms.

Justin reined in his borrowed horse for the first steep descent. Wagons, Mr. Cox had said, would have to negotiate parts of the road with extreme care, and where they must climb, two teams would be required to enable a heavily laden vehicle to reach the top. But the steepest stretches were protected by log rails, and for horses and riders, there was little danger . . . his mother would experience few difficulties, if Andrew adhered to his promise and made her take plenty of time for the journey.

And little Jessica would be with her. He smiled, as he let his horse have its head again. His mother had, as he had hoped, taken to Jessica the instant she had set eyes on her; so had Rachel and William and, of course, Andrew . . . they had all warmly approved of his choice, for all they had been somewhat startled when he had introduced her to them as his wife.

But he had known, during the weeks he had spent in Sydney finishing the repairs to his *Flinders,* that Jessica was the one—the only one—he wanted to wed. He had paid ardent court to her, with Mrs. Macquarie's approval and encouragement. The Governor's lady had wanted to give them a fine wedding from Government House, with all the trappings, and a reception in the ballroom; but as Christmas approached, he had felt no inclination to wait for the ceremony to be performed on their return from the visit to Ulva. There seemed no real reason for delay; Jessica shared his impatience, and neither of them, if the truth were known, had really wanted an elaborate ceremony, which Sydney society might view with disapproval. The marriage of a currency kid and a lady's maid hardly merited the splendor of Government House—better by far, he had argued, a quiet wedding, such as most emancipists were content with, performed in St. Philip's Church by the incumbent, after morning prayer.

And thus it had been. Their banns had been called, and on the Sunday before Christmas, the Reverend William Cowper had joined them together as man and wife, in the presence of the Governor and Mrs. Macquarie, Major Antill—who had acted in place of Jessica's father—and Mr. and Mrs. Spence, Cookie Barnes, and a handful of others.

Mrs. Ovens had served their wedding breakfast in the servants' dining room, not in the ballroom, and they had set off for Parramatta, to spend their wedding night at the Freemason's Arms and travel on to Ulva by the new turnpike road next day.

Justin's smile widened. With the *Flinders* ready for sea again and a snug little cottage near Dawes Point leased to him, life held better prospects than he had ever dared to hope for, and with a wife like his Jessica . . . dear God, he was a fortunate man! And besides . . . He reined his horse in with a smothered exclamation.

A small mounted party was slowly descending the hill ahead of him, and he recognized the leading rider at once. His mother was sitting erectly on the handsome chestnut she called Young Sirius, with Andrew a few paces behind her, and—yes, Jessica, with Rachel and William bringing up the rear.

He stood where he was, watching their approach, and his heart swelled with pride at the picture his mother made on the big, high-stepping chestnut. She was still a fine-looking woman, but until this moment, he had not consciously realized what a consummate horsewoman she was. Light hands, graceful carriage, straight back, and her head held high . . . she seemed part of the animal she rode, putting Andrew to shame, with his workmanlike slouch and overlong leathers.

Cupping his hands about his mouth, Justin hallooed to them, the sound echoing eerily across the intervening distance, flung back by the granite precipice behind him.

"Come on!" he urged, "and I'll show you Bathurst Plain and the promised land!"

Jenny heard him and gave an answering wave. She hoped, as she rode to meet him, that he would never know what the ride had cost her. Andrew knew now, for she had been compelled to tell him, when she could give no answer to his increasingly anxious questions. But he had kept her secret, and because he was aware of how much it meant to her, he had not tried to persuade her to give up her attempt to make the journey—no, the pilgrimage, for that was what it had become—to Bathurst.

Instead, he had done all he unobtrusively could to lessen the strain for her. They had traveled slowly, sometimes making only six or seven miles a day, and for much of the way he had ridden behind her on Young Sirius, offering his broad chest and encircling arms as cushions against her pain. At night, he had seen to it that she was dry and comfortable, building a shelter of bark or boughs where there were no wooden huts left by the road builders, and making her take sips of brandy from his flask when he saw that her breathing was difficult.

Kindest of all, because it went against the grain, was the manner in which Andrew had fended off Rachel's growing fears and potentially awkward questions and William's blunt demands that she turn back. Neither had guessed the truth, Jenny was reasonably certain, although they knew that she was unwell and were worried, supposing that she had caught a chill.

Jessica was easy to deceive. Justin's new wife possessed intuitive understanding and seemed to sense when Jenny was in pain. She asked no questions and offered no advice, but like Andrew, she was there when she was needed, with a hot drink, water in which to wash, or a blanket, thoughtfully warmed at the campfire and a wonderful relief for aching limbs and an overthin body too long exposed to the mountain winds.

That she had managed to travel this far was, Jenny knew, something of a miracle . . . or the answer to prayer, and perhaps her own determination, added to these. She could not have said what impulse drove her; she knew only that, whatever the toll it might take of her, she had to go on.

The dream was there, awaiting fulfillment. The vision she had cherished throughout the long years of her exile was about to become reality, and the alien land was ready to yield up the bounty its mountains had guarded for almost three decades of what had been, for so many of them, a hand-to-mouth existence. It had been so for her, she recalled, and tears came unbidden to ache in her throat, as the memories flooded back.

If the years of toil and near-starvation were to have value and meaning, she wanted to see, with her own eyes, a promise for the future—for the children she had bred, if not for herself.

Justin had understood her longing. He had said he would send word to her when the road was completed, and he had done so, adding that he would meet her on the way. And he was there, waiting to take her—to take all of them—to catch their first glimpse of the land Governor Phillip had believed they would find, if they kept faith.

Jenny lifted her hand in happy greeting, as Justin came trotting toward her, glad now that she had insisted, despite Andrew's concern, on riding Young Sirius alone for the last few miles.

"It's not much farther," Justin said, halting beside her. He smiled at Jessica, and her small face lit up at the sight of him, but she held back, leaving him to ride beside his mother as if, without the need for words, she sensed the significance of this moment and was content to efface herself.

They breasted the hill, and at its summit, Jenny drew rein, looking down at the tiny hamlet of wooden buildings and bark huts, the Union flag flying proudly in the breeze.

Beyond them stretched the plain, mile upon mile of lush green grass, with the river flowing through it into the distance. It was finer and more extensive than even she had dreamed it would be, and she gasped at the wonder of it, scarcely listening as Justin, in an attempt to convince her of the sheer enormity of the discovery, pointed the route he had followed with George Evans for a farther fifty miles.

But Jenny needed no convincing. The dream had indeed become reality, and she turned in her saddle to look at her family, her eyes shining with a light none of them had ever seen before.

"Only imagine what it will mean, to you and to the whole colony! Think of the flocks and herds this land will sustain, the crops it will grow! Look at it, children, for it is your future spread out down there. This is the prosperous land the Governor has told us shall be called Australia . . . and it is for you to build on. It needs only the labors of the husbandman to bring forth the richest and fairest fruits. And . . ." A savage spasm of pain came, robbing her of breath, and her voice trailed off into an agonized silence.

This was the end of the miracle, Jenny knew, as she felt the strength draining out of her. Or perhaps it was only the beginning. She swayed, closing her eyes, and the pain gradually faded, leaving her strangely at peace.

Andrew was off his horse in an instant, lifting his wife down from her saddle. He laid her very gently on the road verge, and Justin, white and shaken, flung himself down beside them.

"What is it?" he asked hoarsely. "For God's sake, Andrew, is she—is Mam ill?"

Andrew did not attempt to deny it. "We must get her into shelter. You know the people down there, Justin. Ride down and ask them for a hut we can take her to—one we can light a fire in. Go with him, Jessica, and Rachel too. William and I will bring her down." He took off his coat and covered her with it, reaching for his flask.

"I'll bring a wagon," Justin said. He climbed onto his horse again and was off down the slope, the two girls after him.

The wagon came, Justin and two of Cox's men with it, but Jenny was unconscious when they finally carried her into one of the huts. There was a fire blazing up inside and a bed prepared from piled blankets, Rachel and Jessica waiting anxiously to help her into it.

It was as day dawned that her soul slipped quietly away, and Andrew, her hand in his, looked up at the four who had shared his nightlong vigil. He said sadly, "She has gone. But this was the way she wanted it, and she knew that it had to come. She knew for over a year and told me only a few weeks ago. God give her brave soul rest!" He rose stiffly to his feet and went outside.

Jessica covered the still face, thinking as she did so that it was happy and at peace, the lines of strain smoothed away, so that now it was a youthful face—and the face of a woman who had, even in death, achieved what she had set out to do.

Rachel was sobbing, William was hard put to retain his habitual composure, and Justin seemed stricken, seeking vainly for words.

Jessica said quietly, "I do truly believe that this was the way your mother wanted to go. She left us to carry on— she told us so, when we were on the hill. So that's what we have to do, is it not? Build for the future!"

None of them spoke, but the four young heads inclined in unison.

EPILOGUE

The first grave in what was to become the Bathurst Town Cemetery had a small granite headstone erected over it, on which was recorded in rough-hewn letters:

Sacred to the Memory of Jenny Hawley,

née Taggart, the Beloved Wife of

Captain Andrew Hawley,

N.S.W. Veteran Company

Born January 2, 1772

Died January 30, 1815, At the End

Of a Long Journey.

And in far-off England, in a country churchyard outside the city of Bath, Somerset, another stone bore witness to the memory of the colony's first Governor. This read:

Beneath lie the Remains of

Arthur Phillip Esq.,

Admiral of the Blue

Who died 31st August, 1814

In his 76th Year.

THE EXILES

Vivian Stuart

In the magnificent wake of *THE THORN BIRDS*, a pioneering epic of virgin Australia and the outcasts who fought an untamed continent to forge a proud new nation.

THE EXILES, first in a breathtaking six-volume series, is the story of Jenny Taggart, driven as a child from her rural Yorkshire home; seeking uneasy refuge in the slums of eighteenth century London; then shipped as a convict to distant, savage Australian shores.

THE EXILES – the bitter birthpangs of the earliest colonies and an unforgettable epic of innocence, virtue and courage.

Futura Publications/A Troubadour Book
Fiction/Historical Romance
0 7088 1914 1

THE SETTLERS

Vivian Stuart

THE SETTLERS continues the unforgettable story of Jenny Taggart, a young convict who travelled from England in *THE EXILES* to settle in the wild continent.

Through years of great turmoil in a raw land drenched with blood, passion and dreams, the settlers struggle to carve out a life for themselves. For Jenny, a woman alone, survival presents even greater problems. The life of this courageous, strong-willed beauty continues to be dominated by the men who surround her. Torn by betrayal and loss, inflamed by love, Jenny is sustained by her unconquerable determination to cling to her perilous dreams of peace for the years to come.

Futura Publications
Fiction
0 7088 2086 7

THE TRAITORS

Vivian Stuart

THE TRAITORS, third in the six-volume Australian series begins in 1807 . . . In the midst of bloodshed and rebellion a new generation struggled to be born . . .

Through heartbreak and tragic loss they had fashioned a new life in the land of their exile. But even now they could not rest securely. The courage of beautiful Abigail Tempest, newly arrived and heiress to a vast land grant . . . the mettle of Justin Broome, with his father's adventurous blood running hot in his veins . . . the loyalty of Andrew Hawley and the passionate faith of Jenny Broome – all would be tested to their very limit.

A new generation struggled to put down roots in precarious soil as treacherous forces defied King and country, threatening to destroy everything the settlers had sacrificed so much to build.

Futura Publications
Fiction
0 7088 2186 3

All Futura Books are available at your bookshop or
newsagent, or can be ordered from the following address:
Futura Books, Cash Sales Department,
P.O. Box 11, Falmouth, Cornwall TR10 9EN.

Please send cheque or postal order (no currency), and
allow 60p for postage and packing for the first book
plus 25p for the second book and 15p for each additional
book ordered up to a maximum charge of £1.90 in U.K.

B.F.P.O. customers please allow 60p for
the first book, 25p for the second book plus 15p per
copy for the next 7 books, thereafter 9p per book.

Overseas customers, including Eire, please allow £1.25
for postage and packing for the first book, 75p for the
second book and 28p for each subsequent title ordered